Books by Gene Wolfe

The Book of the New Sun
    Volume One—The Shadow of the Torturer
    Volume Two—The Claw of the Conciliator
    Volume Three—The Sword of the Lictor

Published by **TIMESCAPE BOOKS**

GENE WOLFE

THE CLAW OF THE CONCILIATOR

Volume Two of
The Book of the New Sun

A TIMESCAPE BOOK
PUBLISHED BY POCKET BOOKS NEW YORK

Another *Original* publication of TIMESCAPE BOOKS

A Timescape Book published by
POCKET BOOKS, a Simon & Schuster division of
GULF & WESTERN CORPORATION
1230 Avenue of the Americas, New York, N.Y. 10020

ISBN: 0-671-47425-1

First Timescape Books paperback printing February, 1982

10   9   8   7   6   5   4   3

POCKET and colophon are registered trademarks
of Simon & Schuster.

Use of the trademark TIMESCAPE is by exclusive license
from Gregory Benford, the trademark owner.

Also available in Timescape trade edition.

Printed in the U.S.A.

But strength still goes out from your thorns,
   and from your abysses the sound of music.
Your shadows lie on my heart like roses
   and your nights are like strong wine.

THE CLAW OF THE CONCILIATOR

I

The Village of Saltus

Morwenna's face floated in the single beam of light, lovely and framed in hair dark as my cloak; blood from her neck pattered to the stones. Her lips moved without speech. Instead I saw framed within them (as though I were the Increate, peeping through his rent in Eternity to behold the World of Time) the farm, Stachys her husband tossing in agony upon his bed, little Chad at the pond, bathing his fevered face.

Outside, Eusebia, Morwenna's accuser, howled like a witch. I tried to reach the bars to tell her to be quiet, and at once became lost in the darkness of the cell. When I found light at last, it was the green road stretching from the shadow of the Piteous Gate. Blood gushed from Dorcas's cheek, and though so many screamed and shouted, I could hear it pattering to the ground. Such a mighty structure was the Wall that it divided the world as the mere line between their covers does two books; before us now stood such a wood as might have been growing since the founding of Urth, trees as high as cliffs, wrapped in pure green. Between them lay the road, grown up in fresh grass, and on it were the bodies of men and women. A burning cariole tainted the clean air with smoke.

Five riders sat destriers whose hooked tushes were encrusted with lazulite. The men wore helmets and capes of indanthrene blue and carried lances whose heads ran with blue fire; their faces were more akin than the faces of brothers. On these riders, the tide of travelers broke as a wave on a rock, some turning left, some right. Dorcas was torn from my arms, and I drew *Terminus Est* to cut down

9

those between us and found I was about to strike Master Malrubius, who stood calmly, my dog Triskele at his side, in the midst of the tumult. Seeing him so, I knew I dreamed, and from that knew, even while I slept, that the visions I had had of him before had not been dreams.

I threw the blankets aside. The chiming of the carillon in the Bell Tower was in my ears. It was time to rise, time to run to the kitchen pulling on my clothes, time to stir a pot for Brother Cook and steal a sausage—a sausage bursting, savory, and nearly burned—from the grill. Time to wash, time to serve the journeymen, time to chant lessons to myself before Master Palaemon's examination.

I woke in the apprentices' dormitory, but everything was in the wrong place: a blank wall where the round port should have been, a square window that should have been a bulkhead. The row of hard, narrow cots was gone, and the ceiling too low.

Then I was awake. Country smells—much like the pleasant odors of flower and tree that used to float across the ruined curtain wall from the necropolis, but mixed now with the hot reek of a stable—drifted through the window. The bells began again, ringing in some campanile not far away, calling the few who retained their faith to beseech the coming of the New Sun, though it was very early still, the old sun had hardly dropped Urth's veil from his face, and save for the bells the village lay silent.

As Jonas had discovered the night before, our water-ewer held wine. I used some to rinse my mouth, and its astringency made it better than water; but I still wanted water to splash on my face and smooth my hair. Before sleeping I had folded my cloak, with the Claw at the center, to use for a pillow. I spread it now, and remembering how Agia had once tried to slip her hand into the sabretache on my belt, thrust the Claw into my boot top.

Jonas still slept. In my experience, people asleep look younger than they do awake, but Jonas seemed older—or perhaps only ancient; he had the face, with straight nose and straight forehead, that I have often noted in old pictures. I buried the smoldering fire in its own ashes and left without waking him.

By the time I had finished refreshing myself from the bucket of the innyard well, the street before the inn was no longer silent, but alive with hooves that splashed through the puddles left by the previous night's rain, and the clacking of scimitar horns. Each animal was taller than a man, black or piebald, rolling-eyed and half blinded by the coarse hair that fell across its face. Morwenna's father, I remembered, had been a drover; it was possible this herd was his, though it seemed unlikely. I waited until the last lumbering beast had passed and watched the men ride by. There were three, dusty and common looking, flourishing iron-tipped goads longer than themselves; and with them, their hard, watchful, low-bred dogs.

Inside the inn once more, I ordered breakfast and got bread warm from the oven, newly churned butter, pickled duck's eggs, and peppered chocolate beaten to a froth. (This last a sure sign, though I did not know it then, that I was among people who drew their customs from the north.) Our hairless gnome of a host, who had no doubt seen me in conversation with the alcalde the night before, hovered over my table wiping his nose on his sleeve, inquiring about the quality of each dish as it was served—though they were all, in truth, very good—promising better food at supper, and condemning the cook, who was his wife. He called me *sieur*, not because he thought as they sometimes had in Nessus that I was an exultant incognito, but because a torturer here, as the efficient arm of the law, was a great person. Like most peons, he could conceive of no more than one social class higher than his own.

"The bed, it was comfortable? Plenty of quilts? We will bring more."

My mouth was full, but I nodded.

"Then we shall. Will three be enough? You and the other sieur, are you comfortable together?"

I was about to say that I would prefer separate rooms (I thought Jonas no thief, but I was afraid the Claw might be too much of a temptation for any man, and I was unused, moreover, to sleeping double) when it occurred to me that he might have difficulty paying for a private accommodation.

"You will be there today, sieur? When they break through the wall? A mason could take down the ashlars, but Barnoch's been heard moving inside and may have strength left. Perhaps he's found a weapon. Why, he could bite the mason's fingers, if nothing else!"

"Not in an official capacity. I may watch if I can."

"Everyone's coming." The bald man rubbed his hands, which slithered together as if they had been oiled. "There's to be a fair, you know. The alcalde announced it. He's got a good head for business, our alcalde has. You take the average man—he'd see you here in my parlor and never think of a thing. Or at least, no more than to have you put an end to Morwenna. Not ours! He sees things. He sees the possibilities of them. You might say that in the wink of an eye the whole fair sprang up out of his head, colored tents and ribbons, roast meat and spun sugar, all together. Today? Why today we'll open the sealed house and pull Barnoch out like a badger. That will warm them up, that will draw them for leagues around. Then we'll watch you do for Morwenna and that country fellow. Tomorrow you'll begin on Barnoch—hot irons you start with usually, don't you? And everybody will want to be there. The day after, finish him off and fold the tents. It doesn't do to let them hang about too long after they've spent their money, or they begin to beg and fight and so on. All well planned, all well thought out! There's an alcalde for you!''

I went out again after breakfast and watched the alcalde's enchanted thoughts take shape. Countryfolk were stumping into the village with fruits and animals and bolts of home-woven cloth to sell; among them were a few autochthons carrying fur pelts and strings of black and green birds killed with the cerbotana. Now I wished I still had the mantle Agia's brother had sold me, for my fuligin cloak drew some odd looks. I was about to step inside once more when I heard the quickstep of marching feet, a sound familiar to me from the drilling of the garrison in the Citadel, but which I had not heard since I had left it.

The cattle I had watched earlier that morning had been going down to the river, there to be herded into barges for the remainder of their trip to the abattoirs of Nessus. These soldiers were coming the other way, up from the water. Whether that was because their officers felt the march would toughen them, or because the boats that had brought them were needed elsewhere, or because they were destined for some area remote from Gyoll, I had no way of knowing. I heard the shouted order to sing as they came into the thickening crowd, and almost together with it the thwacks of the vingtners' rods and the howls of the unfortunates who had been hit.

The men were kelau, each armed with a sling with a two-cubit handle and each carrying a painted leather pouch of incendiary bullets. Few looked older than I and most seemed

younger, but their gilded brigandines and the rich belts and
scabbards of their long daggers proclaimed them members of
an elite corps of the erentarii. Their song was not of battle or
women as most soldiers' songs are, but a true slingers' song.
Insofar as I heard it that day, it ran thus:

> "When I was a lad, my mother said,
> 　'You dry your tears and go to bed;
> I know my son will travel far,
> 　Born beneath a shooting star.'

> "In after years, my father said,
> 　As he pulled my hair and knocked my head,
> 　'They mustn't whimper at a scar,
> 　Who're born beneath a shooting star.'

> "A mage I met, and the mage he said,
> 　'I see for you a future red,
> Fire and riot, raid and war,
> 　O born beneath a shooting star.'

> "A shepherd I met, and the shepherd said,
> 　'We sheep must go where we are led,
> To Dawn-Gate where the angels are,
> 　Following the shooting star.'"

And so on, verse after verse, some cryptic (as it seemed
to me), some merely comic, some clearly assembled purely
for the sake of the rhymes, which were repeated again and
again.

"A fine sight, aren't they?" It was the innkeeper, his bald
head at my shoulder. "Southerners—notice how many have
yellow hair and dotted hides? They're used to cold down
there, and they'll need to be in the mountains. Still, the
singing almost makes you want to join 'em. How many,
would you say?"

The baggage mules were just coming into view, laden with
rations and prodded forward with the points of swords. "Two
thousand. Perhaps twenty-five hundred."

"Thank you, sieur. I like to keep track of them. You
wouldn't believe how many I've seen coming up our road
here. But precious few going back. Well, that's what war is, I
believe. I always try to tell myself they're still there—I mean,
wherever it was they went—but you know and I know there's

a lot that have gone to stay. Still, the singing makes a man want to go with 'em."

I asked if he had news of the war.

"Oh, yes, sieur. I've followed it for years and years now, though the battles they fight never seem to make much difference, if you understand me. It never seems to get much closer to us, or much farther off either. What I've always supposed was that our Autarch and theirs appoints a spot to fight in, and when it's over they both go home. My wife, fool that she is, don't believe there's a real war at all."

The crowd had closed behind the last mule driver, and it thickened with every word that passed between us. Bustling men set up stalls and pavilions, narrowing the street and making the press of people greater still; bristling masks on tall poles seemed to have sprouted from the ground like trees.

"Where does your wife think the soldiers are going, then?" I asked the innkeeper.

"Looking for Vodalus, that's what *she* says. As if the Autarch—whose hands run with gold and whose enemies kiss his heel—would send his whole army to fetch a bandit!"

I scarcely heard a word beyond *Vodalus*.

Whatever I possess I would give to become one of you, who complain every day of memories fading. My own do not. They remain always, and always as vivid as at their first impression, so that once summoned they carry me off spell-bound.

I think I turned from the innkeeper and wandered into the crowd of pushing rustics and chattering vendors, but I saw neither them nor him. Instead I felt the bone-strewn paths of the necropolis under my feet, and saw through the drifting river fog the slender figure of Vodalus as he gave his pistol to his mistress and drew his sword. Now (it is a sad thing to have become a man) I was struck by the extravagance of the gesture. He who had professed in a hundred clandestine placards to be fighting for the old ways, for the ancient high civilization Urth has now lost, has discarded the effectual weapon of that civilization.

If my memories of the past remain intact, perhaps it is only because the past exists only in memory. Vodalus, who wished as I did to summon it again, yet remained a creature of the present. That we are capable only of being what we are remains our unforgivable sin.

No doubt if I had been one of you whose memories fade, I

would have rejected him on that morning as I elbowed my way through the crowd, and so in some fashion would have escaped this death in life that grips me even as I write these words. Or perhaps I would not have escaped at all. Yes, more likely not. And in any case, the old, recalled emotions were too strong. I was trapped in admiration for what I had once admired, as a fly in amber remains the captive of some long-vanished pine.

II

The Man in the Dark

The bandit's house had differed in no way from the common houses of the village. It was of broken mine-stone, single storied, with a flattish, solid-looking roof of slabs of the same material. The door and the only window I could see from the street had been closed with rough masonry. A hundred or so fair-goers stood before the house now, talking and pointing; but there was no sound from within, and no smoke issuing from the chimney.

"Is this commonly done hereabouts?" I asked Jonas.

"It's traditional. You've heard the saying, 'A legend, a lie, and a likelihood make a tradition'?"

"It seems to me it would be easy enough to get out. He could break through a window or the wall itself by night, or dig a passage. Of course, if he expected something like this—and if it's common and he was really engaged in spying for Vodalus, there's no reason he shouldn't—he could have supplied himself with tools as well as a quantity of food and drink."

Jonas shook his head. "Before they close the openings, they go through the house and take everything they can find in the way of food and tools and lights, besides whatever else may be of value."

A resonant voice said, "Having good sense, as we flatter ourselves, we do indeed." It was the alcalde, who had come up behind us without either of us noticing his presence in the crowd. We wished him a good day, and he returned the courtesy. He was a solid, square-built man whose open face was marred by something too clever about the eyes. "I thought I recognized you, Master Severian, bright clothes or no. Are these new? They look it. If they don't give satisfaction, speak out to me about it. We try to keep the traders honest that come to our fairs. It's only good business. If he doesn't make them right for you, whoever he is, we'll duck him in the river, you may be sure. One ðr two ducked a year keep the rest from feeling too comfortable."

He paused to step back and examine me more carefully, nodding to himself as though greatly impressed. "They become you. I must say, you've a fine figure. A handsome face too, save perhaps for a bit too much pallor, which our hot northern weather will soon make right. Anyway, they become you and look to wear well. If you're asked where you had them, you might say Saltus Fair. Such talk does no harm."

I promised I would, though I was far more concerned about the safety of *Terminus Est,* which I had left hidden in our room at the inn, than about my own appearance or the durability of the lay clothes I had bought from a slopman.

"You and your assistant have come to see us draw out the miscreant, I suppose? We'll be at him as soon as Mesmin and Sebald bring the post. A battering ram is what we called it when we passed the word of what was intended, but I'm afraid the truth is that it's nothing more than a tree trunk, and not a big one either—otherwise the village would have had to fee too many men to handle it. Yet it should do the work. I don't suppose you've heard of the case we had here eighteen years gone?"

Jonas and I shook our heads.

The alcalde threw out his chest, as politicians do whenever they see an opportunity to speak for more than a couple of sentences. "I recall it well enough, though I wasn't more than a stripling. A woman. I've forgotten her name, but we called her Mother Pyrexia. The stones were put on her, just like what you see here, for it's largely the same ones doing it, and they did it in the same way. But it was the other end of summer, just at apple-picking time, and that I recall very well because of the people drinking new cider in the crowd, and myself with a fresh apple to eat while I watched.

"Next year when the corn was up, someone wanted to buy the house. Property becomes the property of the town, you know. That's how we finance the work, the ones that do it take what they can find for their share, and the town takes the house and ground.

"To shorten a lengthy tale, we cut a ram and broke through the door in fine fashion, thinking to sweep up the old woman's bones and turn the place over to the new owner." The alcalde paused and laughed, throwing back his head. There was something ghostly in that laughter, possibly only because it blended with the noise of the crowd, and so seemed silent.

I asked, "Wasn't she dead?"

"It depends on what you mean by that. I'll say this—a woman sealed in the dark long enough can become something very strange, just like the strange things you find in rotten wood, back among the big trees. We're miners, mostly, here in Saltus, and used to things found underground, but we took to our heels and came back with torches. It didn't like the light, or the fire either."

Jonas touched me on the shoulder and pointed to a swirl in the crowd. A group of purposeful-looking men were shouldering their way down the street. None had helmets or body armor, but several carried narrow-headed piletes, and the rest had brassbound staves. I was strongly reminded of the volunteer guards who had admitted Drotte, Roche, Eata, and me to the necropolis so long ago. Behind these armed men were four who carried the tree trunk the alcalde had mentioned, a rough log about two spans across and six cubits long.

A collective indrawn breath greeted them; it was followed by louder talk and some good-natured cheering. The alcalde left us to take charge, directing the men with staves to clear a space about the door of the sealed house and using his authority, when Jonas and I pushed forward to get a better view, to make the crowd give way for us.

I had supposed that when all the breakers-ins were in position they would proceed without ceremony. In that, I had reckoned without the alcalde. At the last possible moment he mounted the doorstep of the sealed house, and waving his hat for silence, addressed the crowd.

"Welcome visitors and fellow villagers! In the time it takes to draw breath thrice, you will see us smash this barrier and drag out the bandit Barnoch. Whether he be dead, or, as we have good reason to believe—for he hasn't been in there that long—alive. You know what he has done. He has collaborated with the traitor Vodalus's cultellarii, informing them of the arrivals and departures of those who might become their victims! All of you are thinking now, and rightly!, that such a vile crime deserves no mercy. Yes, I say! Yes, we all say! Hundreds and maybe thousands lie in unmarked graves because of this Barnoch. Hundreds and maybe thousands have met a fate far worse!

"Yet for a moment, before these stones come down, I ask you to reflect. Vodalus has lost a spy. He will be seeking another. On some still night not long, I think, from now, a stranger will come to one of you. It is certain he will have much talk—"

"Like you!" someone shouted, to general laughter.

"Better talk than mine—I'm only a rough miner, as many of you know. Much smooth, persuasive talk, I ought to have said, and possibly some money. Before you nod your head at him, I want you to remember this house of Barnoch's the way it looks now, with those ashlars where the door should be. Think about your own house with no doors and no windows, but with you inside it.

"Then think about what you're going to see done to Barnoch when we take him out. Because I'm telling you—you strangers particularly—what you're about to see here is only the beginning of what you'll be seeing at our fair in Saltus! For the events of the next few days we have employed one of the finest professionals from Nessus! You will see *at least* two persons executed here in the formal style, with the head struck off at a single blow. One's a woman, so we'll be using the chair! That's something a lot of people who boast of their sophistication and the cosmopolitan tincture of their educations have never seen. And you will see this man," pausing, the alcalde struck the sunlit door-stones with the flat of his hand, "this Barnoch, led to Death by an expert guide! It may be that he has made some sort of small hole in the wall by now. Frequently they do, and if so he may be able to hear me."

He lifted his voice to a shout. "If you can, Barnoch, cut your throat now! Because if you don't, you're going to wish you had starved long ago!"

For a moment there was silence. I was in agony at the thought that I should soon have to practice the Art on a follower of Vodalus's. The alcalde raised his right arm over his head, then brought it down in an emphatic gesture. "All right, lads, at it with a will!"

The four who had brought the ram counted *one, two, three* to themselves as if by prearrangement and ran at the walled-up door, losing some of their impetuosity when the two in front mounted the step. The ram struck the stones with a loud thump, but with no other result.

"All right, lads," the alcalde repeated. "Let's try it again. Show them the kind of men Saltus breeds."

The four charged a second time. At this attempt, those in front handled the step more skillfully; the stones plugging the doorway seemed to shudder under the impact, and a fine dust issued from the mortar. A volunteer from the crowd, a burly, black-bearded fellow, joined the original ramsmen, and all five charged; the thump of the ram was not noticeably louder, but it was accompanied by a cracking like the breaking of bones. "One more," the alcalde said.

He was right. The next blow sent the stone it struck into the house, leaving a hole the size of a man's head. After that, the ramsmen no longer bothered with a running start; they knocked the remaining stones out by swinging the ram with their arms until the aperture was large enough for a man to step through.

Someone I had not noticed previously had brought torches, and a boy ran to a neighboring house to kindle them at the kitchen fire. The men with pilettes and staves took them from him. Showing more courage than I would have credited to those clever eyes, the alcalde drew a short truncheon from under his shirt and entered first. We spectators crowded after the armed men, and because Jonas and I had been in the forefront of the onlookers, we reached the opening almost at once.

The air was foul, far worse than I had anticipated. Broken furniture lay on every side, as though Barnoch had locked his chests and cupboards when the sealers came, and they had smashed them to get at his household goods. On a crippled table, I saw the guttered wax of a candle that had burned to the wood. The people behind me were pushing to go in farther; and I, as I discovered somewhat to my surprise, was pushing back.

There was a commotion at the rear of the house—hurried and confused footsteps—a shout—then a high, inhuman scream.

"They've got him!" someone behind me called, and I heard the news being passed to those outside.

A fattish man who might have been a smallholder came running out of the dark, a torch in one hand and a stave in the other. "Out of the way! Get back, all of you! They're bringing him out!"

I do not know what I expected to see. . . . Perhaps a filthy creature with matted hair. What came instead was a ghost. Barnoch had been tall; he was tall still, but stooped and very thin, with skin so pale it seemed to glow as decayed wood does. He was hairless, bald, and beardless; I learned that afternoon from his guards that he had formed the habit of plucking his hairs out. Worst of all were his eyes: protuberant, seemingly blind, and dark as the black abscess of his mouth. I turned away from him as he spoke, but I knew the voice was his. "I will be free," it said. "Vodalus! Vodalus will come!"

How I wished then that I had never been imprisoned myself, for his voice brought back to me all those airless days when I waited in the oubliette beneath our Matachin Tower. I too had dreamed of rescue by Vodalus, of a revolution that would sweep away the animal stench and degeneracy of the present age and restore the high and gleaming culture that was once Urth's.

And I had been saved not by Vodalus and his shadowy army, but by the advocacy of Master Palaemon—and no doubt of Drotte and Roche and a few other friends—who had persuaded the brothers that it would be too dangerous to kill me and too disgraceful to bring me before a tribunal.

Barnoch would not be saved at all. I, who should have been his comrade, would brand him, break him on the wheel, and at last sever his head. I tried to tell myself that he had acted, perhaps, only to get money; but as I did so some metal object, no doubt the steel head of a pilete, struck stone, and I seemed to hear the ringing of the coin Vodalus had given me, the ringing as I dropped it into the space beneath the floor-stone of the ruined mausoleum.

Sometimes when all our attention is thus focused on memory, our eyes, unguided by ourselves, will distinguish from a mass of detail some single object, presenting it with a clarity never achieved by concentration. So it was with me. Out of all the struggling tide of faces beyond the doorway, I saw one, upturned, illuminated by the sun. It was Agia's.

III

The Showman's Tent

The instant was frozen as though we two, and all those about us, stood in a painting. Agia's uptilted face, my own wide eyes; so we remained amid the cloud of countryfolk with their bright clothes and bundles. Then I moved, and she was gone. I would have run to her if I could; but I could only push my way through the onlookers, taking perhaps a hundred poundings of my heart to reach the spot where she had stood.

By then she had vanished utterly, and the crowd was swirling and changing like the water under the bow of a boat. Barnoch had been led forth, screaming at the sun. I took a miner by the shoulder and shouted a question to him, but he had paid no attention to the young woman beside him and had no notion of where she might have gone. I followed the throng who followed the prisoner until I was sure she was not among them, then, knowing nothing better to do, began to search the fair, peering into tents and booths, and making inquiries of the farmwives who had come to sell their fragrant cardamom-bread, and of the hot-meat vendors.

All this, as I write it, slowly convoluting a thread of the vermilion ink of the House Absolute, sounds calm and even methodical. Nothing could be further from the truth. I was gasping and sweating as I did these things, shouting questions to which I hardly stayed for an answer. Like a face seen in dream, Agia's floated before my imagination: wide, flat cheeks and softly rounded chin, freckled, sun-browned skin and long, laughing, mocking eyes. Why she had come, I could not imagine; I only knew she had, and that my glimpse of her had reawakened the anguish of my memory of her scream.

"Have you seen a woman so tall, with chestnut hair?" I repeated it again and again, like the duelist who had called out "Cadroe of Seventeen Stones," until the phrase was as meaningless as the song of the cicada.

"Yes. Every country maid who comes here."

"Do you know her name?"

"A woman? Certainly I can get you a woman."

"Where did you lose her?"

"Don't worry, you'll soon find her again. The fair's not big enough for anybody to stay lost long. Didn't the two of you arrange a place to meet? Have some of my tea—you look so tired."

I fumbled for a coin.

"You don't have to pay, I sell enough as it is. Well, if you insist. It's only an aes. Here."

The old woman rummaged in her apron pocket and produced a flood of little coins, then splashed the tea, hissing hot, from her kettle into an earthenware cup and offered me a straw of some dimly silver metal. I waved it away.

"It's clean. I rinse everything after each customer."

"I'm not used to them."

"Watch the rim then—it'll be hot. Have you looked by the judging? There'll be a lot of people there."

"Where the cattle are? Yes." The tea was maté, spicy and a trifle bitter.

"Does she know you're looking for her?"

"I don't think so. Even if she saw me, she wouldn't have recognized me. I . . . am not dressed as I usually am."

The old woman snorted and pushed a straggling lock of gray hair back under her kerchief. "At Saltus Fair? Of course not! Everybody wears his best to a fair, and any girl with sense would know that. How about down by the water where they've got the prisoner chained?"

I shook my head. "She seems to have disappeared."

"But you haven't given up. I can tell from the way you look at the people going past instead of me. Well, good for you. You'll find her yet, though they do say all manner of strange things have been happening round and about of late. They caught a green man, do you know that? Got him right over there where you see the tent. Green men know everything, people say, if you can but make them talk. Then there's the cathedral. I suppose you've heard about that?"

"The cathedral?"

"I've heard tell it wasn't what cityfolk call a real one—I

know you're from the city by the way you drink your tea—but it's the only cathedral most of us around Saltus ever saw, and pretty too, with all the hanging lamps and the windows in the sides made of colored silk. Myself, I don't believe—or rather, I think that if the Pancreator don't care nothing for me, I won't care nothing for him, and why should I? Still, it's a shame what they did, if they did what's told against them. Set fire to it, you know."

"Are you talking about the Cathedral of the Pelerines?"

The old woman nodded sagely. "There, you said it yourself. You're making the same mistake they did. It wasn't the Cathedral of the Pelerines, it was the Cathedral of the Claw. Which is to say, it wasn't theirs to burn."

To myself I muttered, "They rekindled the fire."

"I beg pardon." The old woman cocked an ear. "I didn't hear that."

"I said they burned it. They must have set fire to the straw floor."

"That's what I heard too. They just stood back and watched it burn. It went up to the Infinite Meadows of the New Sun, you know."

A man on the opposite side of the alleyway began to pound a drum. When he paused I said, "I know that certain persons have claimed to have seen it rise into the air."

"Oh, it rose all right. When my grandson-in-law heard about it, he was fairly struck flat for half a day. Then he pasted up a kind of hat out of paper and held it over my stove, and it went up, and then he thought it was nothing that the cathedral rose, no miracle at all. That shows what it is to be a fool—it never came to him that the reason things were made so was so the cathedral would rise just like it did. He can't see the Hand in nature."

"He didn't see it himself?" I asked. "The cathedral, I mean."

She failed to understand. "Oh, he's seen it when they've been through here, at least a dozen times."

The chant of the man with the drum, similar to that I had once heard Dr. Talos use, but more hoarsely delivered and bereft of the doctor's malicious intelligence, cut through our talk. *"Knows everything! Knows everybody! Green as a gooseberry! See for yourself!"*

(The insistent voice of the drum: BOOM! BOOM! BOOM!)

"Do you think the green man would know where Agia is?"

The old woman smiled. "So that's her name, is it? Now I'll know, if anybody should mention her. He might. You've money, why not try him?"

Why not indeed, I thought.

"Brought from the jun-gles of the North! Never eats! A-kin to the bush-es and the grass-es!" BOOM! BOOM! *"The fu-ture and the re-mote past are one to him!"*

When he saw me approaching the door of his tent, the drummer stopped his clamor. "Only an aes to see him. Two to speak with him. Three to be alone with him."

"Alone for how long?" I asked as I selected three copper aes. A wry grin crossed the drummer's face. "For as long as you wish." I handed him his money and stepped inside.

It had been plain he had not thought I would want to stay long, and I expected a stench or something equally unpleasant. There was nothing beyond a slight odor as of hay curing. In the center of the tent, in a dust-spangled shaft of sunlight admitted by a vent in the canvas roof, was chained a man the color of pale jade. He wore a kilt of leaves, now fading; beside him stood a clay pot filled to the brim with clear water.

For a moment we were silent. I stood looking at him. He sat looking at the ground. "That's not paint," I said. "Nor do I think it dye. And you have no more hair than the man I saw dragged from the sealed house."

He looked up at me, then down again. Even the whites of his eyes held a greenish tint.

I tried to bait him. "If you are truly vegetable, I would think your hair should be grass."

"No." He had a soft voice, saved from womanishness only by its depth.

"You *are* vegetable then? A speaking plant?"

"You are no countryman."

"I left Nessus a few days ago."

"With some education."

I thought of Master Palaemon, then of Master Malrubius and my poor Thecla, and I shrugged. "I can read and write."

"Yet you know nothing about me. I am not a talking vegetable, as you should be able to see. Even if a plant were to follow the one evolutionary way, out of some many millions, that leads to intelligence, it is impossible that it should duplicate in wood and leaf the form of a human being."

"The same thing might be said of stones, yet there are statues."

For all his aspect of despair (and his was a sadder face by far than my friend Jonas's), something tugged at the corners of his lips. "That is well put. You have no scientific training, but you are better taught than you realize."

"On the contrary, all my training has been scientific— although it had nothing to do with these fantastic speculations. What are you?"

"A great seer. A great liar, like every man whose foot is in a trap."

"If you'll tell me what you are, I'll endeavor to help you."

He looked at me, and it was as if some tall herb had opened eyes and shown a human face. "I believe you," he said. "Why is it that you, of all the hundreds who come to this tent, know pity?"

"I know nothing of pity, but I have been imbued with a respect for justice, and I am well acquainted with the alcalde of this village. A green man is still a man; and if he is a slave, his master must show how he came to that state, and how he himself came into possession of him."

The green man said, "I'm a fool, I suppose, to put any confidence in you. And yet I do. I am a free man, come from your own future to explore your age."

"That is impossible."

"The green color that puzzles your people so much is only what you call pond scum. We have altered it until it can live in our blood, and by its intervention have at last made our peace in humankind's long struggle with the sun. In us, the tiny plants live and die, and our bodies feed from them and their dead and require no other nourishment. All the famines, and all the labor of growing food, are ended."

"But you must have sun."

"Yes," the green man said. "And I have not enough here. Day is brighter in my age."

That simple remark thrilled me in a way that nothing had since I had first glimpsed the unroofed chapel in the Broken Court of our Citadel. "Then the New Sun comes as prophesied," I said, "and there is indeed a second life for Urth—if what you say is the truth."

The green man threw back his head and laughed. Much later I was to hear the sound the alzabo makes as it ranges the snowswept tablelands of the high country; its laughter is horrible, but the green man's was more terrible, and I drew away from him. "You're not a human being," I said. "Not now, if you ever were."

He laughed again. "And to think I hoped in you. What a poor creature I am. I thought I had resigned myself to dying here among a people who are no more than walking dust; but at the tiniest gleam, all my resignation fell from me. I am a true man, friend. You are not, and in a few months I will be dead."

I remembered his kin. How often I had seen the frozen stalks of summer flowers dashed by the wind against the sides of the mausoleums in our necropolis. "I understand you. The warm days of sun are coming, but when they are gone, you will go with them. Grow seed while you can."

He sobered. "You do not believe me or even understand that I am a man like yourself, yet you still pity me. Perhaps you are right, and for us a new sun has come, and because it has come we have forgotten it. If I am ever able to return to my own time, I will tell them there of you."

"If you are indeed of the future, why cannot you go forward to your home, and so escape?"

"Because I am chained, as you see." He held out his leg so that I could examine the shackle about his ankle. His berylline flesh was swollen about it, as I have seen the bark of a tree swollen that had grown through an iron ring.

The tent flap opened, and the drummer thrust his head through. "Are you still here? I have others outside." He looked significantly at the green man and withdrew.

"He means that I must drive you off, or he will close the vent through which my sunlight falls. I drive away those who pay to see me by foretelling their futures, and I will foretell yours. You are young now, and strong. But before this world has wound itself ten times more about the sun you shall be less strong, and you shall never regain the strength that is yours now. If you breed sons, you will engender enemies against yourself. If—"

"Enough!" I said. "What you are telling me is only the fortune of all men. Answer one question truthfully for me, and I will go. I am looking for a woman called Agia. Where will I find her?"

For a moment his eyes rolled upward until only a narrow crescent of pale green showed beneath their lids. A faint tremor seized him; he stood and extended his arms, his fingers splayed like twigs. Slowly he said, "Above ground."

The tremor ceased, and he sat again, older looking and paler than before.

"You are only a fraud then," I told him as I turned away. "And I was a simpleton to believe in you even by so little."

"No," the green man whispered. "Listen. In coming here, I have passed through all your future. Some parts of it remain with me, no matter how clouded. I told you only the truth—and if you are indeed a friend of the alcalde of this place, I will tell you something further that you may tell him, something I have learned from the questions of those who have come to question me. Armed men are seeking to free a man called Barnoch."

I took my whetstone from the sabretache at my belt, broke it on the top of the chain-stake, and gave half to him. For a moment he did not comprehend what it was he held. Then I saw the knowledge growing in him, so that he seemed to unfold in his great joy, as though he were already basking in the brighter light of his own day.

IV

The Bouquet

As I left the showman's tent, I glanced up at the sun. The western horizon had already climbed more than half up the sky; in a watch or less it would be time for me to make my appearance. Agia was gone, and any hope of overtaking her had been lost in the frantic time I had spent dashing from one end of the fair to the other; yet I took comfort from the green man's prophecy, which I took to mean that Agia and I should meet again before either of us died, and from the thought that since she had come to watch Barnoch drawn into the light, so, equally, might she come to observe the executions of Morwenna and the cattle thief.

These speculations occupied me at first as I made my way back to the inn. But before I reached the room I shared with Jonas, they had been displaced by recollections of Thecla and my elevation to journeyman, both occasioned by the need to change from my new lay clothes into the fuligin of the guild. So strong is the power of association that it could be exercised by that habit while it was still out of sight on the pegs in the room, and by *Terminus Est* while she remained concealed beneath the mattress.

It used to entertain me, while I was still attendant upon Thecla, to find that I could anticipate much of her conversation, and particularly the first of it, from the nature of the gift I carried when I entered her cell. If it were some favorite food thieved from the kitchen, for example, it would elicit a description of a meal at the House Absolute, and the kind of food I brought even governed the nature of the repast described: flesh, a sporting dinner with the shrieking and

29

trumpeting of game caught alive drifting up from the abattoir below and much talk of brachets, hawks, and hunting leopards; sweets, a private repast given by one of the great Chatelaines for a few friends, deliciously intimate, and soaked in gossip; fruit, a twilit garden party in the vast park of the House Absolute, lit by a thousand torches and enlivened by jugglers, actors, dancers, and pyrotechnic displays.

She ate standing as often as sitting, walking the three strides that took her from one end of her cell to the other, holding the dish in her left hand while she gestured with her right. "Like this, Severian, they all spring into the ringing sky, showering green and magenta sparks, while the maroons boom like thunder!"

But her poor hand could hardly show the rockets rising higher than her towering head, for the ceiling was not much taller than she.

"But I'm boring you. A moment ago, when you brought me these peaches, you looked so happy, and now you won't smile. It's just that it does me good, here, to remember those things. How I'll enjoy them when I see them again."

I was not bored, of course. It was only that it saddened me to see her, a woman still young and endowed with a terrible beauty, so confined. . . .

Jonas was uncovering *Terminus Est* for me when I came into our room. I poured myself a cup of wine. "How do you feel?" he asked.

"What of you? It's your first time, after all."

He shrugged. "I only have to fetch and carry. You've done it before? I wondered, because you look so young."

"Yes, I've done it before. Never to a woman."

"You think she's innocent?"

I was taking off my shirt; when I had my arms freed I mopped my face with it and shook my head. "I'm sure she's not. I went down and talked to her last night—they have her chained at the edge of the water, where the midges are bad. I told you about it."

Jonas reached for the wine himself, his metal hand clinking when it met the cup. "You told me that she was beautiful, and that she had black hair like—"

"Thecla. But Morwenna's is straight. Thecla's curled."

"Like Thecla, whom you seem to have loved as I love your friend Jolenta. I confess you had a great deal more time to fall in love than I did. And you told me she said her husband and child had died of some sickness, probably from bad water. The husband had been quite a bit older than she."

I said, "About your age, I think."

"And there was an older woman there who had wanted him too, and now she was tormenting the prisoner."

"Only with words." Among the guild, apprentices alone wear shirts. I drew on my trousers and put my cloak (which was of fuligin, the color darker than black) around my bare shoulders. "Clients who have been exposed by the authorities like that have usually been stoned. When we see them they're bruised, and often they've lost a few teeth. Sometimes they have broken bones. The women have been raped."

"You say she's beautiful. Perhaps people think she's innocent. Perhaps they took pity on her."

I picked up *Terminus Est,* drew her, and let the soft sheath fall away. "The innocent have enemies. They are afraid of her."

We went out together.

When I had entered the inn, I had to push my way through the mob of drinkers. Now it opened before me. I wore my mask and carried *Terminus Est* unsheathed across my shoulder. Outside, the sounds of the fair stilled as we went forward until nothing remained but a whispering, as though we strode through a wilderness of leaves.

The executions were to take place at the very center of the festivities, and a dense crowd had already gathered there. A caloyer in red stood beside the scaffold clutching his little formulary; he was an old man, as most of them are. The two prisoners waited beside him, surrounded by the men who had taken forth Barnoch. The alcalde wore his yellow gown of office and his gold chain.

By ancient custom, we must not use the steps (although I have seen Master Gurloes assist his vault to the scaffold with his sword, in the court before the Bell Tower). I was, very possibly, the only person present who knew of the tradition; but I did not break it, and a great roar, like the voice of some beast, escaped the crowd as I leaped up with my cloak billowing about me.

"*Increate,*" read the caloyer, "*it is known to us that those who will perish here are no more evil in your sight than we. Their hands run with blood. Ours also.*"

I examined the block. Those used outside the immediate supervision of the guild are notoriously bad: "Wide as a stool, dense as a fool, and dished, as a rule." This one fulfilled the first two specifications in the proverbial description only too well, but by the mercy of Holy Katharine it was actually slightly convex, and though the idiotically hard wood would be sure to dull the male side of my blade, I was in the fortunate position of having before me one subject of either sex, so that I could use a fresh edge on each.

"... *by thy will they may, in that hour, have so purified their spirits as to gain thy favor. We who must confront them then, though we spill their blood today ...*"

I posed, legs wide as I leaned upon my sword as if I were in complete control of the ceremony, though the truth was that I did not know which of them had drawn the short ribbon.

"*You, the hero who will destroy the black worm that devours the sun; you for whom the sky parts as a curtain; you whose breath shall wither vast Erebus, Abaia, and Scylla who wallow beneath the wave; you that equally live in the shell of the smallest seed in the farthest forest, the seed that hath rolled into the dark where no man sees.*"

The woman Morwenna was coming up the steps, preceded by the alcalde and followed by a man with an iron spit who used it to prod her. Someone in the crowd shouted an obscene suggestion.

"*... have mercy on those who had no mercy. Have mercy on us, who shall have none now.*"

The caloyer was finished, and the alcalde began. "Most hatefully and unnaturally . . ."

His voice was high, quite different both from his normal speaking voice and the rhetorical tone he had adopted for the speech outside Barnoch's house. After listening absently for a few moments (I was looking for Agia in the crowd), it struck me that he was frightened. He would have to witness everything that was done to both prisoners at close range. I smiled, though my mask concealed it.

"... of respect for your sex. But you shall be branded on the right cheek and the left, your legs broken, and your head struck from your body."

(I hoped they had had sense enough to remember that a brazier of coals would be required.)

"Through the power of the high justice laid upon my unworthy arm by the condescension of the Autarch—whose thoughts are the music of his subjects—I do now declare . . . I do now declare . . ."

He had forgotten it. I whispered the words: "That your moment has come upon you."

"I do now declare that your moment has come on you, Morwenna."

"If you have pleas for the Conciliator, speak them in your heart."

"If you have pleas for the Conciliator, speak them."

"If you have counsels for the children of women, there will be no voice for them after this."

The alcalde's self-possession was returning, and he got it all: "If you have counsels for the children of women, there will be no voice for them after this."

Clearly but not loudly, Morwenna said, "I know that most of you think me guilty. I am innocent. I would never do the horrible things you have accused me of."

The crowd drew closer to hear her.

"Many of you are my witnesses that I loved Stachys. I loved the child Stachys gave me."

A patch of color caught my eye, purple-black in the strong spring sunshine. It was such a bouquet of threnodic roses as a mute might carry at a funeral. The woman who held them was Eusebia, whom I had met when she tormented Morwenna at the riverside. As I watched her, she inhaled their perfume rapturously, then employed their thorny stems to open a path for herself through the crowd, so that she stood just at the base of the scaffold. "These are for you, Morwenna. Die before they fade."

I hammered the planks with the blunt tip of my blade for silence. Morwenna said, "The good man who read the prayers for me, and who has talked to me before I was brought here, prayed that I would forgive you if I achieved bliss before you. I have never until now had it in my power to grant a prayer, but I grant his. I forgive you now."

Eusebia was about to speak again, but I silenced her with a look. The gap-toothed, grinning man beside her waved, and with something of a start I recognized Hethor.

"Are you ready?" Morwenna asked me. "I am."

Jonas had just set a bucket of glowing charcoal on the scaffold. From it thrust what was presumably the handle of a suitable inscribed iron; but there was no chair. I gave the alcalde a glance I intended to be significant.

I might have been looking at a post. At last I said, "Have we a chair, Your Worship?"

"I sent two men to fetch one. And some rope."

"When?" (The crowd was beginning to stir and murmur.)

"A few moments ago."

The evening before he had assured me that everything would be in readiness, but there was no point in reminding him of that now. There is no one, as I have since found, so liable to fluster on the scaffold as the average rural official. He is torn between an ardent desire to be the center of attention (a position closed to him at an execution) and the quite justified fear that he lacks the ability and training that might enable him to comport himself well. The most cowardly client, mounting the steps in the full knowledge that his eyes are to be plucked out, will in nineteen cases from a score conduct himself better. Even a shy cenobite, unused to the sounds of men and diffident to the point of tears, can be better relied on.

Someone called, "Get it over with!"

I looked at Morwenna. With her famished face and clear complexion, her pensive smile and large, dark eyes, she was a prisoner likely to arouse quite undesirable feelings of sympathy in the crowd.

"We could seat her on the block," I told the alcalde. I could not resist adding, "It's more suited to that anyway."

"There's nothing to tie her with."

I had permitted myself a remark too many already, so I forbore giving my opinion of those who require their prisoners bound.

Instead, I laid *Terminus Est* flat behind the block, made Morwenna sit down, lifted my arms in the ancient salute, took the iron in my right hand, and, gripping her wrists with my left, administered the brand to either cheek, then held up the iron still glowing almost white. The scream had silenced the crowd for an instant; now they roared.

The alcalde straightened himself and seemed to become a new man. "Let them see her," he said.

I had been hoping to avoid that, but I helped Morwenna to rise. With her right hand in mine, as though we were taking part in a country dance, we made a slow, formal circuit of the platform. Hethor was beside himself with delight, and though I tried to shut out the sound of his voice, I could hear him boasting of his acquaintance with me to the people around him. Eusebia held up her bouquet to Morwenna, calling, "Here, you'll need these soon enough."

When we had gone once around, I looked at the alcalde, and after the pause necessitated by his wondering at the occasion for the delay, received the signal to proceed.

Morwenna whispered, "Will it be over soon?"

"It is almost over now." I had seated her on the block again, and was picking up my sword. "Close your eyes. Try to remember that almost everyone who has ever lived has died, even the Conciliator, who will rise as the New Sun."

Her pale, long-lashed eyelids fell, and she did not see the upraised sword. The flash of steel silenced the crowd again, and when the full hush had come, I brought the flat of the blade down upon her thighs; over the smack of it on flesh, the sound of the femurs breaking came as clear as the *crack, crack* of a winning boxer's left-hand, right-hand blows. For an instant Morwenna remained poised on the block, fainted but not fallen; in that instant I took a backward step and severed her neck with the smooth, horizontal stroke that is so much more difficult to master than the downward.

To be candid, it was not until I saw the up-jetting fountain of blood and heard the thud of the head striking the platform that I knew I had carried it off. Without realizing it, I had been as nervous as the alcalde.

That is the moment when, again by ancient tradition, the customary dignity of the guild is relaxed. I wanted to laugh and caper. The alcalde was shaking my shoulder and babbling as I wished to myself; I could not hear what he said—some happy nonsense. I held up my sword, and taking the head by the hair held it up too, and paraded the scaffold. Not a single circuit this time, but again and again, three times, four times. A breeze had sprung up; it dotted my mask and arm and bare chest with scarlet. The crowd was shouting the inevitable jests: "Will you cut my wife's (husband's) hair too?" "Half a measure of sausage when you're done with that." "Can I have her hat?"

I laughed at them all and was feigning to toss the head to them when someone plucked at my ankle. It was Eusebia, and I knew before her first word that she was under that compulsion to speak I had often observed among the clients in our tower. Her eyes were sparkling with excitement, and her face was twisted by her attempt to get my attention, so that she looked simultaneously older and younger than she had appeared before. I could not make out what she was shouting and bent to listen.

"*Innocent! She was innocent!*"

This was no time to explain that I had not been Morwenna's judge. I only nodded.

"*She took Stachys—from me! Now she's dead. Do you understand? She was innocent after all, but I am so glad!*"

I nodded again and made another circuit of the scaffold, holding up the head.

"I killed her!" Eusebia screamed. *"Not you—!"*

I called down to her: "If you like!"

"Innocent! I knew her—so careful. She would have kept something back—poison for herself! She would have died before you got her."

Hethor grasped her arm and pointed to me. *"My master! Mine! My own!"*

"So it was somebody else. Or sickness after all—"

I shouted: "To the Demiurge alone belongs all justice!" The crowd was still noisy, though it had quieted a trifle by this time.

"But she stole my Stachys, and now she's gone." Louder than ever: *"Oh, wonderful! She's gone!"* With that, Eusebia plunged her face into the bouquet as though to fill her lungs to bursting with the roses' cloying perfume. I dropped Morwenna's head into the basket that awaited it and wiped my sword blade with the piece of scarlet flannel Jonas handed me. When I noticed Eusebia again she was lifeless, sprawled among a circle of onlookers.

At the time I thought little of it, only supposing that her heart had failed in her excess of joy. Later that afternoon the alcalde had her bouquet examined by an apothecary, who found among the petals a strong but subtle poison he could not identify. Morwenna must, I suppose, have had it in her hand when she mounted the steps, and must have cast it into the blossoms when I led her around the scaffold after the branding.

Allow me to pause here and speak to you as one mind to another, though we are separated, perhaps, by the abyss of eons. Though what I have already written—from the locked gate to the fair at Saltus—embraces most of my adult life, and what remains to be recorded concerns a few months only, I feel I am less than half concluded with my narrative. In order that it shall not fill a library as great as old Ultan's, I will (I tell you now plainly) pass over many things. I have recounted the execution of Agia's twin brother Agilus because of its importance to my story, and that of Morwenna because of the unusual circumstances surrounding it. I will not recount others unless they hold some special interest. If you delight in another's pain and death, you will gain little satisfaction from me. Let it be sufficient to say that I performed the prescribed operations on the cattle thief, which terminated in his execution; in the future, when I describe my travels, you are to understand that I practiced the mystery of our guild where it was profitable to do so, though I do not mention the specific occasions.

V

The Bourne

That evening, Jonas and I dined alone in our room. It is a very pleasant thing, I found, to be popular with the mob and known to everyone; but it is tiring, too, and after a time one grows weary of answering the same simple-minded questions again and again, and of politely refusing invitations to drink.

There had been a slight disagreement with the alcalde concerning the compensation I was to receive for my work, my understanding having been that in addition to the quarter-payment made when I was engaged, I would receive full payment for each client upon death, while the alcalde had intended, so he said, that full payment should be made only after all three were attended to. I would never have agreed to that, and liked it less than ever in the light of the green man's warning (which out of loyalty to Vodalus I had kept to myself). But after I had threatened not to appear on the following afternoon I was paid, and everything peaceably resolved.

Now Jonas and I were settled over a smoking platter and a bottle of wine, the door was shut and bolted, and the innkeeper had been instructed to deny that I was in his establishment. I would have been completely at ease if the wine in my cup had not recalled to me so vividly the much better wine Jonas had discovered in our ewer the night before, after I had examined the Claw in secret.

Jonas, observing me, I think, as I stared at the pale red fluid, poured a cup of his own and said, "You must remember that you are not responsible for the sentences. If you had not come here, they would have been punished eventually anyway, and probably would have suffered worse in less skilled hands."

I asked him what he thought he was talking about.

"I can see it troubles you . . . what happened today."

"I thought it went well," I said.

"You know what the octopus remarked when he got out of the mermaid's kelp bed: 'I'm not impugning your skill—quite the opposite. But you look as if you could use a little cheering up.'"

"We're always a little despondent afterward. That's what Master Palaemon always said, and I've found it true in my own case. He called it a purely mechanical psychological function, and at the time that seemed to me an oxymoron, but now I'm not sure he wasn't right. Could you see what happened, or did they keep you too busy?"

"I was standing on the steps behind you most of the time."

"You had a good view then, so you must have seen how it was—everything proceeded smoothly after we decided not to wait for the chair. I exercised my skills to applause, and I was the focus of admiration. There's a feeling of lassitude afterward. Master Palaemon used to talk of crowd melancholy and court melancholy, and said that some of us have both, some have neither, and some have one but not the other. Well, I have crowd melancholy; I don't suppose I'll ever have the chance, in Thrax, of discovering whether I also have court melancholy or not."

"And what is that?" Jonas was looking down into his wine cup.

"A torturer, let's say a master at the Citadel, is occasionally brought into contact with exultants of the highest degree. Suppose there's some exceedingly sensitive prisoner who's thought to possess important information. An official of lofty standing is likely to be delegated to attend such a prisoner's examination. Very often he will have had little experience with the more delicate operations, so he will ask the master questions and perhaps confide in him certain fears he has concerning the subject's temperament or health. A torturer under those circumstances feels himself to be at the center of things—"

"Then feels let down when it's over with. Yes, I suppose I can see that."

"Have you ever seen one of these affairs when it was badly botched?"

"No. Aren't you going to eat any of this meat?"

"Neither have I, but I've heard about them, and that's why I was tense. Times when the client has broken away and fled into the crowd. Times when several strokes were needed to part the neck. Times when a torturer lost all confidence and was unable to proceed. When I vaulted onto that scaffold, I had no way of knowing that none of those things was going to happen to me. If they had, I might have been finished for life."

" 'Still, it's a terrible way to earn a living.' That's what the thorn-bush said to the shrike, you know."

"I really don't—" I broke off because I had seen something move on the farther side of the room. At first I thought it was a rat, and I have a pronounced dislike of them; I have seen too many clients bitten in the oubliette under our tower.

"What is it?"

"Something white." I walked around the table to see. "A sheet of paper. Someone has slipped a note under our door."

"Another woman wanting to sleep with you," Jonas said, but by that time I had already picked it up. It was indeed a woman's delicate script, written in grayish ink upon parchment. I held it close to the candle to read.

Dearest Severian:

From one of the kind men who are assisting me, I have learned you are in the village of Saltus, not far away. It seems too good to be true, but now I must discover whether you can forgive me.

I swear to you that any suffering you have endured for my sake was not by my choice. From the first, I wanted to tell you everything, but the others would not hear of it. They judged that no one should know but those who had to know (which meant no one but themselves), and at last told me outright that if I did not obey them in *everything* they would forgo the plan and leave me to die. I knew you would die for me, and so I dared to hope that you would have chosen, if you could choose, to suffer for me too. Forgive me.

But now I am away and almost free—my own mistress so long as I obey the simple and humane instructions of good Father Inire. And so I will tell you everything, in the hope that when you have heard it all you will indeed forgive me.

You know of my arrest. You will remember too how anxious your Master Gurloes was for my comfort, and how frequently he visited my cell to talk to me, or had me brought to him so that he and the other masters might question me. That was because my patron, the good Father Inire, had charged him to be strictly attentive to me.

At length, when it became clear that the Autarch would not free me, Father Inire arranged to do so himself. I do not know what threats were made to Master Gurloes, or what bribes were offered him. But they were sufficient, and a few days before my death—as you thought, dearest Severian—he explained to me how the matter was to be arranged. It was not enough, of course, that I be freed. I must be freed in such a way that no search should be made for me. That meant it needs appear that I was dead; yet the instructions Master Gurloes had received had charged him strictly not to let me die.

You will now be able to fathom for yourself how we cut through this tangle of obstructions. It was arranged that I should be subjected to a device whose action was internal only, and Master Gurloes first so disarmed it that I should suffer no real harm. When you thought me in agony, I was to ask you for means of terminating my wretched life. All went as planned. You provided the knife, and I made a shallow cut on my arm, crouched near the door so some blood would run beneath it, then smeared my throat and fell across the bed for you to see when you looked into my prison.

Did you look? I lay as still as death. My eyes were closed, but I seemed to feel your pain when you saw me there. I nearly wept, and I recall how frightened I was that you might see the tears welling up. At last I heard your footsteps, and I bandaged my arm and washed my face and neck. After a time Master Gurloes came and took me away. Forgive me.

Now I would see you again, and if Father Inire wins a pardon for me as he has solemnly pledged himself to do, there is no reason why we need ever part again. But come to me at once—I am awaiting his messenger, and if he arrives I must fly to the House Absolute to cast myself at the feet of the Autarch, whose name be thrice-blessed balm upon the scorched brows of his slaves.

Speak to *no one* of this, but go northeast from Saltus until you encounter a brook that winds its way to Gyoll.

Trace it against the current, and you will find it to issue from the mouth of a mine.

Here I must impart to you a grave secret, which you must by no means reveal to others. This mine is a treasure house of the Autarch's, and in it he has stored great sums of coined money, bullion, and gems against a day in which he may be forced from the Phoenix Throne. It is guarded by certain servitors of Father Inire's, but you need have no fear of them. They have been instructed to obey me, and I have told them of you, and ordered them to permit you to pass without challenge. Entering the mine, then, follow the water-course until you reach the end, where it issues from a stone. Here I wait, and here I write, in the hope that you will forgive your

THECLA

I cannot describe the surge of joy I felt as I read and reread this letter. Jonas, who saw my face, at first leaped from his chair—I think he supposed I was on the point of fainting—then drew away as he might have from a lunatic. When at last I folded the letter and thrust it in my sabretache, he asked no questions (for Jonas was indeed a friend) but showed by his look that he stood ready to help me.

"I need your animal," I said. "May I take her?"

"Gladly. But—"

I was already unbolting the door. "You cannot come. If all goes well, I'll see that she is returned to you."

As I raced down the stair and into the innyard, the letter spoke in my mind in Thecla's very voice; and by the time I entered the stable I was a lunatic indeed. I looked for Jonas's merychip, but instead saw before me a great destrier, his back higher than my eyes. I had no notion who might have ridden him into this peaceful village, and I gave it no thought. Without hesitating an instant I sprang onto his back, drew *Terminus Est*, and with a stroke severed the reins that tethered him.

I have never seen a better mount. He was out of the stable in one bound, and in two, lunging into the village street. For the space of a breath I feared he would trip on some tent rope, but he was sure-footed as a dancer. The street ran east toward the river; as soon as we were clear of the houses, I urged him to the left. He leaped a wall as a boy might skip across a stick, and I found myself galloping full tilt over a meadow where bulls lifted their horns in the green moonlight.

I am no great rider now, and was still less one then. Despite the high saddle, I think I would have tumbled from the back of an inferior animal before we had covered half a league; but my stolen destrier moved, for all his speed, as smoothly as a shadow. A shadow indeed we must have appeared, he with his black hide, I in my fuligin cloak. He had not slacked his pace before we splashed across the brook mentioned in the letter. I checked him there—partly by grasping his halter, more by speech, to which he harkened as a brother might. There was no path on either side of the water, and we had not traced it far before trees rimmed the banks. I guided him into the brook then (though he was loath to go) where we made our way up foaming races as a man climbs steps, and swam deep pools.

For more than a watch, we waded this brook through a forest much like the one through which Jonas and I had passed after being separated from Dorcas, Dr. Talos, and the rest at the Piteous Gate. Then the banks grew higher and more rugged, the trees smaller, and twisted. There were boulders in the stream; from their squared edges I knew they were the work of hands, and that we were in the region of the mines, with the wreck of some great city below us. Our way was steeper, and for all his mettle he faltered sometimes on sliding stones, so that I was forced to dismount and lead him. In this way we passed through a series of little, dreaming hollows, each dark in the shadows of its high sides, but each flecked in places with green moonlight, each ringing with the sound of water—but with that sound only, and otherwise wrapped in silence.

At last we entered a vale smaller and narrower than any of the others; and at the end of it, a chain or so off where the moonlight spilled upon a sheer elevation, I saw a dark opening. The brook had its origin there, flooding out like saliva from the lips of petrified titan. I found a patch of ground beside the water sufficiently level for my mount to stand and contrived to tie him there, knotting what remained of his reins around a dwarfish tree.

Once, no doubt, a timber trestle had provided access to the mine, but it had rotted away long ago. Though the climb looked impossible in the moonlight, I was able to find a few footholds in the ancient wall and scaled it to one side of the descending jet.

I had my hands inside the opening when I heard, or thought I heard, some sound from the vale behind me. I paused, and turned my head to look back. The rush of the water would have drowned any noise less commanding than a bugle call or an explosion, and it had drowned this, yet still I had sensed something—the note of stone falling upon stone, perhaps, or the splash of something plunging into the water.

The vale seemed peaceful and silent. Then I saw my destrier shift his stance, his proud head and forward-cocked ears coming for an instant into the light. I decided that what I had heard was nothing more than the striking of his steel-shod feet against the rock as he stamped in discontent at being so closely tethered. I drew my body into the mine entrance, and by doing so, as I later learned, saved my life.

A man of any wit, setting out as I had and knowing he must enter such a place, would have brought a lantern and a plentiful supply of candles. I had been so wild at the thought that Thecla still lived that I had none. Thus I crept forward in the dark, and had not taken a dozen steps before the moonlight of the vale had vanished behind me. My boots were in the stream, so I walked as I had when I had led the destrier up it. *Terminus Est* was slung over my left shoulder, and I had no fear that the tip of her sheath might be wet by the stream, for the ceiling of the tunnel was so low that I walked bent double. So I proceeded for a long time, fearing always that I had come wrong, and that Thecla waited for me elsewhere, and would wait in vain.

VI

Blue Light

I grew so accustomed to the sound of the icy water that had you asked me I should have said I walked in silence; but it was not so, and when, most suddenly, the constricted tunnel opened into a large chamber equally dark, I knew it at once from the change in the music of the stream. I took another step, and then another, and raised my head. There was no ragged stone now to strike it. I lifted my arms. Nothing. I grasped *Terminus Est* by her onyx hilt and waved her blade, still in the protection of its sheath. Nothing still.

Then I did something that you, reading this record, will find foolish indeed, though you must recall that I had been told that such guards as might be in the mine had been warned of my arrival and instructed to do me no harm. I called Thecla's name.

And the echoes answered: *"Thecla . . . Thecla . . . Thecla . . ."*

Then silence again.

I remembered that I was to have followed the water until it welled from a rock, and that I had not done so. Possibly it trickled through as many galleries here beneath the hill as it had through dells outside it. I began to wade again, feeling my way at each step for fear I might plunge over my head with the next.

I had not taken five strides when I heard something, far off yet distinct, above the whispering of the now smoothly flowing water. I had not taken five more when I saw light.

It was not the emerald reflection of the fabled forests of the

45

moon, nor was it such a light as guards might carry with them—the scarlet flame of a torch, the golden radiance of a candle, or even the piercing white beam I had sometimes glimpsed by night when the fliers of the Autarch soared over the Citadel. Rather, it was a luminous mist, sometimes seeming of no color, sometimes of an impure yellowish green. It was impossible to say how far it was, and it seemed to possess no shape. For a time it shimmered before my sight; and I, still following the stream, splashed toward it. Then it was joined by another.

It is difficult for me to concentrate on the events of the next few minutes. Perhaps everyone holds in his subconscious certain moments of horror, as our oubliette held, in its lowest inhabited level, those clients whose minds had long ago been destroyed or transformed into consciousness no longer human. Like them, these memories shriek and lash the walls with their chains, but are seldom brought high enough to see the light.

What I experienced under the hill remains with me as they remained with us, something I endeavor to lock within the furthest recesses of my mind but am from time to time made conscious of. (Not long ago, when the *Samru* was still near the mouth of Gyoll, I looked over the sternrail by night; there I saw each dipping of the oars appear as a spot of phosphorescent fire, and for a moment imagined that those from under the hill had come for me at last. They are mine to command now, but I have small comfort in that.)

The light I had seen was joined by a second, as I have described, then the first two by a third, and the first three by a fourth, and still I went on. Soon there were too many of the lights to count; but not knowing what they were, I was actually comforted and encouraged by the sight of them, imagining each perhaps to be a spark from a torch of some kind not known to me, a torch held by one of the guards mentioned in the letter. When I had taken a dozen more steps, I saw that these flecks of light were coalescing into a pattern, and that the pattern was a dart or arrowhead pointed toward myself. Then I heard, very faintly, such a roaring as I used to hear from the tower called the Bear when the beasts were given their food. Even then, I think, I might have escaped if I had turned and fled.

I did not. The roaring grew—not quite any noise of animals, yet not the shouting of the most frenzied human mob. I saw that the flecks of light were not shapeless, as I had imagined before. Rather, each was of that figure called in art a star, having five unequal points.

It was then, much too late, that I halted.

By this time the uncertain, hueless light these stars shed had increased enough for me to see as looming shadows the shapes about me. To either side were masses whose angular sides suggested that they were works of men—it seemed I walked in the buried city (here not collapsed under the weight of the overlaying soil) from which the miners of Saltus delved their treasures. Among these masses stood squat pillars of an ordered irregularity such as I have sometimes noticed in ricks of firewood, from which every stick protrudes yet goes to make the whole. These glinted softly, throwing back the corpse light of the moving stars as something less sinister, or at least more beautiful, then they had received.

For a moment I wondered at these pillars; then I looked at the star-shapes again, and for the first time saw them. Have you ever toiled by night toward what seemed a cottage window, and found it to be the balefire of a great fortress? Or climbing, slipped, and caught yourself, and looked below, and seen the fall a hundred times greater than you had believed? If you have, you will have some notion of what I felt. The stars were not sparks of light, but shapes like men, small only because the cavern in which I stood was more vast than I had ever conceived that such a place could be. And the men, who seemed not men, being thicker of shoulder and more twisted than men, were rushing toward me. The roar I heard was the sound of their voices.

I turned, and when I found I could not run through the water, mounted the bank where the dark structures stood. By that time they were almost upon me, and some were moving wide to my right and left and cut me off from the outer world.

They were terrible in a fashion I am not certain I can explain—like apes in that they had hairy, crooked bodies, long-armed, short-legged, and thick-necked. Their teeth were like the fangs of smilodons, curved and saw-edged, extending a finger's length below their massive jaws. Yet it was not any of these things, nor the noctilucent light that clung to their fur, that brought the horror I felt. It was something in their faces, perhaps in the huge, pale-irised eyes. It told me they were as human as I. As the old are imprisoned in rotting bodies, as women are locked in weak bodies that make them prey for the filthy desires of thousands, so these men were wrapped in the guise of lurid apes, and knew it. As they

ringed me, I could see that knowledge, and it was the worse
because those eyes were the only part of them that did not
glow.

I gulped air to shout *Thecla* once more. Then I knew, and
closed my lips, and drew *Terminus Est.*

One, larger or at least bolder than the rest, advanced on
me. He carried a short-hafted mace whose shaft had once
been a thigh bone. Just out of sword-reach he threatened me
with it, roaring and slapping the metal head of his weapon in a
long hand.

Something disturbed the water behind me, and I turned in
time to see one of the glowing man-apes fording the stream.
He leaped backward as I slashed at him, but the square
blade-tip caught him below the armpit. So fine was that blade,
so magnificently tempered and perfectly edged, that it cut its
way out through the breastbone.

He fell and the water carried his corpse away, but before
the stroke went home I had seen that he waded in the stream
with distaste, and that it had slowed his movements at least as
much as it had slowed mine. Turning to keep all my attackers
in view, I backed into it and began slowly to move toward the
point where it ran to the outside world. I felt that if I could
once reach the constricted tunnel I would be safe; but I knew
too that they would never permit me to do so.

They gathered more thickly around me until there must
have been several hundred. The light they gave was so great
then that I could see that the squared masses I had glimpsed
earlier were indeed buildings, apparently of the most ancient
construction, built of seamless gray stone and soiled everywhere by the dung of bats.

The irregular pillars were stacks of ingots in which each
layer was laid across the last. From their color I judged them
to be silver. There were a hundred in each stack, and surely
many hundreds of stacks in the buried city.

All this I saw while taking a half-dozen steps. At the
seventh they came for me, twenty at least, and from all sides.
There was no time for clean strokes through the neck. I
swung my blade in circles, and its singing filled that underground world and echoed from the stony walls and ceiling,
audible over the bellowing and the screams.

One's sense of time goes mad at such moments. I recall the
rush of the attack and my own frantic blows, but in retrospect
everything seems to have happened in a breath. Two and five
and ten were down, until the water around me was blood-

black in the corpse light, choked with dying and dead; but still they came. A blow on my shoulder was like the smash of a giant's fist. *Terminus Est* slipped out of my hand, and the weight of the bodies bore me down until I was grappling blind under water. My enemy's fangs slashed my arm as two spikes might, but he feared drowning too much, I think, to fight as he would have otherwise. I thrust fingers into his wide nostrils and snapped his neck, though it seemed tougher than a man's.

If I could have held my breath then until I worked my way to the tunnel, I might have escaped. The man-apes seemed to have lost sight of me, and I drifted underwater some small distance downstream. By then my lungs were bursting; I lifted my face to the surface, and they were upon me.

No doubt there comes a time for every man when by rights he should die. This, I have always felt, was mine. I have counted all the life I have held since as pure profit, an undeserved gift. I had no weapon, and my right arm was numbed and torn. The man-apes were bold now. That boldness gave me a moment more of life, for so many crowded forward to kill me that they obstructed one another. I kicked one in the face. A second grasped my boot; there was a flash of light, and I (moved by what instinct or inspiration I do not know) snatched at it. I held the Claw.

As though it gathered to itself all the corpse light and dyed it with the color of life, it streamed forth a clear azure that filled the cavern. For one heartbeat the man-apes halted as though at the stroke of a gong, and I lifted the gem overhead; what frenzy of terror I hoped for (if I really hoped at all) I cannot say now.

What happened was quite different. The man-apes neither fled shrieking nor resumed their attack. Instead they retreated until the nearest were perhaps three strides off, and squatted with their faces pressed against the floor of the mine. There was silence again as there had been when I had first entered it, with no sound but the whispering of the stream; but now I could see everything, from the stacks of tarnished silver ingots near to which I stood, to the very end where the man-apes had descended a ruined wall, appearing to my sight then like flecks of pale fire.

I began to back away. The man-apes looked up at that, and their faces were the faces of human beings. When I saw them thus, I knew of the eons of struggles in the dark from which their fangs and saucer eyes and flap ears had come to be. We, so the mages say, were apes once, happy apes in forests swallowed by deserts so long ago they have no names. Old men return to childish ways when at last the years becloud their minds. May it not be that mankind will return (as an old man does) to the decayed image of what once was, if at last the old sun dies and we are left scuffling over bones in the dark? I saw our future—one future at least—and I felt more sorrow for those who had triumphed in the dark battles than for those who had poured out their blood in that endless night.

I took a step backward (as I have said), and then another, and still none of the man-apes moved to stop me. Then I remembered *Terminus Est*. Were I to have made my escape from the most frantic battle, I would have despised myself if I had left her behind. To walk out unmolested without her was more than I could bear. I began to advance again, watching by the light of the Claw for her gleaming blade.

At this the faces of those strange, twisted men seemed to brighten, and I saw by their looks that they hoped I meant to remain with them, so that the Claw and its blue radiance would be theirs always. How terrible it seems now when I set the words on paper; yet it would not, I think, have been terrible in fact. Bestial though they appeared, I could see adoration on every brute face, so that I thought (as I think now) that if they are worse in many ways than we are, these people of the hidden cities beneath Urth are better in others, blessed with an ugly innocence.

From side to side I searched, from bank to bank; but I saw nothing, though it seemed to me that the light shone from the Claw more brightly, and more brightly still, until at last each tooth of stone that hung from the ceiling of that cavernous space cast behind it a sharp-sided shadow of pitch black. At last I called out to the crouching men, "My sword . . . Where is my sword? Did one of you take her?"

I would not have spoken to them if I had not been half frantic with the fear of losing her; but it seemed they understood. They began to mutter among themselves and to me, and to make signs to me—without rising—to show they would fight no more, extending their bludgeons and spears of pointed bone for me to take.

Then above the murmuring of the water and the muttering of the man-apes, I heard a new sound, and at once they fell silent. If an ogre were to eat of the very legs of the world, the grinding of his teeth would make just such a noise. The bed of the stream (where I still stood) trembled under me, and the water, which had been so clear, received a fine burden of silt, so that it looked as though a ribbon of smoke wound through it. From far below I heard a step that might have been the walking of a tower on the Final Day, when it is said all the cities of Urth will stride forth to meet the dawn of the New Sun.

And then another.

At once the man-apes rose, and crouching low fled toward the farther end of the gallery, silent now and swift as so many flitting bats. The light went with them, for it seemed, as I had somehow feared, that the Claw had flamed for them and not for me.

A third step came from underground, and with it the last gleam winked out; but at that instant, in that final gleam, I saw *Terminus Est* lying in the deepest water. In the dark I bent, and putting the Claw back into the top of my boot, took up my sword; and in so doing I discovered that the numbness had left my arm, which now seemed as strong as it had before the fight.

A fourth step sounded and I turned and fled, groping before me with the blade. What creature it was we had called from the roots of the continent I think I now know. But I did not know then, and I did not know whether it was the roaring of the man-apes, or the light of the Claw, or some other cause that had waked it. I only knew that there was something far beneath us before which the man-apes, with all the terror of their appearance and their numbers, scattered like sparks before a wind.

VII

The Assassins

When I recall my second passage through the tunnel that led to the outer world, I feel it occupied a watch or more. My nerves have never, I suppose, been fully sound, tormented as they have always been by a relentless memory. Then they were keyed to the highest pitch, so that to take three strides seemed to exhaust a lifetime. I was frightened, of course. I have never been called a coward since I was a small boy, and on certain occasions various persons have commented on my courage. I have performed my duties as a member of the guild without flinching, fought both privately and in war, climbed crags, and several times nearly drowned. But I believe there is no other difference between those who are called courageous and those who are branded craven than that the second are fearful before the danger and the first after it.

No one can be much frightened, certainly, during a period of great and immanent peril—the mind is too much concentrated on the thing itself, and on the actions necessary to meet or avoid it. The coward is a coward, then, because he has brought his fear with him; persons we think cowardly will sometimes amaze us by their bravery, if they have had no forewarning of their danger.

Master Gurloes, whom I had supposed to be of the most dauntless courage when I was a boy, was unquestionably a coward. During the period when Drotte was captain of apprentices, Roche and I used to alternate, turn and turn about, in serving Master Gurloes and Master Palaemon; and one night, when Master Gurloes had retired to his cabin but instructed me to stay to fill his cup for him, he began to confide in me.

"Lad, do you know the client Ia? An armiger's daughter and quite good-looking."

As an apprentice I had few dealings with clients; I shook my head.

"She is to be abused."

I had no idea what he meant, so I said, "Yes, Master."

"That's the greatest disgrace that can befall a woman. Or a man either. To be abused. By the torturer." He touched his chest and threw back his head to look at me. He had a remarkably small head for so large a man; if he had worn a shirt or jacket (which of course he never did), one would have been tempted to believe it padded.

"Yes, Master."

"Aren't you going to offer to do it for me? A young fellow like you, full of juice. Don't tell me you're not hairy yet."

At last I understood what he meant, and I told him that I had not realized it would be permissible, since I was still an apprentice; but that if he gave the order, I would certainly obey.

"I imagine you would. She's not bad, you know. But tall, and I don't like them tall. There's an exultant's bastard in that family a generation or so back, you may be sure. Blood will confess itself, as they say, though only we know what all that means. Want to do it?"

He held out his cup and I poured. "If you wish me to, Master." The truth was that I was excited at the thought. I had never possessed a woman.

"You can't. I must. What if I were to be questioned? Then too, I must certify it—sign the papers. A master of the guild for twenty years, and I've never falsified papers. I suppose you think I can't do it."

The thought had never crossed my mind, just as the opposite thought (that he might still retain some potency) had never occurred to me with regard to Master Palaemon, whose white hair, stooped shoulders, and peering lens made him seem like one who had been decrepit always.

"Well, look here," Master Gurloes said, and heaved himself out of his chair.

He was one of those who can walk well and speak clearly even when they are very drunk, and he strode over to a cabinet quite confidently, though I thought for a moment that he was going to drop the blue porcelain jar he took down.

"This is a rare and potent drug." He took the lid off and showed me a dark brown powder. "It never fails. You'll have to use it someday, so you ought to know about it. Just take as much as you could get under your fingernail on the end of a knife, you follow me? If you take too much, you won't be able to appear in public for a couple of days."

I said, "I'll remember, Master."

"Of course it's a poison. They all are, and this is the best—a little more than *that* would kill you. And you mustn't take it again until the moon changes, understand?"

"Perhaps you'd better have Brother Corbinian weigh the dose, Master." Corbinian was our apothecary; I was terrified that Master Gurloes might swallow a spoonful before my eyes.

"Me? I don't need it." Contemptuously, he put the lid on the jar again and banged it down on its shelf in the cabinet.

"That's well, Master."

"Besides" (he winked at me), "I'll have this." From his sabretache he took an iron phallus. It was about a span and a half long and had a leather thong through the end opposite the tip.

It must seem idiotic to you who read this, but for an instant I could not imagine what the thing was for, despite the somewhat exaggerated realism of its design. I had a wild notion that the wine had rendered him childish, as a little boy is who supposes there is no essential difference between his wooden mount and a real animal. I wanted to laugh.

" 'Abuse,' that's their word. That, you see, is where they've left us an out." He had slapped the iron phallus against his palm—the same gesture, now that I think of it, that the man-ape who had threatened me had made with his mace. Then I had understood and had been gripped by revulsion.

But even that revulsion was not the emotion I would feel now in the same situation. I did not sympathize with the client, because I did not think of her at all; it was only a sort of repugnance for Master Gurloes, who with all his bulk and great strength was forced to rely on the brown powder, and still worse, on the iron phallus I had seen, an object that might have been sawed from a statue, and perhaps had been. Yet I saw him on another occasion, when the thing had to be done immediately for fear the order could not otherwise be carried out before the client died, act at once, and without powder or phallus, and without difficulty.

Master Gurloes was a coward then. Still, perhaps his cowardice was better than the courage I would have possessed in his position, for courage is not always a virtue. I had been courageous (as such things are counted) when I had fought the man-apes, but my courage was no more than a mixture of foolhardiness, surprise, and desperation; now, in the tunnel, when there was no longer any cause for fear, I was afraid and nearly dashed my brains out against the low ceiling; but I did not pause or even slacken speed before I saw the opening before me, made visible by the blessed sheen of moonlight. Then, indeed, I halted; and considering myself safe wiped my sword as well as I might with the ragged edge of my cloak, and sheathed her.

That done, I slung her over my shoulder and swung myself out and down, feeling with the toes of my sodden boots for the ledges that had supported me in the ascent. I had just gained the third when two quarrels struck the rock near my head. One must have wedged its point in some flaw in the ancient work, for it remained in place, blazing with white fire. I recall how astonished I was, and also how I hoped, in the few moments before the next struck nearer still and nearly blinded me, that the arbalests were not of the kind that bring a new projectile to the string when cocked, and thus are so swift to shoot again.

When the third exploded against the stone, I knew they were, and dropped before the marksmen who had missed could fire yet again.

There was, as I ought to have known there would be, a deep pool where the stream fell from the mouth of the mine. I got another ducking, but since I was already wet it did no harm, and in fact quenched the flecks of fire that had clung to my face and arms.

There could be no question here of cannily remaining below the surface. The water seized me as if I were a stick and flung me to the top where it willed. This, by the greatest good luck, was some distance from the rock face, and I was able to watch my attackers from behind as I clambered onto the bank. They and the woman who stood between them were staring at the place where the cascade fell.

As I drew *Terminus Est* for the final time that night, I called, "Over here, Agia."

I had guessed earlier that it was she, but as she turned (more swiftly than either of the men with her) I glimpsed her face in the moonlight. It was a terrible face to me (though for all her self-depreciation so lovely) because the sight of it meant that Thecla was surely dead.

The man nearest me was fool enough to try to bring his arbalest to his shoulder before he pulled the trigger. I ducked and cut his legs from under him, while the other's quarrel whizzed over my head like a meteor.

By the time I had straightened up again, the second man had dropped his arbalest and was drawing his hanger. Agia was quicker, making a cut at my neck with an athame before his weapon was free of the scabbard. I dodged her first stroke and parried her second, though *Terminus Est*'s blade was not made for fencing. My own attack made her bound back.

"Get behind him," she called to the second arbalestier. "I can front him."

He did not answer. Instead, his mouth swung open and his point swung wide. Before I realized that it was not at me that he was looking, something feverishly gleaming bounded past me. I heard the ugly sound of a breaking skull. Agia turned as gracefully as any cat and would have spitted the man-ape, but I struck the poisoned blade from her hand and sent it skittering into the pool. She tried to flee then; I caught her by the hair and jerked her off her feet.

The man-ape was mumbling over the body of the arbalestier he had killed—whether he sought to loot it or was merely curious about its appearance I have never known. I set my foot on Agia's neck, and the man-ape straightened and turned to face me, then dropped in the crouching posture I had seen in the mine and held up his arms. One hand was gone; I recognized the clean cut of *Terminus Est*. The man-ape mumbled something I could not understand.

I tried to reply. "Yes, I did that. I am sorry. We are at peace now."

The beseeching look remained, and he spoke again. Blood still seeped from the stump, though his kind must possess a mechanism for pinching shut the veins, as thylacodons are said to do; without the attentions of a surgeon, a man would have bled to death from that wound.

"I cut it," I said. "But it was while we were still fighting, before you people saw the Claw of the Conciliator." Then it came to me that he must have followed me outside for another glimpse of the gem, braving the fear engendered by whatever we had waked below the hill. I thrust my hand into the top of my boot and pulled out the Claw, and the instant I had done so realized what a fool I had been to put the boot and its precious cargo so close to Agia's reach, for her eyes went wide with cupidity at the moment that the man-ape abased himself further and stretched forth his piteous stump.

For a moment we were posed, all three, and a strange group we must have looked in that eerie light. An astonished voice—Jonas's—called "Severian!" from the heights above. Like the trumpet note in a shadow play that dissolves all feigning, that shout ended our tableau. I lowered the Claw and concealed it in my palm. The man-ape bolted for the rock face, and Agia began to struggle and curse beneath my foot.

A rap with the flat of my blade quieted her, but I kept my boot on her until Jonas had joined me and there were two of us to prevent her escape.

"I thought you might need help," he said. "I perceive I was mistaken." He was looking at the corpses of the men who had been with Agia.

I said, "This wasn't the real fight."

Agia was sitting up, rubbing her neck and shoulders. "There were four, and we would have had you, but the bodies of those things, those firefly tiger-men, started pitching out of the hole, and two were afraid and slipped away."

Jonas scratched his head with his steel hand, a sound like the currying of a charger. "I saw what I thought I saw, then. I had begun to wonder."

I asked what he thought he had seen.

"A glowing being in a fur robe making an obeisance to you. You were holding up a cup of burning brandy, I think. Or was it incense? What's this?" He bent and picked up something from the edge of the bank, where the man-ape had crouched.

"A bludgeon."

"Yes, I see that." There was a loop of sinew at the end of the bone handle, and Jonas slipped it over his wrist. "Who are these people who tried to kill you?"

"We would have," Agia said, "if it hadn't been for that cloak. We saw him coming out of the hole, but it covered him when he started to climb down, and my men couldn't see the target, only the skin of his arms."

I explained as briefly as I could how I had become involved with Agia and her twin, and described the death of Agilus.

"So now she's come to join him." Jonas looked from her to

the crimson length of *Terminus Est* and gave a little shrug. "I left my merychip up there, and perhaps I ought to go and look after her. That way I can say afterward that I saw nothing. Was this woman the one who sent the letter?"

"I should have known. I had told her about Thecla. You don't know about Thecla, but she did, and that was what the letter was about. I told her while we were going through the Botanic Gardens in Nessus. There were mistakes in the letter and things Thecla would never have said, but I didn't stop to think of them when I read it."

I stepped away and replaced the Claw in my boot, thrusting it deep. "Maybe you had better attend to your animal, as you say. My own seems to have broken loose, and we may have to take turns riding yours."

Jonas nodded and began to climb back the way he had come.

"You were waiting for me, weren't you?" I asked Agia. "I heard something, and the destrier cocked his ears at the sound. That was you. Why didn't you kill me then?"

"We were up there." She gestured toward the heights. "And I wanted the men I'd hired to shoot you when you came wading up the brook. They were stupid and stubborn as men always are, and said they wouldn't waste their quarrels—that the creatures inside would kill you. I rolled down a stone, the biggest I could move, but by then it was too late."

"They had told you about the mine?"

Agia shrugged, and the moonlight turned her bare shoulders to something more precious and more beautiful than flesh. "You're going to kill me now, so what does it matter? All the local people tell stories about this place. They say those things come out at night during storms and take animals from the cowsheds, and sometimes break into the houses for children. There's also a legend that they guard treasure inside, so I put that in the letter too. I thought if you wouldn't come for your Thecla, you might for that. Can I stand with my back to you, Severian? If it's all the same, I don't want to see it coming."

When she said that, I felt as though a weight had been lifted from my heart: I had not been certain I could strike her if I had to look into her face.

I raised my own iron phallus, and as I did so felt there was one more thing I wanted to ask Agia; but I could not recall what it might be.

"Strike," she said. "I am ready."

I sought good footing, and my fingers found the woman's head at one end of the guard, the head that marked the female edge.

And a little later, again, "Strike!"

But by that time I had climbed out of the vale.

VIII

The Cultellarii

We returned to the inn in silence, and so slowly that the eastern sky was gray before we reached the town. Jonas was unsaddling the merychip when I said, "I didn't kill her."

He nodded without looking at me. "I know."

"Did you watch? You said you wouldn't."

"I heard her voice when you were practically standing beside me. Will she try again?"

I waited, thinking, while he carried the little saddle into the tack room. When he came out, I said, "Yes, I'm sure she will. I didn't exact a promise from her, if that's what you mean. She wouldn't have kept one in any case."

"I would have killed her then."

"Yes," I said. "That would have been the right thing to do."

We walked out of the stable together. There was light enough in the innyard now for us to see the well, and the wide doors that led into the inn.

"I don't think it would have been right—I'm only saying that I would have done it. I would have imagined myself stabbed in my sleep, dying on a dirty bed somewhere, and I would have swung that thing. It wouldn't have been right." Jonas lifted the mace the man-ape had left behind, and chopped with it in a parody, brutal and graceless, of a sword cut. The head caught the light and both of us gasped.

It was of pounded gold.

Neither of us felt any desire to join the festivities the fair still proffered to those who had caroused all night. We retired to the room we shared, and prepared for sleep. When Jonas offered to share his gold with me, I refused. Earlier, I had had money in plenty and the advance on my fee, and he had been living, as it were, upon my largess. Now I was happy that he would no longer feel himself in my debt. I was ashamed, too, when I saw how completely he trusted me with his gold, and remembered how carefully I had concealed (in fact, still concealed) the existence of the Claw from him. I felt bound to tell him of it; but I did not, and contrived instead to slip my foot from my wet boot in such a way that the Claw fell into the toe.

I woke about noon, and after satisfying myself that the Claw was still there, roused Jonas as he had asked me. "There should be jewelers at the fair who'll give me some sort of price for this," he said. "At least, I can bargain with them. Want to come with me?"

"We should have something to eat, and by the time we're through, I'll be due at the scaffold."

"Back to work then."

"Yes." I had picked up my cloak. It was sadly torn, and my boots were dull and still slightly damp.

"One of the maids here can sew that for you. It won't be as good as new, but it will be a lot better than it is now." Jonas swung open the door. "Come along, if you're hungry. What are you looking so thoughtful about?"

In the inn's parlor, with a good meal between us, and the innkeeper's wife exercising her needle on my cloak in another room, I told him what had happened under the hill, ending with the steps I had heard far below ground.

"You're a strange man," was all he said.

"You are stranger than I. You don't want people to know it, but you're a foreigner of some kind."

He smiled. "A cacogen?"

"An outlander."

Jonas shook his head, then nodded. "Yes, I suppose I am. But you—you have this talisman that lets you command nightmares, and you have discovered a hoard of silver. Yet you talk about it to me as someone else might talk about the weather."

I took a bit of bread. "It is strange, I agree. But the strangeness resides in the Claw, the thing itself, and not in me. As for talking about it to you, why shouldn't I? If I were to steal your gold, I could sell it and spend the money, but I don't think things would go well for someone who stole the

Claw. I don't know why I think that, but I do, and of course
Agia stole it. As for the silver—"

"And she put it in your pocket?"

"In the sabretache that hangs from my belt. She thought
her brother would kill me, remember. Then they were going
to claim my body—they had planned that already, so they'd
get *Terminus Est* and my habit. She would have had my sword
and clothes and the gem too, and meanwhile, if it were found,
I would be blamed and not she. I remember . . ."

"What?"

"The Pelerines. They stopped us as we were trying to get
out. Jonas, do you think it's true that some people can read
the thoughts of others?"

"Of course."

"Not everyone is so sure. Master Gurloes used to speak
favorably of the idea, but Master Palaemon wouldn't hear of
it. Still, I think the chief priestess of the Pelerines could, at
least to some degree. She knew Agia had taken something,
and that I had not. She made Agia strip so they could search
her, but they didn't search me. Later they destroyed their
cathedral, and I think that must have been because of the loss
of the Claw—it was the Cathedral of the Claw, after all."

Jonas nodded thoughtfully.

"But none of this is what I wanted to ask you about. I'd like
your opinion of the footsteps. Everyone knows about Erebus
and Abaia and the other beings in the sea who will come to
land someday. Nevertheless, I think you know more about
them than most of the rest of us."

Jonas's face, which had been so open before, was closed
and guarded now. "And why do you think that?"

"Because you've been a sailor, and because of the story
about the beans—the story you told at the gate. You must
have seen my brown book when I was reading it upstairs. It
tells all the secrets of the world, or at least what various
mages have said they were. I haven't read it all or even half of
it, though Thecla and I used to read an entry every few days
and spend the time between readings arguing about it. But
I've noticed that all the explanations in that book are simple,
and seemingly childish."

"Like my story."

I nodded. "Your story might have come out of the book.
When I first carried it to Thecla, I supposed it was intended
for children, or for adults who enjoyed childish things. But
when we had talked about some of the thoughts in it, I

understood that they had to be expressed in that way or they couldn't be expressed at all. If the writer had wanted to describe a new way to make wine or the best way to make love, he could have used complex and accurate language. But in the book he really wrote he had to say, 'In the beginning was only the hexaemeron,' or 'It is not to see the icon standing still, but to see the still standing.' The thing I heard underground . . . was that one of them?"

"I didn't see it." Jonas rose. "I'm going out now to sell the mace, but before I go I'm going to tell you what all housewives sooner or later tell their husbands: 'Before you ask more questions, think about whether you really want to know the answers.'"

"One last question," I said, "and then I promise I won't ask you anything more. When we were going through the Wall, you said the things we saw in there were soldiers, and you implied they had been stationed there to resist Abaia and the others. Are the man-apes soldiers of the same kind? And if they are, what good can human-sized fighters do when our opponents are as large as mountains? And why didn't the old autarchs use human soldiers?"

Jonas had wrapped the mace in a rag and stood now shifting it from one hand to the other. "That's three questions, and the only one I can answer for certain is the second. I'll guess at the other two, but I'm going to hold you to your promise; this is the last time we're going to speak of these things.

"That last question first. The old autarchs, who were not autarchs or called so, did use human soldiers. But the warriors they had created by humanizing animals, and perhaps, in secret by bestializing men, were more loyal. They had to be, since the populace—who hated their rulers—hated these inhuman servitors more still. Thus the servitors could be made to endure things that human soldiers would not. That may have been why they were used in the Wall. Or there may be some other explanation entirely."

Jonas paused and walked to the window, looking not into the street but up at the clouds. "I don't know whether your man-apes are the same kind of hybrid. The one I saw looked quite human to me except for his pelt, so I would be inclined to agree with you that they are human beings who have undergone some change in their essential nature as a result of their life in the mines and their contact with the relics of the city buried there. Urth is very old now. It's very old, and no doubt there have been many treasures hidden in bygone times. Gold and silver do not alter, but their guardians can suffer metamorphoses stranger than those that turn grapes to wine and sand to pearls."

I said, "But we outside endure the dark each night, and the treasures carried up from the mines are brought to us. Why haven't we changed too?"

Jonas did not answer, and I remembered my promise to ask him nothing more. Still, when he turned to face me there was something in his eyes that told me I was being a fool, that we *had* changed. He turned away again and stared out and up once more.

"All right," I conceded, "you don't have to answer that. But what about the other question you pledged yourself to answer? How can human soldiers resist the monsters from the seas?"

"You were correct when you said Erebus and Abaia are as great as mountains, and I admit that I was surprised you knew it. Most people lack the imagination to conceive of anything so large, and think them no bigger than houses or ships. Their actual size is so great that while they remain on this world they can never leave the water—their own weight would crush them. You mustn't think of them battering at the Wall with their fists, or tossing boulders about. But by their thoughts they enlist servants, and they fling them against all rules that rival their own."

Jonas opened the inn's door then and slipped out into the bustle of the street; I remained where I was, resting an elbow on what had been our breakfast table, and recalled the dream I had experienced when I had shared Baldanders's bed. *The land could not hold us,* the monstrous women had said.

Now I am come to a part of my story where I cannot help but write of something I have largely avoided mentioning before. You that read it cannot but have noticed that I have not scrupled to recount in great detail things that transpired years ago, and to give the very words of those who spoke to me, and the very words with which I replied; and you must have thought this only a conventional device I had adopted to make my story flow more smoothly. The truth is that I am one of those who are cursed with what is called perfect recollection. We cannot, as I have sometimes heard foolishly alleged, remember everything. I cannot recall the ordering of the books on the shelves in the library of Master Ultan, for example. But I can remember more than many would credit: the position of each object on a table I walked past when I was a child, and even that I have recalled some scene to mind previously, and how that remembered incident differed from the memory of it I have now.

It was my power of recollection that made me the favorite pupil of Master Palaemon, and so I suppose it can be blamed for the existence of this narrative, for if he had not favored me, I would not have been sent to Thrax bearing his sword.

Some say this power is linked to weak judgment—of that I am no judge. But it has another danger, one I have encountered many times. When I cast my mind into the past, as I am doing now and as I did then when I sought to recall my dream, I remember it so well that I seem to move again in the bygone day, a day old-new, and unchanged each time I draw it to the surface of my mind, its eidolons as real as I. I can even now close my eyes and walk into Thecla's cell as I did one winter evening; and soon my fingers will feel the heat of her garment while the perfume of her person fills my nostrils like the perfume of lilies warmed before a fire. I lift her gown from her and embrace that ivory body, feeling her nipples pressed to my face. . . .

You see? It is very easy to waste hours and days in such rememberings, and sometimes I fall so deeply into them that I am drugged and drunken. So it was now. The footfalls I had heard in the man-apes' cavern still echoed in my mind, and seeking some explanation I returned to my dream, certain now that I knew from whom it had come, and hoping it had revealed more than its shaper apprehended.

Again I bestride the mitred, leather-winged steed. Pelicans fly below us with stiffly formal strokes, and gulls wheel and keen.

Again I fall, tumbling through the abyss of air, whistling toward the sea, yet suspended, for a time, between wave and cloud. I arch my body, bring down my head, let my legs trail behind me like a banner, and so cleave the water and see floating in clear azure the head with hair of snakes and the many-headed beast, and then the swirling sand-garden far below. The giantesses lift arms like the trunks of sycamores, each finger tipped with an amaranthine talon. Then very suddenly, I who had been blind before understood why it was that Abaia had sent me this dream, and had sought to enlist me in the great and final war of Urth.

But now the tyranny of memory overwhelmed my will. Though I could see the titan odalisques and their garden and knew them to be no more than dream-stuff recalled, I could not escape from their fascination and the memory of the dream. Hands grasped me like a doll, and as I dandled thus between the meretrices of Abaia, I was lifted from my broad-armed chair in the inn of Saltus; yet still, for perhaps a hundred heartbeats more, I could not rid my mind of the sea and its green-haired women.

"He sleeps."

"His eyes are open."

A third voice: "Shall we bring the sword?"

"Bring it—there may be work for it."

The titanesses faded. Men in deerskin and rough wool held me on either side, and one with a scarred face held the point of his dirk at my throat. The man on my right had picked up *Terminus Est* with his free hand; he was the black-bearded volunteer who had helped break open the sealed house.

"Someone's coming."

The man with the scarred face glided away. I heard the door rattle, and Jonas's exclamation as he was drawn inside.

"This is your master, isn't it? Well, don't move, my friend, or cry out. We'll kill you both."

IX

The Liege of Leaves

They forced us to stand with our faces to the wall while they bound our hands. Our cloaks were draped over our shoulders afterward to hide the thongs, so that we appeared to walk with our hands clasped behind us, and we were led out into the innyard, where a huge baluchither shifted from foot to foot under a plain howdah of iron and horn. The man who held my left arm reached up and struck the beast at the hollow of the knee with the shaft of a goad to make him kneel, and we were driven onto his back.

When Jonas and I had come to Saltus, our path had threaded hills of debris from the mines, hills composed largely of broken stone and brick. When I had ridden on the false errand of Agia's letter, I had galloped past more of these, though my route had lain chiefly through the forest at its nearest approach to the village. Now we went among the heaps of tailings where there was no path. Here, in addition to much rubble, the miners had cast all they had brought forth from the buried past that might otherwise have defamed their village and occupation. Everything foul lay in tumbled heaps ten times and more the height of the baluchither's lofty back—obscene statues, canted and crumbling, and human bones to which strips of dry flesh and hanks of hair still clung. And with them ten thousand men and women; those who, in seeking a private resurrection, had rendered their corpses forever imperishable lay here like drunkards after their debauch, their crystal sarcophagi broken, their limbs relaxed in grotesque disarray, their clothing rotted or rotting, and their eyes blindly fixed upon the sky.

At first Jonas and I had attempted to question our captors, but they had silenced us with blows. Now that the baluchither wound his way among this desolation, they seemed easier of mind, and I asked again where they were taking us. The man with the scarred face replied, "To the wild, the home of free men and lovely women."

I thought of Agia and asked if he served her; he laughed and shook his head. "My master is Vodalus of the Wood."

"Vodalus!"

"Ah," he said. "You know him then." And he nudged the black-bearded man, who rode in the howdah with us. "Very kindly Vodalus will treat you, no doubt, for offering so blithely to rack one of his servants."

"I know him indeed," I said, and was about to tell the scarred man of my connection with Vodalus, whose life I had preserved in the last year before I became captain of apprentices. But then I came to doubt if Vodalus would remember it, and only said that if I had known Barnoch to be a servant of Vodalus, I would on no account have agreed to perform his excruciation. I lied, of course; for I had known, and had justified accepting my fee by the thought that I would be able to spare Barnoch some suffering. The lie did me no good; all three chortled, even the trainer who bestrode the balu-chither's neck.

When their merriment had subsided, I said, "Last night I rode out of Saltus to the northeast. Are we going that way now?"

"So that's where you were. Our master came seeking you, and came back empty-handed." The scarred man smiled, and I could see that it was not an unpleasant thought that he returned now successful where Vodalus himself had failed.

Jonas whispered, "We go north, as you can see by the sun."

"Yes," said the scarred man, who must have been sharp-eared. "North, but not for long." And then, to pass the time, he described to me the means by which his master dealt with captives, most of which were primitive in the extreme, and more productive of theatrical effects than of true agony.

As if some invisible hand had spread a curtain over us, the shadows of the trees fell upon the howdah. The glitter of billions of shards of glass was left behind with the staring of the dead eyes, and we entered into the coolness and green shade of the high forest. Among those mighty trunks even the baluchither, though he stood three times the height of a man, seemed no more than a little, scurrying beast; and we who rode his back might have been pygmies from some children's tale, bound for the anthill stronghold of a pixie monarch.

And it came to me that these trees had been hardly smaller when I was yet unborn, and had stood as they stood now when I was a child playing among the cypresses and peaceful tombs of our necropolis, and that they would stand yet, drinking in the last light of the dying sun, even as now, when I had been dead as long as those who rested there. I saw how little it weighed on the scale of things whether I lived or died, though my life was precious to me. And of those two thoughts I forged a mood by which I stood ready to grasp each smallest chance to live, yet in which I cared not too much whether I saved myself or not. By that mood, as I think, I did live; it has been so good a friend to me that I have endeavored to wear it ever since, succeeding not always, but often.

"Severian, are you all right?"

It was Jonas who spoke. I looked at him, I think, in some wonder. "Yes. Did I seem ill?"

"For a moment."

"I was only reflecting on the familiarity of this place, seeking to understand it. I think it recalls to me many summer days in our Citadel. These trees are nearly as large as the towers there, and many of the towers are wrapped in ivy, so that in quiet summer weather the light between them has this emerald quality. Too, it is quiet here, as there. . . ."

"Yes?"

"You must have ridden many times in boats, Jonas."

"Occasionally, yes."

"It is something I had long wanted to do, and did for the first time only when Agia and I were ferried to the island where the Botanic Gardens stands, and then later when we crossed the Lake of Birds. The motion is much like the motion of this beast, and it is as silent, save for a splashing, sometimes, when the oar goes into the water. I feel now that I'm traveling through the Citadel in a flood, solemnly rowed."

At that Jonas looked so grave that I burst out laughing at the sight of his face, and stood up, meaning (I think) to look over the side of the howdah and show by some remark about the forest floor that I was merely indulging my fancy.

I had no sooner stood, however, than the scarred man rose too, and holding his dirk's point within a thumb of my throat told me to sit again. To spite him I shook my head.

He flourished his weapon. "Get down or I'll rip your belly open!"

"And lose the glory of bringing me back? I don't think so. Wait until the others tell Vodalus that you had me, and you stabbed me when my hands were tied."

Now came the turn of fate. The bearded man who held *Terminus Est* tried to draw her, and not being acquainted with the proper way to bare so long a sword—which is to grip the quillons in one hand and the throat of the sheath with the other, and by opening the arms to the right and left draw the blade clear—sought to free it by pulling up, as if he were jerking a weed from a field. In this clumsy business he was taken off guard by one of the baluchither's rolling steps, and lurched against the man with the scarred face. The edges of the blade, keen enough to part a hair, cut them both; the man with the scarred face threw himself backward, and Jonas, by hooking one of his feet behind the scarred man's and pressing his leg with the sole of the other, managed to tumble him over the railing of the howdah.

Meantime, the black-bearded man had dropped *Terminus Est* and was staring at his wound, which was very long, though no doubt shallow. I knew that weapon as I know my own hand, and it took only a moment to turn and crouch and grasp the hilt, and then, wedging it between my heels, to cut the thongs that bound my wrists. The black-bearded man drew a dagger then and might have killed me had not Jonas kicked him between the legs.

He bent double, and long before he could straighten himself I was up, with *Terminus Est* ready.

The contraction of his muscles snapped him erect, as often happens when the subject is not made to kneel; I think the spray of blood was the first sign the trainer had (so swiftly had it all taken place) that something was amiss. He looked back at us, and I was able to take him very neatly, swinging the blade one-handed in the horizontal stroke, as I leaned out of the howdah.

His head had no more than struck the ground when the baluchither stepped between two great trees growing so close together that he seemed to squeeze himself like a mouse through a crevice in a wall. Beyond lay a glade more open than anything I had seen in that forest—where grass grew as well as fern, and spots of sunlight, unshaded with green and rich as orpiment, played over the turf. Here Vodalus had caused to be erected his throne, beneath a canopy woven of flowering vines; and here, as it chanced, he sat with the Chatelaine Thea beside him just as we entered, judging and rewarding his followers.

Jonas saw nothing of that, being still sprawled on the floor of the howdah, where he was cutting his hands free with the dagger. I made up for him, for I beheld everything as I stood upright, balanced against the pitching of the baluchither's back and holding up my sword, red now to the hilt. A hundred faces turned toward us, with the face of the exultant on the throne among them, and the heart-shaped face of his consort; and in their eyes I saw what they must have seen at that moment: the great animal bestridden by a headless man, its forequarters dyed with his blood; myself standing erect upon its back, with my sword and fuligin cloak.

Had I slipped down and sought to flee, or tried to goad the baluchither to greater speed, I would have died. Instead, by the virtue of the spirit that had entered me when I saw the long-dead bodies among the refuse of the mines and the eternal trees, I remained as I was; and the baluchither, with no one to guide him, trod forward steadily (Vodalus's followers dodging aside to make a path for him) until the dais supporting the throne and canopy were before him. Then he halted, and the dead man pitched forward and fell on the dais at Vodalus's feet; and I, leaning far out of the howdah, struck the beast behind one leg and the other with the flat of my blade, and he knelt.

Vodalus smiled a thin smile that held many things, but amusement was one of them, and perhaps the foremost. "I sent my men to fetch the headsman," he said. "I perceive they succeeded."

I saluted with my sword, holding the hilt before my eyes as we were taught to do when an exultant came to observe an execution in the Grand Court. "Sieur, they have brought you the anti-headsman—there was a time when your own would have rolled on fresh-turned soil if it had not been for me."

He looked at me more closely then, at my face instead of at my sword and cloak, and after a moment he said, "Yes, you were the youth. Has it been that long?"

"Just long enough, sieur."

"We will talk of this in private, but I have public business to do now. Stand here." He pointed to the ground at the left of the dais.

I climbed from the baluchither with Jonas following me, and two grooms led the beast away. There we waited and heard Vodalus give his orders and transmit his plans, reward and punish, for perhaps a watch. All the boasted human panoply of pillars and arches is no more than an imitation in sterile stone of the boles and vaulting branches of the forest, and here it seemed to me that there was scarcely any difference between the two except that the one was gray or white, and the other brown and pale green. Then I believed I understood why all the soldiers of the Autarch and all the thronging retainers of the exultants could not subdue Vodalus—he occupied the mightiest fortress of Urth, greater by far than our Citadel, to which I had likened it.

At length he dismissed the crowd, each man and woman to his or her own place, and came down from the dais to talk to me, bending over me as I might have bent above a child. "You served me once," he said. "For that I will spare your life whatever else befalls, though it may be necessary that you remain my guest for a time. Knowing that your life is no longer in danger, will you serve me again?"

The oath to the Autarch I had taken on the occasion of my elevation had not the strength to resist the memory of that misty evening with which I have begun this account of my life. Oaths are only mere weak things of honor compared to the benefits we give to others, which are things of the spirit; let us once save another, and we are his for life. I have often heard it said that gratitude is not to be found. That is not true— those who say so have always looked in the mistaken place. One who truly benefits another is for a moment at a level with the Pancreator, and in gratitude for that elevation will serve the other all his days; and so I told Vodalus.

"Good!" he said, and clapped me on the shoulder. "Come. Not far from here we have a meal prepared. If you and your friend will sit with me and eat, I will tell you what must be done."

"Sieur, I have disgraced my guild once. I only ask that I may not be made to disgrace it again."

"Nothing you do will be known," Vodalus said. And that satisfied me.

X

Thea

With a dozen or so others we left the glade on foot, and half a league away found a table set among the trees. I was placed at Vodalus's left hand, and while the others ate, I feigned to and feasted my eyes on him and his lady, whom I had so often recalled as I lay on my cot among the apprentices in our tower.

When I had saved him, mentally at least I had still been a boy, and to a boy all grown men appear lofty unless they are of very low stature indeed. I saw now that Vodalus was as tall as Thecla or taller, and that Thecla's half-sister Thea was as tall as she. Then I knew them to be truly of the exalted blood, and not armigers merely, such as Sieur Racho had been.

It was with Thea that I had first fallen in love, worshipping her because she belonged to the man I had saved. Thecla I had loved, in the beginning, because she recalled Thea. Now (as autumn dies, and winter and spring, and summer comes again, the end of the year as it is its beginning) I loved Thea once more—because she recalled Thecla.

Vodalus said, "You are an admirer of women," and I lowered my eyes.

"I have been little in polite company, sieur. Please forgive me."

"I share your admiration, so there is nothing to forgive. But you were not, I hope, studying that slender throat with the thought of parting it?"

"Never, sieur."

"I am delighted to hear it." He picked up a platter of

thrushes, selected one, and put it upon my plate. It was a sign of special favor. "Still, I own I am a trifle surprised. I would have thought that a man in your profession would look on us poor human beings much as a butcher does on cattle."

"Of that I cannot inform you, sieur. I have not been bred a butcher."

Vodalus laughed. "A touch! I am almost sorry now that you have consented to serve me. If you had only elected to remain my prisoner, we would have had many delightful conversations while I used you—as I had intended to—to cheap for the unfortunate Barnoch's life. As it is, you will be away by morning. Yet I think I have an errand for you that will consort well with your own inclinations."

"If it is your errand, sieur, it must."

"You are wasted on the scaffold." He smiled. "We will find better work for you before long. But if you are to serve me well, you must understand something of the position of the pieces on the board, and the goal of the game we play. Call the sides white and black, and in honor of your garments—so that you shall know where your interests lie—we shall be black. No doubt you have been told that we blacks are mere bandits and traitors, but have you any notion of what it is we strive to do?"

"To checkmate the Autarch, sieur?"

"That would be well enough, but it is only a step and not our final goal. You have come from the Citadel—I know, you see, something of your journeyings and history—that great fortress of bygone days, so you must possess some feeling for the past. Has it never struck you that mankind was richer by far, and happier too, a chiliad gone than it is now?"

"Everyone knows," I said, "that we have fallen far from the brave days of the past."

"As it was then, so shall it be again. Men of Urth, sailing between the stars, leaping from galaxy to galaxy, the masters of the daughters of the sun."

The Chatelaine Thea, who must have been listening to Vodalus though she had showed no sign of it, looked across him to me and said in a sweet, cooing voice, "Do you know how our world was renamed, torturer? The dawn-men went to red Verthandi, who was then named War. And because they thought that had an ungracious sound that would keep others from following them, they renamed it, calling it Present. That was a jest in their tongue, for the same word meant *Now* and *The Gift*. Or so one of our tutors once explained the matter to my sister and me, though I do not see how any language could endure such confusion."

Vodalus listened to her as though he were impatient to speak himself, yet was too well mannered to interrupt her.

"Then others—who would have drawn a people to the innermost habitable world for their own reasons—took up the game as well, and called that world Skuld, the World of the Future. Thus our own became Urth, the World of the Past."

"You are wrong in that, I fear," Vodalus told her. "I have it on good authority that this world of ours has been called by that name from the utmost reaches of antiquity. Still, your error is so charming that I would rather have it that you are correct and I mistaken."

Thea smiled at that, and Vodalus turned again toward me. "Though it does not explain why Urth is called as she is, my dear Chatelaine's tale makes the vital point well, which is that in those times mankind traveled by his own ships from world to world, and mastered each, and built on them the cities of Man. Those were the great days of our race, when our fathers' fathers' fathers strove for the mastery of the universe."

He paused, and because he seemed to expect some comment from me, I said, "Sieur, we are much diminished in wisdom from that age."

"Ah, now you strike to the heart. Yet with all your perspicacity, you mistake it. No, we are not diminished in wisdom. We are diminished in power. Study has advanced without letup, but even as men have learned all that is needful for mastery, the strength of the world has been exhausted. We exist now, and precariously, upon the ruin of those who preceded us. While some skim the air in their fliers, ten thousand leagues in a day, we others creep upon the skin of Urth, unable to go from one horizon to the next before the westernmost has lifted itself to veil the sun. You spoke a moment ago of checkmating that mewling fool the Autarch. I want you to conceive now of two autarchs—two great powers striving for mastery. The white seeks to maintain things as they are, the black to set Man's foot on the road to domination again. I called it the black by chance, but it would be well to remember that it is by night that we see the stars strongly; they are remote and all but invisible in the red light of day. Now, of those two powers, which would you serve?"

The wind was stirring in the trees, and it seemed to me that everyone at the table had fallen silent, listening to Vodalus and waiting for my reply. I said, "The black, surely."

"Good! But as a man of sense you must understand that the way to reconquest cannot be easy. Those who wish no change may sit hugging their scruples forever. *We* must do everything. *We* must dare everything!"

The others had begun to talk and eat again. I lowered my voice until only Vodalus could hear me. "Sieur, there is something I have not told you. I dare not conceal it longer for fear you should think me faithless."

He was a better intriguer than I, and turned away before he answered, pretending to eat. "What is it? Out with it."

"Sieur," I said, "I have a relic, the thing they say is the Claw of the Conciliator."

He was biting the roasted thigh of a fowl as I spoke. I saw him pause; his eyes turned to look at me, though he did not move his head.

"Do you wish to see it, sieur? It is very beautiful, and I have it in the top of my boot."

"No," he whispered. "Yes, perhaps, but not here. . . . No, better not at all."

"To whom should I give it, then?"

Vodalus chewed and swallowed. "I had heard from friends I have in Nessus that it was gone. So you have it. You must keep it until you can dispose of it. Do not try to sell it—it would be identified at once. Hide it somewhere. If you must, throw it into a pit."

"But surely, sieur, it is very valuable."

"It is beyond value, which means it is worthless. You and I are men of sense." Despite his words, there was a tinge of fear in his voice. "But the rabble believe it to be sacred, a performer of all manner of wonders. If I were to possess it, they would think me a desecrator and an enemy of the Theologoumenon. Our masters would think me turned traitor. You must tell me—"

Just at that moment, a man I had not seen previously came running up to the table with a look that indicated he bore urgent news. Vodalus rose and walked a few paces away with him, looking very much, I thought, like a handsome schoolmaster with a boy, for the messenger's head was no higher than his shoulder.

I ate, thinking he would soon return; but after a long questioning of the messenger he walked away with him, disappearing among the broad trunks of the trees. One by one the others rose too, until no one remained but the beautiful Thea, Jonas and me, and one other man.

"You are to join us," Thea said at last in her cooing voice. "Yet you do not know our ways. Have you need of money?"

I hesitated, but Jonas said, "That's something that's always welcome, Chatelaine, like the misfortunes of an older brother."

"Shares will be set aside for you, from this day, of all we take. When you return to us, they will be given to you. Meanwhile I have a purse for each of you to speed you on your way."

"We are going, then?" I asked.

"Were you not told so? Vodalus will instruct you at the supper."

I had supposed the meal we were eating would be the final one of the day, and the thought must have been reflected in my face.

"There will be a supper tonight, when the moon is bright," Thea said. "Someone will be sent to fetch you." Then she quoted a scrap of verse:

> "Dine at dawn to open your eyes,
> Dine at noon that you be strong.
> Dine at eve, and then talk long,
> Dine by night, if you'd be wise. . . .

But now my servant Chuniald will take you to a place where you can rest for your journey."

The man, who had been silent until now, stood and said, "Come with me."

I told Thea, "I would speak with you, Chatelaine, when we have more leisure. I know something that concerns your schoolmate."

She saw that I was serious in what I said, and I saw that she had seen. Then we followed Chuniald through the trees for a distance, I suppose, of a league or more, and at length reached a grassy bank beside a stream. "Wait here," he said. "Sleep if you can. No one will come until after dark."

I asked, "What if we were to leave?"

"There are those all through this wood who know our liege's will concerning you," he said, and turning on his heel, walked away.

Then I told Jonas what I had seen beside the opened grave, just as I have written it here.

"I see," he remarked when I was finished, "why you will join this Vodalus. But you must realize that I am your friend, not his. What I desire is to find the woman you call Jolenta. You want to serve Vodalus, and to go to Thrax and begin a new life in exile, and to wipe out the stain you say you have made on the honor of your guild—though I confess I don't understand how such a thing can be stained—and to find the woman called Dorcas, and to make peace with the woman called Agia while returning something we both know of to the women called Pelerines."

He was smiling by the time he finished this list, and I was laughing.

"And though you remind me of the old man's kestrel, that sat on a perch for twenty years and then flew off in all directions, I hope you achieve these things. But I trust you realize that it is possible—just barely possible, perhaps, but possible—that one or two of them may get in the way of four or five of the others."

"What you're saying is very true," I admitted. "I'm striving to do all those things, and although you won't credit it, I am giving all my strength and as much of my attention as can be of any benefit to all of them. Yet I have to admit things aren't going as well as they might. My divided ambitions have landed me in no better place than the shade of this tree, where I am a homeless wanderer. While you, with your single-minded pursuit of one all-powerful objective . . . look where you are."

In such talk we passed the watches of late afternoon. Birds twittered overhead, and it was very pleasant to have such a friend as Jonas, loyal, reasonable, tactful, and filled with wisdom, humor, and prudence. At that time I had no hint of his history, but I sensed that he was being less than candid about his background, and I sought, without venturing direct questions, to draw him out. I learned (or rather, I thought I did) that his father had been a craftsman; that he had been raised by both parents in what he called the usual way, though it is, in fact, rather rare; and that his home had been a seacoast town in the south, but that when he had last visited it he had found it so much changed that he had no desire to remain.

From his appearance, when I had first encountered him beside the Wall, I had supposed him to be about ten years my elder. From what he said now (and to a lesser extent from some earlier talks we had had) I decided he must be somewhat older; he seemed to have read a good deal of the chronicles of the past, and I was still too naive and unlettered myself, despite the attention Master Palaemon and Thecla had given my mind, to think that anyone much below middle age could have done so. He had a slightly cynical detachment from mankind that suggested he had seen a great deal of the world.

We were still talking when I glimpsed the graceful figure of the Chatelaine Thea moving among the trees some distance away. I nudged Jonas, and we fell silent to watch her. She was coming toward us without having seen us, so that she moved in the blind way people do who are merely following directions. At times a shaft of sunlight fell upon her face, which, if it chanced to be in profile, suggested Thecla's so strongly that the sight of it seemed to tear at my chest. She had Thecla's walk as well, the proud phororhacos stalk that should never have been caged.

"It must be a truly ancient family," I whispered to Jonas. "Look at her! Like a dryad. It might be a willow walking."

"Those ancient families are the newest of all," he answered. "In ancient times there was nothing like them."

I do not believe she was near enough to make out our words, but she seemed to hear his voice, and looked toward us. We waved and she quickened her pace, not running yet coming very rapidly because of the length of her stride. We stood, then sat again when she had reached us and seated herself upon her scarf with her face toward the brook.

"You said you had something to tell me about my sister?" Her voice made her seem less formidable, and seated she was hardly taller than we.

"I was her last friend," I said. "She told me they would try to make you persuade Vodalus to give himself up to save her. Did you know she was imprisoned?"

"Were you her servant?" Thea seemed to weigh me with her eyes. "Yes, I heard they took her to that horrible place in the slums of Nessus, where I understand she died very quickly."

I thought of the time I had spent waiting outside Thecla's door before the scarlet thread of blood came trickling from under it, but I nodded.

"How was she arrested—do you know?"

Thecla had told me the details, and I recounted them just as I had got them from her, omitting nothing.

"I see," Thea said, and was silent for a moment, staring at

the moving water. "I have missed the court, of course. Hearing about those people and that business of muffling her with a tapestry—that's so very characteristic—calls up the reasons I left it."

"I think she missed it sometimes, too," I said. "At least, she talked of it a great deal. But she told me that if she were ever freed she would not go back. She spoke about the country house from which she took her title, and told me how she would refurnish it and give dinners there for the leading persons of the region, and hunt."

Thea's face twisted in a bitter smile. "I have had enough of hunting now for ten lifetimes. But when Vodalus is Autarch, I will be his consort. Then I shall walk beside the Well of Orchids again, this time with the daughters of fifty exultants in my train to amuse me with their singing. Enough of that; it is some months off at least. For the present I have—what I have."

She looked somberly at Jonas and me, and rose very gracefully, indicating by a gesture that we were to remain where we were. "I was happy to hear something now of my half-sister. That house you spoke of is mine now, you know, though I can't claim it. To recompense you, I warn you of the supper we will soon share. You didn't seem receptive of the hints Vodalus flung you. Did you understand them?"

When Jonas said nothing, I shook my head.

"If we, and our allies and masters who wait in the countries beneath the tides, are to triumph, we must absorb all that can be learned of the past. Do you know of the analeptic alzabo?"

I said, "No, Chatelaine, but I have heard tales of the animal of that name. It is said it can speak, and that it comes by night to a house where a child has died, and cries to be let in."

Thea nodded. "That animal was brought from the stars long ago, as were many other things for the benefit of Urth. It is a beast having no more intelligence than a dog, and perhaps less. But it is a devourer of carrion and a clawer at graves, and when it has fed upon human flesh it knows, at least for a time, the speech and ways of human beings. The analeptic alzabo is prepared from a gland at the base of the animal's skull. Do you understand me?"

When she had gone, Jonas would not look at me, nor I at his face; we both knew what feast it was we were to attend that night.

XI

Thecla

After we had sat, so it seemed to me, for a long time (though it was probably no more than a few moments), I could tolerate what I felt no longer. I went to the margin of the brook, and kneeling there on the soft earth spewed out the dinner I had eaten with Vodalus; and when there was nothing more to come forth, I remained where I was, retching and shivering, and rinsing my face and mouth, while the cold, clear water washed away the wine and half-digested meat I had brought up.

When at last I was able to stand, I returned to Jonas and told him, "We must go."

He looked at me as though he pitied me, and I suppose he did. "Vodalus's fighting men are all around us."

"You were not sick, I see, the way I was. But you heard who their allies are. Perhaps Chuniald was lying."

"I've heard our guards walking among the trees—they're not as silent as all that. You have your sword, Severian, and I have a knife, but Vodalus's men will have bows. I noticed that most of those who sat with us at table did. We can try to hide behind the trunks like alouattes. . . ."

I understood what he meant, and said, "Alouattes are shot every day."

"Still, no one hunts them by night. It would be dark in a watch or less."

"You will go with me if we wait until then?" I thrust out my hand.

Jonas clasped it. "Severian, my poor friend, you told me of seeing Vodalus—and this Chatelaine Thea and another man

81

—beside a violated grave. Didn't you know what it was they planned to do with what they got there?"

I had known, of course, but it had been a remote and seemingly irrelevant knowledge then. Now I found I had nothing to say, and indeed almost no thoughts at all outside the hope that night would come quickly.

The men Vodalus sent for us came more quickly still: four burly fellows who might have been peasants and carried berdiches, and a fifth, with something of the armiger about him, who wore an officer's spadroon. Perhaps these men were in the crowd before the dais who had watched us arrive; at any rate, they seemed determined to take no risks with us and surrounded us with their weapons at the ready even while they hailed us as friends and comrades in arms. Jonas put as brave a face on it as a man could, and chatted with them while they escorted us down the forest paths; I could think of nothing but the ordeal ahead, and walked as I might have to the end of the world.

Urth turned her face from the sun's as we traveled. No glimmer of starlight seemed to penetrate the thronging leaves, yet our guides knew the way so well they hardly slowed. With each step I took, I wanted to ask if we would be forced to join in the meal to which we were led, but I knew without asking that to refuse—or even to seem to wish to refuse—would destroy whatever confidence Vodalus had in me, endangering my freedom and perhaps my life.

Our five guards, who had talked only reluctantly at first in response to Jonas's jests and queries, grew more cheerful as I became more desperate, gossiping as if they were on the way to a drinking bout or a brothel. Yet though I recognized the note of anticipation in their voices, the gibes they made were as unintelligible to me as the banter of libertines is to a little child: "Going far this time? Going to drown yourself again?" (This from the man at the back of our party, a mere disembodied voice in the dark.)

"By Erebus, I'm going to sink so far you won't see me until winter."

A voice I recognized as belonging to the armiger asked, "Have any of you seen her yet?" The others had sounded merely boastful, but there was hunger of a kind I had never heard before behind his simple words. He might have been some lost traveler asking about his home.

"No, Waldgrave."

(Another voice.) "Alcmund says a good one, not old or too young."

"Not another tribade, I hope."

"I don't . . ."

The voice broke off, or perhaps I only stopped attending to what it said. I had seen a glimmer through the trees.

After a few strides more, I could make out torches, and hear the sound of many voices. Someone ahead called for us to halt, and the armiger went forward and gave a password softly.

Soon I found myself sitting on forest duff, with Jonas on my right and a low chair of carved wood at my left. The armiger had taken a position on Jonas's right, and the rest of the people present (almost as though they had been waiting for our arrival) had formed a circle whose center was a smokey orange lantern suspended from the boughs of a tree.

No more than a third of those who had been at the audience in the glade were there, but from their dress and weapons it seemed to me that they were largely those of highest rank, together, perhaps, with members of certain favored fighting cadres. There were four or five men to every woman; but the women seemed as warlike as the men, and if anything more eager for the feast to begin.

We had been waiting for some time when Vodalus stepped dramatically out of the darkness and strode across the circle. All present stood, then resumed their seats as he dropped into the carved chair beside me.

Almost at once, a man in the livery of an upper servant in some great house came forward to stand in the center of the circle beneath the orange light. He carried a salver with a large and a small bottle on it, and a crystal goblet. A murmuring began—not a thing for words, I thought, but the sound of a hundred little noises of satisfaction, of quick breathings and tongues on lips. The man with the salver stood motionless until this had run its course, then advanced toward Vodalus with measured steps.

Behind me the cooing voice of Thea said, "The alzabo, of which I told you, is in the smaller bottle. The other holds a compound of herbs that soothe the stomach. Take one full swallow of the mixture."

Vodalus turned to look at her with an expression of surprise.

She entered the circle, passing between Jonas and me, and then between Vodalus and the man who bore the salver, and

at last took a place at Vodalus's left. Vodalus leaned toward
her and would have spoken, but the man with the salver had
begun to mix the contents of the bottles in the goblet, and he
seemed to think the moment inappropriate.

The salver was moved in circles to impart a gentle swirling
motion to the liquid. "Very good," Vodalus said. He took the
goblet from the salver with both hands and raised it to his lips,
then passed it to me. "As the Chatelaine told you, you must
take one full swallow. If you take less, the amount will be
insufficient, and there will be no sharing. If you take more, it
will be of no benefit to you, and the drug, which is very
precious, will be wasted."

I drank from the goblet as he had directed. The mixture
was as bitter as wormwood and seemed cold and fetid,
recalling a winter day long before when I had been ordered to
clean the exterior drain that carried wastes away from the
journeymen's quarters. For a moment I felt that my gorge
would rise as it had beside the brook, though in truth nothing
remained in my stomach to come up. I choked and swallowed
and passed the goblet to Jonas, then discovered that I was
salivating rapidly.

He had as much difficulty as I, or more, but he managed it
at last and passed the goblet to the Waldgrave who had
captained our guards. After that I watched it make its slow
way around the circle. It appeared to hold enough for ten
drinkers; when it was emptied, the man in livery wiped the
rim, filled the goblet again from the bottles on the salver, and
started it once more.

Gradually, he seemed to lose the solid form natural to a
rounded object and become a silhouette only, a mere colored
figure sawn from wood. I was reminded of the marionettes I
had seen in my dream on the night I had shared Baldanders's
bed.

The circle, too, in which we sat, though I knew it to contain
thirty or forty persons, seemed to have been cut from paper
and bent like a toy crown. Vodalus on my left and Jonas at my
right were normal; but the armiger appeared already half
pictured, as did Thea.

As the man in livery reached her, Vodalus rose, and
moving so effortlessly that he might have been propelled by
the night breeze, floated toward the orange lantern. In the
orange light he seemed far away, yet I could feel his gaze as
one feels the heat from the brazier that readies the irons.

"There is an oath to be sworn before the sharing," he said,

and the trees above us nodded solemnly. "By the second life you are to receive, do you swear you will never betray those gathered here? And that you will consent to obey, without hesitation or scruple, to death if need be, Vodalus as your chosen leader?"

I tried to nod with the trees, and when that seemed insufficient I said, "I consent," and Jonas, "Yes."

"And that you will obey as you would Vodalus, any person whatsoever whom Vodalus sets over you?"

"Yes."

"Yes."

"And that you will put this oath above all other oaths, whether sworn before this time or after it?"

"We will," said Jonas.

"Yes," I said.

The breeze was gone. It was as if some unquiet spirit had haunted the gathering, then suddenly vanished. Vodalus was once more in his chair beside me. He leaned toward me. If his voice was slurred, I did not observe it; but something in his eyes told me he was under the influence of the alzabo, perhaps as deeply as I was myself.

"I am no scholar," he began, "but I know it has been said that the greatest causes are often joined by the basest means. Nations are united by trade, the fair ivory and rare woods of altars and reliquaries by the boiled offal of ignoble animals, men and women by the organs of elimination. So we are joined—you and I. So will we both be joined, a few moments hence, to a fellow mortal who will live again—strongly, for a time—in us, by the effluvia pressed from the sweetbreads of one of the filthiest beasts. So blossoms spring from muck."

I nodded.

"This was taught us by our allies, those who wait until man is purified again, ready to join with them in the conquest of the universe. It was brought by the others for foul purposes they hoped to keep secret. I mention this to you because you, when you go to the House Absolute, may meet them, whom the common people call cacogens and the cultured Extra-solarians or Hierodules. You must be careful in no way to bring yourself to their notice, because if they observe you closely they will know by certain signs that you have used alzabo."

"The House Absolute?" Though only for an instant, the thought dispersed the mists of the drug.

"Indeed. I've a fellow there to whom I must transmit

certain instructions, and I have learned that the troupe of players to which you once belonged will be admitted there for a thiasus a few days hence. You will rejoin them and take the opportunity to give what I shall give you," he fumbled in his tunic, "to the one who shall say to you, 'The pelagic argosy sights land.' And should he give you any message in return, you may entrust it to whoever says to you, 'I am from the quercine penetralia.'"

"Liege," I said, "my head is swimming." (Then, lying,) "I cannot remember those words—truly, I have forgotten them already. Did I hear you say that Dorcas and the other will be in the House Absolute?"

Vodalus now pressed into my hand a small object that was not a knife, yet was shaped something like one. I stared at it; it was a steel, such as flint is struck against to kindle fire. "You will remember," he said. "And you will never forget your oath to me. Many of those you see here came, as they believed, only once."

"But, sieur, the House Absolute . . ."

The fluting notes of a upanga sounded from the trees behind the farther side of the circle.

"I must go soon to escort the bride, but have no fear. Some time past you encountered a certain badger of mine—"

"Hildegrin! Sieur, I understand nothing."

"He uses that name among others, yes. He thought it sufficiently unusual to see a torturer so far from the Citadel—and talking of me—as to make it worthwhile to have you watched, though he had no notion you had saved me that night. Unfortunately, the watchers lost you at the Wall; since then they have observed the movements of your traveling companions in the hope you would rejoin them. I supposed that an exile might choose to side with us and so save my poor Barnoch long enough for us to free him. Last night I myself rode into Saltus to speak with you, but I had my mount stolen for my pains and accomplished not a straw. Today, then, it was necessary that we take you by whatever means to prevent you from exercising your skills on my servant; but I still hoped you would make cause with us, and for that reason instructed the men I sent for you to bring you living to me. That cost me three and gained two. The question now is whether the two will outweigh the three."

Vodalus stood then, a little unsteadily; I thanked Holy Katharine that I did not have to stand as well, for I was sure my legs would not hold me. Something dim and white and twice the height of a man was sailing among the trees to the twittering of the upanga. Every neck craned to look at it, and Vodalus drifted to meet it. Thea leaned across his empty chair to speak to me. "Lovely, is she not? They have accomplished wonders."

It was a woman seated on a silver litter borne on the shoulders of six men. For a moment I thought it was Thecla—it looked so like her in the orange light. Then I realized that it was rather her image, made, perhaps, of wax.

"It is said to be perilous," Thea cooed, "when one has known the shared in life; memories held together may amaze the mind. Yet I who loved her will risk that confusion, and knowing from your look when you spoke of her that you would desire it as well, I said nothing to Vodalus."

He had reached up to touch the figurine's arm as it was borne through the circle; with it entered a sweet and unmistakable odor. I recalled the agoutis served at our masking banquets, with their fur of spiced coconut and their eyes of preserved fruits, and knew that what I saw was just such a re-creation of a human being in roasted flesh.

I think I would have gone mad at that moment if it had not been for the alzabo. It stood between my perception and reality like a giant of mist, through which everything could be seen but nothing apprehended. I had another ally as well: it was the knowledge growing in me, the certainty that if I were to consent now and swallow some part of Thecla's substance, the traces of her mind that must otherwise soon fade in decay would enter me and endure, however attenuated, as long as I.

Consent came. What I was about to do no longer seemed filthy or frightening. Instead I opened every part of myself to Thecla, and decked the essence of my being with welcome. Desire came too, born of the drug, a hunger no other food could satisfy, and when I looked around the circle I saw that hunger on every face.

The liveried servant, who I think must have been one of Vodalus's old household gone into exile with him, joined the six who had borne Thecla into the circle and helped lower the litter to the ground. For the space of a few breaths their backs blocked my view. When they parted, she was gone; nothing remained but smoking meats laid upon what might have been a white tablecloth. . . .

I ate and waited, begging forgiveness. She deserved the most magnificent sepulcher, priceless marble of exquisite harmony. In its place she was to be entombed in my torturer's

workroom, with the floor scrubbed and the devices half
disguised under garlands of flowers. The night air was cool,
but I was sweating. I waited for her to come, feeling the drops
roll down my bare chest and staring at the ground because I
was afraid I would see her in the faces of the others before I
felt her presence in myself.

Just when I despaired—she was there, filling me as a
melody fills a cottage. I was with her, running beside the Acis
when we were a child. I knew the ancient villa moated by a
dark lake, the view through the dusty windows of the
belvedere, and the secret space in the odd angle between two
rooms where we sat at noon to read by candlelight. I knew the
life of the Autarch's court, where poison waited in a diamond
cup. I learned what it was for one who had never seen a cell or
felt a whip to be a prisoner of the torturers, what dying
meant, and death.

I learned that I had been more to her than I had ever
guessed, and at last fell into a sleep in which my dreams were
all of her. Not memories merely—memories I had possessed
in plenty before. I held her poor, cold hands in mine, and I no
longer wore the rags of an apprentice, nor the fuligin of a
journeyman. We were one, naked and happy and clean, and
we knew that she was no more and that I still lived, and we
struggled against neither of those things, but with woven hair
read from a single book and talked and sang of other matters.

XII

The Notules

I came from my dreams of Thecla directly to the morning. At one instant we walked mutely together in what surely must have been the paradise the New Sun is said to open to all who, in their final moments, call upon him; and though the wise teach that it is closed to those who are their own executioners, yet I cannot but think that he who forgives so much must sometimes forgive that as well. At the next, I was aware of cold and unwelcome light, and the piping of birds.

I sat up. My cloak was soaked with dew, and dew lay like sweat upon my face. Beside me, Jonas had just begun to stir. Ten paces off two great destriers—one the color of white wine, one of unspotted black—champed their bits and stamped with impatience. Of feast and feasters there was no more sign than of Thecla, whom I have never seen again and now no longer hope to see in this existence.

Terminus Est lay beside me in the grass, secure in her tough, well-oiled sheath. I picked her up and made my way downhill until I found a stream, where I did what I might to refresh myself. When I returned, Jonas was awake. I directed him to the water, and while he was gone I made my farewell to dead Thecla.

Yet some part of her is with me still; at times I who remember am not Severian but Thecla, as though my mind were a picture framed behind glass, and Thecla stands before that glass and is reflected in it. Too, ever since that night, when I think of her without thinking also of a particular time and place, the Thecla who rises in my imagination stands before a mirror in a shimmering gown of frost-white that scarcely covers her breasts but falls in ever-changing cascades below her waist. I see her poised for a moment there; both hands reach up to touch our face.

Then she is whirled away in a room whose walls and ceiling and floor are all of mirrors. No doubt it is her own memory of her image in those mirrors that I see, but after a step or two she vanishes into the dark and I see her no more.

By the time Jonas returned I had mastered my grief and was able to make a show of examining our mounts. "The black for you," he said, "and the cream for me, obviously. Both of them look like they outvalue either of us, though, as the sailor told the surgeon who took off his legs. Where are we going?"

"To the House Absolute." I saw the incredulity in his face. "Did you overhear me talking with Vodalus last night?"

"I caught the name, but not that we were to go there."

I am no rider, as I have said before, but I got one foot into the black's stirrup and swung myself up. The mount I had stolen from Vodalus two nights before had worn a lofty war saddle, fiendishly uncomfortable but very difficult to fall out of; this black carried a nearly flat affair of padded velvet that was both luxurious and treacherous. I had no sooner got my legs around him than he began to dance with eagerness.

It was the worst possible time, perhaps; but it was also the only time. I asked, "How much do you remember?"

"About the woman last night? Nothing." Jonas dodged the black, loosed the cream's reins, and vaulted up. "I didn't eat. Vodalus was watching you, but after they had swallowed the drug, no one was watching me, and anyway I have learned the art of appearing to eat without actually doing it."

I looked at him in astonishment.

"I've practiced several times with you—at breakfast yesterday, for example. I don't have much appetite, and I find it socially useful." As he urged the cream down a forest path, he called over his shoulder, "As it happens, I know the route fairly well, at least for most of the way. But would you mind telling me why we're going?"

"Dorcas and Jolenta will be there," I said. "And I have to do an errand for our liege, Vodalus." Because we were almost certainly watched, I thought it better not to say that I had no intention of performing it.

Here, lest this account of my career run forever, I must pass very quickly over the events of several days. As we rode, I told Jonas all that Vodalus had told me, and much more. We halted at villages and towns as we found them, and where we halted I practiced such of my craft as was in demand—not because the money I earned was strictly necessary to us (for we had the purses the Chatelaine Thea had given us, much of my fee from Saltus, and the money Jonas had obtained for the man-ape's gold) but in order to allay suspicion.

Our fourth morning found us still pressing northward. Gyoll sunned itself to our right like a sluggish dragon guarding the forbidden road that returned to grass upon its bank. The day before, we had seen uhlans on patrol, men mounted much as we were and bearing lances like those that had killed the travelers at the Piteous Gate.

Jonas, who had been ill at ease since we had set out, muttered, "We must hurry if we're to be near the House Absolute tonight. I wish Vodalus had given you the date that celebration begins and some indication of how long it's to last."

I asked, "Is the House Absolute still far off?"

He pointed out an isle in the river. "I think I recall that, and when I was two days from it, some pilgrims told me the House Absolute was nearby. They warned me of the praetorians, and seemed to know what they were talking about."

Following his example, I had allowed my mount to break into a trot. "You were walking."

"Riding my merychip—I suppose I'll never see the poor creature again. She was slower at her best than these animals at their worst, I'll grant you. But I'm not certain they're twice as fast."

I was about to say I did not believe Vodalus would have dispatched us when he did if he had not thought it possible for us to reach the House Absolute in time, when something that at first seemed a great bat came skimming within a handsbreadth of my head.

If I did not know what it was, Jonas did. He shouted words I could not understand and lashed my destrier with the ends of his reins. It bounded forward and nearly threw me, and in

an instant we were galloping madly. I remember shooting
between two trees with not a span to spare on either side and
seeing the thing silhouetted against the sky like a fleck of
soot. A moment later it was rattling among the branches
behind us.

When we cleared the margin of the wood and entered the
dry gully beyond, it was not to be seen; but as we reached the
bottom and began to climb the farther side, it emerged from
the trees, more ragged than ever.

For the space of a prayer it seemed to have lost sight of us,
soaring at an angle to our own path, then swooping toward us
again in a long, flat glide. I had *Terminus Est* clear of her
sheath, and I neck-reined the black between the flying thing
and Jonas.

Swift though our destriers were, it came far more swiftly. If
I had possessed a pointed blade, I think I could have spitted it
as it dove; had I done so I would surely have perished. As it
was, I caught it with a two-handed stroke. It was like cutting
air, and I thought the thing too light and tough for even that
bitter edge. An instant later it parted like a rag; I felt a brief
sensation of warmth, as though the door of an oven had been
opened, then soundlessly shut.

I would have dismounted to examine it, but Jonas shouted
and waved. We had left the lofty forest about Saltus far
behind, and were entering a broken country of steep hills and
ragged cedars. A grove of these stood at the top of the slope;
we plunged into their tangled growth like madmen, flattened
against the necks of our mounts.

Soon the foliage grew so thick they could move no faster
than a walk. Almost at once we reached a sheer rock face and
were forced to halt. When we were no longer smashing
through the tangled limbs, I could hear something else behind
us—a dry rustling, as though a wounded bird were fluttering
among the treetops. The medicinal fragrance of the cedars
oppressed my lungs.

"We must get out," Jonas panted, "or at least keep
moving." The splintered end of a branch had gouged his
cheek; a trickle of blood coursed down it as he spoke. After
looking in both directions he chose the right, toward the
river, and lashed his mount to force it into what appeared to
be an impenetrable thicket.

I let him break a trail for me, reflecting that if the dark
thing caught us I might be able to make some sort of defense
against it. Soon I saw it through the gray-green foliage; a few

moments later there was another, much like the first and only a short distance behind it.

The wood ended, and we were able to flog our mounts to a gallop again. The fluttering scraps of night came after us, but though their smaller size made them appear swifter, they were slower than the single large entity had been.

"We have to find a fire," Jonas shouted above the drumming of the destriers' hooves. "Or a big animal we can kill. If you slashed the belly of one of these beasts, that would probably do it. But if it didn't, we couldn't get away."

I nodded to show that I also opposed killing one of the destriers, though it crossed my mind that my own might soon drop from exhaustion. Jonas was having to allow his to slow now to keep from distancing me. I asked, "Is it blood they want?"

"No. Heat."

Jonas swung his destrier to the right and slapped its flank with his steel hand. It must have been a good blow, for the animal leaped ahead as though stung. We jumped a dry water course, careened sliding and stumbling down a dusty hillside, then struck open, rolling ground where the destriers could show their best speed.

Behind us fluttered the rags of black. They flew at twice the height of a tall tree and seemed to be blown along by the wind, though the rippling of the grass showed that they faced it.

Ahead, the lay of the ground changed as subtly and yet as abruptly as cloth alters at a seam. A sinuous ribbon of green lay as flat as if it had been rolled, and I swung the black down it, shouting in his ears and belaboring him with the flat of my blade. He was drenched with sweat now and streaked with blood from the broken twigs of the cedars. Behind us I could hear Jonas's shouted warnings, but I gave them no heed.

We rounded a curve, and through a break in the trees I saw the gleam of the river. Another curve, with the black beginning to flag again—then, far off, the sight I had been waiting for. Perhaps I should not tell it, but I lifted my sword to Heaven then, to the diminished sun with the worm in his heart; and I called, "His life for mine, New Sun, by your anger and my hope!"

The uhlan (and there was only one alone) must surely have thought me threatening him, as indeed I was. The blue radiance at the tip of his lance increased as he spurred toward us.

Winded though he was, the black swerved for me like a hunted hare. A twitch of the reins, and he was sliding and turning, his hooves scarring the green verdure of the road. In no more than a breath, we had reversed our track and were pounding back toward the things that pursued us. Whether Jonas understood my plan then I do not know, but he fell in with it as though he did, never slackening his own pace.

One of the fluttering creatures swooped, looking for all Urth like a hole torn in the universe; for it was true fuligin, as lightless as my own habit. It was trying for Jonas, I believe, but it came within sword reach, and I parted it as I had before, and again felt a gust of warmth. Knowing from where that heat came, it seemed more evil to me than any vile odor could; the mere sensation on my skin made me ill. I reined sharply away from the river, fearing a bolt from the uhlan's lance at any moment. We had no more than left the road when it came, searing the ground and setting a dead tree ablaze.

I pulled my mount's head up, making him rear and roar. For a moment I looked for the three dark things around the burning tree. They were not there. I glanced toward Jonas then, fearing they had overtaken him after all and were attacking him in some way I could not comprehend.

They were not there either, but his eyes showed me where they had gone: they flitted about the uhlan, and he, as I watched, sought to defend himself with his lance. Bolt after bolt split the air, so that there was a continual crashing like thunder. With each bolt the brightness of the sun was washed away, but the very energies with which he sought to destroy them seemed to give them strength. To my eyes they no longer flew, but flickered as beams of darkness might, appearing first in one place then in another, and always nearer the uhlan, until in less time than I have taken to write of it all three were at his face. He tumbled from his saddle, and the lance fell from his hand and went out.

XIII

The Claw of the Conciliator

I called, "is he dead?", and saw Jonas nod in reply. I would have ridden away then, but he motioned for me to join him and dismounted. When we met by the uhlan's body, he said, "We may be able to destroy those things so they can't be flown against us again or be used to harm anyone else. They're sated now, and I think we might handle them. We need something to put them in—something water-tight, of metal or glass."

I had nothing of that kind and told him so.

"Neither have I." He knelt beside the uhlan and turned out his pockets. Aromatic smoke from the blazing tree wreathed everything like incense, and I had the sensation of being once more in the Cathedral of the Pelerines. The litter of twigs and last summer's leaves on which the uhlan lay might have been the straw-strewn floor; the trunks of the scattered trees, the supporting poles.

"Here," Jonas said, and picked up a brass vasculum. Unscrewing the lid he emptied it of herbs, then rolled the dead uhlan on his back.

"Where are they?" I asked. "Has the body absorbed them?"

Jonas shook his head, and after a moment began, very carefully and delicately, to draw one of the dark things from the uhlan's left nostril. Save for being absolutely opaque, it was like the finest tissue paper.

I wondered at his caution. "If you tear it, won't it just become two?"

"Yes, but it is sated now. Divided, it would lose energy and might be impossible to handle. A lot of people have died, by the way, because they found they could cut these creatures, and chose to stand their ground doing it until they were surrounded by too many to fend off."

One of the uhlan's eyes was half open. I had seen corpses often before, but I could not escape the eerie feeling that he was in some sense watching me, the man who had killed him to save himself. To turn my mind to other things, I said, "After I cut the first one, it seemed to fly more slowly."

Jonas had placed the horror he had drawn out in the vasculum and was extracting a second from the right nostril; he murmured, "The speed of any flying thing depends on its wing area. If that weren't the case, the adepts who use these creatures would tear them into scraps before they sent them forth, I suppose."

"You sound as though you've encountered them before."

"We docked once at a port where they're used in ritual murders. I suppose it was inevitable that someone would bring them home, but these are the first I've seen here." He opened the brass lid and laid the second fuligin thing on the first, which stirred sluggishly. "They'll recombine in there—this is what the adepts do to get them back together. I doubt if you noticed it, but they were torn somewhat in going through the wood and healed themselves in flight."

"There's one more," I said.

He nodded and used his steel hand to force open the dead man's mouth; instead of holding teeth and livid tongue and gums it appeared to be a bottomless gulf, and for a moment my stomach churned. Jonas drew out the third creature, streaked with the dead man's saliva.

"Wouldn't he have had a nostril open, or his mouth, if I hadn't cut the thing a second time?"

"Until they worked their way into his lungs. We're lucky, actually, to have been able to get to him so quickly. Otherwise you would have had to slice the body open to get them out."

A wisp of smoke called to mind the burning cedar. "If it was heat they wanted . . ."

"They prefer life's heat, though they can sometimes be distracted by a fire of living vegetable matter. It's something more than heat, I think, really. Perhaps some radiant energy characteristic of growing cells." Jonas stuffed the third creature into the vasculum and snapped it shut. "We called them notules, because they usually came after dark, when they could not be seen, and the first warning we had was a breath of warmth; but I have no idea what the natives call them."

"Where is this island?"

He looked at me curiously.

"Is it far from the coast? I've always wanted to see Uroboros, though I suppose it is dangerous."

"Very far," Jonas said in a flat voice. "Very far indeed. Wait a moment."

I waited, watching, as he strode to the riverbank. He threw the vasculum hard—it had almost reached midstream when it dropped into the water. When he returned I asked, "Couldn't we have used those things ourselves? It doesn't seem likely that whoever sent them is going to give up now, and we might have need of them."

"'They would not obey us, and the world is better without them anyway,' as the butcher's wife told him when she cut away his manhood. Now we'd best be going. There's somebody coming down the road."

I looked where Jonas had pointed, and saw two figures on foot. He had caught his destrier by the halter as it drank and was ready to climb into the saddle. "Wait," I said. "Or go on a chain or two and wait for me there." I was thinking of the man-ape's bleeding stump, and I seemed to see the dim votive lights of the cathedral hanging, crimson and magenta, among the trees. I reached into my boot, far down where I had pushed it for safety, and drew out the Claw.

It was the first time I had seen it by full daylight. It caught the sun and flashed like a New Sun itself, not blue only but with every color from violet to cyan. I laid it on the uhlan's forehead, and for an instant tried to will him alive.

"Come on," Jonas called. "What are you doing?"

I did not know how to answer him.

"He's not quite dead," Jonas called. "Get off the road before he finds his lance!" He lashed his mount.

Faintly, a voice I seemed to recognize called, "Master!" I turned my head to look down the grass-grown highway.

"Master!" One of the travelers waved an arm, and both began to run.

"It's Hethor," I said; but Jonas had gone. I looked back at the uhlan. Both his eyes were open now, and his chest rose and fell. When I took the Claw from his forehead and thrust it back into my boot top, he sat up. I shouted to Hethor and his companion to leave the road, but they did not appear to understand.

"Who are you?"

"A friend," I said.

Though the uhlan was feeble, he tried to rise. I gave him my hand and pulled him up. For a moment he stared at everything—myself, the two men running toward him, the river, and the trees. The destriers appeared to frighten him, even his own, which stood patiently awaiting its rider. "What is this place?"

"Only a stretch of the old road beside Gyoll."

He shook his head and pressed it with his hands.

Hethor came panting up, like an ill-bred dog that has run when called and now expects a petting for it. His companion, whom he had outreached by a hundred strides or so, wore the gaudy clothes and greasy look of a small trader.

"M-m-master," Hethor said, "you can have no idea how much t-t-trouble, how much deadly loss and difficulty we have had in overtaking you across the mountains, across the wide-blown seas and c-c-creaking plains of this fair world. What am I, your s-slave, but an abandoned sh-shell, the sport of a thousand tides, cast up here in this lonely place because I cannot r-r-rest without you? H-how could you, the red-clawed master, know of the endless labor you've cost us?"

"Since I left you in Saltus afoot and have been well mounted these past few days, I should think a good deal."

"Exactly," he said. "Exactly." He looked significantly at his companion as if my remark had confirmed something he had told him earlier, and sank down to rest upon the ground.

The uhlan said slowly, "I am Cornet Mineas. Who are you?"

Hethor bobbed his head as though he would have bowed. "M-m-master is the noble Severian, servant of the Autarch—whose urine is the wine of his subjects—in the Guild of the Seekers for Truth and Penitence. H-h-hethor is his humble servant. Beuzec is also his humble servant. I suppose the man who rode away is his servant, too."

I gestured for him to be quiet. "We are all only poor travelers, Cornet. We saw you lying here stunned and sought to help you. A moment ago, we thought you dead; it must have been a near thing."

"What is this place?" the uhlan asked again.

Hethor answered eagerly. "The road north of Quiesco. M-m-master, we were on a boat, sailing the wide waters of Gyoll in the blind night. We di-d-disembarked at Quiesco. On her deck and at her sails we worked our p-passage, Beuzec and me. So slowly upriver, while the lucky ones whizzed above on their way to the H-h-house Absolute, but she m-m-made h-h-headway whether we woke or slept, and thus we caught up to you."

"The House Absolute?" the uhlan muttered.

I said, "It's not far from here, I think."

"I am to be especially vigilant."

"I feel sure one of your comrades will be along soon." I caught my mount and clambered onto his lofty back.

"M-m-master, you're not going to l-l-leave us again? Beuzec has seen you perform but twice."

I was about to answer Hethor when I caught sight of a flash of white among the trees across the highway. Something huge was moving there. At once, the thought that the sender of the notules might have other weapons at hand filled my mind, and I dug my heels into the black's flanks.

He sprang away. For half a league or more we raced along the narrow strip of ground that separated the road from the river. When at last I saw Jonas, I galloped across to warn him, and told him what I had seen.

While I spoke he seemed lost in reflection. When I had finished, he said, "I know of nothing like the being you describe, but there may be many importations I know nothing of."

"But surely such a thing wouldn't be wandering free like a strayed cow!"

Instead of replying, Jonas pointed toward the ground a few strides ahead.

A graveled path hardly more than a cubit wide wound among the trees. It was bordered with more wild flowers than I have ever seen growing naturally in company, and it was of pebbles so uniform in size, and of such shining whiteness, that they must surely have been carried from some secret and far-off beach.

After riding a bit closer to examine it, I asked Jonas what such a path here could possibly mean.

"Only one thing, surely—that we are already on the grounds of the House Absolute."

Quite suddenly, I recalled the spot. "Yes," I said. "Once Josepha and I, with some others, made up a fishing party and came here. We crossed by the twisted oak . . ."

Jonas looked at me as though I were mad, and for a moment I felt that I was. I had ridden hunting often before, but this was a charger I sat, and no hunter. My hands raised themselves like spiders to pluck out my eyes—and would have done so if the ragged man beside me had not struck them down with his own hand, which was of steel. "You are not the Chatelaine Thecla," he said. "You are Severian, a journeyman of the torturers, who was unfortunate enough to love her. See yourself!" He held up the steel hand so that I could see a stranger's face, narrow, ugly, and bewildered, reflected in its work-polished balm.

I remembered our tower then, the curved walls of smooth, dark metal. "I am Severian," I said.

"That is correct. The Chatelaine Thecla is dead."

"Jonas . . ."

"Yes?"

"The uhlan is alive now—you saw him. The Claw gave him life again. I laid it on his forehead, but perhaps it was just that he saw it with his dead eyes. He sat up. He breathed and spoke to me, Jonas."

"He was not dead."

"You saw him," I said again.

"I am much older than you are. Older than you think. If there is one thing I have learned in so many voyages, it is that the dead do not rise, nor the years turn back. What has been and is gone does not come again."

Thecla's face was before me still, but it was blown by a dark wind until it fluttered and went out. I said, "If I had only used it, called on the power of the Claw when we were at the banquet of the dead . . ."

"The uhlan had nearly suffocated, but was not quite dead. When I got the notules away from him he was able to breathe, and after a time he regained consciousness. As for your Thecla, no power in the universe could have restored her to life. They must have dug her up while you were still imprisoned in the Citadel and stored her in an ice cave. Before we saw her, they had gutted her like a partridge and roasted her flesh." He gripped my arm. "Severian, don't be a fool!"

At that moment I wanted only to perish. If the notule had reappeared, I would have embraced it. What did appear, far down the path, was a white shape like that I had seen nearer the river. I tore myself away from Jonas and galloped toward it.

XIV

The Antechamber

There are beings—and artifacts—against which we batter our intelligence raw, and in the end make peace with reality only by saying, "It was an apparition, a thing of beauty and horror."

Somewhere among the swirling worlds I am so soon to explore, there lives a race like and yet unlike the human. They are no taller than we. Their bodies are like ours save that they are perfect, and that the standard to which they adhere is wholly alien to us. Like us they have eyes, a nose, a mouth; but they use these features (which are, as I have said, perfect) to express emotions we have never felt, so that for us to see their faces is to look upon some ancient and terrible alphabet of feeling, at once supremely important and utterly unintelligible.

Such a race exists, yet I did not encounter it there at the edge of the gardens of the House Absolute. What I had seen moving among the trees, and what I now—until I at last saw it clearly—flung myself toward, was rather the giant image of such a being kindled to life. Its flesh was of white stone, and its eyes had the smoothly rounded blindness (like sections cut from eggshells) we see in our own statues. It moved slowly, like one drugged or sleeping, yet not unsteadily. It seemed sightless, yet it gave the impression of awareness, however slow.

I have just paused to reread what I have written of it, and I see that I have failed utterly to convey the essence of the thing. Its spirit was that of sculpture. If some fallen angel had overheard my conversation with the green man, he might have contrived such an enigma to mock me. In its every movement it carried the serenity and permanency of art and stone; I felt that each gesture, each position of the head and limbs and torso, might be the last. Or that each might be repeated interminably, as the poses of the gnomens of Valeria's many-faceted dial were repeated down the curving corridors of the instants.

My initial terror, after the white statue's strangeness had washed away my will toward death, was the instinctive one that it would do me hurt.

My second was that it would not attempt to. To be as frightened of something as I was of that silent, inhuman figure, and then to discover that it meant no harm, would have been unbearably humiliating. Forgetting for a moment the ruin it would bring her blade to strike that living stone, I drew *Terminus Est* and reined in the black. The breeze itself seemed to pause as we stood there, the black hardly quivering, myself with sword upraised, as still almost ourselves as statues. The real statue came toward us, its three or four times life-size face stamped with inconceivable emotion and its limbs wrapped in terrible and perfect beauty.

I heard Jonas shout, and the sound of a blow. I had just time to see him on the ground grappling with men in tall, crested helmets that vanished and reappeared even as I looked at them, when something whizzed past my ear; another struck my wrist, and I found myself struggling in a web of cords that constricted like little boas. Someone seized my leg and pulled, and I fell.

When I had recovered enough to be aware of what was taking place, I had a wire noose about my neck, and one of my captors was rummaging through my sabretache. I could see his hands clearly, darting like brown sparrows. His face was visible too, an impassive mask that might have been suspended above me on a conjuror's thread. Once or twice, as he moved, the extraordinary armor he wore gleamed; then I saw it as one sees a crystal beaker immersed in clear water. It was reflective, I think, burnished beyond any merely human skill, so that its own material was invisible and only the greens and browns of the wood could be seen, twisted by the shapes of cuirass, gorget, and greaves.

Despite my protest that I was a member of the guild, the praetorian took all the money I had (though he left me

Thecla's brown book, my fragment of whetstone, oil and flannel, and the other miscellaneous objects in my sabre-tache). Then he skillfully drew off the cords that entangled me and thrust them (as nearly as I could tell) into the armhole of his breastplate, though not before I had seen them. They reminded me of the whip we used to call a "cat," and were a bundle of thongs joined at one end and weighted at the other; I have learned since that this weapon is called the *achico*.

My captor now lifted the wire noose until I stood. I was conscious, as I have been on several similar occasions, that we were in some sense playing a game. We were pretending that I was totally in his power, when in fact I might have refused to rise until he had either strangled me or called over some of his comrades to carry me. I could have done several other things as well—seized the wire and tried to wrest it from him, struck him in the face. I might have escaped, been killed, been rendered unconscious, or plunged into agony; but I could not actually be forced to do as I did.

At least I knew it was a game, and I smiled as he sheathed *Terminus Est* and led me to where Jonas stood.

Jonas said, "We've done no harm. Return my friend's sword and give us back our animals, and we will go."

There was no reply. In silence two praetorians (four fluttering sparrows, as it seemed) caught our destriers and led them away. How like us those animals were, walking patiently they knew not where, their massive heads following thin strips of leather. Nine-tenths of life, so it seems to me, consists of these surrenders.

We were made to go with our captors out of the wood and onto a rolling meadow that soon became a lawn. The statue walked after us, and others of his kind joined him until there were a dozen or more, all huge, all different, and all beautiful. I asked Jonas who the soldiers were and where they were taking us; but he did not answer, and I was nearly throttled for my pains.

So far as I could tell, they were armored from head to foot, yet the perfect polish of the metal imparted to it a seeming softness, an almost liquid yielding, that was profoundly disturbing to the eye and that permitted it to fade into sky and grass at a distance of a few paces. When we had walked half a league across the sward, we entered a grove of flowering plums, and at once the crested helms and flaring pauldrons danced with pink and white.

There we struck a path that curved and curved again. Just as we were on the point of emerging from the grove we halted, and Jonas and I were pushed violently back. I heard the feet of the stony figures that followed us grate on the gravel as they too stopped short; one of the soldiers warned them off with what seemed to me a wordless cry. I peered through the blossoms as well as I could to see what lay ahead.

Before us was a walk much broader than the one we trod. It was, in fact, a garden path grown until it had become a magnificent processional way. The pavement was of white stone, and marble balustrades flanked it to either side. Down it marched a motley company. Most were on foot, but some rode beasts of various sorts. One led a shaggy arctother; another perched upon the neck of a ground sloth greener than the lawns. No sooner had this group passed than other groups followed them. While they were still too far for me to distinguish their faces, I noticed one in which the bowed head of a single individual was lifted above the rest by at least three cubits. A moment later I had recognized another as Dr. Talos, strutting along with his chest thrown out and his head well back. My own dear Dorcas followed close behind him, looking more than ever like a forlorn child wandered from some higher sphere. Fluttering with veils and sparkling with bijoux under her parasol, Jolenta rode a diminutive jennet sidesaddle; and behind them all, patiently wheeling such properties as he could not shoulder, lumbered he whom I had identified first, the giant, Baldanders.

If it was painful for me to see them pass without being able to call out, it must have been torment for Jonas. When Jolenta was nearly opposite us, she turned her head. To me, at that moment, it seemed she must have winded his desire, as among the mountains certain unclean spirits are said to be attracted by the odor of meat that has been cast upon a fire for them. No doubt it was really only the flowering trees among which we stood that caught her attention. I heard the inhalation of Jonas's breath; but the first syllable of her name was cut short by the thud of the blow that followed, and he pitched at my feet. When I recall that scene now, the rattle of his metal hand on the gravel of the path is as vivid as the perfume of the plum blossoms.

After all the troupes of performers had gone, two praetorians picked up poor Jonas and carried him. They did it as easily as they might have carried a child; but I at the time attributed that only to their strength. We crossed the road down which the performers had come and penetrated a hedge of roses higher than a man, covered with immense white blossoms and filled with nesting birds.

Beyond it lay the gardens proper. If I should try to describe them, I should seem only to have borrowed the mad, stammering eloquence of Hethor. Every hill and tree and flower seemed to have been arranged by some master intelligence (which I have since learned is that of Father Inire) to form a breathtaking vision. The observer feels that he is at the center, that everything he sees has been directed toward the point at which he stands; but after he has walked a hundred paces, or a league, he finds himself at the center still; and every vision seems to convey some incommunicable truth, like one of the unutterable insights granted eremites.

So beautiful were these gardens that we had been in them for some time before I realized that no towers were lifted above them. Only the birds and the clouds, and beyond them the old sun and the pale stars, rose higher than their treetops; we might have been wandering through some divine wilderness. Then we reached the crest of a wave of land more lovely than any cobalt wave of Uroboros's, and with breathtaking suddenness a pit opened at our feet. I have called it a pit, but it was not at all like the dark abyss usually associated with that word. Rather, it was a grotto filled with fountains and night flowers, and dotted with people more brilliant than any flowers, people who loitered beside its waters and gossiped among its shades.

At once, as though a wall had collapsed to let light into a tomb, many of the memories of the House Absolute, mine by absorption now from the life of Thecla, coalesced. I understood something that had been implicit in the doctor's play and in many of the stories Thecla had told me as well, though she had never mentioned it directly: The whole of this great palace lay underground—or rather, its roofs and walls were heaped with soil planted and landscaped, so that we had been walking all this time over the seat of the Autarch's power, which I had thought still some distance away.

We did not go down into that grotto, which no doubt opened onto chambers quite unsuited to the detention of prisoners, or into any of the next score or so we passed. At last, however, we came upon one far more grim, though no less beautiful. The stair by which we entered it had been carved to resemble a natural formation of dark rock, irregular and sometimes treacherous. Water dripped from above, and ferns and dark ivy grew in the upper parts of this artificial cavern, where a little sunlight still found its way. In the lower regions, a thousand steps down, the walls were studded with blind fungi; some of these were luminous; some strewed the air with strange, musty odors; some suggested fantastic phallic fetishes.

In the center of this dark garden, supported by scaffolding and green with verdigris, hung a set of gongs. It appeared to me that they were intended to be rung by the wind; yet it seemed impossible that any wind should ever reach them.

So I thought, at least, until one of the praetorians opened a heavy door of bronze and worm-scarred wood in one of the dark stone walls. Then a draft of cold, dry air blew through that doorway and set the gongs to swaying and clashing, so well tuned that their chiming seemed the purposeful composition of some musician, whose thoughts were now in exile here.

In looking up at the gongs (which the praetorians did not prevent me from doing) I saw the statues, forty at least, who had followed us all the way across the gardens. They now rimmed the pit, motionless at last, and looked down on us like a frieze of cenotaphs.

I had expected to be the only occupant of a small cell, I suppose because I unconsciously transferred the practices of our own oubliette to this unknown place. Nothing more different from the actual arrangement could have been imagined. The entrance opened on no corridor of narrow doors, but to a spacious and carpeted one with a second entrance opposite. Hastarii with flaming spears stood as sentries before this second set of doors. At a word from one of the praetorians, they swung them open; beyond lay a vast, shadowy, bare room with a very low ceiling. Several dozen persons, men and women and a few children, were scattered in diverse parts of it—most singly, but some in couples or groups. Families occupied alcoves, and in some places screens of rags had been erected to provide privacy.

Into this we were thrust. Or rather, I was thrust and the unfortunate Jonas was thrown. I tried to catch him as he fell, and I at least prevented his head from striking the floor; as I did so, I heard the doors slam shut behind me.

XV

Fool's Fire

I was ringed by faces. Two women took Jonas from me, and promising to care for him carried him away. The rest began to ply me with questions. What was my name? What clothes were those I wore? Where had I come from? Did I know such a one, or such a one, or such a one? Had I ever been to this town or that? Was I of the House Absolute? Of Nessus? From the east bank of Gyoll or the west? What quarter? Did the Autarch still live? What of Father Inire? Who was archon in the city? How went the war? Had I news of so-and-so, a commander? Of so-and-so, a trooper? Of so-and-so, a chiliarch? Could I sing, recite, play an instrument?

As may be imagined, in such a welter of inquiries I was able to answer almost none. When the first flurry was spent, an old, gray-bearded man and a woman who seemed almost equally old silenced the others and drove them away. Their method, which would surely have succeeded nowhere but here, was to clap each by the shoulder, point to the most remote part of the room, and say distinctly, *"Plenty of time."* Gradually the others fell silent and walked to what seemed the limits of hearing, until at last the low room was as still as it had been when the doors opened.

"I am Lomer," the old man said. He cleared his throat noisily. "This is Nicarete."

I told him my name, and Jonas's.

The old woman must have heard the concern in my voice. "He will be safe, rest assured. Those girls will treat him as well as they can, in the hope that he'll soon be able to talk to them." She laughed, and something in the way she threw

107

back her well-shaped head told me she had once been beautiful.

I began to question them in my turn, but the old man interrupted me. "Come with us," he said, "to our corner. We will be able to sit at ease there, and I can offer you a cup of water."

As soon as he pronounced the word, I realized that I was terribly thirsty. He led us behind the rag screen nearest the doors and poured water for me from an earthenware jug into a delicate porcelain cup. There were cushions there, and a little table not more than a span high.

"Question for question," he said. "That's the old rule. We have told you our names and you have told us yours, and so we begin again. Why were you taken?"

I explained that I did not know, unless it were merely for violating the grounds.

Lomer nodded. His skin was of that pale color peculiar to those who never see the sun; with his straggling beard and uneven teeth, he would have been repulsive in any other setting; but he belonged here as much as the half-obliterated tiles of the floor did. "I am here by the malice of the Chatelaine Leocadia. I was seneschal to her rival the Chatelaine Nympha, and when she brought me here to the House Absolute with her in order that we might review the accounts of the estate while she attended the rites of the philomath Phocas, the Chatelaine Leocadia entrapped me by the aid of Sancha, who—"

The old woman, Nicarete, interrupted him. "Look!" she exclaimed. "He knows her."

And so I did. A chamber of pink and ivory had risen in my mind, a room of which two walls were clear glass exquisitely framed. Fires burned there on marble hearths, dimmed by the sunbeams streaming through the glass but filling the room with a dry heat and the odor of sandalwood. An old woman wrapped in many shawls sat in a chair that was like a throne; a decanter of cut crystal and several brown phials stood on an inlaid table at her side. "An elderly woman with a hooked nose," I said. "The Dowager of Fors."

"You do know her then." Lomer's head nodded slowly, as though it were answering the question put by its own mouth. "You are the first in many years."

"Let us say that I remember her."

"Yes." The old man nodded. "They say she is dead now.

But in my day she was a fine, healthy young woman. The Chatelaine Leocadia persuaded her to it, then caused us to be discovered, as Sancha knew she would. She was but fourteen, and no crime was charged to her. We had done nothing in any case; she had only begun to undress me."

I said, "You must have been quite a young man yourself."

He did not answer, so Nicarete replied for him. "He was twenty-eight."

"And you," I asked. "Why are you here?"

"I am a volunteer."

I looked at her in some surprise.

"Someone must make amends for the evil of Urth, or the New Sun will never come. And someone must call attention to this place and the others like it. I am of an armiger family that may yet remember me, and so the guards must be careful of me, and of all the others while I remain here."

"Do you mean that you can leave, and will not?"

"No," she said, and shook her head. Her hair was white, but she wore it flowing about her shoulders as young women do. "I will leave, but only on my own terms, which are that all those who have been here so long that they have forgotten their crimes be set free as well."

I remembered the kitchen knife I had stolen for Thecla, and the ribbon of crimson that had crept from under the door of her cell in our oubliette, and I said, "Is it true that prisoners really forget their crime here?"

Lomer looked up at that. "Unfair! Question for question—that's the rule, the old rule. We still keep the old rules here. We're the last of the old crop, Nicarete and me, but while we last, the old rules still stand. Question for question. Have you friends who may strive for your release?"

Dorcas would, surely, if she knew where I was. Dr. Talos was as unpredictable as the figures seen in clouds, and for that very reason might seek to have me freed, though he had no real motive for doing so. Most importantly, perhaps, I was Vodalus's messenger, and Vodalus had at least one agent in the House Absolute—him to whom I was supposed to deliver his message. I had tried to cast away the steel twice while Jonas and I were riding north, but had found that I could not; the alzabo, it seemed, had laid yet another spell upon my mind. Now I was glad of that.

"Have you friends? Relations? If you have, you may be able to do something for the rest of us."

"Friends, possibly," I said. "They may try to help me if they ever learn what has happened to me. Is it likely they may succeed?"

In that way we talked for a long time; if I were to write it all here, there would be no end to this history. In that room, there is nothing to do but talk and play a few simple games, and the prisoners do those things until all the savor has gone out of them, and they are left like gristle a starving man has chewed all day. In many respects, these prisoners are better off than the clients beneath our own tower; by day they have no fear of pain, and none is alone. But because most of them have been there so long, and few of our clients had been long confirmed, ours were, for the most part, filled with hope, while those in the House Absolute are despairing.

After what must have been ten watches or more, the glowing lamps in the ceiling began to fade, and I told Lomer and Nicarete I could remain awake no longer. They led me to a spot far from the door, where it was very dark, and explained that it would be mine until one of the other prisoners died and I succeeded to a better position.

As they left, I heard Nicarete say, "Will they come tonight?" Lomer made some reply, but I could not say what that reply was, and I was too fatigued to ask. My feet told me there was a thin pallet on the floor; I sat down and had begun to stretch myself full length when my hand touched a living body.

Jonas's voice said, "You needn't jerk back. It's only me."

"Why didn't you say something? I saw you walking about, but I couldn't break away from the two old people. Why didn't you come over?"

"I didn't say anything because I was thinking. And I didn't come over because I couldn't break away from the women who had me, at first. Afterward, those people couldn't break away from me. Severian, I must escape from here."

"Everyone wants to, I suppose," I told him. "Certainly I do."

"But I *must*." His thin, hard hand—his left hand of flesh—gripped mine. "If I don't, I will kill myself or lose my reason. I've been your friend, haven't I?" His voice dropped to the faintest of whispers. "Will the talisman you carry . . . the blue gem . . . set us free? I know the praetorians didn't find it; I watched while they searched you."

"I don't want to take it out," I said. "It gleams so in the dark."

"I'll turn one of these mats on its side and hold it to shield us."

I waited until I could feel the pallet in position, then drew out the Claw. Its light was so faint I might have shaded it with my hand.

"Is it dying?" Jonas asked.

"No, it's often like this. But when it is active—when it transmuted the water in our carafe and when it awed the man-apes—it shines brightly. If it can procure our escape at all, I don't believe it will do so now."

"We must take it to the door. It might spring the lock." His voice was shaking.

"Later, when the others are all asleep. I'll free them if we can get free ourselves; but if the door doesn't open—and I don't think it will—I don't want them to know I have the Claw. Now tell me why you must escape at once."

"While you were talking to the old people I was being questioned by a whole family," Jonas began. "There were several old women, a man of about fifty, another about thirty, three other women, and a flock of children. They had carried me to their own little niche in the wall, you see, and the other prisoners couldn't come there unless they were invited, which they weren't. I expected that they'd ask me about friends on the outside, or politics, or the fighting in the mountains. Instead I seemed to be only a kind of amusement for them. They wanted to hear about the river, and where I had been, and how many people dressed the way I did. And the food outside—there were a great many questions about food, some of them quite ludicrous. Had I ever seen butchering? And did the animals plead for their lives? And was it true that the ones who make sugar carried poisoned swords and would fight to defend it . . . ?

They had never seen bees, and seemed to think they were about the size of rabbits.

"After a time I began to ask questions of my own and found that none of them, not even the oldest woman, had ever been free. Men and women are put into this room alike, it seems, and in the course of nature they produce children. And though some are taken away, most remain here throughout their lives. They have no possessions and no hope of release. Actually, they don't know what freedom is, and although the older man and one girl told me seriously that they would like to go outside, I don't think they meant to stay. The old women are seventh-generation prisoners, so they said—but one let it slip that her mother had been a seventh-generation prisoner as well.

"They are remarkable people in some respects. Externally they have been shaped completely by this place where they have spent all their lives. Yet beneath that are . . ." Jonas paused, and I could feel the silence pressing in all about us. "Family memories, I suppose you could call them. Traditions from the outside world that have been handed down to them, generation to generation, from the original prisoners from whom they are descended. They don't know what some of the words mean any longer, but they cling to the traditions, to the stories, because those are all they have; the stories and their names."

He fell silent. I had thrust the tiny spark of the Claw back into my boot, and we were in perfect darkness. His labored breathing was like the pumping of the bellows at a forge.

"I asked them the name of the first prisoner, the most remote from whom they counted their descent. It was Kimleesoong . . . Have you heard that name?"

I told him I had not.

"Or anything like it? Suppose it were three words."

"No, nothing like that," I said. "Most of the people I have known have had one-word names like you, unless a part of the name was a title, or a nickname of some sort that had been attached to it because there were too many Bolcans or Altos or whatever."

"You told me once that you thought I had an unusual name. Kim Lee Soong would have been a very common kind of name when I was . . . a boy. A common name in places now sunk beneath the sea. Have you ever heard of my ship, Severian? She was the *Fortunate Cloud*."

"A gambling ship? No, but—"

My eye was caught by a gleam of greenish light so faint that even in that darkness it was scarcely visible. At once there came a murmur of voices echoing and reechoing throughout the wide, low, crooked room. I heard Jonas scrambling to his feet. I did the same, but I was no sooner up than I was blinded by a flash of blue fire. The pain was as severe as I have ever felt; it seemed as though my face were being torn away. I would have fallen if it had not been for the wall.

Somewhere farther off the blue fire flashed again, and a woman cried out.

Jonas was cursing—at least, the tone of his voice told me he was cursing, though the words came in tongues unknown to me. I heard his boots on the floor. There was another flash, and I recognized the lightninglike sparks I had seen the day Master Gurloes, Roche, and I administered the revolutionary to Thecla. No doubt Jonas screamed as I had, but by that time there was such bedlam I could not distinguish his voice.

The greenish light grew stronger, and while I watched, still more than half paralyzed with pain and wracked by as much fear as I can recall ever having experienced, it gathered itself into a monstrous face that glared at me with saucer eyes, then quickly faded to mere dark.

All this was more terrifying than my pen could ever convey, though I were to slave over this part of my account forever. It was the fear of blindness as well as of pain, but we were all, for all that mattered, already blind. There was no light, and we could make none. There was not one of us who could light a candle or so much as strike fire to tinder. All around that cavernous room, voices screamed, wept, and prayed. Over the wild din I heard the clear laughter of a young woman; then it was gone.

XVI

Jonas

I hungered then for light as a starving man for meat, and at last I risked the Claw. Perhaps I should say that it risked me; it seemed I had no control of the hand that slid into my boot top and grasped it.

At once the pain faded, and there came a rush of azure light. The hubbub redoubled as the other wretched inhabitants of the place, seeing that radiance, feared some new terror was to be thrust among them. I pushed the gem down into my boot once more, and when its light was no longer visible began to grope for Jonas.

He was not unconscious, as I had supposed, but lay writhing, some twenty steps from where we had rested. I carried him back (finding him astonishingly light) and when I had covered us both with my cloak touched his forehead with the Claw.

In a short time he was sitting up. I told him to rest, that whatever it was that had been in the prison chamber with us was gone.

He stirred and muttered, "We must get power to the compressors before the air goes bad."

"It's all right," I told him. "Everything is all right, Jonas." I despised myself for it, but I was talking to him as if he were the youngest of apprentices, just as, years before, Master Malrubius had spoken to me.

Something hard and cold touched my wrist, moving as if it were alive. I grasped it, and it was Jonas's steel hand; after a moment I realized he had been trying to clasp my own hand with it. "I feel weight!" His voice was growing louder. "It must be only the lights." He turned, and I heard his hand ring and scrape as it struck the wall. He began talking to himself in a nasal, monosyllabic language I did not understand.

Greatly daring, I drew out the Claw again and touched him with it once more. It was as dull as it had been when we had first examined it that evening, and Jonas became no better; but in time I was able to calm him. At last, long after the remainder of the room had grown quiet, we lay down to sleep.

When I woke, the dim lamps were burning again, though I somehow felt that it was yet night outside, or at least no more than earliest morning.

Jonas lay beside me, still asleep. There was a long tear in his tunic, and I saw where the blue fire had branded him. Recalling the man-ape's severed hand, I made certain no one was observing us and began to trace the burn with the Claw.

It sparkled in the light much more brightly than it had the evening before; and though the black scar did not vanish, it seemed narrower, and the flesh to either side less inflamed. To reach the lower end of the wound, I lifted the cloth a trifle. When I thrust in my hand, I heard a faint note; the gem had struck metal. Drawing back the cloth more, I saw that my friend's skin ended as abruptly as grass does where a large stone lies, giving way to shining silver.

My first thought was that it was armor; but soon I saw that it was not. Rather, it was metal standing in the place of flesh, just as metal stood in the place of his right hand. How far it continued I could not see, and I was afraid to touch his legs for fear of waking him.

Concealing the Claw again, I rose. And because I wanted to be alone and think for a few moments, I walked away from Jonas and into the center of the room. It had been a strange enough place the day before, when everyone was awake and active. Now it seemed stranger still, a ragged blot of a room, frayed with odd corners and crushed under its lowering ceiling. Hoping that exercise would set my mind in motion (as it often does), I decided to pace off the room's length and width, treading softly so as not to wake the sleepers.

I had not gone forty paces when I saw an object that seemed completely out of place in that collection of ragged people and filthy canvas pallets. It was a woman's scarf woven of some rich, smooth material the color of a peach. There is no describing the scent of it, which was not that of any fruit or flower that grows on Urth, but was very lovely.

I was folding this beautiful thing to put in my sabretache when I heard a child's voice say, "It's bad luck. Terrible luck. Don't you know?"

Looking around, then down, I saw a little girl with a pale face and sparkling midnight eyes that seemed too large for it; and I asked, "What's bad luck, Mistress?"

"Keeping findings. They come back for them later. Why do you wear those black clothes?"

"They're fuligin, the hue that is darker than black. Hold out your hand and I'll show you. Now, do you see how it seems to disappear when I trail the edge of my cloak across it?"

Her little head, which small though it was seemed much too big for the shoulders below it, nodded solemnly. "Burying people wear black. Do you bury people? When the navigator was buried there were black wagons and people in black clothes walking. Have you ever seen a burying like that?"

I crouched to look more easily into the solemn face. "No one wears fuligin clothes at funerals, Mistress, for fear they might be mistaken for members of my guild, which would be a slander of the dead—in most cases. Now here is the scarf. See how pretty it is? Is it what you call a finding?"

She nodded. "The whips leave them, and what you ought to do is push them out through the space under the doors. Because they'll come and take their things back." Her eyes were no longer on mine. She was looking at the scar that ran across my right cheek.

I touched it. "These are the whips? The ones who do this? Who are they? I saw a green face."

"So did I." Her laughter held the notes of little bells. "I thought it was going to eat me."

"You don't sound frightened now."

"Mama says the things you see in the dark don't mean anything—they're different almost every time. It's the whips that hurt, and she held me behind her, between her and the wall. Your friend is waking up. Why are you looking so funny?"

(I recall laughing with other people; three were young men, two were women of about my own age. Guibert handed me a scourge with a heavy handle and a lash of braided copper.

Lollian was preparing the firebird, which he would twirl on a long cord.)

"Severian!" It was Jonas, and I hurried over. "I'm glad you're here," he said when I was squatting beside him. "I . . . thought you'd gone away."

"I could hardly do that, remember?"

"Yes," he said. "I remember now. Do you know what this place is called, Severian? They told me yesterday. It's the antechamber. I see you already knew."

"No."

"You nodded."

"I recalled the name when you pronounced it, and I knew it was the right one. I . . . Thecla was here, I think. She never considered it a strange place for a prison, I suppose because it was the only one she had seen before she was taken to our tower, but I find I do. Individual cells, or at least several separate rooms, seem more practical to me. Perhaps I'm only prejudiced."

Jonas pulled himself up until he was sitting with his back to the wall. His face had gone pale under the brown, and it shone with perspiration as he said, "Can't you imagine how this place came to be? Look around you."

I did so, seeing no more than I had seen before: the sprawling room with its dim lamps.

"This used to be a suite—several suites, probably. The walls have been torn away, and a uniform floor laid over all the old ones. I'm sure that's what we used to call a drop ceiling. If you were to lift one of those panels, you'd see the original structure above it."

I stood and tried; but though the tips of my fingers brushed the rectangular panes, I was not tall enough to exert much force on them. The little girl, who had been watching us from a distance of ten paces or so, and listening, I feel sure, to every word, said, "Hold me up and I'll do it."

She ran toward us. I lifted her and found that with my hands around her waist I could easily raise her over my head. For a few seconds her small arms struggled with the square of ceiling above her. Then it went up, showering dust. Beyond it I saw a network of slender metal bars, and through them a vaulted ceiling with many moldings and a flaking painting clouds and birds. The girl's arms weakened, the panel sunk again, with more dust, and my view was cut off.

When she was safely down, I turned back to Jonas. "You're

right. There was an old ceiling above this one, for a room much smaller than this. How did you know?"

"Because I talked to those people. Yesterday." He raised his hands, the hand of steel as well as the hand of flesh, and appeared to rub his face with both. "Send that child away, will you?"

I told the little girl to go to her mother, though I suspect she only crossed the room, then made her way back along the wall until she was within earshot of us.

"I feel as if I were waking up," Jonas said. "I think I said yesterday that I was afraid I would go mad. I think perhaps I'm going sane, and that is as bad or worse." He had been sitting on the canvas pad where we had slept. Now he slumped against the wall just as I have since seen a corpse sit with its back to a tree. "I used to read, aboard ship. Once I read a history. I don't suppose you know anything about it. So many chiliads have elapsed here."

I said, "I suppose not."

"So different from this, but so much like it, too. Queer little customs and usages . . . some that weren't so little. Strange institutions. I asked the ship and she gave me another book."

He was still perspiring, and I thought his mind was wandering. I used the square of flannel I carried to wipe my sword blade to dry his forehead.

"Hereditary rulers and hereditary subordinates, and all sorts of strange officials. Lancers with long, white mustaches." For an instant the ghost of his old humorous smile appeared. "The White Knight is sliding down the poker. He balances very badly, as the King's notebook told him."

There was a disturbance at the farther end of the room. Prisoners who had been sleeping, or talking quietly in small groups, were rising and walking toward it. Jonas seemed to assume that I would go as well, and gripped my shoulder with his left hand; it felt as weak as a woman's. "None of it began so." There was a sudden intensity in his quavering voice. "Severian, the king was elected at the Marchfield. Counts were appointed by the kings. That was what they called the dark ages. A baron was only a freeman of Lombardy."

The little girl I had lifted to the ceiling appeared as if from nowhere and called to us, "There's food. Aren't you coming?" and I stood up and said, "I'll get us something. It might make you feel better."

"It became ingrained. It all endured too long." As I walked toward the crowd, I head him say, "The people didn't know."

Prisoners were walking back with small loaves cradled in one arm. By the time I reached the doorway the crowd had thinned, and I was able to see that the doors were open. Beyond it, in the corridor, an attendant in a miter of starched white gauze watched over a silver cart. The prisoners were actually leaving the antechamber to circle around this man. I followed them, feeling for a moment that I had been set free.

The illusion was dispelled soon enough. Hastarii stood at either end of the corridor to bar it, and two more crossed their weapons before the door leading to the Well of Green Chimes.

Someone touched my arm, and I turned to see the white-haired Nicarete. "You must get something," she said. "If not for yourself, then for your friend. They never bring enough."

I nodded, and by reaching over the heads of several persons I was able to pick up a pair of sticky loaves. "How often do they feed us?"

"Twice a day. You came yesterday just after the second meal. Everyone tries not to take too much, but there is never quite enough."

"These are pastries," I said. The tips of my fingers were coated with sugar icing flavored with lemon, mace, and turmeric.

The old woman nodded. "They always are, though they vary from day to day. That silver biggin holds coffee, and there are cups on the lower tier of the cart. Most of the people confined here don't like it and don't drink it. I imagine a few don't even know about it."

All the pastries were gone now, and the last of the prisoners, save for Nicarete and me, had drifted back into the low-ceilinged room. I took a cup from the lower tier and filled it. The coffee was very strong and hot and black, and thickly sweetened with what seemed to me thyme honey.

"Aren't you going to drink it?"

"I'm going to carry it back to Jonas. Will they object if I take the cup?"

"I doubt it," Nicarete said, but as she spoke she jerked her head toward the soldiers.

They had advanced their spears to the position of guard, and the fires at the spearheads burned more brightly. With her I stepped back into the antechamber, and the doors swung closed behind us.

I reminded Nicarete that she had told me the day before

that she was here by her will, and asked if she knew why the prisoners were fed on pastries and southern coffee.

"You know yourself," she said. "I hear it in your voice."

"No. It's only that I think Jonas knows."

"Perhaps he does. It is because this prison is not supposed to be a prison at all. Long ago—I believe before the reign of Ymar—it was the custom for the Autarch himself to judge anyone accused of a crime committed within the precincts of the House Absolute. Perhaps the autarchs felt that by hearing such cases they would be made aware of plots against them. Or perhaps it was only that they hoped that by dealing justly with those in their immediate circle they might shame hatred and disarm jealousy. Important cases were dealt with quickly, but the offenders in less serious ones were sent here to wait—"

The doors, which had closed such a short time ago, were opening again. A little, ragged, gap-toothed man was pushed inside. He fell sprawling, then picked himself up and threw himself at my feet. It was Hethor.

Just as they had when Jonas and I had come, the prisoners swarmed around him, lifting him up and shouting questions. Nicarete, soon joined by Lomer, forced them away and asked Hethor to identify himself. He clutched his cap (reminding me of the morning when he had found me camping on the grass by Ctesiphon's Cross) and said, "I am the slave of my master, far-traveled, m-m-map-worn Hethor am I, dust-choked and doubly deserted," looking at me all the while with bright, deranged eyes, like one of the Chatelaine Lelia's hairless rats, rats that ran in circles and bit their own tails when one clapped one's hands.

I was so disgusted by the sight of him, and so concerned about Jonas, that I left at once and went back to the spot where we had slept. The image of a shaking, gray-fleshed rat was still vivid as I sat down; then, as though it had itself recalled that it was no more than an image purloined from the dead recollections of Thecla, it flicked out of existence like Domnina's fish.

"Something wrong?" Jonas asked. He appeared to be a trifle stronger.

"I'm troubled by thoughts."

"A bad thing for a torturer, but I'm glad of the company."

I put the sweet loaves in his lap and set the cup by his hand. "City coffee—no pepper in it. Is that the way you like it?"

He nodded, picked up the cup, and sipped. "Aren't you having any?"

"I drank mine there. Eat the bread; it's very good."

He took a bite of one of the loaves. "I have to talk to somebody, so it has to be you even though you'll think I'm a monster when I'm done. You're a monster too, do you know that, friend Severian? A monster because you take for your profession what most people only do as a hobby."

"You're patched with metal," I said. "Not just your hand. I've known that for some time, friend monster Jonas. Now eat your bread and drink your coffee. I think it will be another eight watches or so before they feed us again."

"We crashed. It had been so long, on Urth, that there was no port when we returned, no dock. Afterward my hand was gone, and my face. My shipmates repaired me as well as they could, but there were no parts anymore, only biological material." With the steel hand I had always thought scarcely more than a hook, he picked up the hand of muscle and bone as a man might lift a bit of filth to cast it away.

"You're feverish. The whip hurt you, but you'll recover and we'll get out and find Jolenta."

Jonas nodded. "Do you remember how, when we neared the end of the Piteous Gate, in all that confusion, she turned her head so that the sun shone on one cheek?"

I told him I did.

"I have never loved before, never in all the time since our crew scattered."

"If you can't eat anything more, you ought to rest now."

"Severian." He gripped my shoulder as he had before, but this time with his steel hand; it felt as strong as a vise. "You must talk to me. I cannot bear the confusion of my own thoughts."

For some time I spoke of whatever came into my head, without receiving any reply. Then I remembered Thecla, who had often been oppressed in much the same way, and how I had read to her. Taking out her brown book, I opened it at random.

XVII

The Tale of the Student and His Son

Part I
The Redoubt of the Magicians

Once, upon the margin of the unpastured sea, there stood a city of pale towers. In it dwelt the wise. Now that city had both law and curse. The law was this: That for all who dwelt there, life held but two paths: they might rise among the wise and walk clad with hoods of myriad colors, or they must leave the city and go into the friendless world.

Now one there was who had studied long all the magic known in the city, which was most of the magic known in the world. And he grew near the time at which he must choose his path. In high summer, when flowers with yellow and careless heads thrust even from the dark walls overlooking the sea, he went to one of the wise who had shaded his face with myriad colors for longer than most could remember, and for long had taught the student whose time was come. And he said to him: "How may I—even I who know nothing—have a place among the wise of the city? For I wish to study spells that are *not* sacred all my days, and not go into the friendless world to dig and carry for bread."

Then the old man laughed and said, "Do you recall how, when you were hardly more than a boy, I taught you the art by which we flesh sons from dream stuff? How skillful you were in those days, surpassing all the others! Go now, and flesh such a son, and I will show it to the hooded ones, and you will be as we."

But the student said: "Another season. Let pass another season, and I will do everything you advise."

Autumn came, and the sycamores of the city of pale

towers, that were sheltered from the sea winds by its high wall, dropped leaves like the gold manufactured by their owners. And the wild salt geese streamed among the pale towers, and after them the ossifrage and the lammergeir. Then the old man sent again for him who had been his student, and said: "Now, surely, you must flesh for yourself a creation of dream as I have instructed you. For the others among the hooded ones grow impatient. Save for us, you are the eldest in the city, and it may be that if you do not act now they will turn you out by winter."

But the student answered: "I must study further, that I may achieve what I seek. Can you not for one season protect me?" And the old man who had taught him thought of the beauty of the trees that had for so many years delighted his eyes like the white limbs of women.

At length the golden autumn wore away, and winter came stalking into the land from his frozen capital, where the sun rolls along the edge of the world like a trumpery gilded ball and the fires that flow between the stars and Urth kindle the sky. His touch turned the waves to steel, and the city of the magicians welcomed him, hanging banners of ice from its balconies and heaping its roofs with glaces of snow. The old man summoned his student again, and the student answered as before.

Spring came and with it gladness to all nature, but at spring the city was hung with black; and hatred, and the loathing of one's own powers—that eats like a worm at the heart—fell on the magicians. For the city had but one law and one curse, and though the law held sway all the year, the curse ruled the spring. In spring, the most beautiful maidens of the city, the daughters of the magicians, were clothed in green; and while the soft winds of spring teased their golden hair, they walked unshod through the portal of the city, and down the narrow path that led to the quay, and boarded the black-sailed ship that waited them. And because of their golden hair, and their gowns of green faille, and because it seemed to the magicians that they were reaped like grain, they were called Corn Maidens.

When the man who had long been the student of the old man but was yet unhooded heard the dirges and laments, and looking from his window saw the maidens filing by, he set aside all his books and began to draw such figures as no man had ever seen, and to write in many languages, as his master had taught him aforetime.

Part II
The Fleshing of the Hero

Day after day he labored. When the first light came at the window, his pen had been a drudge already many hours; and when the moon tangled her crooked back among the pale towers, his lamp shone bright. At first it seemed to him that all the skill his master had taught him of old had deserted him, for from the first light to the moonlight he was alone in his chambers save for the moth that fluttered sometimes to show the insignia of Death at his undaunted candle flame.

Then there crept into his dreams, when sometimes he nodded over the table, another; and he, knowing who that other was, welcomed him, though the dreams were fleeting and soon forgotten.

He labored on, and that which he strove to create gathered about him as smoke collects about the new fuel thrown upon a fire almost dead. At times (and particularly when he worked early or late, and when having at long last laid aside all the implements of his art, he stretched himself at length upon the narrow bed provided for those who had not yet earned the many-colored hood) he heard the step, always in another room, of the man he hoped to call into life.

In time these manifestations, originally rare, and, indeed, at first limited almost entirely to those nights when thunder rumbled among the pale towers, became common, and there were unmistakable signs of the other's presence: a book he had not unshelved in decades lying beside a chair; windows and doors that unlocked, as it seemed, of themselves; an ancient alfange, for years past an ornament hardly more deadly than a trompe l'œil picture, found cleansed of its patina, gleaming and newly sharp.

One golden afternoon, when the wind played the innocent games of childhood with the fresh-fledged sycamores, there came a knock at the door of his study. Not daring to turn or express even the smallest part of what he felt by his voice, or even to desist from his work, he called: "Enter."

As doors open at midnight though no living thing stirs, the door began, a thread's width at a time, to swing back. Yet as it

124

moved it seemed to gather strength, so that when it was open (as he judged by the sound) enough that a hand might have been thrust into the room, it seemed that the playful breeze had come in by the window to push life into its wooden heart. And when it was open, as he judged again, wider still, so much so that a diffident helot might have entered with a tray, it seemed a very sea storm seized it and flung it back against the wall. Then he heard strides behind him—quick and resolute—and a voice respectful and youthful, yet deep with a cleanly manhood, addressed him, saying: "Father, I little like to vex you when you are deep in your art. But my heart is sorely troubled and has been so these several days, and I beg you by the love you have for me to suffer my intrusion and counsel me in my difficulties."

Then the student dared turn himself where he sat, and he saw standing before him a youth haughty of port, wide of shoulder, and mighty of thew. Command was in his firm mouth, knowing wit in his bright eyes, and courage in all his face. Upon his brow sat that crown that is invisible to every eye, but can be seen even by the blind; the crown beyond price that draws brave men to a paladin, and makes weak men brave. Then the student said: "My son, have no fear of disturbing me, now or ever, for there is nothing under Heaven that I should rather see than your face. What is it that troubles you?"

"Father," the young man said, "every night for many nights my sleep has been rent with the screams of women, and often I have seen, like a green serpent called by the notes of a pipe, a column of green slip down the cliff below our city to the quay. And sometimes it is vouchsafed me in my dream to go near, and then I see that all who walk in that column are fair women, and that they weep and scream and stagger as they walk, so that I might think them a field of young grain beaten by a moaning wind. What is the meaning of this dream?"

"My son," said the student, "the time has come when I must tell you what I have concealed from you until now, fearing that in the rashness of your youth you might dare too much before the time was ripe. Know that this city is oppressed by an ogre, who each year demands of it its fairest daughters, even as you have seen in your dream."

At this the young man's eyes flashed, and he demanded: "Who is this ogre, and what form has he, and where does he dwell?"

"His name no man knows, for no man can approach near enough. His form is that of a naviscaput, which is to say that to men he appears a ship having upon its deck—which is in truth his shoulders—a single castle, which is his head, and in the castle a single eye. But his body swims in the deep waters with the skate and the shark, with arms longer than the most lofty masts and legs like pilings that reach even to the floor of the sea. His harbor is an isle to the west, where a channel with many a twist and bend, dividing and redividing, reaches far inland. It is on this isle, so my lore teaches me, that the Corn Maidens are made to dwell; and there he rides at anchor in the midst of them, turning his eye ever to left and right to watch them in their despair."

Part III
The Encounter with the Princess

Then the young man fared forth and gathered to him other young men of the city of the magicians to be his crew, and from those who wore the colored hoods he obtained a stout ship, and all that summer he and the young men he had gathered to him armored her, and mounted on her sides the mightiest artillery, and a hundred times practiced the making of sail, and the reefing of sail, and the firing of the guns, until she answered as a blooded mare does to the rein. For the pity they felt for the Corn Maidens, they christened her *Land of Virgins*.

At last, when the golden leaves fell from the sycamores (even as the gold manufactured by magicians falls at last from the hands of men), and the gray salt geese streamed among the pale towers of the city with the lammergeir and the ossifrage screaming after them, the youths set sail. Much befell them on the whale road to the isle of the ogre that has no place here; but at the end of those adventures the lookouts saw before them a country of tawny hills dotted with green; and even as they shaded their eyes to see it, the green grew greater, and greater still. Then the young man whom the student had fleshed from dreams knew that it was indeed the isle of the ogre, and that the Corn Maidens were hastening to the shore for the sight of his sail.

Then were the great guns readied, and the flags of the city of the magicians, that are all of yellow and black, were hung in the rigging. Near they came and nearer, until fearing to run aground they put about and beat along the coast. The Corn Maidens followed them, and following attracted more of their sisterhood until they covered all the land like grain indeed. But the young man did not forget what he had been told: that the ogre lived among the Corn Maidens.

After a half day's sailing, they rounded a point and saw that the coast fell away as a deep channel that did not end, but wound its way among the low hills of the country until it was lost to sight. At the entrance to this channel stood a calotte of white marble surrounded by gardens, and here the young man ordered his companions to cast anchor, and went ashore.

He had no more than set foot on the soil of the isle than there came to meet him a woman of great beauty, swart of skin, black of hair, and luminous of eye. He bowed before her, saying: "Princess or Queen, I see that you are not of the Corn Maidens. Their robes are green; yours is sable. Yet were you to wear a dress of green, I should know you still, for your eyes sorrow not, and the light that is in them is not of Urth."

"You speak truly," the princess said. "For I am Noctua, the daughter of the Night, and the daughter, too, of him whom you have come to slay."

"Then we cannot be friends, Noctua," said the young man. "But let us not be enemies." For though he did not know why, being of the stuff of dreams he was drawn to her; and she, whose eyes held starlight, to him.

At this the princess spread her hands and declared: "Know that my father took my mother by force, and here holds me against my wishes where I would soon go mad were it not that she comes to me at each day's end. If you do not see sorrow in my eyes, it is only because it lies upon my heart. That I may be free, I shall willingly counsel you how you may engage my father and triumph."

All the young men of the city of the magicians grew quiet and gathered to listen to her.

"First you must understand that the waterways of this isle turn and turn again, in such a way that they can never be charted. You can by no means use sail as you wander them, but must kindle your furnaces ere you go farther."

"I have no fear of that," said the young man fleshed from dreams. "Half a forest was laid waste to fill our bins, and those great wheels you see shall walk these waters with the tread of giants."

At that the princess trembled and said: "Oh, speak not of giants, for you know not what you say. Many ships have come as you have, until the oozy bottoms of all these measureless channels are white with skulls. For it is the custom of my father to allow them to wander among the islets and straights until their fuel is spent—however much it may be—and then, coming upon them by night when he can see them by the glow of their dying fires and they not see him, slay them."

Then the heart of the young man fleshed from dreams was troubled, and he said: "We will seek him as we are sworn, but is there no way in which we may escape the fate of those others?"

At this the princess took pity on him, for all who have the stuff of dreams about them seem fair in some degree at least to the daughters of Night, and he fairest of all. Thus she said: "To find my father before your last stick is burned, you need only search out the darkest water, for wherever he passes his great body raises a foul mud, and by observing it you may discover him. But each day you must begin the search at dawn, and at noon desist; for otherwise you may come upon him by twilight, and it will go evilly with you."

"For this counsel I would have given my life," said the young man, and all his companions who had come ashore with him raised a cheer. "For now we will surely overcome the ogre."

At this the solemn face of the princess became more sober yet, and she said: "No, not surely, for he is a dread antagonist in any sea fight. But I know a stratagem that may aid you. You have said that you came well supplied. Have you tar to pay your ship, should she leak?"

"Many barrels," said the young man.

"Then when you fight, see that the wind blows from yourself to him. And when the fight is hottest—which will not be long after you have joined—have your men cast tar into your furnaces. I cannot promise that it will give you the victory, but it will aid you greatly."

At this all the young men thanked her most extravangantly, and the Corn Maidens, who had stood shyly by while the young man fleshed from dreams and the daughter of Night spoke, raised such a cheer as maidens raise, a cheer not strong, but filled with joy.

Then the young men made ready to depart, kindling the

fires in the great furnaces amidships until the white specter
was born that drives good ships ahead no matter what wind
may blow. And the princess watched them from the strand
and gave them her blessing.

But just as the great wheels began to turn, so slowly at first
that they appeared scarcely to move, she called the young
man fleshed from dreams to the railing, saying: "It may be
that you shall find my father. Should you find him, it may be
that you shall defeat him, laying low even such prowess as his.
Yet even so, you may be sorely vexed to find your way to the
sea once more, for the channels of this isle are most won-
drously wrought. Yet there is a way. From my father's right
hand you must flay the tip of the first finger. There you will
see a thousand tangled lines. Be not discouraged, but study it
closely; for it is the map he followed in webbing the waterways, that he himself might always have it by him."

Part IV
The Battle with the Ogre

Inland they turned their bow, and even as the princess had
foretold, the channel they followed soon divided, and divided
again, until there were a thousand forking channels and ten
thousand islets. When the shadow of the mainmast was no
larger than a hat, the young man fleshed from dreams gave
orders that the anchors be cast, and the fires banked, and
there, for a long afternoon, they waited, oiling the guns, and
readying the powder, and preparing all that might be needful
in the hardest fought battle.

At length Night came, and they saw her striding from islet
to islet with her bats about her shoulders and her dire wolves
dogging her steps. No more than an easy carronade shot from
their anchorage she seemed, yet they all observed that she
passed not before Hesperus or even Sirius; but they before
her. For a moment only she turned her face toward them, and
none could be certain what her look conveyed. But all of
them wondered if indeed the ogre had taken her without her
will as her daughter had said; and if so, if she had not lost the
resentment she might be imagined to have felt.

With the first light, the trumpet sounded from the quarter-deck and the banked fires were fed new fuel; but as the dawn breeze stood fair for the channel they held, the young man ordered all plain sail set before the great wheels were ready to take their first step. And when the white specter wakened, the ship pressed forward at double speed.

For many leagues that channel ran, not straight, but near enough that there was no need to furl the sails or even put about. A hundred others crossed it, and at each they studied the water; but each was translucent as crystal. To tell the strange sights they beheld on the islets they passed would require a dozen tales as long as this—women stem-grown like flowers overhung the ship, and in kissing them sought to smear their faces with the powder from their cheeks; men to whom wine had brought death long before lay by springs of wine and drank still, too stupefied to know their lives were past; beasts that would be omens to future times, with twisted limbs and fur of colors never seen, waited the nearer approach of battles, earthquakes, and the murders of kings.

At last the youth who stood first mate to the young man fleshed from dreams approached him where he waited near the steersman, saying: "Far we have traveled on this channel already, and the sun, that had not shown his face when we bent our sails, approaches his zenith. Following it, we have crossed a thousand others, and none has shone a trace of the ogre. May it not be that it is an unlucky course we take? Would not it be wiser to turn aside soon and try another?"

Then the young man answered: "Even now we pass a channel to starboard. Look down, and tell me if its waters are more soiled than our own."

The youth did as he was bid, and said: "Nay, clearer."

"Soon now, another opens to port. To what depth can you see?"

The youth waited until the ship stood opposite the channel of which the young man spoke, and then he answered: "To the utmost. I see the wreck of a ship of long time past, many a fathom down."

"And can you see so far in this channel we sail now?"

Then the youth looked at the waters they cleaved, and they were become as ink; and the very splatters that flew from the laboring wheels might have been rooks and ravens. At once understanding came to him, and he shouted to all the others to stand by the guns, for he could not tell them to make ready, who had made ready so long before.

Ahead lay an islet higher than most, crowned with tall and

somber trees; and here the channel bent gently, so that the wind, that had been dead astern, was at the quarter. The steersman shifted his grip on the wheel, and the watch payed out certain sheets and tightened others, and the ship's prow came around the quick curve of the cliff, and there before them lay a long hull of narrow beam, with a single castle of iron amidships and a single gun larger than any they carried thrusting from its one embrasure.

Then the young man fleshed from dreams opened his lips to shout to the bow-chaser crews that they should fire. Before the words could be spoken, the great gun of their enemy roared, and its sound was not as thunder or as any other sound familiar to the ears of men; but rather, it seemed that they had stood in a tall tower of stone, and it had fallen all around them in a moment.

And the ball of that shot struck the breech of the first gun of their starboard battery, and striking it broke it to pieces and shattered itself as well, so that the fragments of the breaking of both scattered through the ship like dark leaves before a great wind, and many died thereby.

Then the steersman, waiting no order, swung the ship about until her port battery bore, and the guns fired each by the will of the man that pointed it, as wolves howl at the moon. And their shots flew about the single castle of the enemy to either side, and some struck it so that it tolled knells for those who had perished a moment before, and some struck the water before the hull that bore it, and some struck the deck (which was of iron also) and at that contact fled shrieking into the sky.

Then the single gun of their enemy spoke again.

And so it continued, in moments that seemed whole years of time. At last the young man bethought him of the advice of the princess, the daughter of Night; but though the wind blew strong, it was hardly more than astern of his ship, and if he were to shift until it blew from him to his enemy (as the princess had counseled) for many moments no gun would bear but the bow chasers, and then when a battery might be brought to bear, it would be the starboard, of which one gun was destroyed and so many men dead.

But it came to him in that moment that they fought as a hundred others had fought, and that these hundred others were all dead, their ships sunk and their bones scattered among the myriad channels that whorled and tangled the face of the isle of the ogre. Then he gave his order to the steersman; but none answered, for he was dead, and the wheel he had held, held him. So seeing, the young man fleshed from dreams took the spokes in his own hands and presented to their enemy the ship's narrow bow. Then it was seen how the three sisters favor the bold, for the next shot from their enemy, that might have raked her from stem to stern, went to port by the length of an oar. And the next, to starboard by the width of a boat.

Now their enemy, who had stood fast before, neither seeking to fly nor to close, swung about. Seeing that he would escape them if he could, the crew raised a great shout as though already they had won the victory. But marvelous to see, the single castle, which all had until then believed fixed, swung about the other way, so that its great gun, that was greater than any of their own, still bore.

A moment later and its ball had struck them amidships, dashing a gun of the starboard battery from its truck as a drunken man might fling an infant from its cradle and sending it skittering across the deck and smashing everything in its path. Then the guns of the battery—those that remained— spoke all in a chorus of fire and iron. And because the distance was now less than half what it had been (or perhaps only because their enemy, having shown fear, had weakened the fabric of his being), their shot no longer struck his castle with an empty clanging, but with a cracking as though the bell that will toll the end of the world were breaking; and ragged flaws sprang to life on the oiled blackness of the iron.

Then the young man shouted into the gosport to those who had remained faithfully in the engine room feeding the furnaces with tree-wrack, telling them to cast tar into the flames as the princess had counseled them. At first he feared that all there were dead, then that the order was not understood in the din of battle. But a shadow fell upon the sun-brightened water that stretched between their enemy and himself, and he looked upward.

In ancient times, so it is said, a tattered child, the daughter of a fisherman, found on the sand a stoppered flask, and by breaking the seal and drawing forth the cork became queen from ice to ice. Just so, it seemed, an elemental being, strong with the strength of the forging of creation, debouched from the tall smokestacks of their ship, tumbling over himself in dark joy and growing with a rush, as the wind comes.

And the wind came indeed, and it seized him with its uncounted hands and bore him as a solid mass down upon

their enemy. Even when nothing more could be seen—
neither the long, dark hull with its deck of iron, nor the single
guns whose mouth had spoken words to doom them—they
wasted no moment, but fell to their guns and fired into the
blackness. And from time to time they heard the gun of their
enemy also firing; but no flash did they see, and where those
shots struck they could not say.

It may be they have struck nothing yet, and still circle
round the world seeking their target.

They fired until the barrels shone like ingots newly come
from the crucible. Then the smoke that had poured forth so
long diminished, and those below shouted by the gosport that
all the tar was consumed, and the young man fleshed from
dreams ordered that firing cease, and the men who had
worked the guns fell upon the deck like so many corpses, too
exhausted even to beg water.

The black cloud melted. Not as fog melts in the sun, but as
an army strong to evil dissolves before repeated charges,
giving here, stubbornly standing there, still mustering a wisp
of skirmishers when it seems all has given way.

In vain then they searched the new-polished waves for their
enemy. Nothing could they see: not his hull, nor his castle,
nor his gun, nor any plank or spar.

Slowly, so cautiously it might have been thought they
feared an unseen foe, they advanced to the very spot where
he had lain at anchor, noting the shattered trees and furrowed
ground of the islet beyond, where their shot had spent its
energies. When they were over the point at which that long
iron hull had lain, the young man fleshed from dreams
ordered the great wheels reversed, and at last halted, so that
they rested as quietly as their opponent had. Then he strode
to the rail and looked down; but with such an expression that
no one, not even the most brave, dared to look at him.

When he lifted his eyes at last, his face was set and grim,
and with no word to any man he took himself to his cabin and
barred the door. Then the youth that was second to him
ordered the ship put about, that they might return to the
white calotte of the princess; and he ordered also that wounds
be bandaged, and pumps set in motion, and such repairs as
could be made begun. But the dead he kept with them, that
they might be buried on the high sea.

Part V
The Death of the Student

It may be that the channel was not so straight as they believed. Or that they had lost their bearings in the fight, without being aware thereof. Or that the channels twisted (as some alleged) like worms in a litch, when no eye was upon them. Whatever the truth might be, all day they steamed—for the wind had died away—and by the last light saw only that they cruised among islets unknown.

All night they lay to. When morning came, the youth called to him such others as he felt might offer the most valuable counsel; but none of them could suggest anything save calling upon the young men fleshed from dreams (which they were loath to do) or pressing onward until they reached open waters or the calotte of the princess.

That they did all day, striving to hold a straight course, but winding against their will among the many turnings of the channels. And when night came again, their position was no better than before.

But on the morning of the third day, the young man fleshed from dreams came out of his cabin and began to walk up and down the decks as he was wont to do, examining such repairs as they had made to their damage and asking those wounded who by the pain of their wounds were awake early how they fared. Then the youth and those who had advised him came to him, and they explained all that they had done and asked how they might find the sea again, that they might bury the dead and return to their homes in the city of the magicians.

At this he looked up into the very vault of the firmament. And some thought he prayed, and some that he sought to restrain the anger he felt against them, and some only that he hoped to gain inspiration there. But so long did he stare that they waxed afraid, even as they had when he had peered into the water, and one or two began to creep away. Then he said to them: "Behold! Do you not see the sea birds? From every corner of the sky they stream. Follow them."

Until morning was nearly done, they followed the birds

134

insofar as the winding channels permitted. And at last they
saw them wheeling and diving at the water ahead, so their
white wings and ebon heads seemed a cloud low hung in their
course, a cloud fair without but thunderous within. Then the
young man fleshed from dreams told them to load a carronade with powder only, and to fire it; and at the crash of the
gun all those sea birds rose mewing and crying. And where
they had been, the crew saw a great piece of carrion floating,
which seemed to them to have been a beast of the land, for it
had, as they thought, a head and legs four. But it was greater
than many elephants.

When they were near, the young man ordered the boat put
into the water, and when he climbed aboard they saw that he
had thrust into his belt a great alfange whose blade caught the
sun. For a time he labored over the carrion, and when he
returned he carried a chart, the largest any of them had seen,
drawn upon untanned hide.

By dark they reached the calotte of the princess. All waited
on board while her mother visited her; but when that terrible
woman was gone, all who could walk went ashore, and the
Corn Maidens crowded about them, a hundred to each youth,
and the young man fleshed from dreams took the daughter of
Night into his arms and led them all in dances. None of them
ever forgot that night.

The dew found them beneath the trees of the princess'
garden, half smothered in flowers. For a time they slept so,
but when afternoon threw backward the shadows of their
masts they were awake. Then the princess bade farewell to
the isle and swore that though she might visit every country
over which her mother strode, she never would return there;
and the Corn Maidens swore likewise. Too many of them
there were, perhaps, for the ship to hold; yet it held them, so
that all the decks were green with their gowns and gold with
their hair. Many adventures they had in making their way
back to the city of the magicians. This tale might tell how they
cast their dead into the sea with prayers, yet afterward saw
them in the rigging by night; or how certain of the Corn
Maidens wed those princes who, having spent years so long
enchanted that they are loath to leave that life (and have in
that time learned much of gramary), build palaces on lily pads
and are seldom seen by men.

But all those things have no place here. Be it sufficient to
say that as they neared the cliff at whose top stands the city of

the magicians, the student who had fleshed the young man from dreams stood on the battlements, watching for them over the sea. And when he beheld their dark sails, smutted by the burning tar that had blinded their enemy, he believed them blackened in mourning for the young man, and he threw himself down, and so perished. For no man lives long when his dreams are dead.

XVIII

Mirrors

As I read this idle tale I looked at Jonas from time to time, but I never saw the least flicker of expression on his face, though he did not sleep. When it was complete, I said, "I'm not certain I understand why the student at once assumed his son was dead when he saw the black sails. The ship the ogre sent had black sails, but it came only once a year, and had already come."

"I know," Jonas said. His voice held a flatness I had not heard before.

"Do you mean you know the answers to those questions?"

He did not reply, and for a time we sat in silence, I with the brown book (so insistently evocative of Thecla and the evenings we had shared) still held open by a forefinger, he with his back to the cold wall of the prison room, and his hands, one of metal, one of flesh, lying to either side as though he had forgotten them.

At last a small voice ventured to say, "That must be a really old story." It was the little girl who had lifted the ceiling tile for me.

I was so concerned for Jonas that for a moment I was angry at her for interrupting us; but Jonas muttered, "Yes, it is a very old story, and the hero had told the king, his father, that if he failed he would return to Athens with black sails." I am not sure what that remark meant, and it may have been delirium; but since it was almost the last thing I heard Jonas say, I feel I should record it here, as I have transcribed the wonder-tale that prompted it.

137

For a time both the girl and I endeavored to persuade him to speak again. He would not, and at last we desisted. I spent the remainder of the day sitting beside him, and after a watch or so Hethor (whose small store of wit—as I supposed—had soon been exhausted by the prisoners) came to join us. I had a word with Lomer and Nicarete, and they arranged that his sleeping place should be on the opposite side of the room.

Whatever we may say, all of us suffer from disturbed sleep at times. Some in truth hardly sleep, though some who sleep copiously swear that they do not. Some are disquieted by incessant dreams, and a fortunate few are visited often by dreams of delightful character. Some will say they were at one time troubled in sleeping but have "recovered" from it, as though awareness were a disease, as perhaps it is.

My own case is that I usually sleep without memorable dreams (though I sometimes have them, as the reader who has gone this far with me will know) and seldom wake before morning. But on this night my sleep was so different from its usual nature that I have sometimes wondered if it should be called sleep at all. Perhaps it was some other state posing as sleep, as alzabos, when they have eaten of men, pose as men.

If it was the result of natural causes, I attribute it to a combination of unfortunate circumstances. I, who had all my life been accustomed to hard work and violent exercise, had for that day been confined without either. The tale from the brown book had affected my imagination—which was still more stimulated by the book itself and its associations with Thecla, and by the knowledge that I was now within the walls of the House Absolute itself, of which I had heard her speak so often. Possibly most important, my thoughts were oppressed by worry for Jonas, and by the feeling (which had been growing on me all day) that this place was the end of my journey; that I would never reach Thrax; that I would never rejoin poor Dorcas; that I would never restore the Claw, or even rid myself of it; that in fact the Increate, whom the owner of the Claw had served, had decreed that I who had seen so many prisoners die should end my own life as one.

I slept, if it may be called sleep, only for a moment. I had the sensation of falling; a spasm, the instinctive stiffening of a victim cast from a high window, wrenched all my limbs. When I sat up, I could see nothing but darkness. I heard Jonas's breathing, and my fingers told me he was still sitting as I had left him, his back propped by the wall. I lay down and slept again.

Or rather, I tried to sleep, and passed into that vague state that is neither sleeping nor waking. At other times I have found it pleasant, but it was not so now—I was conscious of the need for sleep, and conscious that I was not sleeping. Yet I was not "conscious" in the usual meaning of that term. I heard faint voices in the innyard, and felt, somehow, that soon the bells of the campanile would chime, and it would be day. My limbs jerked again, and I sat up.

For a moment I imagined I had seen a flash of green fire, but there was nothing. I had covered myself with my cloak; I threw it off, and in the instant it took to do so remembered that I was in the antechamber of the House Absolute, and that I had left the inn of Saltus far behind, though Jonas lay beside me still, on his back, his good hand behind his head. The pale blur I saw was the white of his right eye, though the sighing of his breath was that of one who slept. I was still too much asleep myself to wish to talk, and I had a presentiment that he would not answer me in any case.

Lying down again, I surrendered myself to my irritation at being unable to sleep. I thought of the herd driven through Saltus and counted them from memory: one hundred and thirty-seven. Then there were the soldiers who had come singing up from Gyoll. The inkeeper had asked me how many there were and I had guessed at a figure, but I had never counted them until now. He might, or might not, have been a spy.

Master Palaemon, who had taught us so much, had never taught us how to sleep—no apprentice had ever needed to learn that after a day of errands and scrubbing and kitchen work. We had rioted each night for half a watch in our quarters, then slept like the citizens of the necropolis until he came to wake us to polishing floors and emptying slops.

There is a rack of knives over the table where Brother Aybert slices meat. One, two, three, four, five, six, seven knives, all with plainer blades than Master Gurloes's. One with a rivet missing from its handle. One with a handle a little burned because Brother Aybert had once laid it on the stove. . . .

I was wide awake again, or thought I was, and I did not

know why. Beside me Drotte slumbered undisturbed. I closed my eyes once more and tried to sleep as he did.

Three hundred and ninety steps from the ground to our dormitory. How many more to the room where the guns throbbed at the top of the tower? One, two, three, four, five, six guns. One, two, three levels of cells in use in the oubliette. One, two, three, four, five, six, seven, eight wings on each level. One, two, three, four, five six, seven, eight wings on each level. One, two, three, four, five, six, seven, eight, nine, ten, eleven, twelve, thirteen, fourteen, fifteen, sixteen, seventeen cells in each wing. One, two, three bars on the little window of my cell's door.

I woke with a start and a sensation of cold, but the sound that had disturbed me was only the slamming of one of the hatches far down the corridor. Beside me, my boy lover, Severian, lay in the easy sleep of youth. I sat up thinking I would light my candle and look for a moment at the fresh coloring of that chiseled face. Each time he returned to me, he carried a speck of freedom glowing on that face. Each time I took it and blew upon it, and held it to my breast, and each time it pined and died; yet sometime it would not, and then instead of sinking deeper under this load of earth and metal, I would rise through metal and earth to the wind and the sky.

Or so I told myself. If it was not true, still the only joy remaining to me was to gather in that speck.

But when I groped for the candle it was gone, and my eyes and my ears and the very skin of my face told me that my cell itself had vanished with it. There was dim light here—very dim, but not the light from the candle of the torturer in the corridor, the light that filtered through the three bars of my cell's hatch. Faint echoes proclaimed that I was in an area larger than a hundred such cells; my cheeks and forehead, which had worn themselves away in signaling the nearness of my walls, confirmed it.

I stood and smoothed my gown, and began to walk almost as a somnambulist might. . . . One, two, three, four, five, six, seven strides, then the odor of close-kept bodies and confined air told me where I was. It was the antechamber! I felt a wrench of dislocation. Had the Autarch ordered me carried here while I slept? Would the others spare their lashes when they saw me? The door! The door!

My confusion was so great I nearly fell, borne down by the jumble of my mind.

I wrung my hands, but the hands I wrung were not my own. My right hand felt a hand too large and too strong, and at the same instant my left hand felt a similar hand.

Thecla fell from me like a dream. Or I should say, dwindled to nothing, and in dwindling vanished within me until I was myself again, and nearly alone.

Yet I had caught it. The location of the door, the secret door through which the young exultants came by night with their energized lashes of braided wire, was still in my memory. With everything else I have seen or thought. I could escape tomorrow. Or now.

"Please," a voice beside me said, "where did the lady go?"

It was the child again, the little girl with the dark hair and the staring eyes. I asked her if she had seen a woman.

She took my hand in her own tiny one. "Yes, a tall lady, and I'm scared. There's a horrible thing in the dark. Did it find her?"

"You're not afraid of horrible things, remember? You laughed at the green face."

"This is different, a black thing that snuffles in the dark." There was real terror in her voice, and the hand that held mine shook.

"What did the lady look like?"

"I don't know. I could only see her because she was darker than the shadows, but I could tell she was a lady by the way she walked. When I came to see who it was, there was nobody here but you."

"I understand," I told her, "though I doubt that you ever will. Now you must return to your mother and go to sleep."

"It's coming along the wall," she said. Then she released my hand and vanished, but I am sure she did not do as I told her. Instead, she must have followed Jonas and me, for I have glimpsed her twice since I returned here to the House Absolute, where no doubt she exists on stolen food. (It is possible she used to return to the antechamber to eat, but I have ordered that all the people confined there are to be freed, even if it is necessary—as I think it will be—to drive most of them forth at pike point. I have also ordered that Nicarete be brought to me, and when I was writing of our capture, a moment ago, my chamberlain entered to say she waited my pleasure.)

Jonas lay as I had left him, and again I saw the whites of his eyes in the dark. "You said it was necessary to go if you were to remain sane," I told him. "Come. The sender of the notules, whoever that may be, has laid his hands upon another weapon. I have found the way out, and we are going now."

He did not move, and at last I had to take him by the arm and lift him up. Many of those parts of him that were metal must have been forged from those white alloys that deceive the hand by their lightness, for it was like lifting a boy; but the metal parts, and his flesh as well, had been wetted with some thin slime. My foot found the same filthy dampness on the floor nearby and on the wall itself. Whatever it was the child had warned me of had come and gone while I spoke with her, and it had not been for Jonas that it had searched.

The door by which the tormentors entered was not far from our sleeping place, in the center of the rearmost wall of the antechamber. It was unlocked by a word of power, as such ancient things almost always are. I whispered, and we passed through the hidden portal and left it standing open, poor Jonas striding beside me like a thing wholly metal.

A narrow stairway, festooned with the webs of pale spiders and carpeted with dust, led by circuitous turnings downward. That much I recalled, but beyond the stair I could remember nothing. Whatever might come, the stale air tasted of freedom, so that merely to breathe it was pleasure. Worried though I was, I could have laughed aloud.

Secret doors opened at many landings, but there seemed a chance and more than a chance that we might encounter someone as soon as we entered one, and the stair seemed deserted. Before I was seen by any resident of the House Absolute, I wished to be as far from the antechamber as possible.

We had descended perhaps a hundred steps when we reached a door painted with a crimson teratoid sign that appeared to me to be a glyph from some tongue beyond the shores of Urth. At that moment I heard a tread upon the stair. There was neither knob nor latch, but I threw myself against the door, and after an initial resistance it flew open. Jonas followed me; it shut behind us so quickly that it seemed it should have made a great noise, though there was none.

The chamber beyond the door was dim, but the light grew brighter when he had entered. After I had made certain there was no one present but ourselves, I made use of this light to examine him. His face was still fixed, as it had been when he sat with the wall of the antechamber at his back, yet it was not the lifeless thing I had feared. It was the face, almost, of a man about to wake, and tears had left moist furrows down his cheeks.

"Do you know me?" I asked, and he nodded without speaking. "Jonas, I must recover *Terminus Est,* if I can. I've run like any coward, but now that I've had a chance to think, I see I must go back for her. My letter to the archon of Thrax is in her scabbard pocket, and I couldn't bear to part with her anyway. But if you want to try to escape this place, I'll understand. You're not bound to me."

He did not appear to have heard. "I know where we are," he said, and raised one arm stiffly to point toward something I had taken to be a folding screen.

I was delighted to hear his voice, and largely in the hope that he would speak again, I asked, "Where are we, then?"

"On Urth," he answered, and strode across the room to the folded panels. Their backs were set with clustered diamonds, as I now saw, and enameled with such twisted signs as had been on the door. Yet these signs were no stranger than the actions of my friend Jonas when he threw the panels open. The rigidity I had remarked in him only a moment before was gone—yet he had not returned to his old self.

It was then that I knew. We have all watched someone who has lost one hand (as he had) and replaced it with a hook or some other artificial contrivance perform some task that involves both his real hand and the artificial one. So it was with Jonas when I watched him pull back the panels; but the prosthetic hand was the hand of flesh. When I understood that, I understood what he had said much earlier: that in the wreck of his ship his face had been destroyed.

I said, "The eyes . . . They could not replace your eyes. Is that right? And so they gave you that face. Was he killed too?"

He looked about at me in a way that told me he had forgotten I was present. "He was on the ground," he said. "We killed him by accident, coming in. I needed his eyes and larynx, and I took some other parts."

"That was why you were able to tolerate me, a torturer. You are a machine."

"You are no worse than the rest of your kind. Remember that for years before I met you, I had become one of you. Now I am worse than you. You would not have left me, but I am leaving you. Now I have the chance, and it is the chance I sought for years as I went up and down the seven continents of this world seeking the Hierodules and tinkering with clumsy mechanisms."

I thought of all that had happened since I had carried the knife to Thecla; and though I did not follow everything he had said, I told him, "If it is your only chance, then go, and good luck. If I ever see Jolenta, I will tell her you once loved her, and nothing more."

Jonas shook his head. "Don't you understand? I will come back for her when I have been repaired. When I am sane and whole."

Then he stepped into the circle of panels, and a brilliant light kindled in the air above his head.

How foolish to call them mirrors. They are to mirrors as the enveloping firmament is to a child's balloon. They reflect light indeed; but that, I think, is no part of their true function. They reflect reality, the metaphysical substance that underlies the material world.

Jonas closed the circle and moved to its center. For perhaps the time of the briefest prayer, something of wires and flashing, metallic dust danced above the tops of the panels before all was gone and I was alone.

XIX

Closets

I was alone, and I had not been truly alone since I had entered his room in the tumbledown city inn and seen Baldanders's broad shoulders above the blankets. There had been Dr. Talos, then Agia, then Dorcas, then Jonas. The disease of memory gained upon me, and I saw the sharp silhouette of Dorcas, the giant, and the others as I had seen them when Jonas and I were being led through the plum grove. There had been men with animals as well and performers of other kinds, all of them no doubt going to that part of the grounds where (as Thecla had often told me) the outdoor entertainments were held.

I began to search the room with some vague hope of finding my sword. It was not there, and it struck me that there was probably some repository near the antechamber where the goods of the prisoners were kept—most likely on the same level. The stair I had come down would only lead me into the antechamber itself again; the exit from the room of the mirrors took me only to another room, one in which curious objects were stored. Eventually I found a door that opened onto a dark and quiet corridor, carpeted and hung with paintings. I put on my mask and drew my cloak about me, thinking that though the guards who had seized us in the wood had not seemed to know of the existence of the guild, those I might encounter in the halls of the House Absolute itself might not be so ignorant.

In the event, I was never challenged. A man in rich and elaborate clothing drew aside, and several lovely women stared at me curiously; I felt Thecla's memories stirring at the sight of their faces. At last I found another stair—not narrow and secretive like the one that had taken Jonas and me to the chambers of mirrors, but a broad, open flight of wide steps.

I ascended some distance, reconnoitered the corridor there until I was certain I was still lower than the antechamber, then began to climb again when I saw a young woman hurrying down the stair toward me.

Our eyes met.

In that moment, I feel sure, she was as conscious as I that we had exchanged glances thus before. In memory I heard her say again, "My dearest sister," in that cooing voice, and the heart-shaped face sprang into place. It was not Thea, the consort of Vodalus, but the woman who looked like her (and no doubt borrowed her name) whom I had passed on the stair in the House Azure—she descending and I climbing, just as we were now. Harlots then, as well as entertainers, had been summoned for whatever fete was being organized.

Almost purely by chance, I discovered the level of the antechamber. I had no sooner left the stair than I realized I was standing almost precisely where the hastarii had stood while Nicarete and I talked beside the silver cart. This was the point of greatest danger, and I was careful to walk slowly. The wall on my right held a dozen or more doors, each framed in carved woodwork, and each (as I saw when I stopped to examine them) spiked to its frame and sealed with the varnish of years. On my left, the only door was the great one of worm-gnawed oak through which the soldiers had dragged Jonas and me. Opposite it was the entrance to the antechamber, and beyond that stretched another row of spiked doors like the first, at the end of which was another stair. It appeared that the antechamber had grown to occupy all of this level of this wing of the House Absolute.

If there had been anyone in sight, I would not have dared to pause; but since the corridor was empty, I ventured to lean for a moment against the newel post of the second stair. While two soldiers had guarded me, a third had carried *Terminus Est*. It was reasonable to suppose that as Jonas and I were being put through the doorway of the antechamber, this third man would have taken the first few steps at least toward wherever it was that such captured weapons were kept. But I could remember nothing; the soldier had dropped behind when we descended the steps of the grotto, and I had not seen him again. It was possible, even, that he had not come in with us.

In desperation, I returned to the worm-gnawed door and opened it. The musty odor of the well entered the corridor at once, and I heard the song of the green gongs begin. Outside, the world was plunged in night. Save for the corpse candles of the fungi, the rugged walls were invisible, and only a circle of stars overhead showed where the well dropped into the earth.

I closed the door; no sooner had it grated shut than I heard the sound of footsteps on the stair up which I myself had come. There was no place to hide, and if I had darted for the second stair I would have had little chance of reaching it before I was seen. Rather than attempt to duck out through the heavy oak door and close it once more, I decided to remain where I was.

The newcomer was a plump man of fifty or so dressed in livery. Even down the length of the corridor, I saw his face pale at the sight of me. He came hurrying toward me, however, and when he was still twenty or thirty paces off he began to bow, saying, "Can I help you, Your Honor? I am Odilo, the steward here. You, I can see, are on a mission of some confidence to . . . Father Inire?"

"Yes," I said. "But first I must require my sword of you."

I had hoped that he had seen *Terminus Est* and would produce her for me, but he looked blank.

"I was escorted here earlier. At that time I was told that I would have to surrender my sword, but that it would be restored to me before Father Inire required me to use it."

The little man was shaking his head. "I assure you, in my position I would have been informed if any of the other servants—"

"I was told this by a praetorian," I said.

"Ah, I ought to have known. They've been everywhere, answering to no one. We have an escaped prisoner, Your Honor, as I suppose you've heard."

"No."

"A man called Beuzec. They say he's not dangerous, but he and another fellow were found lurking in an arbor. This Beuzec made a dash for it before they locked him up, and got away. They say they'll take him soon; I don't know. I'll tell you, I've lived in our House Absolute all my life, and it has some strange corners—some very strange corners."

"Possibly my sword is in one of them. Will you look?"

He took a half step back, as though I had raised my hand to him. "Oh, I will, Your Honor, I will. I was only trying to make a bit of conversation. It's probably down here. If you'll just follow me . . ."

We walked toward the other stair, and I saw that in my hasty search I had overlooked one door, a narrow one beneath the staircase. It was painted white, so that it was almost of the same shade as the stone.

The steward produced a heavy ring of keys and opened this door. The triangular room inside was much larger than I would have guessed, reaching far back beneath the steps and boasting a sort of loft, accessible by a shaky ladder, toward the rear. Its lamp was of the same type as those I had noticed in the antechamber, but dimmer.

"Do you see it?" the steward asked. "Wait, there's a candle about here somewhere, I think. That one light's not much use, the shelves throw such heavy shadows."

I was examining the shelves as he spoke. They were piled with clothing, with here and there a pair of shoes, a pocket fork, a pen case, a pommander ball.

"When I was just a lad myself, the kitchen boys used to pick the lock and come in here to rummage about. I put a stop to that—got a good lock—but I'm afraid the best things disappeared long ago."

"What is this place?"

"A closet for petitioners, originally. Coats, hats, and boots—you know. Those places always fill up with the things the lucky ones forget to take with them when they go, and then this wing has always been Father Inire's, and I suppose there's always been some that came to see him that never came back out, as well as the ones that come out what never came in." He paused and glanced around. "I had to give the soldiers keys to keep them from kicking down the doors when they were searching for this Beuzec, so I suppose they might have put your sword in here. If they didn't, they probably took it up to their guardroom. This wouldn't be it, I don't imagine?" From a corner he drew out an ancient spadone.

"Hardly."

"It seems to be the only sword here, I'm afraid. I can give you directions for getting to the guardroom. Or I can wake up one of the pages to go and ask, if you like."

The ladder to the loft was shaky, but I scrambled up it after borrowing the steward's candle. Though it seemed exceedingly improbable that the soldier had put *Terminus Est* there, I wanted a few moments to think over the courses of action open to me. .

As I climbed I heard a slight noise from above that I supposed was the scurrying of some rodent; but when I thrust my head and the candle above the level of the loft's floor, I saw the small man who had been with Hethor on the road kneeling in an attitude of intense supplication. That was Beuzec, of course; I had failed to recall the name until I saw him.

"Anything up there, Your Honor?"

"Rags. Rats."

"Just as I thought," the steward said as I stepped from the last rung. "I should have a look myself sometime, but one isn't anxious to climb a thing like that at my age. Would you like to go to the guardroom yourself, or shall I rouse one of the boys?"

"I'll go."

He nodded sagaciously. "That's best, I think. They might not hand it over to a page, or even admit they had it. You're in the Hypogeum Apotropaic now, as I suppose you know. If you don't want to be stopped by the patrols, you had better go indoors, so the best plan would be to go up this stairway we're standing under for three flights, then left. Follow the gallery around for about a thousand paces until you come to the hypethral. With it dark out you might miss it, so keep an eye open for the plants. Turn right in there and go another two hundred paces. There's always a sentry at the door."

I thanked him and managed to get ahead of him on the stair by leaving while he was still fumbling with the lock, then stepped into a corridor off the first landing I reached and allowed him to go past me. When he was well out of the way, I went down again to the corridor of the antechamber.

It seemed to me that if my sword had indeed been carried off to some guardroom, it was very unlikely that I could recover it save by stealth or violence, and I wished to assure myself that it had not been left in some more accessible place before I attempted either. Then too, it seemed possible that Beuzec had seen it in the course of his creeping and hiding, and I wanted to question him about it.

At the same time, I was very much concerned about the prisoners of the antechamber. By that time (as I imagined) they would have discovered the door Jonas and I had left open for them, and would be spreading through this wing of the House Absolute. It could not be long before one was recaptured and a search began for the others.

When I reached the door of the closet beneath the stair, I pressed my ear to the panel hoping to hear Beuzec moving about. There was no sound. I called to him softly by name without eliciting a response, then tried to push the door open with my shoulder. It would not budge, and I was afraid to make noise by running against it. At last I managed to wedge the steel Vodalus had given me between the door and the jamb, and so split out the lock.

Beuzec was gone. After a short search I discovered a hole in the back of the closet that opened into the hollow center of some wall. From there he must have crept into the closet looking for a place large enough for him to stretch his limbs, and to there he had fled again. It is said that in the House Absolute such recesses are inhabited by a species of white wolf that slunk in from the surrounding forests long ago. Perhaps he fell prey to these creatures; I have not seen him since.

That night I did not seek to follow him, but pulled the closet door into place and concealed the damage to the lock as well as I could. It was only then that I noticed the symmetry of the corridor: the entrance to the antechamber in the center, the sealed doors to either side of it, the staircase at either end. If this hypogeum had been set aside for Father Inire (as the steward had said and its name indicated) its selection might have been due, at least in part, to this mirror-image quality. If that were so, then there should certainly be a second closet beneath the other stair.

XX

Pictures

The question was why Odilo the steward had not taken me there; but I did not pause to think on it while I sprinted along the corridor, and when I arrived the answer was plain enough. That door had been broken long before—not just the socket of the lock, but the entire thing smashed so that only two discolored fragments of wood clinging to the hinges showed there had ever been a door there. The lamp within had gone out, leaving the interior to darkness and spiders.

I had actually turned away from it and taken a step or two before I stopped, under the influence of that consciousness of error that often comes to us before we understand in the least in what the error consists. Jonas and I had been thrust into the antechamber late in the afternoon. That night the young exultants had come with their whips. The next morning Hethor had been taken, and at that time, it seemed, Beuzec had bolted from the praetorians, who had been given keys by the steward so they might search the hypogeum for him. When the same steward, Odilo, had met me a few moments before, and I had told him that *Terminus Est* had been taken from me by a praetorian, he had assumed I had come during the day, after Beuzec's escape.

In point of fact, I had not; and therefore, the praetorian who had been carrying *Terminus Est* could not have put her in the locked closet beneath the second stair.

I went back to the closet with the broken door again. By the scant light that filtered in from the corridor, it was apparent that it had once been lined with shelves like its twin; its interior was bare now, the shelving having been stripped

151

away to serve some new use, leaving the shelf brackets to thrust fruitlessly from the walls. I could see no other object of any kind, but I could also see that no guardsman who had to stand inspection would willingly have set foot among its dust and cobwebs. Without bothering to thrust my own head inside, I reached around the jamb of the broken door, and—with an indescribable mingling of triumph and familiarity—felt my hand close upon the beloved hilt.

I was a whole man again. Or rather, more than a man: a journeyman of the guild. There in the corridor I verified that my letter remained in the pocket of the sheath, then drew the shining blade, wiped it, oiled it, and wiped it again, testing its edges with finger and thumb as I walked along. Now let the hunter in the dark appear.

My next objective was to rejoin Dorcas, but I knew nothing of the location of Dr. Talos's company except that they were to perform at a thiasus held in a garden—no doubt one of many gardens. If I went outside now, by night, it would perhaps be as difficult for the praetorians to see me in my fuligin as for me to see them. But I was unlikely to find any aid; and when the eastern horizon dropped below the sun, I would no doubt be apprehended as promptly as Jonas and I had been when we rode onto the grounds. If I stayed within the House Absolute itself, my experience with the steward indicated I might well pass unchallenged, and I might even come across someone who would give me information; indeed, I hit upon the plan of telling anyone I met that I had been summoned to the celebration myself (I supposed it was not unlikely that an excruciation would be a part of the festivities) and that I had left the sleeping quarters assigned to me and lost my way. In that fashion, I might discover where Dorcas and the rest were staying.

Thinking upon this plan I mounted the stair, and at the second landing turned off down a corridor I had not seen previously. It was far longer and more sumptuously furnished than the one before the antechamber. Dark pictures in gold frames hung on the walls, and urns and busts and objects for which I knew no names stood on pedestals between them. The doors opening off the corridor were a hundred or more paces apart, indicating huge rooms beyond; but all were locked, and when I tried their handles I found that they were of a form and metal unknown to me, not shaped to be grasped by human fingers.

When I had walked down this corridor for what seemed at

least half a league, I saw someone ahead of me sitting (as I first thought) upon a high stool. As I drew nearer, I found that what I had taken to be a stool was a stepladder, and that the old man perched on it was cleaning one of the pictures. "Excuse me," I said.

He turned and peered down at me in puzzlement. "Know your voice, don't I?"

Then I knew his, and his face as well. It was Rudesind the curator, the old man I had met so long before, when Master Gurloes had first sent me to fetch books for the Chatelaine Thecla.

"While ago you come looking for Ultan. Didn't you find him?"

"Yes, I found him," I said. "But it wasn't a short time ago."

He seemed to grow angry at that. "I didn't mean today! But it wasn't long. Why, I recollect the landscape I was working on, so it couldn't have been that long."

"So do I," I told him. "Brown desert reflected in the gold visor of a man in armor."

He nodded, and his anger seemed to melt away. Gripping the sides of the ladder, he began to descend, his sponge still in his hand. "Exactly. Exactly the one. Want me to show it to you? It come out very nice."

"We're not in the same place, Master Rudesind. That was in the Citadel. This is the House Absolute."

The old man ignored that. "Come out nice . . . It's down here a ways, somewhere. Those old artists—you couldn't beat 'em for drawing, though their colors has gone off now. And let me tell you, I know art. I've seen armigers, and exultants too, that come and look at them and say this and that, but they don't know a thing. Who's looked at every little bit of these pictures up close?" He thumped his own bosom with the sponge, then bent close to me, whispering though there was no one but ourselves in the long corridor. "Now I'll tell you a secret they don't none of them know—one of these is me!"

To be polite, I said I would like to see it.

"I'm looking for it, and when I find it I'll tell you where. They don't know, but that's why I clean them all the time. Why, I could have retired. But I'm still here, and I work longer than any, except maybe Ultan. He can't see the watchglass." The old man gave a long, cracked laugh.

"I wonder if you could help me. There are performers here

who have been summoned for the thiasus. Do you know where they're quartered?"

"I've heard tell of it," he said doubtfully. "The Green Room is what they call it."

"Can you take me there?"

He shook his head. "There's no picturers there, so I've never been, though there's a picture of it. Come and walk a ways with me. I'll find the picture and point it out to you."

He pulled the edge of my cloak, and I followed him.

"I'd rather you took me to someone who could guide me there."

"I can do that too. Old Ultan has a map somewhere in his library. That boy of his will get it for you."

"This isn't the Citadel," I reminded him again. "How did you come to be here, anyway? Did they bring you here to clean these?"

"That's right. That's right." He leaned on my arm. "There's a logical explanation for everything, and don't you forget it. That must have been the way. Father Inire wanted me to clean his, so here I am." He paused, considering. "Wait a bit, I've got it wrong. I had talent as a boy, that's what I'm supposed to say. My parents, you know, always encouraged me, and I'd draw for hours. I recollect one time I spent all one sunny day sketching in chalk on the back of our house."

A narrower corridor had opened to our left, and he pulled me down it. Though it was less well lit (nearly dark, in fact) and so cramped that one could not stand at anything like the proper distance from them, it was lined with pictures much larger than those in the main corridor, pictures that stretched from floor to ceiling, and that were far wider than my outstretched arms. From what I could see of them, they appeared very bad—mere daubs. I asked Rudesind who it was who had told him he must tell me about his childhood.

"Why, Father Inire," he said, cocking his head up to look at me. "Who do you suppose?" He dropped his voice. "Senile. That's what they say. Been vizier to I don't know how many autarchs since Ymar. Now you be quiet and let me talk. I'll find old Ultan for you.

"An artist—a real one—came by where we lived. My mother, being so proud of me, showed him some of the things I'd done. It was Fechin, Fechin himself, and the portrait he made of me hangs here to this day, looking out at you with my brown eyes. I'm at a table with some brushes and a tangerine on it. I'd been promised them when I was through sitting."

I said, "I don't think I have time to look at it right now."

"So I became an artist myself. Pretty soon, I took to cleaning and restoring the works of the great ones. Twice I've cleaned my own picture. It's strange, I tell you, for me to wash my own little face like that. I keep wishing somebody would wash mine now, make the dirt of the years come off with his sponge. But that's not what I'm taking you to see—it's the Green Room you're after, ain't it?"

"Yes," I said eagerly.

"Well, we've a picture of it right here. Have a look. Then when you see it, you'll know it."

He indicated one of the wide, coarse paintings. It was not of a room at all, but seemed to show a garden, a pleasance bordered by high hedges, with a lily pond and some willows swept by the wind. A man in the fantastic costume of a llanero played a guitar there, as it appeared for no ear but his own. Behind him, angry clouds raced across a sullen sky.

"After this you can go to the library and see Ultan's map," the old man said.

The painting was of that irritating kind which dissolves into mere blobs of color unless it can be seen as a whole. I took a step backward to get a better perspective of it, then another. . . .

With the third step, I realized I should have made contact with the wall behind me, and that I had not. I was standing instead inside the picture that had occupied the opposite wall: a dark room of ancient leather chairs and ebony tables. I turned to look at it, and when I turned back, the corridor where I had stood with Rudesind had vanished, and a wall covered with old and faded paper stood in its place.

I had drawn *Terminus Est* without consciously willing to do so, but there was no enemy to strike. Just as I was on the point of trying the room's single door, it opened and a figure in a yellow robe entered. Short, white hair was brushed back from his rounded brow, and his face might almost have served a plump woman of forty; about his neck, a phallus-shaped vial I remembered hung on a slender chain.

"Ah," he said. "I wondered who had come. Welcome, Death."

With as much composure as I could muster, I said, "I am the Journeyman Severian—of the guild of torturers, as you see. My entrance was entirely involuntary, and to be truthful, I would be very grateful to you if you could explain just how it happened. When I was in the corridor outside, this room appeared to be no more than a painting. But when I took a step or two back to view the one on the other wall, I found myself in here. By what art was that done?"

"No art," the man in the yellow robe said. "Concealed doors are scarcely an original invention, and the constructor of this room did no more than devise a means of concealing an open door. The room is shallow, as you see; indeed, it is shallower than you perceive even now, unless you're already aware that the angles of the floor and ceiling converge, and that the wall at the end is not so high as the one through which you came."

"I see," I said, and in fact I did. As he spoke that crooked room, which my mind, accustomed always to ordinary ones, had tricked me into believing of normal shape, became itself, with a slanted and trapezoidal ceiling and a trapezoidal floor. The very chairs that faced the wall through which I had come were things of little depth, so that one could hardly have sat on them; the tables were no wider than boards.

"The eye is deceived in a picture by such converging lines," the man in the yellow robe continued. "So that when it encounters them in reality, with little actual depth and the additional artificiality of monochromatic lighting, it believes it sees another picture—particularly when it has been conditioned by a long succession of true ones. Your entrance with that great weapon caused a real wall to rise behind you to detain you until you had been examined. I need hardly add that the other side of the wall is painted with the picture you believed you saw."

I was more astounded than ever. "But how could the room know I carried my sword?"

"That is more complex than I can well explain . . . far more so than this poor room. I can only say that the door is wrapped with metal strands, and that these know when the other metals, their brothers and sisters, pass their circle."

"Did you do all this?"

"Oh, no. All these things . . ." He paused. "And a hundred more like them, make up what we call the Second House. They are the work of Father Inire, who was called by the first Autarch to create a secret palace within the walls of the House Absolute. You or I, my son, would no doubt have built a mere suite of concealed rooms. He contrived that the hidden house should be everywhere coextensive with the public one."

"But you aren't he," I said. "Because now I know who you

are! Do you recognize me?" I drew off my mask so he could see my face.

He smiled and said, "You came but once. The khaibit did not please you, then."

"She pleased me less than the woman she counterfeited— or rather, I loved the other more. Tonight I have lost a friend, yet it seems to be a time for meeting old acquaintances. May I ask how you've come here from your House Azure? Were you summoned for the thiasus? I saw one of your women earlier tonight."

He nodded absently. An oddly angled mirror set above a trumeau at one side of the strange, shallow room caught his profile, delicate as a cameo, and I decided he must be an androgyne. Pity welled up in me, with a sense of helplessness, as I thought of him opening the door to men, night after night, at his establishment in the Algedonic Quarter. "Yes," he said. "I will remain here for the celebration, then go."

My mind was full of the picture old Rudesind had shown me in the corridor outside, and I said, "Then you can show me where the garden is."

I sensed at once that he had been caught off guard, possibly for the first time in many years. There was pain in his eyes, and his left hand moved (though only slightly) toward the vial at his throat. "So you have heard of that . . ." he said. "Even supposing that I knew the way, why should I reveal it to you? Many will seek to flee by that road if the pelagic argosy sights land."

XXI

Hydromancy

Several seconds passed before I rightly understood what it was the androgyne had said. Then the remembered scent of Thecla's roasted flesh rose sickening-sweet in my nostrils, and I seemed to feel the unquiet of the leaves. Forgetting in the stress of the moment how futile such precautions must be in that deception-filled room, I looked about, seeking to assure myself that no one could overhear us, then found that without my having willed it (consciously, I had intended to question him before betraying my connection with Vodalus) my hand had taken the knife-shaped steel from the innermost compartment of my sabretache.

The androgyne smiled. "I felt you might be the one. For days now I have been expecting you, and I have kept the old man outside and many others under instructions to bring promising strangers to me."

"I was imprisoned in the antechamber," I said. "And so lost time."

"But you escaped, I see. It isn't likely you'd be released before my man came to search it. It's well you did—there isn't much time left . . . the three days of the thiasus, then I must go. Come, and I will show you the way to the Garden, though I am by no means sure you will be permitted to enter."

He opened the door by which he had come in, and this time I saw that it was not truly rectangular. The room beyond was hardly larger than the one we had left; but its angles seemed normal, and it was richly furnished.

"You came to the correct part of the Secret House at least," the androgyne said. "Otherwise we would have had to

158

walk a weary way. Your pardon, while I read the message you brought."

He crossed to what I at first supposed was a glass-topped table, and put the steel under it on a shelf. At once a light kindled, shining down from the glass, though there was no light above it. The steel grew until it seemed a sword, and its striations, in place of mere teeth on which to strike sparks from a flint, I saw to be lines of flowing script.

"Stand back," the androgyne said. "If you have not read this before, you must not read it now."

I did as he bid, and for some time watched him bending over the little object I had carried away from Vodalus's glade. At last he said, "There is no help for it then . . . we must fight on two flanks. But this is none of your affair. Do you see that cabinet with the eclipse carved on its door? Open it and lift down the book you find there. Here, you may put it on this stand."

Although I feared some trap, I opened the door of the cabinet he had indicated. It held one monstrous book—a thing nearly as tall as I and a good two cubits wide—that stood with its cover of mottled blue-green leather facing me much as a corpse might had I opened the lid of an upright casket. Sheathing my sword, I gripped this great volume with both hands and placed it on the stand. The androgyne asked if I had seen it previously, and I told him I had not.

"You looked fearful of it, and tried . . . as it appeared to me . . . to keep your face from it when you carried it." He threw back the cover as he spoke. The first page, thus revealed, was written in red in a character I did not know. "This is a warning to the seekers of the path," he said. "Shall I read it to you?"

I blurted, "It seemed to me that I saw a dead man in the leather, and that he was myself."

He closed the cover again and ran his hand over it. "These pavonine dyeings are but the work of craftsmen long gone . . . the lines and swirls beneath them, only the scars of the suffering animals' back, the marks of ticks and whips. But if you are fearful, you need not go."

"Open it," I said. "Show me the map."

"There is no map. This is the thing itself," he said, and with that he threw back the cover and the first page as well.

I was blinded, almost, as I have been on dark nights by a discharge of lightning. The inner pages seemed of pure silver, beaten and polished, that caught every wisp of illumination in

the room and flung it back amplified a hundred times.
"They're mirrors," I said, and in saying it realized that they
were not, but those things for which we have no word but
mirrors, those things that less than a watch before had
returned Jonas to the stars. "But how can they have power,
when they do not face each other?"

The androgyne answered, "Consider how long they faced
each other when the book was closed. Now the field will
withstand the tension we put on it for some time. Go, if you
dare."

I did not dare. As he spoke, something shaped itself in
shining air above the open pages. It was neither a woman nor
a butterfly, but it partook of both, and just as we know when
we look at the painted figure of a mountain in the background
of some picture that it is in reality as huge as an island, so I
knew that I saw the thing only from far off—its wings beat, I
think, against the proton winds of space, and all Urth might
have been a mote disturbed by their motion. Then as I had
seen it, so it saw me, much as the androgyne a moment before
had seen the swirls and loops of writing on the steel through
his glass. It paused and turned to me and opened its wings
that I might observe them. They were marked with eyes.

The androgyne closed the book with a crash, like a door
slammed shut. "What did you see?" he asked.

I could think only that I no longer had to look into the
pages, and said, "Thank you, sieur. Whoever you may be, I
am your servant from this time forward."

He nodded. "Perhaps sometime I may remind you of that.
But I will not ask you again what it was you saw. Here, wipe
your forehead. The sight has marked you."

He handed me a clean cloth as he spoke, and I wiped my
brow with it as he told me, because I could feel the moisture
running down my face. When I looked at the cloth, it was
crimson with blood.

As though he had read my thoughts, he said, "You are not
wounded. The physicians' term is haematidrosis, I believe.
Under the stress of strong emotion, minute veins in the skin
of the afflicted part . . . of the skin everywhere, sometimes
. . . rupture during a profuse sweating. You will have a nasty
bruise there, I'm afraid."

"Why did you do that?" I asked. "I thought you were going
to show me a map. I only want to find the Green Room, as
old Rudesind out there says it's called, where the players are
quartered. Did Vodalus's message say you were to kill the

bearer?" I was fumbling for my sword as I spoke, but when my hands gripped the familiar hilt, I found I was too weak to draw the blade.

The androgyne laughed. It was pleasant laughter at first, wavering somewhere between a woman's and a boy's, but it trailed off into tittering, as a drunken man's sometimes does. Thecla's memories stirred in me; almost, they woke. "Was that all you wished?" he said when he had control of himself again. "You asked me for a light for your candle, and I tried to give you the sun, and now you are burned. The fault was mine . . . I sought, perhaps, to postpone my time, yet even so I would not have let you travel so far had I not read in the message that you have carried the Claw. And now I am most truly sorry, but I cannot help but laugh. Where will you go, when you have found the Green Room, Severian?"

"Where you send me. As you remind me, I have sworn service to Vodalus." (In fact, I feared him, and feared that the androgyne would inform him if I professed disobedience.)

"But if I have no orders for you? Have you already disposed of the Claw?"

"I could not," I said.

There was a pause. He did not speak.

"I'll go to Thrax," I said. "I have a letter to the archon there; he's supposed to have work for me. For the honor of my guild, I would like to go."

"That is well. How great, in truth, is your love of Vodalus?"

Again I felt the haft of the ax in my hand. For you others, as I am told, memory dies; mine scarcely dims. The mist that shrouded the necropolis that night blew against my face again, and everything I had felt when I received the coin from Vodalus and watched him walk away to a place where I could not follow returned to me. "I saved him once," I said.

The androgyne nodded. "Then here is what you are to do. You must go to Thrax as you planned, telling everyone . . . even yourself . . . that you are going to fill the position that waits you there. The Claw is perilous. Are you aware of it?"

"Yes. Vodalus told me that if it became known we possess it, we might lose the support of the populace."

For a moment the androgyne stood silent again. Then he said, "The Pelerines are in the north. If you are given the opportunity, you must restore the Claw to them."

"That is what I had hoped to do."

"Good. There is something else you must do as well. The

Autarch is here, but long before you reach Thrax he will be in the north too, with the army. If he comes near Thrax, you are able to go to him. In time you will discover the way in which you must take his life."

His tone betrayed him as much as Thecla's thoughts. I wanted to kneel, but he clapped his hands, and a bent little man slipped silently into the room. He wore a cowled habit like a cenobite's. The Autarch spoke to him, something I was too distracted to understand.

In all the world, there can be few sights more beautiful than that of the sun at dawn seen through the thousand sparkling waters of the Vatic Fountain. I am no esthete, but my first sight of its dance (of which I had so often heard), must have acted as a restorative. I still recall it for my pleasure, just as I saw it when the cowled servitor opened a door for me—after so many leagues of the contrived corridors of the Second House—and I watched the silver streams trace ideographs across the solar disc.

"Straight ahead," the cowled figure murmured. "Follow the path through the Gate of Trees. You will be safe among the players." The door shut behind me and became the grassy slope of a hillock.

I stumbled toward the fountain, which refreshed me with windblown spray. I was surrounded by a pavement of serpentine; for a time I stood there, seeking to read my fortune in the dancing shapes, and at last I fumbled in my sabretache for an offering. The praetorians had taken all my money, but while I felt among the few possessions I yet carried there (a flannel, the fragment of whetstone, and a flask of oil for *Terminus Est;* a comb and the brown book for myself) I spied a coin wedged between the green blocks at my feet. After only a little effort I was able to draw it out—a single asimi, worn so thin that hardly a trace of the imprint remained. With a whispered wish, I threw it into the very center of the fountain. A jet caught it there and tossed it skyward, so that it flashed for a moment before it fell. I began to read the symbols the water made against the sun.

A sword. That seemed clear enough. I would continue a torturer.

A rose then, and beneath it a river. I would climb Gyoll as I had planned, since that was the road to Thrax.

Now angry waves, becoming soon a long, sullen swell. The

sea, perhaps; but one could not reach the sea, I thought, by climbing toward the source of the river.

A rod, a chair, a multitude of towers, and I began to think the oracular powers of the fountain, in which I had never greatly believed, to be wholly false. I turned away; but as I turned, I glimpsed a many-pointed star, growing even larger.

Since I have returned to the House Absolute, I have twice revisited the Vatic Fountain. Once I came at the first light, approaching it through the same door through which I first glimpsed it. But I have never again dared to ask it questions.

My servants, who confess one and all that they have dropped their orichalks into it when the garden was clear of guests, tell me one and all that they have received no true prophecy for their money. Yet I am unsure, recalling the green man, who drove off his visitors with his accounts of their futures. May it not be that these servants of mine, seeing only a lifetime of trays and brooms and ringing bells, reject it? I have asked my ministers as well, who doubtless cast in chrisos by the handful, but their answers are doubtful and mixed.

It was hard indeed to keep my back to the fountain and its lovely, cryptic messages and walk toward the old sun. Huge as a giant's face and darkly red it showed as the horizon dropped away. The poplars of the grounds were silhouetted against it, making me think of the figure of Night atop the khan on this western bank of Gyoll, which I had so often seen with the sun behind it at the close of one of our swimming parties.

Not realizing that I was now deep within the bounds of the House Absolute and well away from the patrols about the periphery, I feared I might be stopped at any moment, and perhaps cast back into the antechamber—whose secret door, I felt sure, would have been discovered and sealed by now. Nothing of the kind occurred. So far as I could see, no one stirred in all the leagues of hedge and velvet lawn, flower and trickling water, except myself. Lilies far taller than I, their star-shaped faces spangled with unshaken dew, overhung the path; its perfect surface showed behind me only the disturbance of my own feet. Nightingales, some free, some suspended from the branches of trees in golden cages, were singing still.

Once I saw before me, with something of the old feeling of

horror, one of the walking statues. Like a colossal man (though it was not a man) too graceful and too slow to be human, it came across a small secretive lawn as if moving to the inaudible notes of some strange processional. I confess I hung back until it had passed, wondering if it could sense me where I stood in the shadow, and if it cared that I stood so.

Just when I had despaired of finding the Gate of Trees, I saw it. There was no mistaking it. Even as lesser gardeners espalier pears against a wall, the greater gardeners of the House Absolute, who have generations in which to complete their work, had molded the huge limbs of oaks until every twig conformed to an inspiration wholly architectural, and I, walking on the rooftops of the greatest palace of Urth, with not a stone in sight, saw looming to one side that great, green entranceway built of living wood as if of masonry.

I ran then.

XXII

Personifications

Through the wide, dripping arch of the Gate of Trees I ran, and out onto a broad expanse of grass, now spangled with tents. Somewhere a megathere roared and shook its chain. There seemed to be no other sound. I halted and listened, and the megathere, no longer disturbed by my footfalls, settled back into the deathlike sleep of its kind. I could hear the dew running from the leaves, and the faint, interrupted twitter of birds.

Something else there was as well. A faint *whick, whick,* quick and irregular, that grew louder as I listened for it. I began to thread a path among the silent tents, following the sound. I must have misjudged it, however, for Dr. Talos saw me before I saw him.

"My friend! My partner! They are all asleep—your Dorcas and the rest. All but you and I. Over here!"

He flourished his cane as he spoke; the *whick, whick* had been his chopping at the heads of flowers.

"You have rejoined us just in time. Just in time! We perform tonight, and I would have been forced to hire one of these fellows to take your part. I'm delighted to see you! I owe you some money—do you recall? Not much, and between you and I, I think it false. But it is owed just the same, and I always pay."

"I'm afraid I don't recall," I said, "so it can't be a great sum. If Dorcas is all right I'm quite willing to forget it, provided you'll give me something to eat and show me where I can sleep for a couple of watches."

The doctor's sharp nose dipped for an instant to express

165

regret. "Sleep you may have in plenty until the others wake you. But I'm afraid we've no food. Baldanders, you know, eats like a fire. The Thiasus Marshal has promised to bring something today for all of us." He waved his stick vaguely at the irregular city of tents. "But I'm afraid that won't be before midmorning at the earliest."

"It's probably just as well. I'm really too tired to eat, but if you'll show me where I can lie down—"

"What got your head? Never mind—we'll mask it with greasepaint. This way!" He was already trotting before me. I followed him through a maze of tent ropes to a heliotrope dome. Baldanders's barrow stood at the door, and at last I felt certain I had found Dorcas again.

When I woke, it was as though we had never been separated. Dorcas's delicate loveliness was unchanged; Jolenta's radiance threw it into shadow as always, yet made me wish, when the three of us were together, that she would leave so that I might rest my eyes on Dorcas. I took Baldanders to one side, an hour or so after we were all awake, and asked him why he had left me in the forest beyond the Piteous Gate.

"I was not with you," he said slowly. "I was with my Dr. Talos."

"And so was I. We might have sought him together and been of help to each other."

There was a long hesitation; I seemed to feel the weight of those dull eyes on my face, and thought in my ignorance what a terrible thing it would be if Baldanders possessed energy and the will to anger. At last he said, "Were you with us when we left the city?"

"Of course. Dorcas and Jolenta and I were all with you."

Another hesitation. "We found you there, then."

"Yes, don't you remember?"

He shook his head slowly, and I noticed that his thatch of coarse black hair was touched with gray. "I woke one morning and there you were. I was thinking. You left me soon."

"The circumstances were different then—we had arranged to meet again." (I felt a pang of guilt when I recalled that I had never intended to honor that promise.)

"We have met again," Baldanders said dully; and then, seeing that the answer failed to satisfy me, added, "There is nothing here real to me but Dr. Talos."

"Your loyalty is very commendable, but you might have remembered that he wanted me with him as well as yourself." I found it impossible to be angry with this dim, gentle giant.

"We will collect money here in the south, and then we will build again, as we have built before, when they have forgotten."

"This is the north. But that's right, your house was destroyed, wasn't it?"

"Burned," Baldanders said. I could almost see the flames reflected in his eyes. "I am sorry if you came to harm. For so long I have thought only of the castle and my work."

I left him sitting there and went to inspect the properties of our theater—not that they seemed in need of it, or that I could have detected any but the most obvious lacks. A number of showmen were gathered around Jolenta, and Dr. Talos drove them away and ordered her to go into the tent. A moment later, I heard the smack of his cane on flesh; he came out grinning but still angry.

"It isn't her fault," I said. "You know how she looks."

"Too gaudy. Too gaudy by far. Do you know what I like about you, Sieur Severian? You prefer Dorcas. Where is she, by the way? Have you seen her since you came back?"

"I warn you, Doctor. Don't strike her."

"I wouldn't think of it. I'm only afraid she may be lost."

His surprised expression convinced me that he was telling the truth. I told him, "We only got to talk for a moment. She's gone to fetch water."

"That's courageous of her," he said, and when I looked puzzled he added, "She's afraid of it. Surely you've noticed. She's clean, but even when she washes, the water is only thumb deep; when we cross bridges, she holds onto Jolenta and trembles."

Dorcas returned then, and if the doctor said anything more I did not hear it. When she and I had met that morning, neither of us had been able to do much more than smile, and touch with incredulous hands. Now she came to me, putting down the pails she carried, and seemed to devour me with her eyes. "I have missed you so," she said. "I've been so lonely without you."

I laughed to think of anyone missing me, and held up the edge of my fuligin cloak. "You missed this?"

"Death, you mean. Did I miss death? No, I missed you." She took the cloak from my hand and used it to draw me toward the line of poplars that formed one wall of the Green

Room. "There is a bench I found where there are beds of herbs. Come and sit with me. They can spare us for a while after so many days, and eventually Jolenta will come out and find the water, which was for her anyway."

As soon as we were away from the bustle of the tents, where jugglers tossed their knives and acrobats their children, we were wrapped in the stillness of the gardens. They are perhaps the largest tract of land anywhere planned and planted for beauty, save for those wildernesses that are the gardens of the Increate and whose cultivators are invisible to us. Overlapping hedges formed a narrow door. We passed into a grove of trees with white, perfumed boughs that reminded me sadly of the flowering plums through which the praetorians had dragged Jonas and me, though those had seemed planted for ornament, and these, I thought, for the sake of their fruit. Dorcas had broken a twig bearing half a dozen of the blossoms and thrust it into her pale golden hair.

Beyond the orchard was a garden so old that I felt sure it had been forgotten by everyone save the servants who tended it. The stone seat there had been carved with heads, but they had worn away until they were almost featureless. A few beds of simple flowers remained, and with them fragrant rows of kitchen herbs—rosemary, angelica, mint, basil, and rue, all growing in a soil black as chocolate from the labor of countless years.

There was a little stream too, where Dorcas had no doubt drawn her water. Its source may once have been a fountain—now it was only a species of spring, rising in a shallow stone bowl to splash over the lip and eventually wind its way through little canals lined with rough masonry to water the fruit trees. We sat in the stone seat, I leaned my sword against its arm, and she took my hands in hers.

"I am afraid, Severian," she said. "I have such terrible dreams."

"Since I've been gone?"

"All the time."

"When we slept side by side in the field, you told me you had awakened from a good dream. You said it was very detailed and seemed real."

"If it was good, I have forgotten it now."

I had already noticed that she was careful to keep her eyes away from the water spilling from the ruined fountain.

"Every night, I dream I am walking through streets of

shops. I am happy, or at least content. I have money to spend, and there is a long list of things I wish to buy. Again and again I recite the list to myself, and I try to decide in what parts of the quarter I can get each in the best quality for the lowest price.

"But gradually, as I go from shop to shop, I grow aware that everyone who sees me hates me and holds me in contempt, and I am aware that it is because they believe me to be an unclean spirit who has wrapped itself in the woman's body they see. At last I enter a tiny shop conducted by an old man and an old woman. She sits making lace while he spreads their wares on the counter for me. I hear the sound her thread makes behind me as it is pulled through the work."

I asked, "What is it you have come to buy?"

"Tiny clothes." Dorcas held her small, white hands half a span apart. "Doll's clothing, perhaps. I particularly remember little shirts of fine wool. At last I choose one and hand the old man money. But it is not money at all—only a lump of filth."

Her shoulders were shaking, and I put my arm about her to comfort her.

"I want to scream then that they are wrong, that I am not the foul specter they take me for. Yet I know that if I do, whatever I may say will be taken as the final proof that they are right, and the words choke me. The worst part is that just then the hissing of the thread stops." She had taken my free hand again, and now she gripped it as though to drive her meaning into me. "I know that no one could understand who has not had the same dream, but it is terrible. Terrible."

"Perhaps now that I am here with you again, these dreams will end."

"And then I sleep, or at least fall into blackness. If I do not wake then, there is a second dream. I am in a boat poled across a spectral lake—"

"There is no mystery in that, at least," I said. "You rode in such a boat with Agia and me. It belonged to a man named Hildegrin. Surely you must remember that trip."

Dorcas shook her head. "It is not that boat but a much smaller one. An old man poles it, and I lie at his feet. I am awake, but I cannot move. My arm trails in the black water. Just as we are about to touch shore, I fall from the boat, but the old man does not see me, and as I sink through the water I know that he has never known I was there at all. Soon the

light is gone, and I am very cold. Far above me, I hear a voice
I love calling my name, but I cannot remember whose voice it
is."

"It's my voice, calling to wake you."

"Perhaps." The whip mark Dorcas had carried from the
Piteous Gate burned on her cheek like a brand.

For a while we sat without speaking. The nightingales were
silent now, but linnets were singing in all the trees, and I saw
a parrot, clad in scarlet and green like a little messenger in
livery, flash among the branches.

At last Dorcas said, "What a frightful thing water is. I
should not have brought you here, but it was the only place
nearby where I could think to go. I wish we had sat on the
grass under those trees."

"Why do you hate it? It seems beautiful to me."

"Because it is here in the sunshine, but by its own nature it
runs down and down forever, away from the light."

"But it rises again," I said. "The rain we see in spring is the
same water we saw running the gutters the year before. Or so
Master Malrubius taught us."

Dorcas's smile flashed like a star. "That is good to believe,
whether it's true or not. Severian, it's silly for me to say
you're the best person I know, because you're the only good
person I know. But I think if I met a thousand others, you
would still be the best. That was what I wanted to talk to you
about."

"If you need my protection, you have it. You know that."

"It isn't that at all," Dorcas said. "In a way I want to give
you mine. Now *that* sounds silly, doesn't it? I have no family,
I have no one except you, and yet I think I can protect you."

"You know Jolenta, and Dr. Talos and Baldanders."

"They are no one. Don't you feel that, Severian? Even I
am no one, but they are less than I. The five of us were in the
tent last night, and yet you were alone. You told me once that
you don't have much imagination, but you must have sensed
that."

"Is that what you want to protect me from—loneliness? I
would welcome such protection."

"Then I will give you all I can, for as long as I can. But most
of all, I want to protect you from the opinion of the world.
Severian, do you remember what I told you of my dream?
How all the people in the shops, and on the street, believed
that I was only some hideous ghost? They may be right."

She was shaking, and I held her.

"That is part of the reason the dream is so painful. The other part comes from knowing that in some other way they are wrong. The foul specter is in me. It is me. But there are other things in me too, and they are what I am as much as it is."

"You could never be a foul specter, or anything foul."

"Oh, yes," she said seriously, and looked up at me. Her small, tilted face was never more beautiful than it was then in the sunlight, or more pure. "Oh, yes I could, Severian. Just as you can be what they call you. What you sometimes are. Do you remember how we saw the cathedral leap into the sky and burn away in an instant? And how we went walking down a road between trees until we saw a light ahead, and it was Dr. Talos and Baldanders, ready to put on their show with Jolenta?"

"You held my hand," I said. "And we talked about philosophy. How could I forget?"

"When we came to the light and Dr. Talos saw us—do you remember what he said?"

I cast my mind back to that evening, the end of the day on which I had executed Agilus. In memory I heard the roar of the crowd, Agia's scream, and then the roll of Baldanders's drum. "He said that everyone had come now, and that you were Innocence, and I was Death."

Dorcas nodded solemnly. "That's right. But you're not really Death, you know, no matter how often he calls you that. You're no more death than a butcher is because he cuts the throats of steers all day. To me you're Life, and you're a young man named Severian, and if you wanted to put on different clothes and become a carpenter or a fisherman, no one could stop you."

"I have no desire to leave my guild."

"But you could. Today. That's the thing to remember. People don't want other people to be people. They throw names over them and lock them in, but I don't want you to let them lock you in. Dr. Talos is worse than most. In his own way, he's a liar . . ."

She left the accusation unfinished, and I ventured, "I once heard Baldanders say he seldom lied."

"In his own way, I said. Baldanders is right, Dr. Talos doesn't lie the way other people understand lying. Calling you Death wasn't a lie, it was a . . . a . . ."

"Metaphor," I suggested.

"But it was a dangerous, *bad* metaphor, and it was aimed at you like a lie."

"Do you think Dr. Talos hates me, then? I would have said he was one of the few people who've showed me real kindness since I left the Citadel. You, Jonas—who's gone now—an old woman I met while I was imprisoned, a man in a yellow robe—who also called me Death, by the way—and Dr. Talos. It's a short list, actually."

"I don't think he hates in the way we understand it," Dorcas replied softly. "Or for that matter, that he loves. He wants to manipulate everything he comes upon, to change it with his will. And since tearing down is easier than building, that's what he does most often."

"Baldanders seems to love him, though," I said. "I used to have a crippled dog, and I've seen Baldanders look at the doctor the way Triskele used to look at me."

"I understand you, but it doesn't strike me that way. Have you ever thought of how you must have looked, when you looked at your dog? Do you know anything about their past?"

"Only that they lived together near Lake Diurturna. The people there appear to have set fire to their house to drive them away."

"Do you think Dr. Talos could be Baldanders's son?"

The idea was so absurd that I laughed, happy to have the release from tension.

"Just the same," Dorcas said, "that's how they act. Like a slow-thinking, hard-working father with a brilliant, erratic son. At least so it seems to me."

It was not until we had left the bench and were walking back to the Green room (which no more resembled the picture Rudesind had shown me than any other garden would have) that it occurred to me to wonder whether Dr. Talos's calling Dorcas "Innocence" had not been a metaphor of the same kind.

XXIII

Jolenta

The old orchard and the herb garden beyond it had been so silent, so freighted with oblivion, that they had recalled to me the Atrium of Time, and Valeria with her exquisite face framed in furs. The Green Room was pandemonium. Everyone was awake now, and sometimes it seemed that everyone was shouting. Children climbed the trees to free the caged birds, pursued by their mothers' brooms and their fathers' missiles. Tents were being struck even while rehearsals continued, so that I saw a seemingly solid pyramid of striped canvas collapse like a flag thrown down and reveal beyond it the grass-green megathere rearing on his hind legs while a dancer pirouetted on his forehead.

Baldanders and our tent were gone, but in a moment Dr. Talos came rushing up and hurried us away down twisted walks, past balustrades and waterfalls and grottoes filled with raw topazes and flowering moss, to a bowl of clipped lawn where the giant labored to erect our stage under the eyes of a dozen white deer.

It was to be a much more elaborate stage than the one I had played upon within the Wall of Nessus. Servants from the House Absolute, it seemed, had brought timbers and nails, tools and paint and cloth in quantities much greater than we could possibly make use of. Their generosity had waked the doctor's bent toward the grandiose (which never slumbered deeply) and he alternated between assisting Baldanders and me with the heavier constructions and making frantic additions to the manuscript of his play.

The giant was our carpenter, and though he moved slowly,

he worked so steadily, and with such great strength—driving a spike as thick as my forefinger with a blow or two and cutting a timber it would have taken me a watch to saw through with a few strokes of his ax—that he might have been ten slaves toiling under the whip.

Dorcas found a talent for painting that I at least was surprised by. Together, we erected the black plates that drink the sun, not only to gather energy for the night's perform-ance, but to power the projectors now. These contrivances can provide a backdrop of a thousand leagues as easily as the interior of a hut, but the illusion is complete only in total darkness. It is best, therefore, to strengthen it with painted scenes behind, and Dorcas created those with skill, standing waist high in mountains as she thrust her brushes through the daylight-faded images.

Jolenta and I were of less value. I had no painter's hand, and too little understanding of the necessities of the play even to assist the doctor in arranging our properties. Jolenta, I think, rebelled physically and psychically against any kind of work, and certainly against this. Those long legs, so slender below the knees, so rounded to bursting above them, were inadequate to bear much weight beyond that of her own body; her jutting breasts were in constant danger of having their nipples crushed between lumber or smeared with paint. Nor had she any of that spirit that animates the members of a group forwarding the group's purpose. Dorcas had said that I had been alone the night before, and perhaps she had been more nearly correct than I supposed, but Jolenta was more solitary still. Dorcas and I had each other, Baldanders and the doctor their crooked friendship, and we came together in the performance of the play. Jolenta had only herself, the inces-sant performance whose sole goal was to garner admiration.

She touched my arm, and without speaking rolled enor-mous emerald eyes to indicate the edge of our natural amphitheater, where a grove of chestnuts lifted white candles among their pale leaves.

I saw that none of the others were looking at us and nodded. After Dorcas, Jolenta walking beside me seemed nearly as tall as Thecla, though she took small steps instead of Thecla's swinging strides. She was a head taller than Dorcas at least, her coiffure made her seem taller still, and she wore boots with high, riding heels.

"I want to see it," she said. "It's the only chance I shall ever have."

That was a palpable lie, but as though I believed it I said, "The opportunity is symmetric. Today and only today the House Absolute has the opportunity to see you."

She nodded; I had enunciated a profound truth. "I need someone—someone the ones I don't want to talk to will be afraid of. I mean all these showmen and mummers. When you were gone, no one but Dorcas would go with me, and no one is afraid of her. Could you draw that sword and carry it over your shoulder?"

I did so.

"If I don't smile, make them leave. Understand?"

Grass much longer than that in the natural amphitheater, but softer than fern, grew among the chestnuts; the path was of quartz pebbles shot with gold.

"If only the Autarch saw me, he would desire me. Do you think he will come to our play?"

To please her I nodded, but added, "I have heard he has little use for women, however beautiful, save as advisors, spies, and shield maids."

She stopped and turned, smiling. "That's just it. Don't you see? I can make anyone desire me, and so he, the One Autarch, whose dreams are our reality, whose memories are our history, will desire me too, unmanned or not. You have wanted women other than me, haven't you? Wanted them badly?"

I admitted I had.

"And so you think you desire me as you wished for them." She turned and began to walk again, hobbling a little, as it seemed she always did, but invigorated for the moment by her own argument. "But I make every man stiffen and every woman itch. Women who have never loved women wish to love me—did you know that? The same ones come to our performances again and again, and send me their food and their flowers, scarfs, shawls, and embroidered kerchiefs with oh, such sisterly, motherly notes. They're going to *protect* me, protect me from my physician, from his giant, from their husbands and sons and neighbors. And the *men!* Baldanders has to throw them in the river."

I asked if she were lame, and as we emerged from the chestnuts, I looked about for some conveyance for her, but there was nothing.

"My thighs are chafed and it hurts to walk. I have an unguent for them that helps a bit, and a man bought a jennet for me to ride, but I don't know where it's pastured now. I'm really only comfortable when I can keep my legs apart."

"I could carry you."

She smiled again, displaying perfect teeth. "We'd both enjoy that, wouldn't we? But I'm afraid it wouldn't look dignified. No, I'll walk—I just hope I don't have to walk far. I *won't* walk far, in fact, no matter what happens. No one seems to be about but the mummers anyway. Perhaps the important people are sleeping late to prepare for the night's festivities. I'll have to sleep myself, four watches at least, before I go on."

I heard the sound of water sliding over stones, and having no better goal to seek made for it. We passed through a hawthorn hedge whose spotted white blossoms seemed from a distance to present an insurmountable barrier, and saw a river hardly wider than a street, on which swans sailed like sculptures of ice. There was a pavilion there, and beside it three boats, each shaped like the wide flower of the nenuphar. Their interiors were lined with the thickest silk brocade, and when I stepped into one I found that they exuded the odor of spices.

"Wonderful," Jolenta said. "They won't mind if we take one, will they? Or if they do, I'll be brought before someone important, just as it is in the play, and when he sees me he'll never let me leave. I'll make Dr. Talos stay with me, and you if you want. They'll have some use for you."

I told her I would have to continue my journey north and lifted her into the boat, putting my arm about a waist quite as slender as Dorcas's.

She lay down at once upon the cushions, where the uplifted petals gave her perfect complexion shade. It made me think of Agia, laughing in the sun as we descended the Adamnian Steps and boasting of the wide-brimmed hat she would wear next year. Agia had no feature that was not inferior to Jolenta's; she had been hardly taller than Dorcas, with hips over-wide and breasts that would have seemed meager beside Jolenta's overflowing plenitude; her long, brown eyes and high cheekbones were more expressive of shrewdness and determination than passion and surrender. Yet Agia had engendered a healthy rut in me. Her laughter, when it came, was often tinged with spite; but it was real laughter. She had sweated with her heat; Jolenta's desire was no more than the desire to be desired, so that I wished, not to comfort her loneliness as I had wished to comfort Valeria's, nor to find expression for an aching love like the love I had felt for Thecla, nor to protect her as I wished to protect Dorcas; but to shame and punish her, to destroy her self-possession, to fill her eyes with tears and tear her hair as one burns the hair of corpses to torment the ghosts that have fled them. She had boasted that she made tribadists of women. She came near to making an algophilist of me.

"This is my last performance, I know. I feel it. The audience is sure to hold someone . . ." She yawned and stretched. It appeared so certain her straining bodice would be unable to contain her that I averted my eyes. When I looked again, she was sleeping.

A slender oar trailed behind the boat. I took it and found that despite the circularity of the hull above the water, there was a keel below. In the center of the river the current ran strongly enough that I needed only to steer our slow progress along a series of gracefully sweeping meanders. Just as the hooded servant and I had passed unseen through suites and alcoves and arcades when he had escorted me along the hidden ways of the Second House, so now the sleeping Jolenta and I passed without noise or effort, almost completely unobserved, through leagues of garden. Couples lay on the soft grass beneath the trees and in the more refined comfort of summerhouses and seemed to think our craft hardly more than a decoration sent idly downstream for their delectation, or if they saw my head above the curved petals assumed us intent upon our own affairs. Lone philosophers meditated on rustic seats, and parties, not invariably erotic, proceeded undisturbed in clerestories and arboriums.

Eventually I came to resent Jolenta's sleep. I abandoned the oar and knelt beside her on the cushions. There was a purity in her sleeping face, however artificial, that I had never observed when she was awake. I kissed her, and her large eyes, hardly open, seemed almost Agia's long eyes, as her red-gold hair appeared almost brown. I loosened her clothing. She seemed half drugged, whether by some soporific in the heaped cushions or merely by the fatigue induced by our walk in the open and the burden of so great a quantity of voluptuous flesh. I freed her breasts, each nearly as large as her own head, and those wide thighs, which seemed to hold a new-hatched chick between them.

When we returned, everyone knew where we had been, though I doubt that Baldanders cared. Dorcas wept in

private, vanishing for a time only to emerge with inflamed
eyes and a heroine's smile. Dr. Talos, I think, was simultaneously enraged and delighted. I received the impression (which
I hold to this day) that he had never enjoyed Jolenta, and that
it was only to him, of all the men of Urth, that she would have
given herself entirely willingly.

We spent the watches that remained before nightfall in
listening to Dr. Talos chaffer with various officials of the
House Absolute, and in rehearsal. Since I have already said
something of what it was to act in Dr. Talos's play, I propose
to give an approximation of the text here—not as it existed on
the fragments of soiled paper we passed from hand to hand
that afternoon, which often contained no more than hints for
improvisations, but as it might have been recorded by some
diligent clerk in the audience; and as it was, in fact, recorded
by the demonic witness who dwells behind my eyes.

But first you must visualize our theater. Urth's laboring
margin has climbed once more above the red disc; long-
winged bats flit overhead, and a green quarter moon hangs
low in the eastern sky. Imagine the slightest of valleys, a
thousand paces or more from lip to lip, set among the gentlest
turf-covered rolling hills. There are doors in these hills, some
no wider than the entrance to an ordinary private room, some
as wide as the doors of a basilica. These doors are open, and a
mist-tinged light spills from them. Flagged paths wind down
toward the tiny arch of our proscenium; they are dotted with
men and women in the fantastic costumes of a masque—
costumes drawn largely from remote ages, so that I, with no
more than the smattering of history furnished me by Thecla
and Master Palaemon, scarcely recognize one of them. Servants move among these masquers carrying trays loaded with
cups and tumblers, heaped with delicious-smelling meats and
pastries. Black seats of velvet and ebony, as delicate as
crickets, face our stage, but many in the audience prefer to
stand, and throughout our performance the spectators come
and go without interruption, many remaining to hear no more
than a dozen lines. Hylas sing in the trees, the nightingales
trill, and atop the hills the walking statues move slowly
through many poses. All the parts in the play are taken by Dr.
Talos, Baldanders, Dorcas, Jolenta, or me.

XXIV

Dr. Talos's Play: Eschatology and Genesis

Being a dramatization (as he claimed) of certain parts of the lost Book of the New Sun

Persons in the Play:

Gabriel	A Statue
The Giant Nod	A Prophet
Meschia, the First Man	The Generalissimo
Meschiane, the First Woman	Two Demons (disguised)
Jahi	The Inquisitor
The Autarch	His Familiar
The Contessa	Angelic Beings
Her Maid	The New Sun
Two Soldiers	The Old Sun
	The Moon

The back of the stage is dark. GABRIEL *appears bathed in golden light and carrying a crystal clarion.*

GABRIEL: Greetings. I have come to set the scene for you—after all, that is my function. It is the night of the last day, and the night before the first. The Old Sun has set. He will appear in the sky no more. Tomorrow the New Sun will rise, and my siblings and I will greet him. Tonight . . . tonight no one knows. Everyone sleeps.

Footsteps, heavy and slow. Enter NOD.

GABRIEL: Omniscience! Defend your servant!

NOD: Do you serve him? So do we Nephilim. I will not harm you, then, unless he suggests it.

GABRIEL: You are of his household? How does he communicate with you?

179

NOD: To tell the truth, he doesn't. I'm forced to guess at
    what he wishes me to do.

GABRIEL: I was afraid of that.

NOD: Have you seen Meschia's son?

GABRIEL: Have I seen him? Why, you great ninny, he isn't
    even born yet. What do you want with him?

NOD: He is to come and dwell with me, in my land east of
    this garden. I will give him one of my daughters to wife.

GABRIEL: You have the wrong creation, my friend—you're
    fifty million years too late.

NOD: *(Nods slowly, not understanding.)* If you should see
    him—

*Enter MESCHIA and MESCHIANE, with JAHI following. All are
naked, but JAHI wears jewelry.*

MESCHIA: What a lovely place! Delightful! Flowers, foun-
    tains, and statues—isn't it wonderful?

MESCHIANE: *(Timidly.)* I saw a tame tiger with fangs longer
    than my hand. What shall we call him?

MESCHIA: Whatever he wants. *(To GABRIEL:)* Who owns this
    beautiful spot?

GABRIEL: The Autarch.

MESCHIA: And he permits us to live here. That's very
    gracious of him.

GABRIEL: Not exactly. There's someone following you, my
    friend. Do you know it?

MESCHIA: *(Not looking.)* There's something behind you too.

GABRIEL: *(Flourishing the clarion that is his badge of office.)*
    Yes, *He* is behind me!

MESCHIA: Close, too. If you're going to blow that horn to
    call help, you'd better do it now.

GABRIEL: Why, how perceptive of you. But the time is not
    quite ripe.

*The golden light fades, and GABRIEL vanishes from the stage.
NOD remains motionless, leaning on his club.*

MESCHIANE: I'll start a fire, and you had better begin to build
    us a house. It must rain often here—see how green the
    grass is.

MESCHIA: *(Examining NOD.)* Why, it's only a statue. No
    wonder he wasn't afraid of it.

MESCHIANE: It might come to life. I heard something once
    about raising sons from stones.

MESCHIA: Once! Why you were only born just now. Yester-
    day, I think.

MESCHIANE: Yesterday! I don't remember it. . . . I'm such a child, Meschia. I don't remember anything until I walked out into the light and saw you talking to a sunbeam.

MESCHIA: That wasn't a sunbeam! It was . . . to tell the truth, I haven't thought of a name for what it was yet.

MESCHIANE: I fell in love with you then.

Enter the AUTARCH.

AUTARCH: Who are you?

MESCHIA: As far as that goes, who are *you?*

AUTARCH: The owner of this garden.

MESCHIA bows, and MESCHIANE curtsies, though she has no skirt to hold.

MESCHIA: We were speaking to one of your servants only a moment ago. Now that I come to think of it, I am astonished at how much he resembled your august Self. Save that he was . . . ah . . .

AUTARCH: Younger?

MESCHIA: In appearance, at least.

AUTARCH: Well, it is inevitable, I suppose. Not that I am attempting to excuse it now. But I was young, and though it would be better to confine oneself to women nearer one's own station, still there are times—as you would understand, young man, if you had ever been in my position—when a little maid or country girl, who can be wooed with a handful of silver or a bolt of velvet, and will not demand, at the most inconvenient moment, the death of some rival or an ambassadorship for her husband . . . Well, when a little person like that becomes a most enticing proposition.

While the AUTARCH has been speaking, JAHI has been creeping up behind MESCHIA. Now she lays a hand on his shoulder.

JAHI: Now you see that he, whom you have esteemed your divinity, would countenance and advise all I have proposed of you. Before the New Sun rises, let us make a new beginning.

AUTARCH: Here's a lovely creature. How is it, child, that I see the bright flames of candles reflected in each eye, while your sister there still puffs cold tinder?

JAHI: She is no sister of mine!

AUTARCH: Your adversary then. But come with me. I will give these two my leave to camp here, and you shall wear a rich gown this night, and your mouth shall run with wine, and that slender figure shall be rendered a shade less graceful, perhaps, by larks stuffed with almonds and candied figs.

JAHI: Go away, old man.

AUTARCH: What! Do you know who I am?

JAHI: I am the only one here who does. You are a ghost and less, a column of ashes upheld by the wind.

AUTARCH: I see, she is mad. What does she want you to do, friend?

MESCHIA: *(Relieved.)* You hold no resentment toward her? That is good of you.

AUTARCH: None at all! Why, a mad mistress should be a most interesting experience—I am looking forward to it, believe me, and there are few things to look forward to when you've seen and done all I have. She doesn't bite, does she? I mean, not hard?

MESCHIANE: She does, and her fangs run with venom.

JAHI springs forward to claw her. MESCHIANE darts offstage, pursued.

AUTARCH: I shall have my piquenaires search the garden for them.

MESCHIA: Don't worry, they'll both be back soon. You'll see. Meanwhile I am, actually, glad to have a moment alone with you like this. There are some things I've been wanting to ask you.

AUTARCH: I grant no favors after six—that's a rule I've had to make to keep my sanity. I'm sure you understand.

MESCHIA: *(Somewhat taken aback.)* That's good to know. But I wasn't going to ask *for* something, really. Only for information, for divine wisdom.

AUTARCH: In that case, go ahead. But I warn you, you must pay a price. I mean to have that demented angel for my own tonight.

MESCHIA drops to his knees.

MESCHIA: There is something I have never understood. Why must I talk to you when you know my every thought? My first question was: Knowing her to be of that brood you have banished, should I not still do what she proposes? For she knows I know, and it is in my heart to believe that she puts forward right action in the thought that I will spurn it because it comes from her.

AUTARCH: *(Aside.)* He is mad too, I see, and because of my yellow robes thinks me divine. *(To MESCHIA:)* A little adultery never hurt any man. Unless of course it was his wife's.

MESCHIA: Then mine would hurt her? I—

Enter the CONTESSA and her MAID.

CONTESSA: My Sovereign Lord! What do you do here?

MESCHIA: I am at prayer, daughter. Take off your shoes at
least, for this is holy ground.

CONTESSA: Liege, who is this fool?

AUTARCH: A madman I found wandering with two women as
mad as he.

CONTESSA: Then they outnumber us, unless my maid be
sane.

MAID: Your grace—

CONTESSA: Which I doubt. This afternoon she laid out a
purple stole with my green capote. I was to look like a
post decked with morning-glories, it would seem.

*MESCHIA, who has been growing angrier as she speaks, strikes
her, knocking her down. Unseen behind him, the AUTARCH
flees.*

MESCHIA: Brat! Don't trifle with holy things when I am near,
or dare do anything but what I tell you.

MAID: Who are you, sir?

MESCHIA: I am the parent of the human race, my child. And
you *are* my child, as she is.

MAID: I hope you will forgive her—and me. We had heard
you were dead.

MESCHIA: That requires no apology. Most are, after all. But
I have come round again, as you see, to welcome the
new dawn.

NOD: *(Speaking and moving after his long silence and immo-
bility.)* We have come too early.

MESCHIA: *(Pointing.)* A giant! A giant!

CONTESSA: Oh! Solange! Kyneburga!

MAID: I'm here, Your Grace. Lybe is here.

NOD: Too early for the New Sun by some time still.

CONTESSA: *(Beginning to weep.)* The New Sun is coming! We
shall melt like dreams.

MESCHIA: *(Seeing that NOD intends no violence.)* Bad dreams.
But it will be the best thing for you. you understand that,
don't you?

CONTESSA: *(Recovering a little.)* What I don't understand is
how you, who suddenly seem so wise, could mistake the
Autarch for the Universal Mind.

MESCHIA: I know that you are my daughters in the old
creation. You must be, since you are human women, and
I have had none in this.

NOD: His son will take my daughter to wife. It is an honor
our family has done little to deserve—we are only

humble people, the children of Gea—but we will be
exulted. I will be . . . What will I be, Meschia? The
father-in-law of your son. It may be, if you don't object,
that someday my wife and I will visit our daughter on the
same day you come to see him. You wouldn't refuse us,
would you, a place at the table? We would sit on the
floor, naturally.

MESCHIA: Of course not. The dog does that already—or will,
when we see him. *(To the* CONTESSA:) Has it not struck
you that I may know more of him you call the Universal
Mind than your Autarch does of himself? Not only your
Universal Mind, but many lesser powers wear our humanity like a cloak when they will, sometimes only as
concerns two or three of us. We who are worn are
seldom aware that, seeming ourselves to ourselves, we
are yet Demiurge, Paraclete, or Fiend to another.

CONTESSA: That is wisdom I have gained late, if I must fade
with the New Sun's rising. Is it past midnight?

MAID: Nearly so, Your Grace.

CONTESSA: *(Pointing to the audience.)* All these fair folk—
what will befall them?

MESCHIA: What befalls leaves when their year is past, and
they are driven by the wind?

CONTESSA: If—

MESCHIA *turns to watch the eastern sky, as though for the first
sign of dawn.*

CONTESSA: If—

MESCHIA: If what?

CONTESSA: If my body held a part of yours—drops of
liquescent tissue locked in my loins . . .

MESCHIA: If it did, you might wander Urth for a time longer,
a lost thing that could never find its way home. But I will
not bed you. Do you think that you are more than a
corpse? You are less.

MAID *faints.*

CONTESSA: You say you are the father of all things human. It
must be so, for you are death to woman.

The stage darkens. When the light returns, MESCHIANE *and* JAHI
*are lying together beneath a rowan tree. There is a door in the
hillside behind them.* JAHI's *lip is split and puffed, giving her a
pouting look. Blood trickles from it to her chin.*

MESCHIANE: How strong I would be still to search for him, if
only I knew you would not follow me.

JAHI: I move with the strength of the World Below, and will

follow you to the second ending of Urth, if need be. But if
you strike me again you will suffer for it.

MESCHIANE lifts her fist, and JAHI cowers back.

MESCHIANE: Your legs were shaking worse than mine when
we decided to rest here.

JAHI: I suffer far more than you. But the strength of the
World Below is to endure past endurance—even as I am
more beautiful than you, I am a more tender creature by
far.

MESCHIANE: We've seen that, I think.

JAHI: I warn you again, and there will be no third warning.
Strike me at your peril.

MESCHIANE: What will you do? Summon up Erinys to destroy me? I have no fear of that. If you could, you would
have done it long before.

JAHI: Worse. If you strike me again, you will come to enjoy
it.

Enter FIRST SOLDIER and SECOND SOLDIER, armed with pikes.

FIRST SOLDIER: Look here!

SECOND SOLDIER: *(To the women:)* Down, down! Don't
stand, or like a heron I'll skewer you. You're coming
with us.

MESCHIANE: On our hands and knees?

FIRST SOLDIER: None of your insolence!

*He prods her with his pike, and as he does there is a groaning
almost too deep for hearing. The stage vibrates in sympathy
with it, and the ground shakes.*

SECOND SOLDIER: What was that?

FIRST SOLDIER: I don't know.

JAHI: The end of Urth, you fool. Go ahead and spear her.
It's the end of you anyway.

SECOND SOLDIER: Little you know! It's the beginning for
us. When the order came to search the garden, special mention was made of you two, and orders given to
bring you back. Ten chrisos you'll be worth, or I'm a
cobbler.

*He seizes JAHI, and as soon as he does so, MESCHIANE darts off
into the darkness. FIRST SOLDIER runs after her.*

SECOND SOLDIER: Bite me, will you!

He strikes JAHI with the shaft of his weapon. They struggle.

JAHI: Fool! She's escaping!

SECOND SOLDIER: That's Ivo's worry. I've got my prisoner,
and he let his escape, if he doesn't catch her. Come on,
we're going to see the chiliarch.

JAHI: Will you not love me before we leave this winsome spot?

SECOND SOLDIER: And have my manhood cut off and shoved into my mouth? Not I!

JAHI: They'd have to find it first.

SECOND SOLDIER: What's that? *(Shakes her.)*

JAHI: You take the office of Urth, who will not trouble herself for me. But wait—release me only for a moment and I will show you wonderful things.

SECOND SOLDIER: I can see them now, for which I give all thanks to the moon.

JAHI: I can make you rich. Ten chrisos will be as nothing to you. But I have no power while you grasp my body.

SECOND SOLDIER: Your legs are longer than the other woman's, but I've seen that you don't move so readily on them. Indeed, I think that you can scarcely stand.

JAHI: No more can I.

SECOND SOLDIER: I'll hold your necklace—the chain looks stout enough. If that's sufficient, show me what you can do. If it's not, come with me. You'll be no freer while I have you.

JAHI raises both hands, with the little fingers, index fingers, and thumbs extended. For a moment there is silence, then a strange, soft music filled with trillings. Snow falls in gentle flakes.

SECOND SOLDIER: Stop that!

He seizes one arm and jerks it down. The music stops abruptly. A few last snowflakes settle on his head.

SECOND SOLDIER: That was not gold.

JAHI: Yet you saw.

SECOND SOLDIER: There's an old woman in my home village who can work the weather too. She's not as quick as you, I admit, but then she's a lot older, and feeble.

JAHI: Whoever she may be, she is not a thousandth part as old as I.

Enter the STATUE, moving slowly and as though blind.

JAHI: What is that thing?

SECOND SOLDIER: One of Father Inire's little pets. It can't hear you or make a sound. I'm not even sure it's alive.

JAHI: Why, neither am I, for all of that.

As the STATUE passes near her, she strokes its cheek with her free hand.

JAHI: Lover . . . lover . . . lover. Have you no greeting for me?

STATUE: E-e-e-y!

SECOND SOLDIER: What's this? Stop! Woman, you said you
    had no power while I held you.

JAHI: Behold my slave. Can you fight him? Go ahead—
    break your spear on that broad chest.

The STATUE *kneels and kisses* JAHI'S *foot.*

SECOND SOLDIER: No, but I can outrun him.

He throws JAHI *across his shoulder and runs. The door in the
hill opens. He enters, and it slams shut behind him. The
STATUE hammers it with mighty blows, but it does not yield.
Tears stream down his face. At last he turns away and begins to
dig with his hands.*

GABRIEL: *(Offstage.)* Thus stone images keep faith with a
    departed day, Alone in the desert when man has fled
    away.

As the STATUE *continues to dig, the stage grows dark. When the
lights come up again, the* AUTARCH *is seated on his throne. He
is alone on stage, but silhouettes projected on screens to either
side of him indicate that he is surrounded by his court.*

AUTARCH: Here I sit as though the lord of a hundred worlds.
    Yet not master even of this.

*The tramp of marching men is heard offstage. There is a
shouted order.*

AUTARCH: Generalissimo!

Enter a PROPHET. *He wears a goat skin and carries a staff whose
head has been rudely carved into a strange symbol.*

PROPHET: A hundred portents are abroad. At Incusus, a calf
    was dropped that had no head, but mouths in his knees.
    A woman of known propriety has dreamed she is with
    child by a dog, last night a shower of stars fell hissing
    onto the southern ice, and prophets walk abroad in the
    land.

AUTARCH: You yourself are a prophet.

PROPHET: The Autarch himself has seen them!

AUTARCH: My archivist, who is most learned in the history of
    this spot, once informed me that over a hundred proph-
    ets have been slain here—stoned, burned, torn by
    beasts, and drowned. Some have even been nailed like
    vermin to our doors. Now I would learn of you some-
    thing of the coming of the New Sun, so long prophesied.
    How is it to come about? What does it mean? Speak, or
    we shall give the old archivist another mark for his tally,
    and train the pale moonflower to climb that staff.

PROPHET: I despair of satisfying you, but I shall attempt it.

AUTARCH: Do you not know?

PROPHET: I know. But I know you for a practical man, concerned with the affairs of this universe alone, who seldom looks higher than the stars.

AUTARCH: For thirty years I have prided myself on that.

PROPHET: Yet even you must know that cancer eats the heart of the old sun. At its center, matter falls in upon itself, as though there were there a pit without bottom, whose top surrounds it.

AUTARCH: My astronomers have long told me so.

PROPHET: Think on an apple rotten from the bud. Fair still without, until it collapses into foulness at last.

AUTARCH: Every man who finds himself still strong in the latter half of life has thought on that fruit.

PROPHET: So much then for the old sun. But what of its cancer? What know we of that, save that it deprives Urth of heat and light, and at last of life?

Sounds of struggle are heard offstage. There is a scream of pain, and a crash as though a large vase had been knocked from its pedestal.

AUTARCH: We will learn what that commotion is soon enough, Prophet. Continue.

PROPHET: We know it to be far more, for it is a discontinuity in our universe, a rent in its fabric bound by no law we know. From it nothing comes—all enters in, nought escapes. Yet from it anything may appear, for it alone of all the things we know is no slave to its own nature.

Enter NOD, *bleeding, prodded by pikes held offstage.*

AUTARCH: What is this miscreation?

PROPHET: The very proof of those portents I spoke to you. In future times, so it has long been said, the death of the old sun will destroy Urth. But from its grave will rise monsters, a new people, and the New Sun. Old Urth will flower then as a butterfly from its dry husk, and the New Urth shall be called Ushas.

AUTARCH: Yet all we know will be swept aside? This ancient house in which we stand? Yourself? Me?

NOD: I have no wisdom. Yet I heard a wise man—soon to be a relative of marriage—say not long ago that all that is for the best. We are but dreams, and dreams possess no life by their own right. See, I am wounded. *(Holds out his hand.)* When my wound heals, it will be gone. Should it with its bloody lips say it is sorry to heal? I am only trying to explain what another said, but that is what I think he meant.

Deep bells toll offstage.

AUTARCH: What's that? You, Prophet, go and see who's ordered that clamor, and why. *Exit PROPHET.*

NOD: I feel sure your bells have begun the welcome of the New Sun. It is what I came to do myself. It is our custom, when an honored guest arrives, to roar and beat our chests, and pound the ground and the trunks of trees all about with gladness, and lift the greatest rocks we can, and send them down the gorges in honor of him. I will do that this morning, if you will set me free, and I feel sure Urth herself will join me. The very mountains will leap into the sea when the New Sun rises up today.

AUTARCH: And from where did you come? Tell me, and I'll release you.

NOD: Why, from my own country, to the east of Paradise.

AUTARCH: And where is that?

NOD points to the east.

AUTARCH: And where is Paradise? In the same direction?

NOD: Why, this is Paradise—we are in Paradise, or at least under it.

Enter the GENERALISSIMO, who marches to the throne and salutes.

GENERALISSIMO: Autarch, we have searched all the land above this House Absolute, as you ordered. The Contessa Carina has been found, and, her injuries not being serious, escorted to her apartments. We have also found the colossus you see before you, the bejeweled woman you described, and two merchants.

AUTARCH: What of the other two, the naked man and his wife?

GENERALISSIMO: There is no trace of them.

AUTARCH: Repeat your search, and this time look well.

GENERALISSIMO: *(Salutes.)* As my Autarch wills.

AUTARCH: And have the jeweled woman sent to me.

NOD begins to walk offstage, but is stopped by pikes. The GENERALISSIMO draws his pistol.

NOD: Am I not free to leave?

GENERALISSIMO: By no means!

NOD: *(To AUTARCH.)* I told you where my country lies. Just east of here.

GENERALISSIMO: More than your country lies. I know that area well.

AUTARCH: *(Fatigued.)* He has told the truth as he knows it. Perhaps the only truth there is.

NOD: Then I am free to go.

AUTARCH: I think that he whom you came to welcome will arrive whether you are free or not. Yet there is a chance—and such creatures as you cannot be allowed to roam abroad in any case. No, you are not free, nor ever again will be.

NOD rushes from the stage, pursued by the GENERALISSIMO. *Shots, screams, and crashes. The figures around the* AUTARCH *fade. In the midst of the uproar, the bells toll again.* NOD *REENTERS WITH A LASER BURN ACROSS ONE CHEEK. The* AUTARCH *strikes him with his scepter; each blow produces an explosion and a burst of sparks.* NOD *seizes the* AUTARCH *and is about to dash him to the stage when two* DEMONS *disguised as merchants enter, throw him down, and restore the* AUTARCH *to his throne.*

AUTARCH: Thank you. You will be richly rewarded. I had given up hope of being rescued by my guards, and I see I thought rightly. May I ask who you are?

FIRST DEMON: Your guards are dead. That giant has smashed their skulls against your walls and broken their spines upon his knees.

SECOND DEMON: We are two traders merely. Your soldiers took us up.

AUTARCH: Would that they were traders, and in their places I had such soldiers as you! And yet, you are in appearance so slight I would think you incapable of even ordinary strength.

FIRST DEMON: *(bowing.)* Our strength is inspired by the master we serve.

SECOND DEMON: You will wonder why we—two common-place traders in slaves—should have been found wandering your grounds by night. The fact is that we came to warn you. Our travels but lately took us to the northern jungles, and there, in a temple older than man, a shrine overgrown with rank vegetation until it seemed hardly more than a leafy mound, we spoke to an ancient shaman who foretold great peril to your realm.

FIRST DEMON: With that intelligence we hastened here to give you the alarm before it should be too late, arriving at the very wince of time.

AUTARCH: What must I do?

SECOND DEMON: This world that you and we treasure has now been driven round the sun so often that the warp and woof of its space grow threadbare and fall as dust and feeble lint from the loom of time.

FIRST DEMON: The continents themselves are old as raddled women, long since stripped of beauty and fertility. The New Sun comes—

AUTARCH: I know!

FIRST DEMON: —and he will send them crashing into the sea like foundered ships.

SECOND DEMON: And from the sea lift new—glittering with gold, silver, iron, and copper. With diamonds, rubies, and turquoises, lands wallowing in the soil of a million millennia, so long ago washed down to the sea.

FIRST DEMON: To people these lands, a new race is prepared. The humankind you know will be shouldered aside even as the grass, that has prospered on the plain so long, yields to the plow and so gives way to wheat.

SECOND DEMON: But what if the seed were burned? What then? The tall man and the slight woman you met not long ago are such seed. Once it was hoped that it might be poisoned in the field, but she who was dispatched to accomplish it has lost sight of the seed now among the dead grass and broken clods, and for a few sleights of hand has been handed over to your Inquisitor for strict examination. Yet the seed might be burned still.

AUTARCH: The thought you suggest has already passed through my own mind.

FIRST & SECOND DEMON: *(In chorus.)* Of course!

AUTARCH: But would the death of those two truly halt the coming of the New Sun?

FIRST DEMON: No. But would you wish it? The new lands shall be yours.

The screens grow radiant. Wooded hills and cities of spires appear. The AUTARCH *turns to face them. There is a pause. He draws a communicator from his robes.*

AUTARCH: May never the New Sun see what we do here. . . . Ships! Sweep over us with flame till all is sere.

As the two DEMONS *vanish,* NOD *sits up. The cities and hills fade, and the screens show the image of the* AUTARCH *multiplied many times. The stage goes dark.*

When the lights go up again, the INQUISITOR *sits at a high desk in the center of the stage. His* FAMILIAR, *dressed as a torturer and masked, stands beside the desk. To either side are various instruments of torment.*

INQUISITOR: Bring in the woman said to be a witch, Brother.

FAMILIAR: The Contessa waits outside, and as she is of exalted blood, and a favorite of our sovereign's, I beg you see her first.

Enter the CONTESSA.

CONTESSA: I heard what was said, and as I could not think you would be deaf, Inquisitor, to such an appeal, I have made bold to come in at once. Do you think me bold for that?

INQUISITOR: You toy with words. But yes, I own I do.

CONTESSA: Then you think wrongly. Eight years since my girlhood have I abode in this House Absolute. When first the blood seeped from out my loins and my mother brought me here, she warned me never to come near these apartments of yours, where the blood has trickled from so many, caring nothing for the phases of the fickle moon. And never have I come till now, and now, trembling.

INQUISITOR: Here the good need have no fear. Yet even so, I think you grown bold by your own testimony.

CONTESSA: And am I good? Are you? Is he? My confessor would tell you I am not. What does yours tell you, or is he in fear? And is your familiar a better man than you?

FAMILIAR: I would not wish to be.

CONTESSA: No, I am not bold—nor safe here, as I know. It is fear that drives me to these grim chambers. They have told you of the naked man who struck me. Has he been taken?

INQUISITOR: He has not been brought before me.

CONTESSA: Scarcely a watch ago some soldiers found me moaning in the garden, where my maid sought to comfort me. Because I feared to be outside by dark, they carried me to my own suite by way of that gallery called the Road of Air. Do you know it?

INQUISITOR: Well.

CONTESSA: Then you know, too, that it is everywhere over-hung with windows, so that all the chambers and corridors that abut on it may receive the benefit. As we passed by, I saw in one the figure of a man, tall and clean-limbed, wide of shoulder and slender of waist.

INQUISITOR: There are many such men.

CONTESSA: So I thought. But in a little time, the same figure appeared in another window—and another. Then I appealed to the soldiers who carried me to fire upon it. They thought me mad and would not, but the party they sent to take that man returned with empty hands. Still he looked at me through the windows, and appeared to sway.

INQUISITOR: And you believe this man you saw to be the man who struck you?

CONTESSA: Worse. I fear it was not he, though it resembled him. Besides, he would be kind to me, I am sure, if only I treated his madness with respect. No, on this strange night, when we, who are the winter-killed stalks of man's old sprouting, find ourselves so mixed with next year's seed, I fear that he is something more we do not know.

INQUISITOR: That may be so, but you will not find him here, nor the man who struck you. (*To his* FAMILIAR:) Bring in the witch-woman, Brother.

FAMILIAR: Such are they all—though some are worse than others.

He exits and returns leading MESCHIANE *by a chain.*

INQUISITOR: It is alleged against you that you so charmed seven of the soldiers of our sovereign the Autarch that they betrayed their oath and turned their weapons upon their comrades and their officers. (*He rises, and lights a large candle at one side of his desk.*) I now most solemnly adjure you to confess this sin, and if you have so sinned, what power aided you to accomplish it, and the names of those who taught you to call upon that power.

MESCHIANE: The soldiers only saw I meant no harm, and were afraid for me. I—

FAMILIAR: Silence!

INQUISITOR: No weight is given to the protestations of the accused unless they are made under duress. My familiar will prepare you.

FAMILIAR seizes MESCHIANE *and straps her into one of the contrivances.*

CONTESSA: With so little time left to the world, I shall not waste it in watching this. Are you a friend to the naked man of the garden? I am going to seek him, and I will tell him what has become of you.

MESCHIANE: Oh, do! I hope that he will come before it is too late.

CONTESSA: And *I* hope he will accept me, in your stead. No

doubt both hopes are equally forlorn, and we shall soon be sisters in despair.

Exit the CONTESSA.

INQUISITOR: I go too, to speak to those that were her rescuers. Prepare the subject, for I shall return shortly.

FAMILIAR: There is another, Inquisitor. Of similar crimes, but less, perhaps, in potency.

INQUISITOR: Why did you not tell me? I might have instructed both together. Bring her in.

FAMILIAR *exits and returns leading* JAHI. *The* INQUISITOR *searches among the papers on his desk.*

INQUISITOR: It is alleged against you that you so charmed seven of the soldiers of our sovereign the Autarch that they betrayed their oath and turned their weapons upon their comrades and their officers. I now most solemnly adjure you to confess this sin, and if you have so sinned, what power aided you to accomplish it, and the names of those who taught you to call upon that power.

JAHI: *(Proudly.)* I have done all you accuse me of and more than you know. The power I dare not name lest this upholstered rathole be blasted to bits. Who taught me? Who teaches a child to call upon her father?

FAMILIAR: Her mother?

INQUISITOR: I would not know. Prepare her. I shall return soon.

Exit the INQUISITOR.

MESCHIANE: They fought for you too? How sad that so many had to die!

FAMILIAR: *(Locking* JAHI *in a contrivance on the other side of the desk.)* He had your paper again. I'll point his error out to him—diplomatically, you may be sure—when he comes back.

JAHI: You charmed the soldiers? Then charm this fool, and free us.

MESCHIANE: I have no chant of power, and I charmed but seven of fifty.

Enter NOD, *bound, driven by* FIRST SOLDIER *with a pike.*

FAMILIAR: What's this?

FIRST SOLDIER: Why, such a prisoner as you've never had before. He's killed a hundred men as we might puppies. Have you shackles big enough for him?

FAMILIAR: I'll have to link several pairs together, but I'll contrive something.

NOD: I am no man, but less and more—being born of the
     clay, of Mother Gea, whose pets are the beasts. If your
     dominion is over men, then you must let me go.

JAHI: We're not men either. Let us go too!

FIRST SOLDIER: *(Laughing.)* We can see you're not. I wasn't
     in doubt for a moment.

MESCHIANE: She's no woman. Don't let her trick you.

FAMILIAR: *(Snapping the last fetter on NOD.)* She won't.
     Believe me, the time of tricks is over.

FIRST SOLDIER: You'll have some fun, won't you, when I'm
     gone.

He reaches for JAHI, *who spits like a cat.*

FIRST SOLDIER: I don't suppose you'd be a good fellow and
     turn your back for a moment?

FAMILIAR: *(Preparing to torture* MESCHIANE.*)* If I were such a
     good fellow as that, I'd find myself broken on my own
     wheel soon enough. But if you wait here until my master
     the Inquisitor returns, you may find yourself lying beside
     her as you wish.

*FIRST SOLDIER hesitates, then realizes what is meant, and
hurries out.*

NOD: That woman will be the mother of my son-in-law. Do
     not harm her. *(He strains at his chains.)*

JAHI: *(Stifling a yawn.)* I've been up all night, and though
     the spirit is as willing as ever, this flesh is ready for rest.
     Can't you hurry with her and get to me?

FAMILIAR: *(Not looking.)* There is no rest here.

JAHI: So? Well, it's not quite as homelike as I would expect.

*JAHI yawns again, and when she moves a hand to cover her
mouth, the shackle falls away.*

MESCHIANE: You have to hold her—don't you understand?
     The soil has no part in her, so iron has no power over
     her.

FAMILIAR: *(Still looking at* MESCHIANE, *whom he is tortur-
     ing.)* She is held, never fear.

MESCHIANE: Giant! Can you free yourself? The world de-
     pends on it!

NOD strains at his bonds, but cannot break them.

JAHI: *(Walking out of her shackles.)* Yes! It is I who answer,
     because in the world of reality I am far larger than any of
     you. *(She walks around the desk and leans over the
     FAMILIAR's shoulder.)* How interesting! Crude, but inter-
     esting.

The FAMILIAR *turns and gapes at her, and she flees, laughing. He runs clumsily after her, and a moment later returns crestfallen.*

FAMILIAR: *(Panting.)* She's gone.

NOD: Yes. Free.

MESCHIANE: Free to pursue Meschia and ruin everything, as she did before.

FAMILIAR: You don't realize what this means. My master will return soon, and I am a dead man.

NOD: The world is dead. So she has told you.

MESCHIANE: Torturer, you have one chance yet—listen to me. You must free the giant as well.

FAMILIAR: And he will kill me and release you. I will consider it. At least it will be a quick death.

MESCHIANE: He hates Jahi, and though he isn't clever he knows her ways, and he is very strong. What's more, I can tell you an oath that he will never break. Give him the key to his shackles, then stand by me with your sword at my neck. Make him swear to find Jahi, return her here, and bind himself again.

The FAMILIAR *hesitates.*

MESCHIANE: You've nothing to lose. Your master doesn't even know he's supposed to be here. But if she's gone when he returns . . .

FAMILIAR: I'll do it! *(He detaches a key from the ring at his belt.)*

NOD: I swear as I hope to be linked by marriage to the family of Man, so that we giants may be called the Sons of the Father, that I will capture the succubus for you, and return her here, and hold her so that she shall not escape again, and bind myself as I am bound now.

FAMILIAR: Is that the oath?

MESCHIANE: Yes!

The FAMILIAR *throws the key to* NOD, *then draws his sword and holds it ready to strike* MESCHIANE.

FAMILIAR: Can he find her?

MESCHIANE: He *must* find her!

NOD: *(Unlocking himself.)* I will catch her. That body weakens, as she said. She may whip it far, but she will never learn that whipping will not do everything. *(Exits.)*

FAMILIAR: I must continue with you. I hope you understand. . . .

The FAMILIAR *tortures* MESCHIANE, *who screams.*

FAMILIAR: *(Sotto voce.)* How fair she is! I wish that we . . .
     were met when better things might be.

*The stage darkens; JAHI's running feet are heard. After a time,
a faint light shows NOD loping through the corridors of the
House Absolute. Moving images of urns, pictures, and furniture behind him show his progress. JAHI appears among them,
and he exits stage right in pursuit. JAHI enters stage left, with
SECOND DEMON walking in lockstep behind her.*

JAHI: Where can he have gone? The gardens are burned
     black. You have no flesh beyond a seeming—cannot you
     make yourself an owl and seek him out for me?

SECOND DEMON: *(Mocking.)* Who-o-o?

JAHI: Meschia! Wait until the Father hears how you have
     treated me, and betrayed all our efforts.

SECOND DEMON: From you? It was you who left Meschia,
     lured away by the woman. What will you say? "The
     woman tempted me?" We have done with that so long
     ago that no one remembers it save you and I, and now
     you have spoiled the lie by making it come true.

JAHI: *(Turning on him.)* You little foul sniveler! You scrab-
     bler at windows!

SECOND DEMON: *(Jumping back.)* And now you are exiled to
     the land of Nod, east of Paradise.

*NOD's footfalls are heard offstage. JAHI hides behind a clepsy-
dra, and SECOND DEMON produces a pike and stands with it in
the attitude of a soldier as NOD enters.*

NOD: How long have you been standing there?

SECOND DEMON: *(Saluting.)* As long as you want, sieur.

NOD: What news is there?

SECOND DEMON: All you want, sieur. A giant as high as a
     steeple has killed the throne-guards, and the Autarch's
     missing. We've searched the gardens so often that if only
     we'd been carrying dung instead of spears, the daisies'd
     be as big as umbrellas. Ducks' clothes is down and hopes
     is up—so's the turnips. Tomorrow should be fair, warm,
     and bright . . . *(looks significantly toward the clepsydra)*
     and a woman with no clothes on has been running
     through the halls.

NOD: What is that thing?

SECOND DEMON: A water clock, sieur. See, you, knowing
     what time it is, can tell by that how much water's flowed.

NOD: *(Examining the clepsydra.)* There is nothing like this in
     my land. Do these puppets move by water?

SECOND DEMON: Not the big one, sieur.

JAHI bolts offstage, pursued by NOD, *but before he is fully out of sight of the audience, she dives between his legs, reentering. He continues off, giving her time to hide in a chest. Meanwhile,* SECOND DEMON *has disappeared.*

NOD: *(Reentering.)* Ho! Stop! *(Runs to opposite side of stage and returns.)* My fault! My fault! In the garden there— she passed close by me once. I could have reached out and crushed her like a cat—a worm—a mouse—a snake. *(Turns on audience.)* Don't laugh at me! I could kill you all! The whole poisoned race of you! Oh, to strew the valleys with your white bones! But I am done—I am done! And Meschiane, who trusted in me, is undone!

NOD strikes the clepsydra, sending brass pans and water flying across the stage.

NOD: What good is this gift of speech, except that I can curse myself. Good mother of all the beasts, take it from me. I would be as I was, and shout wordless among the hills. Reason shows reason can only bring pain—how wise to forget and be happy again!

NOD seats himself on the chest in which JAHI *hides, and buries his face in his hands. As the lights dim, the chest begins to splinter beneath his weight.*

When the lights come up again, the scene is once more the INQUISITOR's *chamber.* MESCHIANE *is on the rack. The* FAMILIAR *is turning the wheel. She screams.*

FAMILIAR: That made you feel better, didn't it? I told you it would. Besides, it lets the neighbors know we're awake in here. You wouldn't believe it, but this whole wing is full of empty rooms and sinecures. Here the master and I do our business still. We do it still, and that's why the Commonwealth stands. And we want them to know it.

Enter the AUTARCH. *His robes are torn and stained with blood.*

AUTARCH: What place is this? *(He sits on the floor, his head in his hands in an attitude reminiscent of* NOD's.*)*

FAMILIAR: What place? Why, the Chambers of Mercy, you jackass. Can you come here without knowing where you are?

AUTARCH: I have been so hunted through my house this night that I might be anywhere. Bring me some wine—or water, if you've no wine here—and bar the door.

FAMILIAR: We have claret, but no wine. And I can hardly bar the door, since I expect my master back.

AUTARCH: *(More forcefully.)* Do as I tell you.

FAMILIAR: *(Very softly.)* You are drunk, friend. Go out.

AUTARCH: I am—What does it matter? The end is here. I am a man neither worse nor better than you.

NOD's heavy tread is heard in the distance.

FAMILIAR: He has failed—I know it!

MESCHIANE: He has succeeded! He would not come back so soon with empty hands. The world may yet be saved!

AUTARCH: What do you mean?

Enter NOD. The madness he prayed for is upon him, but he drags JAHI behind him. The FAMILIAR runs forward with shackles.

MESCHIANE: Someone must hold her, or she will escape as she did before.

The FAMILIAR drapes chains on NOD and snaps closed the locks, then chains one of NOD's arms across his body in such a way that he holds JAHI. NOD tightens the grip.

FAMILIAR: He's killing her! Let go, you great booby!

The FAMILIAR snatches up the bar with which he has been tightening the rack and belabors NOD with it. NOD roars, tries to grasp him, and lets the unconscious JAHI slip down. The FAMILIAR seizes her by the foot and pulls her to where the AUTARCH sits.

FAMILIAR: Here, you, you'll do.

He jerks the AUTARCH erect and swiftly imprisons him in such a way that one hand is clamped about JAHI's wrist, then returns to torture MESCHIANE. Unseen behind him, NOD is freeing himself of his chains.

XXV

The Attack on the Hierodules

Though we were outdoors, where sounds are so easily lost against the immensity of the sky, I could hear the clatter Baldanders made as he feigned to struggle with his bonds. There were conversations in the audience, and I could hear those as well—one about the play, which discovered in it significances I had never guessed and which Dr. Talos, I would say, had never intended; and another about some legal case that a speaker with the drawling intonation of an exultant seemed certain the Autarch was about to judge wrongly. As I turned the windlass of the rack, letting the pawl drop with a satisfying clack, I risked a sidelong look at those who watched us.

No more than ten chairs were in use, but lofty figures stood at the sides of the seating area, and behind it. There were a few women in court dresses much like the ones I had once seen in the House Azure, dresses with very low décolletages and full skirts that were often slit, or relieved with panels of lace. Their hair was simply dressed, but it was set off with flowers, jewels, or brilliantly luminous larvae.

Most of those in our audience seemed men, and more arrived momentarily. Many were as tall as or taller than Vodalus. They stood wrapped in their cloaks as though they were chilled by the soft spring air. Their faces were shadowed beneath broad-brimmed, low-crowned petasoses.

Baldanders's chains fell with a crash, and Dorcas shrieked to let me know he was free. I turned toward him, then cowered away, wrenching the nearest flambeau from its socket to fend him off. It guttered as the oil in its bowl nearly drowned the flame, sputtering to renewed life when the brimstone and mineral salts Dr. Talos had gummed around the rim took fire.

The giant was feigning madness, as his role required. His coarse hair hung about his eyes; and they, behind its screen, blazed so wildly I could see them despite it. His mouth hung slack, drooling spittle and showing his yellowed teeth. Arms twice the length of my own groped toward me.

What frightened me—and I was frightened, I admit, and wished heartily I had *Terminus Est* in my hands instead of the iron flambeau—was what I can only call the expression beneath the lack of expression on his face. It was there like the black water we sometimes glimpse moving beneath the ice when the river freezes. Baldanders had found a terrible joy now in being as he was; and when I faced him I realized for the first time that he was not so much feigning madness on the stage as feigning sanity and his dim humility off it. I wondered then how much he had influenced the writing of the play, though it may be only that Dr. Talos had (as he surely had) understood his patient better than I.

We were not, of course, to terrify the Autarch's courtiers as we had the country people. Baldanders would wrest the flambeau from me, pretend to break my back, and end the scene. He did not. Whether he was as mad as he pretended or was genuinely enraged at our growing audience, I cannot say. Perhaps both those explanations are correct.

However that might be, he jerked the flambeau from me and turned on them, flourishing it so the burning oil flew about him in a shower of fire. My sword, with which I had threatened Dorcas's head a few moments before, lay near my feet, and I stooped for it instinctively. By the time I had straightened up again, Baldanders was in the midst of the audience. The flambeau had gone out, and he swung it like a mace.

Someone fired a pistol. The bolt set his costume afire, but must have missed his body. Several exultants had drawn their swords, and someone—I could not see who—possessed that rarest of all weapons, a dream. It moved like tyrian smoke, but very much faster, and in an instant it had enveloped the giant. It seemed then that he stood wrapped in all that was past and much that had never been: a gray-haired woman sprouted from his side, a fishing boat hovered just over his head, and a cold wind whipped the flames that wreathed him. Yet the visions, which are said to leave soldiers dazed and

helpless, a burden to their cause, did not seem to affect
Baldanders. He strode forward still, and the flambeau
smashed clear a path for him.

Then, in the moment more that I watched (for I soon
recovered enough self-command to flee that mad fight) I saw
several figures throw aside their capes and—as it appeared—
their faces too. Under those faces, which when they were no
longer worn seemed of a tissue as insubstantial as that of the
notules, were such monstrosities as I had not thought existence could support: a circular mouth rimmed with needle
teeth; eyes that were themselves a thousand eyes, clustered
like the scales of a pine cone; jaws like tongs. These things
have remained in my memory as everything remains, and I
have stared again at them in the dark watches of the night. I
am very glad, when at last I rouse myself to turn my face
toward the stars and moon-drenched clouds instead, that I
could see only those nearest our footlights.

I have already said that I fled. But that slight delay, during
which I picked up *Terminus Est* and stood observing Baldanders's mad attack, almost cost me dearly; by the time I
turned to take Dorcas to safety, she was gone.

I ran then not so much from Baldanders's fury, or from the
cacogens in the audience, or from the Autarch's praetorians
(who I felt would surely arrive soon), but in pursuit of
Dorcas. Searching for her and calling her name as I went, I
found nothing but the groves and fountains and abrupt wells
of that endless garden; and at last, winded and with aching
legs, I slowed to a walk.

It is impossible for me to set down on paper all the
bitterness I felt then. To have found Dorcas and lost her so
soon seemed more than I could bear. Women believe—or at
least often pretend to believe—that all our tenderness for
them springs from desire; that we love them when we have
not for a time enjoyed them, and dismiss them when we are
sated, or to express it more precisely, exhausted. There is no
truth in this idea, though it may be made to appear true.
When we are rigid with desire, we are apt to pretend a great
tenderness in the hope of satisfying that desire; but at no
other time are we in fact so liable to treat women brutally,
and so unlikely to feel any deep emotion but one. As I
wandered through the nighted gardens, I felt no physical need
for Dorcas (though I had not enjoyed her since we had slept
in the fortress of the dimarchi, beyond the Sanguinary Fields)
because I had poured out my manhood again and again with

Jolenta in the nenuphar boat. Yet if I had found Dorcas I would have smothered her with kisses; and for Jolenta, whom I had been prone to dislike, I now had conceived a certain affection.

Neither Dorcas nor Jolenta appeared, nor did I see hastening soldiers or even the revelers we had come to entertain. The thiasus, it seemed clear, had been confined to some certain part of the grounds; and I was now far from that part. Even now, I am unsure how far the House Absolute extends. There are maps, but they are incomplete and contradictory. There are no maps of the Second House, and even Father Inire tells me that he has long ago forgotten many of its mysteries. In wandering its narrow corridors, I have seen no white wolves; but I have found stairs leading to domes beneath the river, and hatches opening into what appears to be untouched forest. (Some of these are marked above ground by ruinous, half-overgrown marble steles; some are not.) When I have closed such hatches and retreated regretfully into an artificial air still laced with the odors of vegetable growth and decay, I have often wondered whether some passage or other does not reach the Citadel. Old Ultan hinted once that his library stacks extended to the House Absolute. What is that but to say that the House Absolute extended to his library stacks? There are parts of the Second House that are not unlike the blind corridors in which I searched for Triskele; perhaps they are the same corridors, though if they are, I ran a greater risk than I then knew.

Whether these speculations of mine are rooted in fact or not, I had no notion of them at the time of which I write now. In my innocence I supposed that the borders of the House Absolute, which extended both in space and in time so much further than the uninformed would guess, could be strictly delimited; and that I was approaching, or would soon approach, or had already passed them. Thus I walked all that night, directing my course northward by the stars. And as I walked, I reviewed my life in just the way I have so often attempted to prevent myself from doing while I waited for sleep. Again Drotte and Roche and I swam in the clammy cistern beneath the Bell Keep; again I replaced Josephina's toy imp with the stolen frog; again I stretched forth my hand to grasp the haft of the ax that would have slain the great Vodalus and so saved a Thecla not yet imprisoned; again I saw the ribbon of crimson creep from under Thecla's door, Malrubius bending over me, Jonas vanishing into the infinity between dimensions. I played again with pebbles in the courtyard beside the fallen curtain wall, as Thecla dodged the hooves of my father's mounted guard.

Long after I had seen the last balustrade, I feared the soldiers of the Autarch; but after some time, when I had not so much as glimpsed a distant patrol, I grew contemptuous of them, believing their ineffectiveness to be a part of that general disorganization I had observed in the Commonwealth so often. With or without my help, Vodalus, I felt, would surely destroy such bunglers—indeed, could do so now, if he would only strike.

And yet the androgyne in the yellow robe, who had known Vodalus's password and received his message as if expecting it, was unquestionably the Autarch, the master of those soldiers and in fact of the entire Commonwealth insofar as it recognized a master. Thecla had seen him often; those memories of Thecla's were now my own, and it was he. If Vodalus had won already, why did he remain in hiding? Or was Vodalus merely a creature of the Autarch's? (If so, why did Vodalus refer to the Autarch as though he were a servitor?) I tried to persuade myself that everything that had passed in the chamber of the picture and the rest of the Second House had been a dream; but I knew it was not so, and the steel was gone.

Thinking of Vodalus reminded me of the Claw, which the Autarch himself had urged me to return to the order of priestesses called Pelerines. I drew it out. Its light was soft now, neither flashing as it had been in the mine of the man-apes nor dull as it had been when Jonas and I had examined it in the antechamber. Though it lay upon the palm of my hand, it seemed to me now a great pool of blue water, purer than the cistern, purer far than Gyoll, into which I might dive . . . though in doing so I should in some incomprehensible fashion be diving *up*. It was at once comforting and disquieting, and I pushed it into my boot top again and walked on.

Dawn found me on a narrow path that straggled through a forest more sumptuous in its decay even than that outside the Wall of Nessus. The cool fern arches I had seen there were absent here, but fleshy-fingered vines clung to the great mahoganies and rain-trees like hetaerae, turning their long limbs to clouds of floating green and lowering rich curtains spangled with flowers. Birds unknown to me called overhead, and once a monkey who might, save for his four hands, have been a wizened, red-bearded man in fur, spied on me from a fork as high as a spire. When I could walk no farther, I found a dry, well-shaded spot between pillar-thick roots and wrapped myself in my cloak.

Often I have had to hunt down sleep as though it were the most elusive of chimeras, half legend and half air. Now it sprang upon me. I had no sooner closed my eyes than I faced the maddened giant again. This time I held *Terminus Est,* but she seemed no more than a wand. Instead of the stage, we stood upon a narrow parapet. To one side flamed the torches of an army. On the other a sheer drop terminated in a spreading lake that at once was and was not the azure pool of the Claw. Baldanders lifted his terrible flambeau, and I had somehow become the childish figure I had seen beneath the sea. The gigantic women, I felt, could not be far away. The mace crashed down.

It was broad afternoon, and flame-colored ants were making a caravan across my chest. After two or three watches spent in walking among the pale leaves of that noble yet doomed forest, I struck a broader path, and in another watch (when the shadows were lengthening) I halted, sniffed the air, and found that the odor I had detected was indeed the reek of smoke. I was wracked with hunger by that time, and I hurried forward.

XXVI

Parting

Where the path crossed another, four people sat on the ground around a tiny fire. I recognized Jolenta first—her aura of beauty made the clearing seem a paradise. At almost the same moment, Dorcas recognized me and came running to kiss me, and I glimpsed Dr. Talos's foxlike face over Baldanders's massive shoulder.

The giant, whom I ought to have known at once, was changed almost out of recognition. His head was swathed in dirty bandages, and in place of the baggy black coat he had worn, his wide back was covered with a sticky ointment that resembled clay and smelled like stagnant water.

"Well met, well met," Dr. Talos called. "We've all been wondering what became of you." Baldanders indicated with a slight inclination of his head that it was actually Dorcas who had been wondering, which I think I might have guessed without the hint.

"I ran," I said. "So did Dorcas, I know. I'm surprised the rest of you weren't killed."

"We very nearly were," the doctor admitted, nodding.

Jolenta shrugged, making the simple movement seem an exquisite ceremony. "I ran away, too." She cupped her huge breasts with her hands. "But I don't think I'm well suited to running, do you? Anyway, in the dark I soon bumped against an exultant who told me I would have to run no farther, that he would protect me. But then some spahis came—I would like to have their animals harnessed to my carriage someday, they were very fine—and they had with them a high official of the sort that cares nothing for women. I hoped then that I would be taken to the Autarch—whose pores outshine the stars themselves—the way it nearly happens in the play. But they made my exultant leave, and instead it was back to the theater where he," she gestured toward Baldanders, "and the doctor were. The doctor was putting salve on him, and the soldiers were going to kill us, although I could see they didn't really want to kill me. Then they let us go, and here we are."

Dr. Talos added, "We found Dorcas at daybreak. Or rather, she found us, and we have been traveling slowly toward the mountains ever since. Slowly, because ill though he is, Baldanders is the only one of us with the strength to carry our baggage, and though we have discarded much of it, there remain certain items we must keep."

I said I was surprised to hear Baldanders was merely ill, since I had been certain he was dead.

"Dr. Talos stopped him," Dorcas said. "Isn't that right, Doctor? That's how he was captured. It's surprising that both of them weren't killed."

"Yet as you see," Dr. Talos said, smiling, "we yet walk among the living. And though we are somewhat the worse for wear, we are rich. Show Severian our money, Baldanders."

Painfully, the giant shifted his position and took out a bulging leather purse. After looking at the doctor as though for additional instructions, he loosened the strings and poured into his huge hand a shower of new-minted chrisos.

Dr. Talos took one of the coins and held it up so it caught the light. "How long do you think a man from one of the fishing villages about Lake Diuturna would build walls for that?"

I said, "At least a year, I should imagine."

"Two! Every day, winter and summer, rain or shine, provided we dole it out in bits of copper, as we shall. We'll have fifty such men to help rebuild our home. Wait until you see it next!"

Baldanders added in his heavy voice, "If they will work."

The red-haired doctor whirled on him. "They'll work! I've learned something since last time, let me tell you!"

I interposed. "I assume that a part of that money is mine, and that a part belongs to these women—does it not?"

Dr. Talos relaxed. "Oh, yes. I had forgotten. The women have already had their shares. Half of this is yours. After all, we wouldn't have had it without you." He scooped the coins out of the giant's hand and began to create two stacks on the ground before him.

I supposed that he meant only that I had contributed to the success of his play, such as it was. But Dorcas, who must have sensed that something more lay behind the credit he had given me, asked, "Why do you say that, Doctor?"

The fox-face smiled. "Severian has friends in high places. I own I have thought so for some time—a torturer wandering the roads like a vagrant was a bit too much even for Baldanders to swallow, and I have, I fear, an excessively narrow throat."

"If I have such friends," I said, "I am unaware of them."

The stacks were level now, and the doctor pushed one toward me and the other back to the giant. "At first, when I found you abed with Baldanders, I thought you might have been sent to warn us against performing my play—in some respects it is, as you may have observed, at least in appearance critical of the Autarchy."

"Somewhat," Jolenta lisped sarcastically.

"Yet, surely, to send a torturer from the Citadel to frighten a couple of strolling mountebanks would be an absurd overreaction. Then I realized that we, by the very fact that we were staging the play, served to conceal you. Few would suspect that a servant of the Autarch would associate himself with such an enterprise. I wrote in the Familiar's part so that we should hide you better by giving your habit a reason for existence."

"I know nothing of this," I said.

"Of course. I have no desire to force you to violate your trust. But as we were setting up our theater yesterday, a highly placed servant from the House Absolute—an agamite, I think, and they are always close to the ear of authority—came asking if our troupe was the one in which you performed, and if you were with us. You and Jolenta had absented yourselves, but I answered in the affirmative. He asked then how great a share you had of what we made, and when I told him, said that he was instructed to pay us now for the night's performance. Very fortunate that proved, since this great ninny went charging out into our audience."

It was one of the few times I saw Baldanders appear hurt by his physician's jibes. Though it clearly cost him pain to do so, he swung his big body about until he faced away from us.

Dorcas had told me that when I had slept in Dr. Talos's tent, I had slept alone. Now I sensed that the giant felt so; that for him the clearing held only himself and certain small animals, pets of whom he was tiring.

"He has paid for his rashness," I said. "He looks badly burned."

The doctor nodded. "Actually, Baldanders was fortunate. The Hierodules dialed down their beams and tried to turn him back instead of killing him. He lives now through their forbearance, and will regenerate."

Dorcas murmured, "Heal, you mean? I trust so. I feel more pity for him than I can say."

"Yours is a tender heart. Too tender, perhaps. But Baldanders is still growing, and growing children have great recuperative powers."

"Still growing?" I asked. "His hair is partly gray."

The doctor laughed. "Then perhaps he is growing grayer. But now, dear friends," he rose and dusted his trousers, "now we have come, as some poet aptly puts it, to the place where men are pulled apart by their destinations. We had halted here, Severian, not only because we were fatigued, but because it is here that the route toward Thrax, where you are going, and that toward Lake Diuturna and our own country diverge. I was loath to pass this point, the last at which I had hopes of seeing you, without making a fair division of our gains—but that is accomplished now. Should you communicate again with your benefactors in the House Absolute, will you own that you have been equitably dealt with?"

The stack of chrisos was still on the ground before me. "There is a hundred times more here than I ever expected to receive," I said. "Yes. Certainly." I picked up the coins and put them into my sabretache.

A glance passed between Dorcas and Jolenta, and Dorcas said, "I am going to Thrax with Severian, if that is where Severian is going."

Jolenta held up a hand to the doctor, obviously expecting that he would help her to rise.

"Baldanders and I will be traveling alone," he said, "and we will walk all night. We will miss all of you, but the time of parting is upon us. Dorcas, my child, I am delighted that you will have a protector." (Jolenta's hand was by this time on his thigh.) "Come, Baldanders, we must be away."

The giant lumbered to his feet, and though he made no

moan, I could see how much he suffered. His bandages were wet with mingled sweat and blood. I knew what I had to do, and said, "Baldanders and I must speak privately for a moment. Could I ask the rest of you to move off a hundred paces or so?"

The women began to do as I had asked, Dorcas walking down one path and Jolenta (whom Dorcas had helped up) down another; but Dr. Talos remained where he was until I repeated my request that he go.

"You wish me to leave as well? It's quite useless. Baldanders will tell me anything you tell him as soon as we are together again. Jolenta! Come here, dear."

"She is leaving at my request, just as I asked you to."

"Yes, but she's going the wrong way, and I cannot have it. Jolenta!"

"Doctor, I only wish to help your friend—or your slave, or whatever he is."

Quite unexpectedly, Baldanders's deep voice issued from beneath his swirl of bandages. "I am his master."

"Exactly so," said the doctor, as taking up the stack of chrisos he had pushed toward Baldanders, he dropped it into the giant's trousers pocket.

Jolenta had hobbled back to us with tears streaking her lovely face. "Doctor, can't I go with you?"

"Of course not," he said as coolly as if a child had asked for a second slice of cake. Jolenta collapsed at his feet.

I looked up at the giant. "Baldanders, I can help you. A friend of mine was burned as much as you are not long ago, and I was able to help him. But I won't do it while Dr. Talos and Jolenta look on. Will you come with me, only a short way, back down the path toward the House Absolute?"

Slowly, the giant's head swung from side to side.

"He knows the lenitive you offer," Dr. Talos said, laughing. "He himself has provided it to many, but he loves life too much."

"Life is what I offer—not death."

"Yes?" The doctor raised an eyebrow. "Where is your friend?"

The giant had picked up the handles of his barrow. "Baldanders," I said, "do you know who the Conciliator was?"

"That was long ago," Baldanders answered. "It does not matter." He started down the path Dorcas had not taken. Dr.

Talos followed him for a few strides, with Jolenta clinging to his arm, then stopped.

"Severian, you have guarded a good many prisoners, according to what you've told me. If Baldanders were to give you another chrisos, would you hold this creature until we are well gone?"

I was still sick with the thought of the giant's pain and my own failure; but I managed to say, "As a member of the guild, I can accept commissions only from the legally constituted authorities."

"We will kill her then, when we are out of your sight."

"That is a matter between you and her," I said, and started after Dorcas.

I had hardly caught up with her before we heard Jolenta's screams. Dorcas halted and grasped my hand more tightly, asking what the sound was; I told her of the doctor's threat.

"And you let her go?"

"I didn't believe he meant it."

As I said that, we had turned and were already retracing our way. We had not gone a dozen strides before the screams were succeeded by a silence so profound we could hear the rustling of a dying leaf. We hurried on; but by the time we reached the crossing, I felt certain we were too late, and so I was, if the truth be known, only hurrying because I knew Dorcas would be disappointed in me if I did not.

I was wrong in thinking Jolenta dead. As we rounded a turn in the path we saw her running toward us, her knees together as if her legs were hampered by her generous thighs, her arms crossed over her breasts to steady them. Her glorious red-gold hair fell across her eyes, and the thin organza shift she wore had been slashed to tatters. She fainted when Dorcas embraced her. "Those devils, they've beaten her," Dorcas said.

"A moment ago we were afraid they would kill her." I looked at the welts on the beautiful woman's back. "These are the marks of the doctor's cane, I think. She's lucky he didn't set Baldanders on her."

"But what can we do?"

"We can try this." I fished the Claw from my boot top and showed it to her. "Do you remember the thing we found in my sabretache? That you said was no true gem? This is what it was, and it seems to help injured people, sometimes. I wanted to use it on Baldanders, but he wouldn't let me."

I held the Claw over Jolenta's head, then ran it along the bruises on her back, but it flamed no brighter and she seemed no better. "It isn't working," I said. "I'll have to carry her."

"Put her over your shoulder, or you'll be holding her just where she's been hurt worst."

Dorcas carried *Terminus Est,* and I did as she suggested, finding Jolenta nearly as heavy as a man. For a long while we trudged thus beneath the pale green canopy of the leaves before Jolenta's eyes opened. Even then she could hardly walk or stand without help, however, or so much as comb back that extraordinary hair with her fingers to let us better see the tear-stained oval of her face.

"The doctor won't let me come with him," she said.

Dorcas nodded. "It seems not." She might have been talking to someone far younger than herself.

"I will be destroyed."

I asked why she said that, but she only shook her head. After a time she said, "May I go with you, Severian? I don't have any money. Baldanders took away what the doctor had given me." She shot a sidelong glance at Dorcas. "She has money too—more than I got. As much as the doctor gave you."

"He knows that," Dorcas said. "And he knows any money I have is his, if he wants it."

I changed the subject. "Perhaps both of you should know that I may not be going to Thrax, or at least, not directly. Not if I can discover the whereabouts of the order of Pelerines."

Jolenta looked at me as if I were mad. "I've heard they roam the whole world. Besides, they accept only women."

"I don't want to join them, only to find them. The last news I had was that they were on the way north. But if I can find out where they are, I'll have to go there—even if it means turning south again."

"I'm going where you go," Dorcas declared. "Not to Thrax."

"And I'm going nowhere," Jolenta sighed.

As soon as we no longer had to support Jolenta, Dorcas and I drew somewhat ahead of her. When we had been walking for some time, I turned to look back at her. She was no longer weeping, but I hardly recognized the beauty who had once accompanied Dr. Talos. She had held her head proudly, and even arrogantly. Her shoulders had been thrown back and her magnificent eyes had flashed like emeralds. Now her shoulders drooped with weariness and she looked at the ground.

"What was it you spoke of with the doctor and the giant?" Dorcas asked as we walked.

"I've already told you," I said.

"Once you called out so loudly that I could hear what you said. It was 'Do you know who the Conciliator was?' But I couldn't tell if you didn't know yourself, or were only seeking to discover if they knew."

"I know very little—nothing, really. I've seen pictures that are supposed to be of him, but they differ so much they can hardly be of the same man."

"There are legends."

"Most of them I've heard sound very foolish. I wish Jonas were here; he would take care of Jolenta, and he would know about the Conciliator. Jonas was the man we met at the Piteous Gate, the man who rode the merychip. For a time he was a good friend to me."

"Where is he now?"

"That's what Dr. Talos wanted to know. I don't know, and I don't wish to speak of it. Tell me about the Conciliator, if you want to talk."

No doubt it was foolish, but as soon as I mentioned that name, I felt the silence of the forest like a weight. The sighing of a little wind somewhere among the uppermost branches might have been the sigh from a sickbed; the pale green of the light-starved leaves suggested the pallid faces of starved children.

"No one knows much about him," Dorcas began, "and I probably know less than you do. I don't even remember now how I learned what I know. Anyway some people say he was hardly more than a boy. Some say he was not a human being at all—not a cacogen, but the thought, tangible to us, of some vast intelligence to whom our actuality is no more real than the paper theaters of the toy sellers. The story goes that he once took a dying woman by the hand and a star by the other, and from that time forward he had the power to reconcile the universe with humanity, and humanity with the universe, ending the old breach. He had a way of vanishing, then reappearing when everyone thought he was dead— reappearing sometimes after he had been buried. He might be encountered as an animal, speaking the human tongue, and he appeared to some pious woman or other in the form of roses."

I recalled my masking. "Holy Katharine, I suppose, at her execution."

"There are darker legends, too."

"Tell them to me."

"They frightened me," Dorcas said. "Now I don't even remember them. Doesn't that brown book you carry with you make any mention of him?"

I drew it out and saw that it did, and then, since I could not comfortably read while we walked, I thrust it back in my sabretache again, resolving to read that section when we camped, as we would have to soon.

XXVII

Toward Thrax

Our path ran through the stricken forest for as long as the light lasted; a watch after dark we reached the edge of a river smaller and swifter than Gyoll, where by moonlight we could see broad cane fields on the farther side waving in the night wind. Jolenta had been sobbing with weariness for some distance, and Dorcas and I agreed to halt. Since I would never have risked *Terminus Est*'s honed blade on the heavy limbs of the forest trees, we would have had little firewood there; such dead branches as we had come across had been soaked with moisture and were already spongy with decay. The riverbank provided an abundance of twisted, weathered sticks, hard and light and dry.

We had broken a good many and laid our fire before I remembered I no longer had my striker, having left it with the Autarch, who must also, I felt certain, have been the "highly placed servant" who had filled Dr. Talos's hands with chrisos. Dorcas had flint, steel, and tinder among her scant baggage, however, and we were soon comforted by a roaring blaze. Jolenta was fearful of wild beasts, though I labored to explain to her how unlikely it was that the soldiers would permit anything dangerous to live in a forest that ran up to the gardens of the House Absolute. For her sake we burned three thick brands at one end only, so that if need arose we could snatch them from the fire and threaten the creatures she dreaded.

No beasts came, our fire drove off the mosquitoes, and we lay upon our backs and watched the sparks mount into the

air. Far higher, the lights of fliers passed to and fro, filling
the sky for a moment or two with a ghostly false dawn as the
ministers and generals of the Autarch returned to the House
Absolute or went forth to war. Dorcas and I speculated about
what they might think when they looked down—for only an
instant as they were whirled away—and saw our scarlet star;
and we decided that they must wonder about us much as we
wondered about them, pondering who we might be, and
where we went, and why. Dorcas sang a song for me, a song
about a girl who wanders through a grove in spring, lonely for
her friends of the year before, the fallen leaves.

Jolenta lay between our fire and the water, I suppose
because she felt safer there. Dorcas and I were on the
opposite side of the fire, not only because we wanted to be
out of her sight as nearly as possible, but because Dorcas, as
she told me, disliked the sight and sound of the cold, dark
stream slipping by. "Like a worm," she said. "A big ebony
snake that is not hungry now, but knows where we are and
will eat us by and by. Aren't you afraid of snakes, Severian?"

Thecla had been; I felt the shade of her fear stir at the
question and nodded.

"I've heard that in the hot forests of the north, the Autarch
of All Serpents is Uroboros, the brother of Abaia, and that
hunters who discover his burrow believe they have found a
tunnel under the sea, and descending it enter his mouth and
all unknowing climb down his throat, so that they are dead
while they still believe themselves living; though there are
others who say that Uroboros is only the great river there that
flows to its own source, or the sea itself, that devours its own
beginnings."

Dorcas edged closer as she recounted all this, and I put my
arm about her, knowing that she wanted me to make love to
her, though we could not be sure Jolenta was asleep on the
other side of the fire. Indeed, from time to time she stirred,
seeming because of her full hips, narrow waist, and billowing
hair, to undulate like a serpent herself. Dorcas lifted her
small tragically clean face to mine, and I kissed her and felt
her press herself to me, trembling with desire.

"I am so cold," she whispered.

She was naked, though I had not seen her undress. When I
put my cloak about her, her skin felt flushed—as my own
was—from the heat of the blaze. Her little hands slipped
under my clothes, caressing me.

"So good," she said. "So smooth." And then (though we had coupled before), "Won't I be too small?", like a child.

When I woke, the moon (it was almost beyond belief that it was the same moon that had guided me through the gardens of the House Absolute) had nearly been overtaken by the mounting horizon of the west. Its berylline light streamed down the river, giving to every ripple the black shadow of a wave.

I felt uneasy without knowing why. Jolenta's fears of beasts no longer seemed so foolish as they had, and I got up and, after making certain she and Dorcas were unharmed, found more wood for our dying fire. I remembered the notules, which Jonas had told me were often sent forth by night, and the thing in the antechamber. Night birds sailed overhead—not only owls, such as we had in plenty nesting in the ruined towers of the Citadel, birds marked by their round heads and short, broad, silent wings, but birds of other kinds with two-forked and three-forked tails, birds that stooped to skim the water and twittered as they flew. Occasionally, moths vastly larger than any I had seen before passed from tree to tree. Their figured wings were as long as a man's arms, and they spoke among themselves as men do, but in voices almost too high for hearing.

After I had stirred the fire, made sure of my sword, and looked for a time on Dorcas's innocent face with its great, tender eyelashes closed in sleep, I lay down again to watch the birds voyage among the constellations and enter that world of memory that, no matter how sweet or how bitter it may be, is never wholly closed to me.

I sought to recall that celebration of Holy Katharine's day that fell the year after I became captain of apprentices; but the preparations for the feast were hardly begun before other memories came crowding unbidden around it. In our kitchen I lifted a cup of stolen wine to my lips—and found it had become a breast running with warm milk. It was my mother's breast then, and I could hardly contain my elation (which might have wiped the memory away) at having reached back at last to her, after so many fruitless attempts. My arms sought to clasp her, and I would, if only I could, have lifted my eyes to look into her face. My mother certainly, for the children the torturers take know no breasts. The grayness at the edge of my field of vision, then, was the metal of her cell wall. Soon she would be led away to scream in the Apparatus or gasp in Allowin's Necklace. I sought to hold her back, to mark the moment so I might return to it when I chose; she faded even as I tried to bind her to me, dissolving as mist does when the wind rises.

I was a child again . . . a girl . . . Thecla. I stood in a magnificent chamber whose windows were mirrors, mirrors that at once illuminated and reflected. Around me were beautiful women twice my height or more, in various stages of undress. The air was thick with scent. I was searching for someone, but as I looked at the painted faces of the tall women, lovely and indeed perfect, I began to doubt if I should know her. Tears rolled down my cheeks. Three women ran to me and I stared from one to another. As I did, their eyes narrowed to points of light, and a heart-shaped patch beside the lips of the nearest spread webfingered wings.

"Severian."

I sat up, uncertain of the point at which memory had become dream. This voice was sweet, yet very deep, and though I was conscious of having heard it before, I could not at once recall where. The moon was nearly behind the western horizon now, and our fire was dying a second death. Dorcas had thrown aside her ragged bedding, so that she slept with her sprite's body exposed to the night air. Seeing her thus, her pale skin rendered more pale still by the waning moonlight, save where the glow of the embers flushed it with red, I felt such desire as I had never known—not when I had clasped Agia to me on the Adamnian Steps, not when I had first seen Jolenta on Dr. Talos's stage, not even on the innumerable occasions when I had hastened to Thecla in her cell. Yet it was not Dorcas I desired; I had enjoyed her only a short time ago, and though I fully believed she loved me, I could not be certain she would have given herself so readily if she had not more than suspected I had entered Jolenta on the afternoon before the play, and if she had not believed Jolenta to be watching us across the fire.

Nor did I desire Jolenta, who lay upon her side and snored. Instead I wanted them both, and Thecla, and the nameless meretrix who had feigned to be Thecla in the House Azure, and her friend who had taken the part of Thea, the woman I had seen on the stair in the House Absolute. And Agia, Valeria, Morwenna, and a thousand more. I recalled the witches, their madness and their wild dancing in the Old

Court on nights of rain; the cool, virginal beauty of the red-robed Pelerines.

"*Severian.*"

It was no dream. Sleepy birds, perched on branches at the margin of the forest, had stirred at the sound. I drew *Terminus Est* and let her blade catch the cold dawn light, so that whoever had spoken should know me armed.

All was quiet again—quieter now than it had ever been by night. I waited, turning my head slowly in my attempt to locate the one who had called my name, though I was conscious it would have been better if I could have appeared to know the correct direction already. Dorcas stirred and moaned, but neither she nor Jolenta woke; there was no other sound but the crackling of the fire, the dawn wind among the leaves, and the lapping water.

"Where are you?" I whispered, but there was no reply. A fish jumped with a silver splash, and all was silent again.

"*Severian.*"

However deep, it was a woman's voice, throbbing with passion, moist with need; I remembered Agia and did not sheathe my sword.

"*The sandbar . . .*"

Though I feared it was merely a trick to make me turn my back on the trees, I let my eyes search the river until I saw it, about two hundred paces from our fire.

"*Come to me.*"

It was no trick, or at least not the trick I had at first feared. It was from downstream that the voice spoke.

"*Come. Please. I cannot hear you where you stand.*"

I said, "I did not speak," but there was no reply. I waited, reluctant to leave Dorcas and Jolenta alone.

"*Please. When the sun reaches this water, I must go. There may be no other chance.*"

The little river was wider at the sandbar than below or above it, and I could walk upon the yellow sand itself, dryshod, nearly to the center. To my left the greenish water gradually narrowed and deepened. To my right lay a deep pool perhaps twenty paces wide, from which water flowed swiftly yet smoothly. I stood on the sand with *Terminus Est* gripped in both hands, her square point buried between my feet. "I'm here," I said. "Where are you? Can you hear me now?"

As though the river itself were replying, three fish leaped at once, then leaped again, making a series of soft explosions on the surface. A moccasin, his brown back marked with linked rings of gold and black, glided up almost at my boot toes, turned as if to menace the jumping fish and hissed, then entered the ford on the upper side of the bar and swam away in long undulations. Through the body, he had been as thick as my forearm.

"Do not fear. Look. See me. Know that I will not harm you."

Green though the water had been, it grew greener still. A thousand jade tentacles writhed there, never breaking the surface. As I watched, too fascinated to be afraid, a disc of white three paces across appeared among them, rising slowly toward the surface.

It was not until it was within a few spans of the ripples that I understood what it was—and then only because it opened its eyes. A face looked through the water at me, the face of a woman who might have dandled Baldanders like a toy. Her eyes were scarlet, and her mouth was bordered by full lips so darkly crimson I had not at first thought them lips at all. Behind them stood an army of pointed teeth; the green tendrils that framed her face were her floating hair.

"I have come for you, Severian," she said. *"No, you are not dreaming."*

XXVIII

The Odalisque of Abaia

I said, "Once before I dreamed of you." Dimly, I could see her naked body in the water, immense and gleaming.

"We watched the giant, and so found you. Alas, we lost sight of you too soon, when you and he separated. You believed then that you were hated, and did not know how much you were loved. The seas of the whole world shook with our mourning for you, and the waves wept salt tears and threw themselves despairing upon the rocks."

"And what is it you want of me?"

"Only your love. Only your love."

Her right hand came to the surface as she spoke, and floated there like a raft of five white logs. Here, truly, was the hand of the ogre, whose fingertip held the map of his domain.

"Am I not fair? Where have you beheld skin clearer than mine, or redder lips?"

"You are breathtaking," I said truthfully. "But may I ask why you were observing Baldanders when I met him? And why you were not observing me, though it seems you wished to?"

"We watch the giant because he grows. In that he is like us, and like our father-husband, Abaia. Eventually he must come to the water, when the land can bear him no longer. But you may come now, if you will. You will breathe—by our gift—as easily as you breathe the thin, weak wind here, and whenever you wish you shall return to the land and take up your crown. This river Cephissus flows to Gyoll, and Gyoll to the peaceful sea. There you may ride dolphin-back through current-swept fields of coral and pearl. My sisters and I will show you the

forgotten cities built of old, where a hundred trapped genera-
tions of your kin bred and died when they had been forgotten
by you above."

"I have no crown to take up," I said. "You mistake me for
someone else."

"All of us will be yours there, in the red and white parks
where the lionfish school."

As the undine spoke, she slowly lifted her chin, allowing
her head to fall back until the whole plane of face lay at an
equal depth, and only just submerged. Her white throat
followed, and crimson-tipped breasts broke the surface, so
that little lapping waves caressed their sides. A thousand
bubbles sparkled in the water. In the space of a few breaths
she lay at full length upon the current, forty cubits at least
from alabaster feet to twining hair.

No one who reads, this, perhaps, will understand how I
could be drawn to so monstrous a thing; yet I wanted to
believe her, to go with her, as a drowning man wants to gasp
air. If I had fully credited her promises, I would have plunged
into the pool at that moment, forgetting everything else.

"You have a crown, though you know not of it yet. Do you
think that we, who swim in so many waters—even between the
stars—are confined to a single instant? We have seen what you
will become, and what you have been. Only yesterday you lay
in the hollow of my palm, and I lifted you above the clotted
weed lest you die in Gyoll, saving you for this moment."

"Give me the power to breathe water," I said, "and let me
test it on the other side of the sandbar. If I find you have told
the truth, I will go with you."

I watched those huge lips part. I cannot say how loudly she
spoke in the river that I should hear her where I stood in air;
but again fish leaped at her words.

"It is not so easily done as that. You must come with me,
trusting, though it is only a moment. Come."

She extended her hand toward me, and at the same
moment I heard Dorcas's agonized voice crying for help.

I turned to run to her. Yet if the undine had waited, I think
I might have turned back. She did not. The river itself seemed
to heave from its bed with a roar like breaking surf. It was as
though a lake had been flung at my head, and it struck me like
a stone and tumbled me in its wash like a stick. A moment
later, when it receded, I found myself far up the bank, soaked
and bruised and swordless. Fifty paces away the undine's
white body rose half out of the river. Without the support of

the water her flesh sagged on bones that seemed ready to snap under its weight, and her hair hung lank to the soaking sand. Even as I watched, water mingled with blood ran from her nostrils.

I fled, and by the time I reached Dorcas at our fire, the undine was gone save for a swirl of silt that darkened the river below the sandbar.

Dorcas's face was nearly as white. "What was that?" she whispered. "Where were you?"

"You saw her then. I was afraid . . ."

"How horrible." Dorcas had thrown herself into my arms, pressing her body to mine. "Horrible."

"That wasn't why you called, though, was it? You couldn't have seen her from here until she rose out of the pool."

Dorcas pointed mutely toward the farther side of the fire, and I saw the ground was soaked with blood where Jolenta lay.

There were two narrow cuts in her left wrist, each about the length of my thumb; and though I touched them with the Claw, it seemed the blood that welled from them would not clot. When we had soaked several bandages torn from Dorcas's scant store of clothing, I boiled thread and needle in a little pan she had and sewed the edges of the wounds shut. Through all this Jolenta seemed less than half conscious; from time to time her eyes opened, but they closed again almost immediately, and there was no recognition in them. She spoke only once, saying, "Now you see that he, whom you have esteemed your divinity, would countenance and advise all I have proposed to you. Before the New Sun rises, let us make a new beginning." At the time, I did not recognize it as one of her lines.

When her wound no longer bled, and we had shifted her to clean ground and washed her, I went back to the place where I had found myself when the water receded, and after some searching discovered *Terminus Est* with only her pommel and two fingers' width of hilt protruding from the wet sand.

I cleaned and oiled the blade, and Dorcas and I discussed what we should do. I told her of my dream, the night before I met Baldanders and Dr. Talos, and then about hearing the undine's voice while she and Jolenta slept, and what she had said.

"Is she still there, do you think? You were down there when you found your sword. Could you have seen her through the water if she were near the bottom?"

I shook my head. "I don't believe she is. She injured herself in some way when she tried to leave the river to stop me, and from the pallor of her skin, I doubt she would stay long in any water shallower than Gyoll's under the sun of a clear day. But no, if she had been there I don't think I would have seen her—the water was too roiled."

Dorcas, who had never looked more charming than at this moment, sitting on the ground with her chin propped on one knee, was silent for a time, and seemed to watch the eastern clouds, dyed cerise and flame by the eternal mysterious hope of dawn. At length she said, "She must have wanted you very badly."

"To have come up out of the water like that? I think she must have been on land before she had become so large, and she forgot for a moment at least that she could no longer do it."

"But before that she swam up filthy Gyoll, and then up this narrow little river. She must have been hoping to seize you when we crossed, but she found she could not get above the sandbar, and so she called you down. Altogether, it can't have been a pleasant trip for someone accustomed to swimming between the stars."

"You believe her, then?"

"When I was with Dr. Talos and you were gone, he and Jolenta used to tell me what a simple-minded person I was for believing people we met on the road, and things that Baldanders said, and things they said themselves, too. Just the same, I think that even the people who are called liars tell the truth much more often than they lie. It's so much easier! If that story about saving you wasn't true, why tell it? It could only frighten you when you thought back on it. And if she *doesn't* swim between stars, what a useless thing to say. Something's bothering you, though. I can see it. What is it?"

I did not want to describe my meeting with the Autarch in detail, so I said, "Not long ago I saw a picture—in a book—of a being who lives in the gulf. She was winged. Not like birds' wings, but enormous continuous planes of thin, pigmented material. Wings that could beat against the starlight."

Dorcas looked interested. "Is it in your brown book?"

"No, another book. I don't have it here."

"Just the same, it reminds me that we were going to see what your brown book has to say about the Conciliator. Do you still have it?"

"I did, and I drew it out. It was damp from my wetting, so I opened it and laid it where the sun would strike its leaves, and the breezes that had sprung up as Urth's face looked on his again would play over them. After that, the pages turned gently as we talked, so that pictures of men and women and monsters took my eye between our words, and thus engraved themselves on my mind, so that they are there yet. Occasionally too, phrases, and even short passages, glowed and faded as the light caught, then released, the sheen of the metallic ink: "soulless warrior!" "lucid yellow," "by noyade." Later: "These times are the ancient times, when the world is ancient." And: "Hell has no limits, nor is circumscribed; for where we are is Hell, and where Hell is, there we must be."

"You don't want to read it now?" Dorcas asked.

"No. I want to hear what happened to Jolenta."

"I don't know. I was sleeping and dreaming of . . . the kind of thing I always do. And I went into a toy shop. There were shelves along the wall with dolls on them, and a well in the center of the floor with dolls sitting on the coping. I remember thinking that my baby was too young for dolls, but they were so pretty, and I had not had one since I was a little girl, so I would buy one and keep it for the baby, and meanwhile I could take it out sometimes and look at it, and perhaps make it stand before the mirror in my room. I pointed to the most beautiful one, which was one of those on the coping, and when the shopman picked it up for me I saw it was Jolenta, and it slipped from his hands. I saw it falling down very far, toward the black water. Then I woke up. Naturally I looked to see if she was all right . . ."

"And you found her bleeding?"

Dorcas nodded, her pale golden hair glinting in the light. "So I called for you—twice—and then I saw you down by the sandbar, and that thing came out of the water after you."

"There's no reason for you to look so pale," I told her. "Jolenta was bitten by an animal, that's clear. I've no idea of what kind, but judging from the bite it was a fairly small one, and no more to be feared than any other little animal with sharp teeth and a bad disposition."

"Severian, I remember being told that there were blood bats farther north. When I was just a child, someone used to frighten me by telling me about them. And then when I was older, once a common bat got into the house. Somebody killed it, and I asked my father if it were a blood bat, and if there were really any such things. He said there were, but they lived in the north, in the steaming forests at the center of the world. They bit sleeping people and grazing animals by night, and their spittle was poisoned so that the wounds of their teeth bled on."

Dorcas paused, looking up into the trees. "My father said that the city had been creeping northward along the river for all of history, having begun as an autochthon village where Gyoll joins the sea, and how terrible it would be when it entered the region where the blood bats fly and they could roost in the derelict buildings. It must be terrible already for the people of the House Absolute. We cannot have walked so very far from there."

"The Autarch has my sympathy," I said. "But I don't think I have ever heard you talk so much about your past life before. Do you remember your father now, and the house where the bat was killed?"

She stood; though she tried to look brave, I could see that she was trembling. "I remember more each morning, after my dreams. But, Severian, we must go now. Jolenta will be weak. She must have food, and clean water to drink. We can't stay here."

I was ravenously hungry myself. I put the brown book back into my sabretache and sheathed *Terminus Est*'s freshly oiled blade. Dorcas packed her little bundle of belongings.

Then we set out, fording the river well above the sandbar. Jolenta was unable to walk alone; we had to support her on either side. Her face was drawn, and though she had regained consciousness when we lifted her, she seldom spoke. When she did it was only a word or two. For the first time, I noticed how thin her lips were, and now the lower lip had lost its firmness and hung away from her teeth, showing the livid gums. It seemed to me that her entire body, yesterday so opulent, had softened like wax, so that instead of appearing (as she once had) a woman to Dorcas's child, she seemed a flower too long blown, the very end of summer to Dorcas's spring.

As we walked thus along a narrow, dusty track with sugarcane already higher than my head to either side, I found myself thinking over and over of how I had desired her in the short time I had known her. Memory, so perfect and vivid as to be more compelling than any opiate, showed me the woman as I had believed I had seen her first, when Dorcas and I had come around a grove of trees by night to find Dr. Talos's stage gleaming with lights in a pasture. How strange it had seemed to see her by daylight as perfect as she had ap-

peared in the flattering glow of the flambeaux the night
before, when we set off northward on the most glorious
morning I can remember.

Love and desire are said to be no more than cousins, and I
had found it so until I walked with Jolenta's flaccid arm about
my neck. But it is not really true. Rather, the love of women
was the dark side of a feminine ideal I had nourished for
myself on dreams of Valeria and Thecla and Agia, of Dorcas
and Jolenta and Vodalus's leman of the heart-shaped face and
cooing voice, the woman I now knew to be Thecla's half-sister
Thea. So that as we trudged between the walls of cane, when
desire had fled and I could only look at Jolenta with pity, I
found that though I had believed I cared only for her
importunate, rose-flushed flesh and the awkward grace of her
movements, I loved her.

XXIX

The Herdsmen

For most of the morning we walked through the cane, meeting no one. Jolenta grew neither stronger nor weaker, so far as I could judge; but it seemed to me that hunger, and the fatigue of supporting her, and the pitiless glare of the sun were telling upon me, for twice or thrice, when I glimpsed her from the corner of an eye, it seemed that I was not seeing Jolenta at all, but someone else, a woman I recalled but could not identify. If I turned my head to look at her, this impression (which was always very slight) vanished altogether.

So we walked, talking little. It was the only time since I had received her from Master Palaemon that *Terminus Est* seemed burdensome to me. My shoulder grew raw under the baldric.

I cut cane for us, and we chewed it for the sweet juice. Jolenta was always thirty, and since she could not walk unless we aided her, and could not hold her stalk of cane when we did, we were forced to stop often. It was strange to see those long legs, so beautifully molded, with their slender ankles and ripe thighs, so useless.

In a day we reached the end of the cane and emerged onto the edge of the true pampa, the sea of grass. Here there were still a few trees, though they were so widely scattered that each was in sight of no more than two or three others. To each of these trees the body of some beast of prey was lashed with rawhide, its forepaws outspread like arms. They were mostly the spotted tigers common in that part of the country; but I saw atroxes, too, with hair like man's, and sword-toothed

228

smilodons. Most were hardly more than bones, but some lived and made those sounds that, as the people believe, serve to frighten other tigers, atroxes, and smilodons which, if they were not so frightened, would prey upon the cattle.

These cattle represented a far greater danger to us than the cats did. The herd bulls will charge anything that comes near them, and we were forced to give each herd we came across as much room as would prevent their short-sighted eyes from seeing us, and to move downwind of each. On these occasions, I was forced to let Dorcas prop Jolenta's weight as best she could, so I could walk ahead of them and somewhat nearer the animals. Once I had to leap aside and strike off the head of a bull as it charged. We built a fire of dry grass and roasted some of the meat.

The next time I recalled the Claw, and the way in which it had ended the attack of the man-apes. I drew it out, and the fierce black bull trotted to me and nuzzled my hand. We put Jolenta on his back with Dorcas to hold her on, and I walked beside his head, holding the gem where he could see its blue light.

A living smilodon was bound to the next tree we reached, which was nearly the last we saw, and I was afraid he would frighten the bull. Yet when we passed him I seemed to feel his eyes upon my back, yellow eyes as large as pigeon's eggs. My own tongue was swollen with his thirst. I gave Dorcas the gem to hold and went back and cut him down, thinking all the while that he would surely attack me. He fell to the ground too weak to stand, and I, who had no water to give him, could only walk away.

A little after noon, I noticed a carrion bird circling high above us. It is said they smell death, and I remembered that once or twice when the journeymen were very busy in the examination room, it was necessary for us apprentices to turn out to throw stones at those who settled on the ruined curtain wall, lest they give the Citadel a reputation more evil than it already possessed. The thought that Jolenta might die was repugnant to me, and I would have given much for a bow, so that I might perhaps pick the bird out of the air; but I had nothing of the kind, and could only wish.

After an interminable time, this first bird was joined by two much smaller ones, and from their bright head color, occasionally visible even from so far below, I knew them to be Cathartidae. Thus the first, whose wings had three times the spread of theirs, was a mountain teratornis, the breed that is said to attack climbers, raking their faces with poisoned talons and striking them with the elbows of its great pinions until they fall to their deaths. From time to time the other two approached it too closely, and it turned upon them. When that occurred, we sometimes heard a shrill cry come drifting down from the ramparts of their castle of air. Once, in a macabre mood, I gestured for the birds to join us. All three dove, and I brandished my sword at them and gestured no more.

When the western horizon had climbed nearly to the sun, we reached a low house, scarcely more than a hut, built of turf. A wiry man in leather leggings sat on a bench before it, drinking maté and pretending to watch the colors in the clouds. In truth, he must have seen us long before we saw him, for he was small and brown and blended well with his small, brown home, while we had been silhouetted against the sky.

I thrust away the Claw when I saw this herdsman, though I was not certain what the bull would do when it was no longer in his sight. In the event he did nothing, plodding ahead with the two women on his back as before. When we reached the sod house I lifted them down, and he raised his muzzle and sniffed the wind, then looked at me from one eye. I waved toward the undulating grass, both to show him I had no more need of him and to let him see that my hand was empty. He wheeled and trotted away.

The herdsman took his pewter straw from between his lips. "That was an ox," he said.

I nodded. "We needed him to carry this poor woman, who is ill, and so we borrowed him. Is he yours? We hoped you wouldn't mind, and after all, we did him no harm."

"No, no." The herdsman made a vaguely deprecating gesture. "I only asked because when I first saw you I thought he was a destrier. My eyes are not as good as they once were." He told us how good they once were, which was very good indeed. "But as you say, it was an ox."

This time Dorcas and I nodded together.

"You see what it is to become old. I would have licked the blade of this knife," he slapped the metal hilt that protruded above his broad belt, "and pointed it to the sun to swear that I saw something between the ox's legs. But if I were not such a fool I would know that no one can ride the bulls of the pampas. The red panther does it, but then he holds on with his claws, and sometimes he dies even so. No doubt it was an udder the ox inherited from his mother. I knew her, and she had one."

I said I was a city man, and very ignorant of everything that concerned cattle.

"Ah," he said, and sucked his maté. "I am a man more ignorant than you. Everyone around here but me is one ignorant eclectic. You know these people they call eclectics? They don't know anything—how can a man learn with neighbors like that?"

Dorcas said, "Please, won't you let us take this woman inside where she can lie down? I'm afraid she's dying."

"I told you I don't know nothing. You should ask this man here—he can lead an ox—I almost said a bull—like a dog."

"But he can't help her! Only you can."

The herdsman cocked an eye at me, and I understood that he had established to his own satisfaction that it was I, and not Dorcas, who had tamed the bull. "I'm very sorry for your friend," he said, "who I can see must have been a lovely woman once. But even though I've been sitting here cracking jokes with you, I have a friend of my own, and right now he's lying inside. You're afraid your friend is dying. I know mine is, and I'd like to let him go with no one to bother him."

"We understand, but we won't disturb him. We may even be able to help him."

The herdsman looked from Dorcas to me and back again. "You are strange people—what do I know? No more than one of those ignorant eclectics. Come in, then. But be quiet, and remember you're my guests."

He rose and opened the door, which was so low I had to stoop to get through it. A single room constituted the house, and it was dark and smelled of smoke. A man much younger and, I thought, much taller than our host lay on a pallet before the fire. He had the same brown skin, but there was no blood beneath the pigment; his cheeks and forehead might have been smeared with dirt. There was no bedding beyond that on which the sick man lay, but we spread Dorcas's ragged blanket on the earthen floor and laid Jolenta on it. For a moment her eyes opened. There was no consciousness in them, and their once clear green had faded like shoddy cloth left in the sun.

Our host shook his head and whispered, "She won't last longer than that ignorant eclectic Manahen. Maybe not as long."

"She needs water," Dorcas told him.

"In back, in the catch barrel. I'll get it."

When I heard the door shut behind him, I drew out the Claw. This time it flashed with such searing, cyaneous flame that I feared it would penetrate the walls. The young man who lay on the pallet breathed deeply, then released his breath with a sigh. I put the Claw away again at once.

"It hasn't helped her," Dorcas said.

"Perhaps the water will. She's lost a great deal of blood."

Dorcas reached down to smooth Jolenta's hair. It must have been falling out, as the hair of old women and of people who suffer high fevers often does; so much clung to Dorcas's damp palm that I could see it plainly despite the dimness of the light. "I think she's always been ill," Dorcas whispered. "Ever since I've known her. Dr. Talos gave her something that made her better for a time, but now he has driven her away—she used to be very demanding, and he has had his revenge."

"I can't believe he meant it to be as severe as this."

"Neither can I, really. Severian, listen; he and Baldanders will surely stop to perform and spy out the land. We might be able to find them."

"To spy?" I must have looked as surprised as I felt.

"At least, it always seemed to me that they wandered as much to discover what passed in the world as to get money, and once Dr. Talos as much as admitted that to me, though I never learned just what they were looking for."

The herdsman came in with a gourd of water. I lifted Jolenta to a sitting position, and Dorcas held it to her lips. It spilled and soaked Jolenta's tattered shift, but some of it went down her throat as well, and when the gourd was empty and the herdsman filled it again, she was able to swallow. I asked him if he knew where Lake Diuturna lay.

"I am only an ignorant man," he said. "I have never ridden so far. I have been told that way," pointing, "to the north and the west. Do you wish to go there?"

I nodded.

"You must pass through a bad place, then. Perhaps through many bad places, but surely through the stone town."

"There is a city near here, then?"

"There is a city, yes, but no people. The ignorant eclectics who live near there believe that no matter which way a man goes, the stone town moves itself to wait in his path." The herdsman laughed softly, then sobered. "That is not so. But the stone town bends the way a man's mount walks, so he finds it before him when he thinks he will go around it. You understand? I think you do not."

I remembered the Botanic Gardens and nodded. "I understand. Go on."

"But if you are going north and west, you must pass through the stone town anyway. It will not even have to bend the way you walk. Some find nothing there but the fallen walls. I have heard that some find treasures. Some come back with fresh stories and some do not come back. Neither of these women are virgins, I think."

Dorcas gasped. I shook my head.

"That is well. It is they who most often do not return. Try to pass through by day, with the sun over the right shoulder by morning and later in the left eye. If night comes, do not stop or turn to one side. Keep the stars of the Ihuaivulu before you when they first grow bright."

I nodded and was about to ask for further information when the sick man opened his eyes and sat up. His blanket fell away, and I saw there was a bloodstained bandage over his chest. He started, stared at me, and shouted something. Instantly, I felt the cold blade of the herdsman's knife at my throat. "He won't harm you," he told the sick man. He used the same dialect, but because he spoke more slowly I was able to understand him. "I don't believe he knows who you are."

"I tell you, Father, it is the new lictor of Thrax. They have sent for one, and the clavigers say he's coming. Kill him! He'll kill all of them who haven't died already."

I was astounded to hear him mention Thrax, which was still so far away, and wanted to question him about it. I believe I could have talked to him and his father and made some sort of peace, but Dorcas struck the older man on the ear with the gourd—a futile, woman's blow that did nothing more than smash the gourd and cause little pain. He slashed at her with his crooked, two-edged knife, but I caught his arm and broke it, then broke the knife, too, under the heel of my boot. His son, Manahen, tried to rise, but if the Claw had restored his life it had, at least, not made him strong, and Dorcas pushed him down on his pallet again.

"We will starve," the herdsman said. His brown face was twisted by the effort he made not to cry out.

"You cared for your son," I told him. "Soon he will be well enough to care for you. What was it he did?"

Neither man would tell.

I set the bone and splinted it, and Dorcas and I ate and slept outside that night after telling father and son that we would kill them if we so much as heard the door open, or if any harm was done Jolenta. In the morning, while they were still asleep, I touched the herdsman's broken arm with the Claw. There was a destrier picketed not far from the house, and riding him I was able to catch another for Dorcas and Jolenta. As I led it back, I noticed the sod walls had turned green overnight.

XXX

The Badger Again

Despite what the herdsman had told me, I hoped for some place like Saltus, where we might find pure water and a few aes would buy us food and rest. What we found instead was scarcely the remnant of a town. Coarse grass grew between the enduring stones that had been its pavements, so that from a distance it seemed hardly different from the surrounding pampa. Fallen columns lay among this grass like the trunks of trees in a forest devastated by some frenzied storm; a few others still stood, broken and achingly white beneath the sun. Lizards with bright, black eyes and serrated backs lay frozen in the light. The buildings were mere hillocks from which more grass sprouted in soil caught from the wind.

There was no reason I could see to turn from our course, and so we continued northwest, urging our destriers forward. For the first time I became conscious of the mountains ahead. Framed in a ruined arch, they were no more than a faint line of blue on the horizon; yet they were a presence, as the mad clients on the third level of our oubliette were a presence though they were never taken up a single step, or even out of their cells. Lake Diuturna lay somewhere in those mountains. So did Thrax; the Pelerines, so far as I had been able to discover, wandered somewhere among their peaks and chasms, nursing the wounded of the endless war against the Ascians. That too lay in the mountains. There hundreds of thousands perished for the sake of a pass.

But now we had come to a town where no voice sounded but the raven's. Although we had carried water in skin bags from the herdsman's house, it was nearly gone. Jolenta was weaker, and Dorcas and I agreed that if we did not find more by nightfall, it was likely she would die. Just as Urth began to roll across the sun, we came upon a broken sacrificial table whose basin still caught rain. The water was stagnant and stinking, but in our desperation we allowed Jolenta to drink a few swallows, which she immediately vomited. Urth's turning revealed the moon, now well past the full, so that we gained her weak greenish gleam as we lost the sunlight.

To have come upon a simple campfire would have seemed a miracle. What we actually saw was stranger but less startling. Dorcas pointed to the left. I looked, and a moment later beheld, as I thought, a meteor. "It's a falling star," I said. "Did you see one before? They come in showers sometimes."

"No! That's a building—can't you see it? Look for the dark place against the sky. It must have a flat roof, and someone's up there with flint and steel."

I was about to tell her that she imagined too much, when a dull red glow no bigger, it seemed, than the head of a pin, appeared where the sparks had fallen. Two breaths more, and there was a tiny tongue of flame.

It was not far, but the dark and the broken stones we rode over made it seem so, and by the time we reached the building the fire was bright enough for us to see that three figures crouched about it. "We need your help," I called. "This woman is dying."

All three raised their heads, and a crone's screech asked, "Who speaks? I hear a man's voice, but I see no man. Who are you?"

"Here," I called, and threw back my fuligin cloak and hood. "On your left. I've dark clothes, that's all."

"So you do . . . so you do. Who's dying? Not little pale hair . . . big red-gold. We've wine here and a fire, but no other physic. Go around, that's where the stair is."

I led our animals around the corner of the building as she had indicated. The stone walls cut off the low moon and left us in blind darkness, but I stumbled on rough steps that must have been made by piling stones from fallen structures against the side of the building. After hobbling the two destriers, I carried Jolenta up, Dorcas going before us to feel the way and warn me of danger.

The roof, when we reached it, was not flat; and the pitch was great enough for me to fear falling at every step. Its hard, uneven surface seemed to be of tiles—once one loosened, and

I heard it grating and clattering against the others until it fell over the edge and smashed on the uneven slabs below.

When I was an apprentice and too young to be entrusted with any but the most elementary tasks, I was given a letter to take to the witches' tower, across the Old Court from our own. (I learned much later that there was a good reason for selecting only boys well below the age of puberty to carry the messages our proximity to the witches required.) Now, when I know of the horror our own tower inspired not only in the people of the quarter but to an equal or greater degree in the other residents of the Citadel itself, I find a flavor of quaint naïveté in the recollection of my own fear; yet to the small and unattractive boy I was, it was very real. I had heard terrible stories from the older apprentices, and I had seen that boys unquestionably braver than I were afraid. In that most gaunt of all the Citadel's myriad towers, strangely colored lights burned by night. The screams we heard through the ports of our dormitory came not from some underground examination room like our own, but from the highest levels; and we knew that it was the witches themselves who screamed thus and not their clients, for in the sense we used that word, they had none. Nor were those screams the howlings of lunacy and the shrieks of agony, as ours were.

I had been made to wash my hands so they would not soil the envelope, and I was very conscious of their dampness and their redness as I picked my way among the puddles of freezing water that dotted the courtyard. My mind conjured up a witch who should be immensely dignified and humiliating, who would not shrink from punishing me in some particularly repulsive way for daring to carry a letter to her in red hands and would send me back with a scornful report to Master Malrubius as well.

I must have been very small indeed: I had to jump to reach the knocker. The smack of the witches' deeply worn doorstep against the thin soles of my shoes remains with me still.

"Yes?" The face that looked into mine was hardly higher than my own. It was one of those—outstanding of its kind among all the hundreds of thousands of faces I have seen—that are at once suggestive of beauty and disease. The witch to whom it belonged seemed old to me and must actually have been about twenty or a little less; but she was not tall, and she carried herself in the bent-backed posture of extreme age.

Her face was so lovely and so bloodless that it might have been a mask carved in ivory by some master sculptor.

Mutely, I held up my letter.

"Come with me," she said. Those were the words I had feared, and now that they had actually been given voice, they seemed as inevitable as the procession of the seasons.

I entered a tower very different from our own. Ours was oppressively solid, of plates of metal so closely fitted that they had, ages ago, diffused into one another to become one mass, and the lower floors of our tower were warm and dripping. Nothing seemed solid in the witches' tower, and few things were. Much later, Master Palaemon explained to me that it was far older than most other parts of the Citadel, and had been built when the design of towers was still little more than the imitation in inanimate materials of human physiology, so that skeletons of steel were used to support a fabric of flimsier substances. With the passing of the centuries, that skeleton had largely corroded away—until at last the structure it had once stiffened was held up only by the piecemeal repairs of past generations. Oversized rooms were separated by walls not much thicker than draperies; no floor was level, and no stair straight; each bannister and railing I touched seemed ready to come off in my hand. Gnostic designs in white, green, and purple had been chalked on the walls, but there was little furniture, and the air seemed colder than that outside.

After climbing several stairs and a ladder lashed together from the unpeeled saplings of some fragrant tree, I was ushered into the presence of an old woman who sat in the only chair I had yet seen there, staring through a glass tabletop at what appeared to be an artificial landscape inhabited by hairless, crippled animals. I gave her my letter and was led away; but for a moment she had glanced at me, and her face, like the face of the young-old woman who had brought me to her, has of course remained graven in my mind.

I mention all this now because it seemed to me, as I laid Jolenta on the tiles beside the fire, that the women who crouched over it were the same. It was impossible; the old woman to whom I had handed my letter was almost certainly dead, and the young one (if she were still living) would be changed beyond recognition, as I was myself. Yet the faces that turned toward me were the faces I recalled. Perhaps there are but two witches in the world, who are born into it again and again.

"What is the matter with her?" the younger woman asked, and Dorcas and I explained as well as we could.

Long before we finished, the older one had Jolenta's head in her lap and was forcing wine from a clay bottle into her throat. "It would harm her if it were strong to harm," she said. "But this is three parts pure water. Since you do not wish to see her die, you are fortunate, possibly, to have come across us so. Whether she is also fortunate, I cannot say."

I thanked her, and inquired where the third person who had been at their fire had gone.

The old woman sighed, and stared at me for a moment before returning her attention to Jolenta.

"There were only the two of us," the younger woman said. "You saw three?"

"Very clearly, in the firelight. Your grandmother—if that is who she is—looked up and spoke to me. You and whoever was with you lifted your heads, then bowed them again."

"She is the Cumaean."

I had heard the word before, but for a moment I could not remember where, and the younger woman's face, immobile as an oread's in a picture, gave me no clue.

"The seeress," Dorcas supplied. "And who are you?"

"Her acolyte. My name is Merryn. It is significant, possibly, that you, who are three, saw three of us at the fire, while we who are two at first saw but two of you." She looked to the Cumaean as if for confirmation, and then, as if she had received it, back to us, though I saw no glance pass between them.

"I'm quite sure I saw a third person who was larger than either of you," I said.

"This is a strange evening, and there are those who ride the night air who sometimes choose to borrow a human seeming. The question is why such a power would wish to show itself to you."

The effect of her dark eyes and serene face was so great that I think I might have believed her if it had not been for Dorcas, who suggested with an almost imperceptible movement of her head that the third member of the group about the fire might have escaped our observation by crossing the roof and hiding on the farther side of the ridge.

"She may live," the Cumaean said without lifting her gaze from Jolenta's face. "Though she does not wish it."

"It's a good thing for her that the two of you had so much wine," I said.

The old woman did not rise to the bait, saying only, "Yes, it is. For you and possibly even for her."

Merryn picked up a stick and stirred the fire. "There is no death."

I laughed a little, mostly, I think, because I was no longer quite so worried about Jolenta. "Those of my trade think otherwise."

"Those of your trade are mistaken."

Jolenta murmured, *"Doctor?"* It was the first time she had spoken since morning.

"You do not need a physician now," Merryn said. "Someone better is here."

The Cumaean muttered, "She seeks her lover."

"Who is not this man in fuligin then, Mother? I thought he seemed too common for her."

"He is but a torturer. She seeks a worse."

Merryn nodded to herself, then said to us, "You will not wish to move her farther tonight, but we must ask that you do. You will find a hundred better camping places on the other side of the ruins, and it would be dangerous for you to stay here."

"A danger of death?" I asked. "But you tell me there is none—so if I believe you, why should I fear? And if I cannot believe you, why should I believe you now?" Nevertheless, I rose to go.

The Cumaean looked up. "She's right," she croaked. "Though she does not know it, and only speaks by rote like a starling in a cage. Death is nothing, and for that reason you must fear it. What is more to be feared?"

I laughed again. "I can't argue with someone as wise as you. And because you gave us what help you could, we will go now because you wish it."

The Cumaean permitted me to take Jolenta from her, but said, "I do not wish it. My acolyte still believes the universe hers to command, a board where she can move counters to form whatever patterns suit her. The Magi see fit to number me among themselves when they write their short roll, and I should lose my place on it if I did not know that people like ourselves are only little fish, who must swim with unseen tides if we are not to exhaust ourselves without finding sustenance. Now you must wrap this poor creature in your cloak and lay her by my fire. When this place passes out of the shadow of Urth, I will look to her wound again."

I remained standing, holding Jolenta, uncertain whether we should go or stay. The Cumaean's intentions seemed friendly enough, but her metaphor had carried an unpleasant reminder of the undine; and as I studied her face I had come to doubt that she was an old woman at all, and to recall only too clearly the hideous faces of the cacogens who had removed their masks when Baldanders had rushed among them.

"You shame me, Mother," Merryn said. "Shall I call to him?"

"He has heard us. He will come without your call."

She was right. I already detected the scrape of boots on the tiles of the other side of the roof.

"You are alarmed. Would it not be better to put down the woman as I instructed you, so you might take up your sword to defend your paramour? But there will be no need."

By the time she had finished speaking, I could see a tall hat and a big head and broad shoulders silhouetted against the night sky. I laid Jolenta near Dorcas and drew *Terminus Est*.

"No need of that," a deep voice said. "No need at all, young fellow. I'd have come out sooner to renew our acquaintance, but I didn't know the Chatelaine here wanted it. My master—and yours—sends his greetings." It was Hildegrin.

XXXI

The Cleansing

"You may tell your master I delivered his message," I said.

Hildegrin smiled. "And have you a message to return, armiger? Remember, I'm from the quercine penetralia."

"No," I said. "None."

Dorcas looked up. "I do. A person I met in the gardens of the House Absolute told me I would encounter someone who identified himself thus, and that I was to say to him, 'When the leaves are grown, the wood is to march north.'"

Hildegrin laid a finger beside his nose. "*All* the wood? Is that what he said?"

"He gave me the words I have already recited to you, and nothing more."

"Dorcas," I asked, "why didn't you tell me this?"

"I've hardly had an opportunity to talk to you alone since we met at the crossing of the paths. And besides, I could see it was a dangerous thing to know. I couldn't see any reason to put that danger on you. It was the man who gave Dr. Talos all that money who told me. But he didn't give Dr. Talos the message—I know because I listened when they talked. He only said that he was your friend, and told me."

"And told you to tell me."

Dorcas shook her head.

Hildegrin's thick-throated chuckle might almost have come from underground. "Well, it don't hardly matter now, does it? It's been delivered, and for myself I don't mind tellin' you I wouldn't have minded if it had waited a little longer. But we're all friends here, except maybe for the sick girl, and I don't think she can hear what's said, or understand what we're talkin' about if she could. What did you say her name was? I couldn't hear you too clear when I was over there on the other side."

"That was because I didn't say it at all," I told him. "But her name is Jolenta." As I pronounced *Jolenta*, I looked at her, and seeing her in the firelight realized she was Jolenta no longer—nothing of the beautiful woman Jonas had loved remained in that haggard face.

"And a bat bite did it? They've grown uncommon strong lately then. I've been bit a couple of times myself." I looked at Hildegrin sharply, and he added, "Oh, yes, I've seen her before, young sieur, as well as yourself and little Dorcas. You didn't think I let you and that other gal leave the Botanic Gardens alone, did you? Not with you talkin' of goin' north and fightin' a officer of the Septentrions. I saw you fight and saw you take that fellow's head off—I helped to catch him, by the bye, because I thought he might be from the House Absolute for true—and I was in the back of the people that watched you on the stage that night. I didn't lose you till the affair at the gate the next day. I seen you and I seen her, though there's not much left of her now except the hair, and I think even that's changed."

Merryn asked the Cumaean, "Shall I tell them, Mother?"

The old woman nodded. "If you can, child."

"She has been imbued with a glamour that rendered her beautiful. It is fading fast now because of the blood she lost, and because she has had a great deal of exercise. By morning only traces will remain."

Dorcas drew back. "Magic, you mean?"

"There is no magic. There is only knowledge, more or less hidden."

Hildegrin was staring at Jolenta with a thoughtful expression. "I didn't know looks could be changed so much. That might be useful, that might. Can your mistress do it?"

"She could do much more than this, if she willed it."

Dorcas whispered, "But how was this done?"

"There have been substances drawn from the glands of beasts added to her blood, to change the pattern in which her flesh was deposited. Those gave her a slender waist, breasts like melons, and so on. They may have been used to add calf to her legs as well. Cleaning and the application of health-ening broths to the skin freshened her face. Her teeth were cleaned too, and some were ground down and given false crowns—one has fallen away now, if you'll look. Her hair was dyed, and thickened by sewing threads of colored silk into her scalp. No doubt much body hair was killed as well, and that at least will remain so. Most important, she was promised beauty while entranced. Such promises are believed with faith greater than any child's, and her belief compelled yours."

"Can nothing be done for her?" Dorcas asked.

"Not by me, and it is not a task of the kind the Cumaean undertakes, save in great need."

"But she will live?"

"As the Mother told you—though she will not wish it."

Hildegrin cleared his throat and spat over the side of the roof. "That's settled then. We've done what we can for her, and it's all we can do. So what I say is let's get on with what we come for. Like you said, Cumaean, it's good these others showed up. I got the message I was supposed to, and they're friends of the Liege of Leaves, just like me. The armiger here can help me fetch up this Apu-Punchau, and what with my two fellows bein' killed on the road, I'll be glad to have him. So what's to keep us from goin' ahead?"

"Nothing," the Cumaean murmured. "The star is in the ascendant."

Dorcas said, "If we're going to assist you with something, shouldn't we know what it is?"

"Bringin' back the past," Hildegrin told her grandly. "Divin' back into the time of old Urth's greatness. There was somebody who used to live in this here place we're sittin' on that knew things that could make a difference. I intend to have him up. It'll be the high point, if I may say it, of a career that's already considered pretty spectacular in knowin' circles."

I asked, "You're going to open the tomb? Surely, even with alzabo—"

The Cumaean reached out to smooth Jolenta's forehead. "We may call it a tomb, but it was not his. His house, rather."

"You see what with me workin' so near," Hildegrin explained, "I've been in the way to do this Chatelaine a favor now and again. More than one, if I may say it, and more than two. Finally I figured the time had come for me to collect. I mentioned my little plan to the Master of the Wood, you may be sure. And here we are."

I said, "I had been given to understand that the Cumaean served Father Inire."

"She pays her debts," Hildegrin announced smugly. "Quality always does. And you don't have to be a wise woman to know it might be wise to have a few friends on the other side, just in case that's the side that wins."

Dorcas asked the Cumaean, "Who was this Apu-Punchau, and why is his palace still standing when the rest of the town is only tumbled stones?"

When the old woman did not reply, Merryn said, "Less than a legend, for not even scholars now remember his story. The Mother has told us that his name means the Head of Day. In the earliest eons he appeared among the people here and taught them many wonderful secrets. Often he vanished, but always he returned. At last he did not return, and invaders laid waste to his cities. Now he shall return for the last time."

"Indeed. Without magic?"

The Cumaean looked up at Dorcas with eyes that seemed as bright as the stars. "Words are symbols. Merryn chooses to delimit magic as that which does not exist . . . and so it does not exist. If you choose to call what we are about to do here magic, then magic lives while we do it. In ancient days, in a land far off, there stood two empires, divided by mountains. One dressed its soldiers in yellow, the other in green. For a hundred generations they struggled. I see that the man with you knows the tale."

"And after a hundred generations," I said, "an eremite came among them and counseled the emperor of the yellow army to dress his men in green, and the master of the green army that he should clothe it in yellow. But the battle continued as before. In my sabretache, I have a book called *The Wonders of Urth and Sky*, and the story is told there."

"That is the wisest of all the books of men," the Cumaean said. "Though there are few who can gain any benefit from reading it. Child, explain to this man, who will be a sage in time, what we do tonight."

The young witch nodded. "All time exists. That is the truth beyond the legends the epopts tell. If the future did not exist now, how could we journey toward it? If the past does not exist still, how could we leave it behind us? In sleep the mind is encircled by its time, which is why we so often hear the voices of the dead there, and receive intelligence of things to come. Those who, like the Mother, have learned to enter the same state while waking live surrounded by their own lives, even as the Abraxas perceives all of time as an eternal instant."

There had been little wind that night, but I noticed now

that such wind as there had been had died utterly. A stillness hung in the air, so that despite the softness of Dorcas's voice her words seemed to ring, "Is that what this woman you call the Cumaean will do, then? Enter that state, and speaking with the voice of the dead tell this man whatever it is he wishes to know?"

"She cannot. She is very old, but this city was devastated whole ages before she came to be. Only her own time rings her, for that is all her mind comprehends by direct knowledge. To restore the city, we must make use of a mind that existed when it was whole."

"And is there anyone in the world that old?"

The Cumaean shook her head. "In the world? No. Yet such a mind exists. Look where I point, child, just above the clouds. The red star there is called the Fish's Mouth, and on its one surviving world there dwells an ancient and acute mind. Merryn, take my hand, and you, Badger, take the other. Torturer, take the right hand of your sick friend, and Hildegrin's. Your paramour must take the sick woman's other hand, and Merryn's. . . . Now we are linked, men to one side, women to the other."

"And we'd best do somethin' quick," Hildegrin grumbled. "There's a storm comin', I would say."

"We shall, as quickly as may be. Now I must use all your minds, and the sick woman's will be of little help. You will feel me guiding your thought. Do as I bid you."

Releasing Merryn's hand for a moment, the old woman (if she were in truth a woman at all) reached into her bodice and drew out a rod whose tips vanished into the night as if they were at the borders of my field of vision, though it was hardly longer than a dagger. She opened her mouth; I thought she meant to hold the rod between her teeth, but she swallowed it. A moment later I could detect its glowing image, muted and tinged with crimson, below the sagging skin of her throat.

"Close eyes, all of you. . . . There is a woman here I do not know, a high woman chained . . . never mind, Torturer, I know her now. Do not shrink from my hand. . . . None of you shrink from my hand. . . ."

In the stupor that had followed Vodalus's banquet, I had known what it was to share my mind with another. This was different. The Cumaean did not appear as I had seen her, or as a young version of herself, or (as it seemed to me) as anything. Rather, I found my thought surrounded by hers, as a fish in a bowl floats in a bubble of invisible water. Thecla was there with me, but I could not see her whole; it was as if she were standing behind me and I saw her hand over my shoulder at one moment, and felt her breath on my cheek at the next.

Then she was gone and everything with her. I felt my thought hurled off into the night, lost among the ruins.

When I recovered, I was lying on the tiles near the fire. My mouth was wet with the foam of my spittle mixed with my own blood, for I had bitten my lips and tongue. My legs were too weak to stand, but I raised myself to a sitting posture again.

At first I thought the others were gone. The roof was solid under me, but they had become, to my sight, as vaporous as ghosts. A phantom Hildegrin sprawled on my right—I thrust my hand into his chest and felt his heart beat against it like a moth that struggled to escape. Jolenta was dimmest of all, hardly present. More had been done to her than Merryn had guessed; I saw wires and bands of metal beneath her flesh, though even they were dim. I looked to myself then, at my legs and feet, and found I could see the Claw burning like a blue flame through the leather of my boot. I grasped it, but there was no strength in my fingers; I could not take it forth.

Dorcas lay as if in sleep. There was no foam flecking her lips, and she was more solid in appearance than Hildegrin. Merryn had collapsed into a black-clad doll, so thin and dim that slender Dorcas seemed robust beside her. Now that intelligence no longer animated that ivory mask, I saw that it was no more than parchment over bone.

As I had suspected, the Cumaean was not a woman at all; yet neither was she one of the horrors I had beheld in the gardens of the House Absolute. Something sleekly reptilian coiled about the glowing rod. I looked for the head but found none, though each of the patternings on the reptile's back was a face, and the eyes of each face seemed lost in rapture.

Dorcas woke while I looked from one to another. "What has happened to us?" she said. Hildegrin was stirring.

"I think we are seeing ourselves from a perspective longer than a single instant's."

Her mouth opened, but there was no cry.

Although the threatening clouds had brought no wind, dust was swirling through the streets below us. I do not know how to describe it except by saying that it seemed as if an uncountable host of minute insects a hundredth the size of midges had been concealed in the crevices of the rough pavement, and now were drawn by the moonlight to their nuptial flight. There was no sound, and no regularity in their motions, but after a time the undifferentiated mass formed swarms that swept to and fro, growing always larger and more dense, and at last sank again to the broken stones.

It seemed then that the insects no longer flew, but crawled over one another, each trying to reach the center of the swarm. "They are alive," I said.

But Dorcas whispered, "Look, they are dead."

She was correct. The swarms that had seethed with life a moment before now showed bleached ribs; the dust motes, linking themselves just as scholars piece together shards of ancient glass to re-create for us a colored window shattered thousands of years before, formed skulls that gleamed green in the moonlight. Beasts—aelurodons, lumbering spelaeae, and slinking shapes to which I could put no name, all fainter than we who watched from the rooftop—moved among the dead.

One by one they rose, and the beasts vanished. Feebly at first, they began to rebuild their town; stones were lifted again, and timbers molded of ashes were laid into sockets in the restored walls. The people, who had seemed hardly more than ambulant corpses when they rose, gathered strength from their work and became a bandylegged race who walked like sailors and rolled cyclopean stones with the might of their wide shoulders. Then the town was complete, and we waited to see what would happen next.

Drums broke the stillness of the night; by their tone I knew that when they had last beat a forest had stood about the town, for they reverberated as sounds only reverberate among the boles of great trees. A shaman with a shaven head paraded the street, naked and painted with pictographs in a script I had never seen, so expressive that the mere shapes of the words seemed to shout their meanings.

Dancers followed him, a hundred or more capering in lockstep, single file, the hands of each on the head of the dancer before him. Their faces were upturned, making me wonder (as I wonder still) if they did not dance in imitation of the hundred-eyed serpent we called the Cumaean. Slowly they coiled and twined, up and down the street, around the shaman and back again until at last they reached the entrance to the house from which we watched them. With a crash like thunder, the stone slab of the door fell. There was an odor as of myrrh and roses.

A man came forth to greet the dancers. If he had possessed a hundred arms, or had worn his head beneath his hands, I could not have been more astonished, for his was a face I had known since childhood, the face of a funeral bronze in the mausoleum where I played as a boy. There were massive gold bracelets on his arms, bracelets set with jacinths and opals, carnelians and flashing emeralds. With measured strides he advanced until he stood in the center of the procession, with the dancers swaying about him. Then he turned toward us and lifted his arms. He was looking at us, and I knew that he, alone of all the hundreds there, truly saw us.

I had been so entranced by the spectacle below me that I had not noticed when Hildegrin left the roof. Now he darted—if so large a man can be said to dart—into the crowd and laid hold of Apu-Punchau.

What followed I hardly know how to describe. In a way it was like the little drama in the house of yellow wood in the Botanic Gardens; yet it was far stranger, if only because I had known then that the woman and her brother, and the savage, were chant-caught. And now it seemed almost that it was Hildegrin, Dorcas, and I who were wrapped in magic. The dancers, I am sure, could not see Hildegrin; but they were somehow aware of him, and cried out against him, and slashed the air with stone-toothed cudgels.

Apu-Punchau, I felt certain, *did* see him, just as he had seen us on the rooftop and as Isangoma had seen Agia and me. Yet I do not believe he saw Hildegrin as I saw him, and it may be that what he saw seemed as strange to him as the Cumaean had to me. Hildegrin held him, but he could not subdue him. Apu-Punchau struggled, but he could not break free. Hildegrin looked up to me and shouted for help.

I do not know why I responded. Certainly I no longer consciously desired to serve Vodalus and his purposes. Perhaps it was the lingering effect of the alzabo, or only the memory of Hildegrin's rowing Dorcas and me across the Lake of Birds.

I tried to push the bandylegged men away, but one of their random blows caught the side of my head and knocked me to my knees. When I rose again, I seemed to have lost sight of Apu-Punchau among the leaping, shrieking dancers. Instead there were two Hildegrins, one who grappled with me, one who fought something invisible. Wildly, I threw off the first and tried to come to the aid of the second.

"Severian!"

Rain beating upon my upturned face awakened me—big drops of cold rain that stung like hail. Thunder rolled across the pampas. For a moment I thought I had gone blind; then a flash of lightning showed me wind-lashed grass and tumbled stones.

"Severian!"

It was Dorcas. I started to rise, and my hand touched cloth as well as mud. I seized it and pulled it free—a long, narrow strip of silk tipped with tassels.

"Severian!" There was terror in the cry.

"Here!" I called. "I'm down here!" Another flash showed me the building and Dorcas's frantic figure silhouetted on the roof. I circled the blind walls and found the steps. Our mounts were gone. On the roof, so were the witches; Dorcas, alone, bent over the body of Jolenta. By lightning, I saw the dead face of the waitress who had served Dr. Talos, Baldanders, and me in the café in Nessus. It had been washed clean of beauty. In the final reckoning there is only love, only that divinity. That we are capable only of being what we are remains our unforgivable sin.

Here I pause again, having taken you, reader, from town to town—from the little mining village of Saltus to the desolate stone town whose very name had long ago been lost among the whirling years. Saltus was for me the gateway to the world beyond the City Imperishable. So too, the stone town was a gateway, a gateway to the mountains I had glimpsed through its ruined arches. For a long way thereafter, I was to journey among their gorges and fastnesses, their blind eyes and brooding faces.

Here I pause. If you wish to walk no farther with me, reader, I do not blame you. It is no easy road.

Appendixes

Social Relationships in the Commonwealth

One of the translator's most difficult tasks is the accurate expression of matter concerned with caste and position in terms intelligible to his own society. In the case of *The Book of the New Sun,* the lack of supportive material renders it doubly difficult, and nothing more than a sketch is presented here.

So far as can be determined from the manuscripts, the society of the Commonwealth appears to consist of seven basic groups. Of these, one at least seems completely closed. A man or woman must be born an *exultant,* and if so born, remains an exultant throughout life. Although there may well be gradations within this class, the manuscripts indicate none. Its women are called "Chatelaine," and its men by various titles. Outside the city I have chosen to call Nessus, it carries on the administration of day-to-day affairs. Its hereditary assumption of power is deeply at variance with the spirit of the Commonwealth, and sufficiently accounts for the tension evident between the exultants and the autarchy; yet it is difficult to see how local governance might be better arranged under the prevailing conditions—democracy would inevitably degenerate into mere haggling, and an appointive bureaucracy is impossible without a sufficient pool of educated but relatively unmoneyed executives to fill its offices. In any case, the wisdom of the autarch no doubt includes the principle that an entire sympathy with the ruling class is the most deadly disease of the state. In the manuscripts, Thecla, Thea, and Vodalus are unquestionably exultants.

The *armigers* seem much like exultants, though on a lesser

251

scale. Their name indicates a fighting class, but they do not appear to have monopolized the major roles in the army; no doubt their position could be likened to that of the samurai who served the daimyos of feudal Japan. Lomer, Nicarete, Racho, and Valeria are armigers.

The *optimates* appear to be more or less wealthy traders. Of all the seven, they make the fewest appearances in the manuscripts, though there are some hints that Dorcas originally belonged to this class.

As in every society, the *commonality* constitute the vast bulk of the population. Generally content with their lot, ignorant because their nation is too poor to educate them, they resent the exultants' arrogance and stand in awe of the Autarch, who is, however, in the final analysis their own apotheosis. Jolenta, Hildegrin, and the villagers of Saltus all belong to this class, as do countless other characters in the manuscripts.

Surrounding the Autarch—who appears to distrust the exultants, and no doubt with good reason—are the *servants of the throne*. They are his administrators and advisors, both in military and civil life. They appear to be drawn from the commonality, and it is noteworthy that they treasure such education as they have obtained. (For contrast, see Thecla's contemptuous rejection of it.) Severian himself and the other inhabitants of the Citadel, with the exception of Ultan, might be said to belong to this class.

The *religious* are almost as enigmatic as the god they serve, a god that appears fundamentally solar, but not Apollonian. (Because the Conciliator is given a Claw, one is tempted to make the easy association of the eagle of Jove with the sun; it is perhaps too pat.) Like the Roman Catholic clergy of our own day, they appear to be members of various orders, but unlike them they seem subject to no uniting authority. At times there is something suggestive of Hinduism about them, despite their obvious monotheism. The Pelerines, who play a larger part in the manuscripts than any other holy community, are clearly a sisterhood of priestesses, accompanied (as such a roving group would have to be in their place and time) by armed male servants.

Lastly, the *cacogens* represent, in a way we can hardly more than sense, that foreign element that by its very foreignness is most universal, existing in nearly every society of which we have knowledge. Their common name seems to indicate that they are feared, or at least hated, by the commonality. Their presence at the Autarch's festival would seem to show that they are accepted (though perhaps under duress) at court. Although the populace of Severian's time appears to consider them a homogeneous group, it appears likely that they are in fact diverse. In the manuscripts, the Cumaean and Father Inire represent this element.

The honorific I have translated as *sieur* would seem to belong only to the highest classes, but to be widely misapplied at the lower levels of society. *Goodman* properly indicates a householder.

Money, Measures, and Time

I have found it impossible to derive precise estimates of the values of the coins mentioned in the original of *The Book of the New Sun*. In the absence of certainty, I have used *chrisos* to designate any piece of gold stamped with the profile of an autarch; although these no doubt differ somewhat in weight and purity, it appears they are of roughly equal value.

The even more various silver coins of the period I have lumped together as *asimi*.

The large brass coins (which appear from the manuscripts to furnish the principal medium of exchange among the common people) I have called *orichalks*.

The myriad small brass, bronze, and copper tokens (not struck by the central government, but by the local archons at need, and intended only for provincial circulation) I have called *aes*. A single aes buys an egg; an orichalk, a day's work from a common laborer; an asimi, a well-made coat suitable for an optimate; a chrisos, a good mount.

It is important to remember that measures of length or distance are not, strictly speaking, commensurable. In this book, *league* designates a distance of about three miles; it is the correct measure for distances between cities, and within large cities such as Nessus.

The *span* is the distance between the extended thumb and forefinger—about eight inches. A *chain* is the length of a measuring chain of 100 links, in which each link measures a span; it is thus roughly 70 feet.

An *ell* represents the traditional length of the military arrow; five spans, or about 40 inches.

The *pace,* as used here, indicates a single step, or about two and a half feet. The *stride* is a double step.

The most common measure of all, the distance from a man's elbow to the tip of his longest finger (about 18 inches), I have given as a *cubit.* (It will be observed that throughout my translation I have preferred modern words that will be understandable to every reader in attempting to reproduce—in the Roman alphabet—the original terms.)

Words indicative of duration seldom occur in the manuscripts; one sometimes intuits that the writer's sense of the passage of time, and that of the society to which he belongs, has been dulled by dealings with intelligences who have been subjected to, or have surmounted, the Einsteinian time paradox. Where they occur, a *chiliad* designates a period of 1,000 years. An *age* is the interval between the exhaustion of some mineral or other resource in its naturally occurring form (for example, sulfur) and the next. The *month* is the (then) lunar one of 28 days, and the *week* is thus precisely equal to our own week: a quarter of the lunar month, or seven days. A *watch* is the duty period of a sentry: one-tenth of the night, or approximately one hour and 15 minutes.

G.W.

About the Author

Gene Wolfe was born in New York City and raised in Houston, Texas. He spent two and a half years at Texas A&M, then dropped out and was drafted. As a private in the Seventh Division during the Korean War, he was awarded the Combat Infantry Badge. The GI Bill permitted him to attend the University of Houston after the war, where he earned a degree in Mechanical Engineering. He is currently a senior editor on the staff of *Plant Engineering Magazine*.

Although he has written a "mainstream" novel, a young-adult novel, and many magazine articles, Wolfe is best known as a science-fiction writer, the author of over a hundred science-fiction short stories and of *The Fifth Head of Cerberus*. In 1973 his *The Death of Doctor Island* won the Nebula (given by the Science Fiction Writers of America) for the best science-fiction novella of the year. His novel *Peace* won the Chicago Foundation for Literature Award in 1977; and his "The Computer Iterates the Greater Trumps" has been awarded the Rhysling for science-fiction poetry.

His next collection of short stories will be published under the title *The Gene Wolfe Book of Days*.